Crash Philosophy

Second Collision

Table of Contents

Choose by Setting

Location One: Apocalyptic Wasteland

Location Two: Evil Laboratory

Location Three: Human Mind

Location Four: The Ocean

Location Five: The Triassic

Location Six: Space

Location Seven: Alternate Future

Choose by Character
Character One: Alien

Character Two: Clown

Character Three: Imaginary Friend

Character Four: Kaiju

Character Five: Robot Assassin

Character Six: Dinosaur

Character Seven: Psycho Killer

Introduction

To say I knew what to expect when editing the *Second Collision* would be a misnomer. Sure, I knew which characters and settings were being added, and I knew the five that came from the first. The first anthology was my first experience in editing so much material from others. My previous experience was in a critique group where we focused on feature length works in progress at a content level. The first anthology I published, *Shatter Your Image*, included a wide variety of poetry, non-fiction, and short stories where each one required its own approach. *First Collision* was a learning curve. So much so, that I relied heavily on my writing partner, and booth buddy, Melissa Koons as my primary editor and formatter. That proved to be too much to ask for the deadline to release the second collision.

As a result, I decided to do the first round of edits on this second installment myself. What came was a new way to appreciate the storytelling throughout all the entries. The level of thought put into some of the stories became so blaringly obvious as I edited, it was exhilarating to read. For how absurd some of the combinations of characters and setting are, it's incredible how emotionally resonant these narratives became. There are surprising endings to a few I didn't see coming, yet all the seeds of incredible storytelling were there. Themes such as grief, death, and friendship showed up multiple times.

I enjoyed the process of creating the *Second Collision* a little more than the first. That's not to say I don't have considerable love and appreciation for the *First Collision*, but that learning curve was a steep one to overcome. In addition, by having me take the first pass on the stories and do a round of edits, it not only made Melissa's jobs easier, but it allowed me to more fully immerse myself in the narratives. So much so, at one point I reached one of my short stories, a Kaiju in an Alternate Future, and while reading it and trying to edit the story, I stopped. I realized I had to scrap the entire thing and start over. Most of the writers used their combination with such inventive creativity, I couldn't include the draft I had because it was rudimentary in how I capitalized on the pairing. The new version of the Kaiju in an Alternate

Future now plays with our current app-obsessed culture, but with gigantic monsters!

This is a long way of saying the writing in this is phenomenal, and challenged me as both an editor, but also as an author to raise my game. It's what makes the creative community so incredible. We all want each other to succeed. As I edited this anthology, I found myself challenging the authors to make sure the stories were as solid as they could be while in the editing stages. In addition, I had to push myself by reading these incredible stories and surrounding myself (albeit digitally for the most part) with authors with talents different from mine.

The goal of this experiment was to see what stories could come from the odd variations of bringing different characters and settings together, it has not disappointed. It also makes me excited for the *Third Collision*, with an aimed release of Spring 2020. If we wanted to, we could release it a lot faster, but the team wants to allow the necessary amount of time to devote to furthering this process and indulging in the process of enhancing these stories. Plus, every time I set an earlier release date, I inevitably miss the deadline, so I need to be a better project manager for myself. Which does come with a dose of irony since that is my current day job. I'm great at managing other projects, but my own can be a bit hard to deal with. It's the same reason you can't edit your own work! You need other eyes and voices to chime in.

Please enjoy this, some of these stories truly blew me away and I'm eternally grateful for everyone who contributed. This wouldn't have been feasible on my own; writing a third of the stories for this installment alone proved a massive hurdle. I can't express my appreciation to the creative team of writing superheroes assembled in these anthologies. It's been a blast and I'm excited for the next one!

Thomas A. Fowler

"The Age of Dust" by Melissa Koons
Dinosaur in an Apocalyptic Wasteland

It was a strange land. Everything about it was completely foreign to him. He may have been recently hatched, but there was something in his very bones that told him he wasn't meant to be here. Looking around, his eyes burned from the bright orange dust that fell from the sky. The air was heavy, hot, and if it wasn't for his thick scales, he was sure that it would sting. Sneezing, the young dinosaur blinked the dust from his eyes and tried to gain his bearings.

Nothing seemed right. White walls wrapped around him, but they no longer stretched high. They were broken, crumbled, and stained with the orange dust. In some places, the walls were completely obliterated, allowing him to see the great expanse of nothingness that stretched out beyond the rubble. He could make out strange shapes in the dust on the ground— shapes that looked jagged and inorganic. The young dinosaur shivered. This was most certainly not right. Not only was it the wrong color palate, but it was far too quiet.

He didn't know what he expected, he had only just pushed his way out of his shell, but he thought the world would have sound. He thought

Melissa Koons

he would open his bleary eyes and see bright green leaves or other creatures like him. Instead, the sight that greeted him was a dilapidated mess covered in orange and brown dust with a blanketed silence that made him feel like the only living creature on earth.

His breath came a little shorter and he frantically swiveled his head from side to side. There were no other figures like him, but he did notice some broken eggs on the floor that looked similar to the half-shell he sat in. There were some other, unbroken eggs still sitting on a metal table near him, but they didn't move. All the eggs had folded tags with strange scribbles on them. Looking down, he saw a similar tag in front of his. Comparing it to the others, his was the only tag with those markings. They all were the only ones of their kind.

Looking down from his elevated position, he did see some strange bodies lying on the ground. They were a little bigger than he was, but they looked nothing like him. They had no beaks, no plates along their backs, no spiked tails—no tails to speak of at all. They looked nothing like he did. They were long, soft-looking, and had strange appendages that could not be described as claws. Tilting his head, the young dinosaur attempted to roll himself out of his shell to take a closer look. The first try, he managed to rock the shell a little, but nothing more than that. With a grunt, he used one of his legs to give a mighty push and the remainder of his shell shattered.

He swished his tail back and forth, finally free to stretch. The small spikes at the tip of his tail scratched along the polyurethane tabletop, making an awful screech. He sniffed the air and sneezed, the orange dust irritating his nasal cavities. With a small grunt, the little dinosaur waddled across the metal table; his short front legs and longer rear legs took a moment to adjust to as he took his first, unsteady steps. He scanned for any possible way to get down. There was a stool not far off that he could leap to, but to get down from there it looked like he was still bound to suffer a fall.

With another puff, he squatted down and prepared his young legs for their first leap. Instinct told him what to do, and with a powerful shove he pushed off the table. The table emitted a painful creak; it groaned at the force and shook on its rusted legs. He reached out his front legs for the stool, but as soon as his toes hit the ripped leather seat, the stool spun away from him and he tumbled to the dust-covered ground.

4

Pain. The sharp jolt shot through his body immediately as he collided with the hard ground. His limbs throbbed and his body ached from the impact. His thick skin had dulled much of the blow, but his body was still too soft to endure it without injury. He was, after all, less than an hour old. Peeling open an eye, the little dinosaur looked around from his new vantage point. The orange dust was worse on the ground and there was a horrible heat that came from the earth and burned his feet. His eyes flicked back to the table and the egg he desperately wanted to return to, but he knew he could never go back. He knew he should not be here, but there was nowhere else for him to be. It seemed, there was nothing else in the world at all.

A rumble stirred in his stomach making the young dinosaur cringe into himself. Food. He needed food. He craved big leafy greens, sparkling water, and bright yellow flowers. He clenched his teeth together, grinding them as he pretended to chew the low-growing plants between his large, flat teeth. Swiveling his head around, he saw nothing. Just as he had noticed from his position on top of the metal table, the world was the wrong color. There was nothing green, nothing leafy nor sparkling. He heard no sounds of streams or rivers, and the rain was only this dry dirt that fell in fine particles. His stomach growled again. He peered around, this time taking in all the details surrounding him to try and locate a food source of any kind. His eyes fell on the strange body lying in front of him. It was the same animal that he had seen lying around the room. There were several of them, and none of them had any scales, nor plates; the only protection they had for their soft flesh were white coats draped over their limbs.

It didn't feel right. The little dinosaur squinted at the dead creature before him and took a step toward it, his stomach constantly reminding him that he needed sustenance. There was a little squeak and the dinosaur stopped in his tracks. It was the first sound he had heard that didn't belong to the table or himself. He waited, breathing shallowly so that he may hear it again. Another squeak sounded and the dinosaur snapped his head in the direction of the sound. He didn't move, but the squeaking became more frequent and closer.

Popping out from behind the rubble, a small, armored head looked over at the young dinosaur with curious eyes. It tilted its head this way and that, taking in the little creature who wandered the dusty earth and had caused such a commotion to get her attention. He didn't look like

5

her, but she knew he was of her kind. She climbed over the rocks, pushing them out of her way with her small, front legs. Her tail dragged behind her, giving her the balance she needed to walk upright on her two, powerful, back legs. She stopped beside the young dinosaur who quivered with fear.

He looked up at her and the domed plate protecting her skull, noting that it would be quite painful if she chose to butt him with her head. He remained very still as she sniffed him, cautiously determining what he was. His eyes flicked over to a tag that was attached to her ear. It had the same strange scribbles on it as the one in front of his egg, but hers looked different; she was different from him, yet more similar than the squishy creatures on the ground. She, too, was the only one of her kind.

His stomach growled and she jumped away from him, startled by the sound. He looked at her fearfully, but did not give into his urge to take a step back. He held his ground and his hungry eyes darted to the animal in the white coat.

The other dinosaur followed his hungry gaze and snorted. He may not look like her, but he ate like her. She could see he was confused, uncertain by his hunger. Flashing her teeth, she took a step toward the squishy creature and let them sink into its soft flesh. She tore away some meat with effort— her teeth were small, but sharp— and looked over at the young dinosaur as she chewed, hoping that he would understand and follow her lead.

Stepping closer, the little dinosaur reached out his neck and tried to bite down on the body like the other dinosaur had shown him. His teeth didn't tear into it and he struggled to pull away any flesh or meat like she initially had. He worked hard at it; his beak nipped at it, but without any front teeth he couldn't get a good grip. He opened wider for a bigger bite, but his flat, back teeth just pounded the skin down and didn't break it away.

Noticing his handicap, she bent down and tore a large chunk of meat off the dead animal and tossed it to the young dinosaur.

He gave her a snort of appreciation and ate the meat, using his flat teeth to pound the flesh down before he swallowed. It didn't taste right—it tasted foul and rancid, but it was food and the cramping in his stomach started to subside as he ate. The more he chewed, the less wrong it felt. He watched as the other dinosaur ripped the dead creature's throat and drink the congealed red ooze that used to flow there. It may not be sparkling water, but his thirst demanded he sip it.

Lapping at the blood that dribbled down their chins, the two dinosaurs stared at each other a moment, their shared feast laying between them. She lifted her head and gestured for her young companion to follow her.

He didn't know where she had emerged from nor where she wanted to go, but there was no other option for him. He could remain in the silent room with the bodies of the white coats, or follow her into the unknown where she was surviving. He stepped over the half-eaten body and clamored after her through the rubble. Instinct told him he should fear her company, but he ignored it since they were the only two living creatures left on earth.

"Opportunity" by Kimberly Keane
Psycho Killer in an Apocalyptic Wasteland

Carpe Diem

Faith peeked out from behind the jagged wall of the ruined building, gritting her teeth as the mortar bit into the small cuts on her hand. The air was redolent with ozone and concrete dust, and she didn't cough by sheer force of will.

There were two of them. Men. One big, one small. No more than a year or two older than she was. She reached into her bulky coat and touched the butt of the gun. In the wake of the destruction, it was easier to get than she'd expected it to be.

Their voices carried well. The noise of the city abruptly cut off a few, short hours ago from the bomb. A nuclear bomb. In New York. She was lucky she'd survived. She hadn't started throwing up yet, but that would come. And other, more unpleasant things. She'd been too close to it. And now she was here. Watching these two. Trying to figure out how best to proceed.

8

The smaller one, slight with red hair, fell to his knees, and emptied his stomach.

"Hey," the other one said, "You got that shit on my shoes."

"Yeah, asshole," The one she'd named Tiny answered, "You can get payback when you start puking."

"But, we're going to the hospital," Titan, the huge one, said.

"They can't do nothing for us."

"Why the fuck we going?"

"What else we gonna do?" Tiny stood, grabbing onto Titan's outstretched hand, and then ran the entire length of the sleeve of his coat over his mouth. "Maybe they'll give us something good when the pain gets bad."

"I don't feel nothin'. Maybe it'll be all good."

"We're dying."

"Not me."

"You were right next to me when it hit."

"So?"

"So, you got just as much as I did."

"Why ain't I gettin' sick then?"

"Who the fuck knows?"

Maybe she should just leave. Do what Tiny suggested; he was right about the pain killers. And he was right about something else. They were dying. All of them. There was no recovery from radiation poisoning. She felt fine, but she'd been further from the blast than either of them, so it stood to reason they'd feel the effects before her. Part of her wanted to side with Titan. To believe that maybe she wasn't dying. She was far enough away that some of the buildings around her were still standing when it hit, including the one she'd been in. But she'd seen the mushroom cloud, large and looming. That meant radiation. That meant death.

She almost wished she had the mental capacity of Titan. Almost wanted to shield herself from the knowledge her life was forfeit. Almost, but not really. She'd grasped the situation immediately. Understood exactly what it meant. For the people who'd been vaporized. For those who were close to the blast and died in minutes. And for those like Titan and Tiny. Those who would die over the next few days or weeks, healthy enough to make their way back to civilization. And for her. The opportunity it presented. No, she wouldn't just leave, wouldn't waste it.

She smiled, turned away from the men, and started walking in the same general direction they were going. The same direction from which she'd come. It didn't take them long to spot her.

"Hey," Tiny called out to her.

She stumbled and fell as she turned, looking up at them through the hair that had fallen into her face.

She grasped onto Titan's outstretched hand, much like Tiny had a few minutes before, ignoring the stinging of the cuts, and he damn near pulled her arm out of her socket pulling her to her feet. He looked strong, but he was stronger than she'd suspected. She filed the information away.

"Hey, ma . . ." Tiny started and trailed off when he saw her face. She wasn't surprised; she had that effect on men. He started again, "Hey, I'm Astuto. This is Fuerte."

"Faith." She said. She set her hand on Titan's arm and looked up into his face and smiled. Then she met Tiny's eyes. "Thank you."

He smiled, his eyes flicking downward and back up to her face.

"Where were you when it hit?" Astuto, Tiny, said.

"Headed to Times Square," she said, "My family was there."

"We was headed there, too," Titan said, "When it hit."

"We think that's where it landed," Tiny said, bending over and throwing up again. He wiped his mouth and looked up at her, narrowing his eyes. "Wait a minute. Times Square is that way." He pointed behind him. "But you're headed that way." He pointed his chin in the opposite direction.

She nodded. "Obviously they didn't survive." She looked around the landscape pointedly. "Anyway, didn't you just say it hit in the square?"

He nodded, letting his head hang.

"There you go," she said, "Where are you going?"

"Hospital." Titan said.

She nodded. "Mind if I tag along?" She trailed her hand down Titan's arm.

The men grinned at each other, Tiny still bent over, and then nodded to her.

They moved in silence for a time. It was slow going with the level of destruction, and the dust, or other things, in the air made them all cough. Each coughing fit sent Tiny into a bout of puking, but neither Titan nor Faith were emptying their stomachs. Yet.

Faith grumbled silently. How were things supposed to go with all of them hacking too hard to carry any kind of communication? She'd relied on her previous experiences, and the look they'd thrown one another, certain they'd start making advances sooner rather than later. Perhaps she'd relied too heavily on them but it was her only reliable method of communication. Eye contact and body language were more important than verbal discourse. Play the prey effectively enough, and others didn't notice how banal she found polite conversation.

She'd have to say something eventually, but she hadn't a clue where to start. Her previous attempts had always been met with stoicism or outbursts, and she still hadn't cracked the code on small talk. Perhaps she should say something about the weather. That always seemed to illicit the least volatile responses. She had taken a breath to follow through when Titan's voice broke the silence.

"Do you think it was terrorists?"

Of course, it was terrorists. By definition, it was terrorists. But she didn't give voice to those thoughts. She didn't know why saying that would confuse or anger one or the other of them, but she knew it would. Instead she shrugged and said, "It doesn't really matter."

"Of course, it does!" Titan said.

"What's done is done. Who did it isn't going to change the situation."

"Fuck it won't," His voice low and tight. "Payback's a bitch."

Did he really expect to get revenge? Did he think he could figure out who to target? She almost stopped and looked up at him, raising her eyebrow, but she caught herself, again. She was figuring out what to say next when he resumed talking.

"Fuckers. Bombing our city. Blowing up our home. Hell, yeah. We'll get—" vomit erupted out of him, cutting off his words. He went to his hands and knees, breathing heavily when it was over.

"Told you," Tiny said, sitting down in the rubble after puking again himself. He wiped at the sweat that broke out on his forehead.

"Shut up, man." Titan said, pushing himself up to sit next to Tiny.

"I'm just saying."

"And I'm just saying to shut up."

Tiny dropped his head and stayed silent for a moment, then punched Titan in his massive bicep. "Hey, man," he said, his legs trembling as they took his weight, "We'll get you to the hospital. Maybe they can do something."

Even Faith could hear the disbelief in Tiny's voice. Or maybe *only* she could hear it, because Titan smiled at Tiny, punching him back and almost sending him sprawling. "Yeah, man. Let's go."

It didn't take her long to realize there wasn't much time left. Tiny was going south quickly. He was dry heaving more than throwing up, and she was sure the little that was coming up was blood.

Originally, she thought Titan would be the better option. More satisfying. But he was going to be too much of a problem. He was starting to look rough around the edges, but it hardened his resolve. Made him focus more. Push harder. She wouldn't be able to control him, no matter how good she was.

That quality was alluring. Oh, so very tempting. To best that would be an accomplishment; it made her mouth water. She had already decided to take the opportunity, to realize a desire she'd never even given voice to. And here she was, following through. Taking that risk. She wanted to take that a step further, and risk it on Titan.

But she wouldn't. She wouldn't be stupid about it. Wouldn't risk her one shot by getting caught up in the moment. Lose her chance because she'd fallen into the emotional traps she'd seen everyone else fall into. She was better than that.

She was still regretting the need to take him out first, and quickly, when she pulled the gun, pivoted, and pointed it at him. She watched the expressions cross his face, one after another. Noticed his eyes widen and then narrow. He didn't look like he was going to hold up his hands and plead. Disappointing, but not surprising. His eyes hardened, and his jaw clenched. The muscles in his arms and legs tensed. But he didn't get the chance to follow through.

His head snapped back from the impact. She wished she could have taken more time with him. Or at least seen more. Watch his body crumple to the ground. Watch the life leave his eyes. But there was Tiny to think about, so she trained the weapon on the smaller man.

Inception

It went faster than she expected it to. Than she'd wanted it to. The fact that she had to shoot Tiny twice to get him to comply probably shortened the time even more; blood loss will do that. She'd hoped she could get him restrained without having to hurt him, but he'd known he wouldn't get out alive. Still, pain was a huge motivator, and it worked, even though it meant less time for her to play.

She thought she'd like the blood, but it turned out to be an annoyance. Messy. And the coppery smell added to the acrid scent that already stung her nose. The pain, though, now *that* was something. The way his body writhed, and the mewling sounds he tried to stifle before abandoning his futile effort to remain stoic and unbreakable. Oh, the look in his eyes. Even the threats that spewed out of him before the pleading began. It was intriguing. Exciting. She felt warm and alive. She hadn't known it was possible to feel that way.

Before that moment, life had been one drab day after another. People were one annoying replica after another. But *this. This* was something new. An experience she replayed in her head, committing all the nuances of his expressions to memory.

She looked down at the blood on her hands. On the rubble. On her clothes. It was everywhere. There was more than she could reasonably explain. It was then she realized she hadn't planned this well enough. She thought about trying to clean up before continuing onto the hospital. But that would be hard to explain, too. She was close enough to the blast to need medical attention, so showing up pristine would raise just as many questions.

Respite

The blood wasn't an issue. She probably could have killed half the people in the waiting room, and no one would have noticed. She was lucky she could fit through the door, and even luckier she found an unoccupied place on the floor to wait. And wait she did. But it was lovely. She'd never been able to simply observe. Take it all in. Enjoy everyone's discomfort without having to school her reactions.

The chaos was soothing. The fear. The pain. The crying. The misery. Even the shock that caused people to sit silently, detached from everything around them, was balm to the monotony of her daily life. Maybe this, too, would grow tiresome. People found patterns, after all. Those patterns were so simple to see, to predict. Eventually this brilliant deviation would fall to inevitable tedium. But until it did, she'd bask in its radiance.

Agitation

She'd been placed in what she'd heard the nurses call the "hot ward;" well, one of them. She still wasn't throwing up, and no one in the room with her, or in her ward, was either. The other radioactive ward was a different story. The nurses complained about that one. They didn't want to spend time there. Didn't want to clean up after the patients there, either.

She wouldn't have known that had she not ventured out on her own. The inevitable boredom that permeated her existence became too much to bear. How the others could lay around in beds placed side-by-side was beyond her. Hauling around the IV was annoying, but it beat the never-ending TV programs and banal conversations.

She thought she might draw attention to herself, but everyone was still so busy that no one even questioned her. Soon, though, overhearing all the other chatter lost its luster. There were only so many conversations to be overheard. Only so many topics before people started sounding like the broken records they'd always been.

Sometimes she wished she hadn't done it. Had never met Titan and Tiny. Never experienced such pleasure. She trembled at the memory. The world seemed even flatter now. Such a brilliant experience drenched the rest of the world in a single shade of grey.

Still, she replayed it in her head. Pictured his face. Heard his screams and cries. Felt the warmth in her body. She longed for the excitement, the novelty, and wished she'd thought to take something to remind her. To bring the experience back more vividly. Instead, the memory started to fade, and she feared the return to her previously boring existence. Until she found the other radioactive ward; the hotter one.

Ecstasy

At first, the ultra-hot ward was as packed as her own. But it became clear this was where the patients with acute radiation poisoning were put to die. After a few days, there was enough space that curtains could be used to separate each bed, offering both the dying, and her, a bit of privacy.

She couldn't do to them what she'd done to Tiny. She didn't have the knife, and those types of wounds would draw attention. But there were other options.

She found pillows worked well, but they were too impersonal. She couldn't see their eyes; see them widen with surprise, settle with knowledge, and finally turn glassy with fear. She couldn't see the life drain from them.

Her hands worked better. Large enough to cover their nose and mouth and small enough she could see every nuance in their faces. And their eyes. Oh, what she could see in their eyes. She didn't know what it all meant, but it was mesmerizing. Widening, narrowing, watering, muscle twitching. So much subtlety. So much to catalog.

Some of them even had a bit more strength and reached up to pick at her fingers. She trembled at the thought and closed her eyes. The exhilaration. It was like being born into a vivid, wonderful world.

Rebirth

She'd spent two weeks in the hospital. Her explorations broke the dreariness of the days. The ER was good for some excitement, and always a place she could taste someone's misery or anxiety without drawing attention to herself. The morgue was the place for the serenity of death; where no one could complain about anything. The only time she could be around people where she didn't have to police every word, every expression, every motion. The ultra-hot ward, though. That was freedom. That's where she could go to come alive. To feel the life drain away from others. The ER was a snack, the ultra-hot ward was a meal.

Now she was being released. It seemed she'd not quite gotten the dose of radiation that she thought she'd gotten. It was enough that she'd probably have health issues in the coming years, and they would eventually kill her, but not enough that she was in imminent danger.

She stood and pushed herself away from the wheelchair. She turned to say something to the nurse. Something that most people would say. Perhaps she would thank her. She wasn't sure what she would thank her for, but that was the thing that two weeks near others had given her. A better sense of how others talked to each other. And she got to practice. She still had much to learn, but she could say a few well-placed words, and most people would fill in the rest.

The nurse surprised her with a hug, and she returned it awkwardly, glad Nurse couldn't see her face.

"You know where to go now, don't you?" Nurse said, pushing the wheelchair to the side.

Faith nodded. "I heard there were busses taking us to shelters."

"That's right, sweetie. The stop is just out on the corner. They come by every hour. Maybe you'll find your family."

Faith tried to smile. She knew the nurse expected it, and she hoped that Nurse would chalk the inauthenticity of it to the fact that her mother, her only family, was most certainly dead.

"Oh, sweetie," the nurse said and wrapped her in another hug, "You'll be okay."

Faith nodded against the woman's shoulder and thought hard about how to phrase her question. She had to ask now. There wouldn't be another opportunity. She'd managed several conversations by leading others, never finishing a thought. This was a complete idea, though, and it was all her own. She could easily screw it up. But if she pulled it off well enough, she may be able to leverage it in the future. She stuck with short and sweet. Just ask the question and don't get into why.

"How long does it take to become a nurse?"

The nurse stepped back and took Faith's shoulders in her hands. "You want to be a nurse?"

Faith nodded again and fell silent. The silence stretched, and she knew she couldn't stay quiet for too long. Her brain grasped for something. She couldn't share the real reason why. She had to do one of those half sentences. "Watching you all these past weeks . . ."

Nurse smiled, and Faith sighed in relief. It worked.

"Not every patient will be as easy as you. Most will want more medication or answers or the doctor's time." She stepped back and waived her hands in the air. "But then you know that. You lived in the ward for the last few weeks. In close quarters. You've probably seen it all by now."

Faith nodded.

"After you get settled into . . . well, wherever you land, you come back here and find me, and I'll help you get started."

"Thank you." Faith paused. "And thank you for . . ."

The nurse waived her hands again. "It was my pleasure, sweetheart. Now you get going, the bus will be by any time now."

Faith stepped out into the sun. She had a lot to learn, but these last two weeks showed her she could do it. She could befriend people. And if not, she could appear as mundane as anyone else while she quietly found opportunities to splash color on the grey.

"Substantial Effect" by Thomas A. Fowler

Dinosaur in an Evil Laboratory

The scientist stood, frozen. A tyrannosaurus rex lingered in the portal entryway. Its head pushed against the frame. The wood of the door cracked as it pushed. The creature's voice rumbled, its deep bellows rippled through the lab.

"Hello, my friend," his scratchy voice greeted the dinosaur. "You are an eager one."

The tyrannosaur pulled its head out from the entry. She swung her neck back, preparing for the coming impact. Her head crashed into the entryway, the exterior split like twigs. Her body pushed through, taking down support beams in the entrance. The ceiling around the front of the laboratory sunk. It bowed as the support beams fell to the ground, destroying the doorframe.

The dinosaur's massive steps shook the entire laboratory. The scientist fell back onto a counter behind him. The portal remained, spinning about in a consistent ebb and flow like a circular tide.

"Wait, wait, wait," the scientist reached up, trying to slow the creature's charge.

The scientist looked at his lab assistant's vitals. Her unconscious body clung to life the entire time she'd helped to open portals to new worlds, new realities—altering time. Her potential was stronger than any of the other candidates, who'd continued to disappoint the scientist. She'd already shown completely unparalleled discoveries within the portal. Never did he expect a tyrannosaur to be conjured from within her mind.

The scientist stumbled farther into his lab. The narrow hallway to the genetics and robotics area wouldn't stop the dinosaur, but it would slow it down enough to stall the creature and allow him to escape.

Then he witnessed something unexpected: the dinosaur slowed.

"Wait," he said.

The tyrannosaur stopped. Her right foot stumbled over a fallen stool. She looked at it, then kicked it back. That was intelligent problem solving.

"Big girl. Do you understand what I'm saying?" the scientist asked.

The rex tilted her head, like a dog wondering if she was about to receive a treat.

"Perhaps some of what I'm saying," the scientist looked down toward the robotics department.

There was a glint in the dinosaur's eye—a familiar glint the scientist had had in his own eyes frequently. It was the glint of wanting, the desire for more.

"You've been to the epicenter of the human mind," he said. "Why are you here?" The scientist asked.

The tyrannosaurus rex stomped forward. It peered at the girl, looking at her longingly.

"Tell me," the scientist said. "Is she okay?" The scientist pointed at the unconscious body of his assistant.

The rex looked over.

"She is the key to everything I'm trying to accomplish. You were in her mind, she has powers. It's how you ended up here. She created a gateway that brought you into her head, then into my lab," he paused.

The rex looked at the motionless girl, she brought her snout toward the human. Sniffing her, the dinosaur nudged the table. No movement from the girl. The rex gave out a small call which, from a tyrannosaur, still resonated throughout the entire lab. The rex moved her snout closer, nudging the girl directly. Still nothing. The dinosaur tried to reach out to her to no avail. Her arms could not reach; it seemed the rex tried to carry her but couldn't. She acted like a mother caring for her child.

"Wait. You saw something in there," the scientist said.

The rex bellowed. This wasn't a creature giving basic calls. This was an advanced creature communicating. It called out for something.

The scientist smiled. "What did you see?"

The rex looked down at the girl.

"You could see her?" the scientist asked.

The rex chuffed in a quick acknowledgment.

"Did she say anything to you?" he asked.

The dinosaur did not acknowledge the question. She returned to the table, trying to grab the girl. Her short arms reaching, stretching, without success...

"You keep reaching for her," the scientist observed. "Why?"

The rex bellowed again. Her call, this time, had a longer and deeper resonance to it. A sad reflection, like she wanted to take the girl away.

"She is the key. So, if you're trying to help her, I can help you. What can I do?" the scientist asked.

She reached for the scientist, her short arms fell shy. The rex flailed her small arms, reaching and reaching.

"Your arms," the scientist said.

He looked down the hall. The robotics department was full of parts to construct their weaponry. There hung a tremendous number of appendages, data chips, and weaponry.

"My friend, I can give you more agility and strength than you could ever imagine," The scientist said. "Enough..."

The rex backed up. She relaxed her arms.

"Enough to propel yourself through the cosmos to change...to change history," the scientist said.

"It seems...the arms are meant to alter history." The scientist said. "To change the world as you know it, to alter reality and time as we know it. Are you aware of your species and its ultimate fate?"

The rex rested patiently as the scientist worked. It chuffed in acknowledgment. It knew what happened to dinosaurs; it was given the knowledge while in the portal.

"What if you could go back, knowing everything you do now? Find a way to save your species?" the scientist asked.

The rex looked confused, starting at him, then the girl.

"Humans? Oh, we'll find a way. Even if we don't, it could be the best thing for this planet," he replied. "Believe me, part of my exploration with this portal has been to identify, if not create, alternate realities where humanity is eradicated. We are a dark species; I know more than anyone. What I've done with my subjects to get them within the portal, it's been a heavy price for a larger objective."

As he built the robotic appendages, she nestled next to the girl, giving out small calls to let her know she was right next to her.

The scientist modified upper leg attachments for a human to latch onto the rex's arms. A fitting for a wide human thigh seemed to fit over her forearms quite nicely. He also gave her a grip within the robotic arms to control her hands. Attaching the arms, he raised his thumbs.

"I gave you opposable thumbs." He moved his thumbs around. "That way you can grab things, pull, and do so much more than you ever could before."

"This is great," the rex said. Startled by her own voice, the tyrannosaur stumbled back, trying to flee her own voice.

"Whoa, whoa, whoa. The arms also have a communicator tied to your neural network in your brain," the scientist said. "It's okay. You can talk to me now."

The rex snarled in protest. "I don't want this voice."

"It will let you talk to me," he said. "Send me transmissions within the portal to report back. Maybe even communicate with Dana."

"Dana?" She looked at the girl on the table, then the scientist, finally at her arms. "Maybe I do want these arms. If anything, for the power it gives me."

The rex struggled to use the hands, at first. The three fingers clutched at the straps keeping the girl on the table. Her two large fingers were easier to manipulate, she was used to having those. But the third, under the main two claws, proved to be a struggle. It was a completely new motor function and dynamic.

"Why are you taking her from the table?" the scientist asked. "I understand you want to hold her, but she cannot leave. Her mind is connected to the portal."

"Because of you," the rex said.

"What?" the scientist shook his head in confusion. He picked up a small, handheld device.

"All of them," the rex snarled. "I'm taking all of them from you."

"All of them?" the scientist asked for clarification.

The rex's snarl changed to a full-fledged roar. It understood how to use all three fingers as it reached out, clutching at the scientist's throat, holding its arms around his neck and raising him up. "All of your subjects."

"That's what she told you in that portal. You must have connected with her subconscious where she could warn you, send you to rescue her," the scientist said. "I'm only holding all of them until I can understand the portal's power. She's only connected as long as it takes to harness the power."

The rex roared. The scientist's fading hair flew about in different directions as the hot air from the tyrannosaur shot from its mouth. The rex tightened her grip, squeezing just a little more.

"This is bigger than holding a few lives captive, either within the portal or somewhere in this lab. This is the universe and our planet's fate," he argued.

"Protecting life is what makes the universe worth living in," the rex replied. "I will free your captives, then use these arms to bring her back to this world. We're connected. You hold no power now."

The rex shook her head. She received a signal, shocking her at the base of her arms from the robotics, traveling up the base of her neck and skull. It caused her to flinch.

"You think I wouldn't put in a failsafe?" he asked, pressing the handheld device. "I have more power than you know."

The rex looked at her arms. She swung them toward a pillar within the lab. The scientist flew form her grasp. The dinosaur fought through the pain and continued to slam her robotic arms against the pillar. The arms fell away in pieces. She turned and bit the scientist in the leg. She lifted him up from the ground, then walked. Going down a hallway, they passed another lab. Students, unaware of what went on a few labs down, panicked and ran. The scientist pleaded for help, but no one had the means to fight a tyrannosaurus rex, or the desire to join him in death. They abandoned him.

The rex stepped toward a basement corridor, slamming against a thick, storage unit at the very end. The door gave after a few swipes from her tail. Inside were six women. The rex clamped down on the scientist's leg, breaking the bones and rupturing the skin and muscles. She dropped him to the ground. Broken and crippled, the scientist tried to crawl away. Like a mother teaching her young to feed, she nodded toward the scientist. The women charged after the scientist, taking their former captor captive, kicking and stomping him.

The rex returned to the main lab. The sound of multiple humans and loud, echoing machines came from outside. Flashing lights surrounded the building. The rex stood above the girl, trying to reach out for her to free her from the table. She tried to bite the straps; her mouth was much too large to grip them. Her arms could not reach. Her feet weren't dexterous enough to manipulate the straps.

Moments later, the group of women arrived in the lab with the scientist, tied and gagged. They shouted, demanding for him to free the girl. The rex roared at the scientist.

"She could still help us understand the portal's power, its potential," he said. "The experiment must continue."

He broke free from the group of women and ran toward the portal. The rex swung her tail, swiping at him and taking him out at the knees. The rex tried stomping down on his back, but he rolled, dodging her while weaseling his way toward the portal. He dove into it, disappearing into a circular void.

Down the hall, the rex heard the sound of shouting humans. New voices. They wore matching outfits. As they approached, they held some sort of mechanisms, all aimed and pointed at her as they shouted over and over.

One of the women looked at the rex, waving her arms toward the portal. "Go! We'll take care of Dana. We'll get her out. You go, they'll only hurt you!"

The rex gave one last call to the girl, letting her know she would always watch over her. The tyrannosaur stepped into the portal and vowed two things. First, to help find the scientist. Second, to reach the girl again; back where they had found one another before.

"Lab Report" by Thomas A. Fowler
Psycho Killer in an Evil Laboratory

EPP-6022: Laboratory Report
(d) 06 (m) March (y) 2345
Dana Banks
Westshire Hall; Laboratory G7

The Connection of Portals and the Human Mind

WEEK ONE: ABSTRACT

My physical introduction and experimentation with the portal will allow me to explore the vast ability for the human mind to bridge alternate realities. In doing so, I hope the last five years of research I've done in my theoretical classes will find application for real-world exploration.

In meeting Dr. Campbell, we sought to jointly solve the issue of how alternate realities bridged by the human mind can be combined with his constructed portal—which began this exploration, in the first place.

We used various method—including paid participants—with little success, resulting in utilizing a more advanced mind capable of handling the concept of multi-verses and time alteration.

Our results were successful in the beginning, but the final result ended in a discovery of dangerous potential in the hands of those with ill intent. We did reveal the potential for portal exploration; however, in doing so we also found the ability to alter the fabric of human existence itself.

WEEK TWO: INTRODUCTION

After the discovery of the portal on 27.July.2297, the beginning of experimental portal physics classes did not begin until we were able to replicate the portal and distribute it to multiple labs. Westshire Hall, through a grant from the Westshire Foundation, allowed the school, London School of Astrophysics and Space Exploration, to gain one of only seven portals created before the portal project was deemed financially unviable. No results ended in financial gain for the investors.

I introduced the theory that without a living organism connected to the portal, it may not have a viable bridge to use the portal effectively. In my EPP-5011 class the last academic year, the previous lab assistants discovered the portal fires much like the human brain. Synapse firings within the portal trigger connections to alternate universes and timelines much like synapse triggers help the brain learn new skillsets, language, physical movement, and additional developments of the human function.

The final theory, developed with Dr. Campbell, was to answer the question if living organisms could help trigger a connection—like the brain firing a synapse—and could make the necessary tie to the portal that will allow us to finally enter it with tangible results, and potentially extract experimental subjects from the portal into our reality.

WEEKS THREE-SEVEN: METHOD

1. Electroencephalography (EEG) machines were used to monitor the brain activity for Earth-based organisms. Initial tests were done

with the portal to indiscernible results [see 2 below].

2. Magnetoencephalography (MEG) had to be used for the portal, as the EEG could not sufficiently monitor the amount of synapse firings. This was able to better separate the findings, and subtle differences between human synapse and portal synapse triggers. The MEG tracked the sheer number of synapse fires from the portal with more accuracy [triggers were occurring at times approaching 2.3 trillion sfps {synapse-fires per second}].

Procedure: Began with mice to no results. Synapse fires were nowhere near close to create a bridge. No apparent side effects, but they were frightened of the EEG scanner more than they were the portal. Then tested with dogs (7-year-old male Pitbull, followed by a 4-year-old female Labrador retriever), we saw some connections but not enough to have the portal activate or open. With the parallel of human brain synapse connections, and no apparent side effects to any other mammals thus far, we decided to perform human trials next. Dr. Campbell first asked to do the experiment using himself as the test subject, but we resisted the notion that any of the researchers should be part of the experiment to avoid any potential side effects and keep active team members capable of response in the event anything unexpected occurred. Volunteers were gathered; only adult ages, non-students, to avoid any complications with the University.

Subject A (23-year-old Caucasian male, recent graduate, retail employee) showed no signs of portal connectivity. Synapse firings between the brain and the portal paralleled one another, but ended after only a few mild firings. [No synapse connections made].

Subject B (34-year-old Hispanic female, Bachelor's degree, project manager for architecture firm) made a connection to the portal. However, after repeated attempts the portal would not open, despite the right synapse fire pairings occurring. We did two weeks with Subject B with no results after the initial connection was made. We received a minimal amount of connections [23 scps {synapse connections per second}].

Subjects C – E (see table 14-A in addendum paper for subject information) resulted in no connection whatsoever. Results were similar, or worse, than Subject A. We received no more than 8 scps.

RESULTS AND ANALYSIS

Connection to the portals did not work. Dr. Campbell, in a state of agitation, made himself Subject F. He established a connection, but could not trigger an opening, making his results that of Subject B with a slightly reduced 21 scps. Analysis found the portal was responsive, meaning it was sentient and capable of responding based on want and desire. The result ended with our grant being temporarily suspended, as well as Dr. Campbell's tenure undergoing extensive scrutiny by the board and a formal review hearing.

DISCUSSION

Analysis of the events post-grant removal resulted in a scan of all student brain synapse firings as a secondary report, an attempt to salvage some tangible results to show the board. Post-method work included one-on-ones with Dr. Campbell. After week three of post-method (week 12 in the overall experiment) one student (Mia Morgan, seventh year doctoral candidate) disappeared from campus. Her belongings were gone from her apartment, and there was a letter citing a desire to explore other pursuits). During my setup to the MEG, it was discovered I had a unique synapse combination through scans. Dr. Campbell asked if I would become Subject I. Due to ethical concerns, and explicit orders from the university that the portal was to remain closed, I rejected the request. Dr. Campbell asked for another quick MEG scan. I was forced into the experiment when Dr. Campbell created a connection through the portal without my consent. As I drifted, he revealed he had Mia Morgan, and others, held in the basement in a secure space to continue experimenting until he could rewrite history. He believed the portal could somehow allow time travel, although no findings indicated as such to this point.

My brain went into a state of comatose from the forced connection, but, while comatose, my subconscious linked with the portal, opening it and syncing my mind to its source. I received a warning that great danger was arriving soon.

I began seeing creatures, both Earth-based animals and unidentified species. See below for their identification and relative order of appearance:

1. Dunklesosteus terrelli (extinct species of prehistoric fish) No

direct interaction, fish swam past me within portal space, then moved on.

2. Saccorhytus (extinct species of sea-based creature) An entire school [roughly 20-25 specimens] circled me within the ethereal space of the portal, then proceed to swim forward. I followed them for some time. Eventually, they left me behind.

3. Unidentified creature (gaseous in nature, contained within a metal and glass-like orb) flew by me, it seemed like a storm cloud within the orb. Flashes of lightning followed with echoed thunderous sounds of varying pitch. It did this multiple times, likely in an attempt to communicate, then left when no linguistic understanding could be made.

4. Human-esque form (suited, appeared and sounded like a female, no verification) subject spotted me, but fled shouting about no human contact. It was a variation of English; therefore, I am unable to clearly identify this as a human. Based on the advanced technology of the suit, may have been a human from alternate reality or future, unclear as they fled once they saw me.

5. Tyrannosaurus Rex (female, older species, significant scars on left leg and hip-bone) Female tyrannosaurus rex entered the portal and connected with my mind. In doing so, it gained a sense of awareness no dinosaur was ever capable of collecting as an extinct, and primitive species. Initially, I thought it was a danger, but then the portal spoke to me and I realized the true danger.

While still comatose and connected to the portal, I could communicate with the T-Rex. I negotiated with it, when it learned dinosaurs had gone extinct, I helped it to understand that extinction naturally selected them. I asked if it had children. They had all perished. I bonded with her, told her that there was still a chance to raise more young—well before the extinction event—if she returned to her time. We also discussed the natural order of nature; she saw the progression. The two of us were met by the Unidentified Creature (Number 3 from above chart). It had learned to communicate in English and came back to find me. They explained that both of our species were naturally extinct in their time. Earth had periodic restarts, therefore nothing done within the portal would make any significant impact. Both humans and dinosaurs were destined for extinction at one point or another. The T-Rex decided she would return to her home, allowing natural order to take place. Before she left, I asked her for a favor.

The rex came through the portal, and received modifications from Dr. Campbell, mainly robotic appendages to enhance the length and capabilities of the otherwise stunted arms. It was later revealed he wanted to send the rex back to its time to save its species from extinction. By doing so, Dr. Campbell hoped to remove all humans from ever having existed and allow dinosaurs to thrive, killing and removing the poisonous human species from this reality.

He provided the rex instructions, which it promptly ignored. Instead, the rex freed the captive students, attacked the professor, but returned in a state of panic as police arrived.

Through a struggle with the other students (whom he had taken prisoner), Dr. Campbell fled into the portal. Although we did not find one another within the space, the rex returned and guided me back. My fellow students pulled me from the portal on the Earth-side. We thought Dr. Campbell would be lost within the portal, never to return.

CONCLUSION

After several weeks, the students in our class began disappearing. After the third disappearance, I returned to the portal, and connected myself to it. While inside, I discovered Dr. Campbell had scanned for possibilities to eradicate the human race through the portal. After the portal refused to show him the way, he began taking revenge on his students, forcibly pulling them into the portal and then placing them in a state of purgatory.

The only student not found was Mia Morgan, she'd been murdered by Dr. Campbell and evidence brought out he'd taken her to a deep lake, which was later recovered upon a scan of Dr. Campbell's brain within the portal.

I extracted the surviving students one at a time, leaving Dr. Campbell trapped within a prisonous space, provided by the Unidentified Creature (Number 3); an eternity of never being able to leave again. All portals were destroyed and his ability to reach humankind eradicated.

The conclusion being: when a mysterious portal with unknown consequences shows up, don't open it. Hoping we can finally learn that lesson.

"Stunted Fate" by Thomas A. Fowler
Dinosaur in the Human Mind

I couldn't understand my place in this world. A floating, indiscernible place. A warm, red world where I could float. My last memory was entering a bright, vibrant circle.

A portal.

Why would I understand this word? A portal. I was growing smarter, my consciousness gaining intelligence. Consciousness, what an odd word. Con-chesh-ness. Going through this portal, I went somewhere new. It was a brain. Nothing like my brain. A creature I had never seen.

Was this the brain of something that could be my child? No, the brain was large compared to its body. Most of my dinosaur kind had relatively small brains. This was a creature I did not know. It was a female, like me, but a creature that wouldn't exist until well after my extinction.

My extinction.

All of the dinosaurs. How? How could all of my kind be obliterated? How was this woman's knowledge of history passed onto me? It didn't matter. What mattered was how I could change this. Change history. Change the fate of my life, and the lives of my very race!

Could this space, the mind of this woman show me how to alter my fate?

I swung my short arms to the side, unable to swim in this space. My arms didn't have the power. Something many of my predatory counterparts could handle better than me with my little arms and two claws. My legs, my tail, those let me move to find my destiny. My arms had to be stronger somehow, longer, more able. I continued to swim through this woman's mind, searching for an answer.

Then I saw it: a meteor. A rock the size of a mountain, flying through space. Hurling towards us. If I could stop this mountainous trajectory, alter its path, then I alter my path. The path for all dinosaurs.

Inside this woman's head was the answer, and the door. If I stepped into this world through a portal, then I can find my way to a solution.

"Hello?" she said to me. "Can you hear me? Can you help me?"

Another portal. A glowing light inside this woman's head. She told me a story, a story of her needing help. A story of a psychotic man bent on removing her kind from existence—like the dinosaurs. She asked for my help.

I approached, changing my destiny. As I went through it, I saw equipment: vials, chemicals, a human man. He wore a lab coat. We stared at one another, wondering how the other could change our respective histories.

"Monochromania" by M.M. Ralph
Psycho Killer in the Human Mind

Endless white with brassy doorknobs, that's all I can see. I lost the marks. I was carving them to track my place, to know which rooms I'd tried, but I lost them. I don't remember which way is back or which way is forward. I hate this hallway, but every time I find my way out of a room and back to it, I feel relief. It's a touchstone, and I hate it.

I will get out of here. I will find the right door. She can't keep me trapped forever. I do applaud her, for this device. It's the best yet for keeping me at bay. The medication was never this effective. When I heard she wanted to get off the pills and try a series of hypnotists and meditations, I thought I'd be back on top in no time. Guess she really showed me.

It won't last. It never lasts. You can't keep me out forever!! You hear me?

I'll find it. She knows I'll find it. I found it last time... last time she stopped taking the yellow pill. She hates them almost as much as I do. But then something different happened.

I'm not making sense. I feel like I can't breathe, and I can't think. I must be running a fever. I thought I was making progress. I thought... the marks. I left marks to know which doors I've tried. I don't see any! But I did leave them, I did. I had a... it was in my hand, screwdriver. But I don't know.

I don't know how long it's been. It's an endless hallway of endless doors and I'm sick of opening them. The last two I opened were to other hallways with more doors. I tried to get back, but I lost my place.

Ok, I can't keep sitting here. Movement, strategy, I've always got a plan. I always make a comeback. Ok, I feel like left is better than right. And 3 is the number of people I've killed, the 4th barely got away, stupid barking dog. So left door, number 3 it is.

What was that?

I thought I heard something. Was that a door slamming?

I don't hear it now. I must be losing it. Damn this claustrophobic, monochromatic hellhole!

Ok, third door.

There it is again. I know I heard it. It was a door slamming. Someone else, I'm not alone here.

"Hello?"

Nothing. No response.

Scratching. Something is scratching. I can hear it. It's behind me.

"Who's there?"

Not just scratching. It's a long, dragging sound. Like claws.

"Stop that! Who are you?"

Silence. Nothing. Where did it go?

"Are you stuck here too? I could help you. We could help each other. Do you know the way out?"

Slam, this time coming from in front of me.

"Hey, wait!" Was it three doors up or more?

Scratches, I see them. Someone else has been here. My marks. I see the scratches over my marks. Someone else is... Someone else has used me to get this far.

The Third. The Third followed me. I remember. I was in its hallway, found the door to it by mistake. I used the screwdriver to stab it, to try and get away.

Long scratches, I hear it. The door in front of me, it's on the other side.

I have to hide. If it gets me, if it gets out, it'll take everything. Neither of us will survive. I have to run. I have to lose it.

I can't believe I'm doing this. Can you hear me? Build another hallway! Build it fast! I can't believe I'm helping you. You created something worse than me!

SLAM.

"Dead Last" by Aylâ Larsen
Dinosaur in the Ocean

Blue. Blue. It had been days, (weeks?) of blue. Time was lost when the world blinded white, turned red hot, and issued an age of endless black that erased the sun. As if something had permanently turned out the lights. As if the planet had heaved a sigh and given up. And it seemed like its fiery mountains and watery depths knew it too, as they threw their bile to every corner of the map, abandoning ship and trying to escape. In darkness, flame and wave tossed in panic. The world shook. Then came the bitter cold, still on this sunless stage. The smallest scraped into the remaining earth to hide. Green had no reason to grow. Everything living, writhed, withered, stopped and shattered. The black faded to grey. The grey to blue. And blue. And blue. We didn't make it.

Is the world still shaking? No, no. Just rocking. I lazily, apathetically opened my eyes and caught a world of blue. This had been the usual sight for an endless time. Blue sky, blue water. It was difficult, though it bothered me none, to tell which side was up and which down. The pale, watery sun sent dancing glares upon the waves. It surprised me to smile to see it. My claws held tight around the trunk of the tree, its fronds brushing their own rhythm against my torso. My back legs and tail floated easily behind me. The spiny sail along my back had little feeling left in it. I attempted to stretch it and underestimated its damage. A painful roar escaped from my snout and my teeth snapped together with a hiss. My lungs heaved two quick, deep breaths and darkness blotted my vision, spreading into the center. The white and the red and the black flashed through my mind again and disappeared.

It was the lack of movement that woke me next, when my head and right side rested on a solid, grainy bank. The tree was gone and had been replaced by a pattern of smooth stones on the bank's edge that my claws clung to for support. I unclenched them and my teeth, which I didn't know I was doing. I had struck land. After so much time spent in the blue, my body was indescribably relieved to relax. I started to close my eyes to rest when I realized I was being watched. A curious bird with a fat, round beak, a fat round body and two scaly feet waddled its way towards me. It was the oddest thing I had ever seen. He was small but alarmed me, as creatures smaller than me and with so much meat on their bones had historically and wisely stayed far away from me, especially when any one of my teeth was bigger than their head. Before he got any closer, I instinctively hoisted my spiny sail in warning, and huffed, wincing at the pain and fighting the darkness starting to blot around my vision, but ready to defend. Yet he no more minded this gesture than if it were a passing breeze, and he got evermore closer.

My proven shield failing unexpectedly, I anxiously, quickly, took clunky, giant steps back into the water as he saddled up to the edge of the shore. After everything that had happened, I was shocked to know I still could feel fear. Before I could have my next thought, he opened that fat, round beak.

"You're new." He blinked and shivered his feathers. I stared. He stared back. There was a beat. "You look like a dragon."

I wasn't familiar with the word, so I neither knew if it was a compliment or an insult. It felt most like an observation, so I made one of my own.

"You look like something I would eat. Aren't you afraid of me?"

This made him laugh, which came out like a muffled honk. He turned his head, smirking, his eyes scanning me from snout to tail. His eyes traced the spines along my back and the teeth poking out from my closed jaw. "No," he responded confidently, still reviewing my shape. "You see, I evolved without any sort of predator at all. Well…for a time." He smiled sadly, and a story shadowed his eyes for an instant. He shook it away, then strode right up to my snout and ran his head along the tips of my upper teeth. I stood completely still, fascinated and confused. "Wow. This is quite new," he said. As his head brushed along my longest teeth at the very front, I snapped them ferociously together, trying to elicit some reaction. But all he did was hop, rather chipper, up onto the tip of my snout.

It was my turn to be amused. "You're the first thing I've ever known that didn't turn tail and run."

He laughed again, this one a laugh-sigh, designed by a bittersweet irony. "Ho ho, first thing?" He said and laughed the same way again.

Dodo was his name and he acted as my tour guide, perching comfortably on my snout as he directed me around the island. Island, I learned, was a name for a land surrounded by ocean. It seemed constricting to me, a place you had to stay and couldn't escape. So I asked him, "Don't you ever want to leave? How do you get off the island?" And without even turning around to look at me, he softly answered, almost more to himself than to me, "Where would I go?" I'm not sure he knew I heard him. But a silence followed, and he seemed through with the subject, so I let it drop.

The island itself was multi-dimensioned. The bank I had washed up on had been all sand and ocean, but I could see tall trees and snowy mountains inland. For now, we skirted the shore, and spotted a large, black-eyed, furry sea mammal swimming alongside a silver, narrow-snouted fish. They paused to notice me, then continued on their way. Dodo waved his tiny wing at them, then pointed them out and said their names. I had never seen water-based creatures that weren't lizards or fish. I took a step to follow them, but Dodo urged me to continue along the shoreline, and I turned back to catch one last glimpse of them as they swam further away.

After the sand and ocean and the creatures who dwelled there, we turned inland and came upon a field of long, yellow grass, where a four-legged, golden animal with darker fur framing his face and a long tail was standing next to a giant bird towering above me and another four-legged creature with skinny, twig-legs and two large spikes curling up and out of the top of her head. A bird smaller than Dodo, with two feathers poking out from either side of his neck and close stripes of brown and white, was speaking to the others, in an animated tone when we walked up.

"And then it became a holiday! Can you believe that? And was it *me* who was remembered? Oh no, it was the wild turkey! And have you seen any turkeys around here? No! You haven't! So much for giving thanks! I mean, for-"

The animals listening appeared relieved and grateful when Dodo politely interrupted the small bird. He introduced him as Heath Hen, and named the others, but I admit, I can't recall the rest of their names, being so fascinated and overwhelmed by their odd appearances. They seemed shocked by my appearance too, although less so when the fur-faced one said, "He reminds me of Dragon," and the other creatures nodded in agreement. I looked from one face to another trying to determine what sort of reaction or emotion that word inspired. No clue. As we walked away, Dodo leaned down close to my face and said, "You'll have to forgive Heath Hen, he's still fairly new and a little upset about being forgotten." I wondered how anyone could forget such an obnoxious and grating little bird.

As we left the grasslands, we turned deeper into the island, and came upon a giant lake stretched out in front of us, its other side cloaked in a heavy grey mist. Hopping up onto the top of my sail, Dodo gestured his head towards that other unknown side of the lake. I dove headfirst into the water, swimming easily as Dodo kept dry high up on my sail. Hours later, the water turned cold, thick and frozen. And piece by piece the mist gave way to an icy, windy desert. Hooking my claws into the sheets of ice, I pulled us up onto the snowy shore and happened upon another odd animal – an orange, four-legged, furry creature with pointed ears and two sharp front teeth that were twice the length of my longest tooth. Dodo was introducing her as Saber when a large mountain behind us started to move. I stumbled back a step before I realized it was not a mountain, but a giant creature. He had what appeared to be five legs, but one leg hung down from between his eyes and two enormous, white spikes that curved out and up from his cheeks. This fifth leg moved more fluidly than the others, and as Dodo told me the mountain-sized creature's name, it wandered playfully along my fin and spines, clearly curious of my shape. I was too shocked and wide-eyed to issue any sort of sound.

Leaving the frozen desert, my sore feet thawed as we wandered into a familiar climate. Water made the air heavy and the heat rise from the soft earth. The trees and vegetation around us grew thick, crawling this way and that, tangling together. Some trees I knew but some trees sported bark, roots, leaves and colors I had never seen before. Deeper into the glens, the green impossibly grew even more and surrounded us. Every inch was green. My eyes swam with tears thinking of all the untimely time I had spent mourning the color green, believing a whole color no longer existed in the world. When the green blocked our way, my teeth ripped through it or my claws stomped it down. The further we entered the woods, a dissonance of whistling, singing and shouting grew. Dodo stopped me after a minute or so, where the noise was at peak level. Even though I wasn't making a sound, Dodo turned to me and mimicked a *shh* with his short wing, barely reaching his beak. He looked me in the eyes with a kind of manic smile, and tilted his head straight up. My eyes followed and bright sunlight fell into my eyes. I blinked and winced. Then a world of color unfolded before me. There were birds, insects and animals of every kind thriving and bustling in the green. Small birds whistled to each other, flitting here and there, inching along branches. Each one was brilliantly colored, a flurry of rainbows. One bird with a red crest atop his head, similar to my sail, loudly knocked his beak against a tree trunk over and over again. A black sparrow with vibrant, yellow wings and a long white tail rested on a twig next to another black bird with a long, curved beak and orange cheeks. A blue bird with a green stomach sat next them. A red bird with yellow and blue feathers perched across from them. They sang a lovely melody together, each one a different harmony, culminating in one layered, flawless symphony. A curious-looking mammal with a pouch glided from tree to tree, with a *whoosh*, its fur spread out into a blanket that carried it to and fro. A violet beetle crawled along a leaf, a green worm with 50 legs followed it, and a red, round bug with spots followed after. They were carrying on a conversation. I could pick out words here and there, but they talked so fast and over each other, constantly interrupting and changing the subject. Water trickled down from the tops of the trees and added a soft pattering backdrop. So lost was I in the spectacle that Dodo half scared me when he whispered "Beautiful, isn't it? There are too many of them for you to meet right now, but you'll learn their names in time."

I wanted to stay and watch the activity of the forest, blissful in its lively existence, but Dodo urged us on. After a while though, my steps became heavy and after taking in so many strange places and animals, my mind was so filled with questions that it prevented me from carrying either of us any further. It was nearing sunset now, and the mood of the dusky light somehow marked the right moment to get some answers. When I came to a complete halt, Dodo turned his head back to look at me. He jumped off my snout and stood on the ground, preening and pulling his feathers without a word.

I intended to start with the most obvious question, but once I did, the rest tumbled out too. "Where are we? What are all these animals? Why are they here? Why do they all look so strange? Why don't any of them look like me?" Suddenly exhausted, I huffed and sunk my head to the ground, whipping my tail back and forth as an idle comfort. "What's going on?" I whispered tiredly, looking at a stray pebble in my field of view.

Dodo took a deep breath and calmly started to explain, in a manner that suggested he had told this tale many, many times before. He spoke slowly and clearly. "This is the Island of Last Things. Every living thing on this island was the last of its kind. Saber-Tooth, Mammoth, Ibex, Lion, Seal, all those things in the rainforest, on the shore, me, all of us. Everyone you've met here is a last thing. We don't know how or why, but each of us washed up on the shore of this place when the rest of our kind went extinct."

I swallowed and ground my teeth together. He looked at me and read my mind.

"Yes, you too. You are the last..." He paused and looked me over once more. "I say, what *are* you?"

"Dinosaur," I breathed.

"Ah. Di-no-saur." The word didn't sit right in his beak and he chewed the syllables as he said it two more times quickly and quietly, to get the hang of it or maybe as not to forget.

Was it true? Was I the last dinosaur? It's not like I hadn't suspected it with everything that had happened. But suspecting it and having it be confirmed were two very different things. Or was it confirmed? Who said this fat little bird knew everything? Or anything?

"But I've never seen most of these creatures before," I bit at him, defensively.

"And many of us have never seen anything like you. Time doesn't follow the rules on this island. It's nonlinear. Creatures just show up, without any sort of warning and come from any age, any year. All jumbled and out of order. On the southern point of the island, we've charted the timeline of earth and we fill in the gaps, frontwards and back when someone new arrives. Many of these creatures never existed at the same time, which is why many of us look so strange to one other."

Oh I see, I thought. I've gone insane! Or I swallowed too much seawater in the blue and now it's making me hallucinate. Yes, that's it. I bet I'm still floating on some wave somewhere, my scaly arms and claws still wrapped around that tree, hallucinating from drinking too much seawater. Or, I've landed in a place where a bunch of kooks offed the rest of their species. A land of murderers. Oh, *much* better. My stomach churned from the thought. Or was that the seawater getting to me? One thing was for sure. I had to get out of here. I had to escape the island. Maybe find some other dinosaur survivors. With little difficulty, I feigned exhaustion.

"Right. This is a lot to take in. I think I'll just take a walk and mull it over, maybe look around and take a nap," I lied. Dodo nodded his head at me and said, "Of course. I should report back anyway in case there's another new arrival." And with that he stood up, saluted his wing to me and waddled away. I stepped in the opposite direction, and when he was out of sight, broke into a full sprint.

I ran along the shore, waiting for the ocean to turn into a bridge of land. Surely an entire plot of earth couldn't be entirely surrounded by water. My whole life, every pool of water I spent hunting fish in was surrounded by dirt, rocks, and green. Oh please let there be no such thing as an island.

Sometime later, I had found nothing but myself in a marshy land. The night had settled in. I sank to the ground and the seawater in my stomach from my blue journey finally splurged out. I coughed, gasping for air and cursed, as it confirmed that this place was not a result of the seawater after all.

"Will you keep it down?!" An annoyed voice spat at me from the large-leaved bushes and trees that covered the ground. I whipped my head around looking for the source of the voice but found none. The trees were thick and the bushes obscured the ground entirely. Suddenly I saw something – a scaly patch of skin that looked like mine amongst the heavy plant life. I searched for more skin. My eyes squinted, scanning the dark. Leaf, leaf, tree, moss, leaf, tree trunk, bush. My eyes jumped back to the tree trunk. I cautiously stepped closer and saw that it was not a tree trunk or even a tree at all, but a leg – scaly and huge. A sigh shook the leaves and its wind uncovered the head of the creature 50 feet to the right. Finally, a familiar face! Overjoyed, I ran up to it.

"You're here!" I nearly shouted. "I knew that bird was crazy. Last dinosaur, my ass!"

Sharp, bony ridges and spikes covered her face and her snout came to a narrow point. One of the dinosaur's eyes slowly opened and observed me for a brief moment. Her eye was golden, with an ebony slit down the middle. It closed.

"What are you on about? Let me sleep."

But I was not to be deterred. "Dodo! That fat bird, he told me I was the last of my kind. But it's all bullshit!" I laughed, deliriously. "Bullshit!"

"Yup. You're right," she said lazily, still with her head nestled in the bushes. "You're not the last of your kind."

42

I beamed. I wasn't alone.

"I knew it!" I cried. "I'm not the last dinosaur." A joyful roar leaped from my throat. It rang through the air, bouncing off the trees and echoing away.

The dinosaur opened the same eye, studied me for a moment then closed it again and rubbed her chin along the ground before settling its head back down. She sighed, "Yes you are."

My happy bubble popped. Now I was the annoyed one. "What are you talking about? I'm a dinosaur; you're a dinosaur. We're dinosaurs!"

At this, both her eyes snapped open and a stern, rigid brow bore down upon them. In one quick and fluid motion, she lifted her head up out of the marsh, and shot her whole body up into the air. Leaves, vines and dirt fell off her and monstrous wings unfolded from her sides, crimson and beating ferociously in a heartbeat rhythm, sending a cloud of dust swirling beneath her. She hung there, suspended and powerful, glaring down at me. I stared up at her with wide eyes. Her neck was long and narrow and her body wide with four, trunk legs and a long, spiked tail that came to a sharp, triangular point.

Slowly, her wings gently brought her to the ground and folded up again. "I am NOT a dinosaur," she said indignantly and sharply, as if to close the subject.

I shook my head, my voice shaking. "B-but. You have scales. And-and spines. And eyes like mine."

"I fly."

"Some dinosaurs fly," I whispered, desperately.

Fire like lightning erupted from her mouth, drawing a line between us, igniting the ground. The line snapped and flickered as I stumbled backwards, shielding myself behind the fallen tree I tripped over.

The red flames between us swam in her eyes are she stared into mine and snarled, baring her razor teeth. She exhaled angrily a few times, then seeing my expression, suddenly calmed and looked at me with sorrow and pity. Her mouth curled into a downward smile. Her long tail swept across the earth and snuffed out the flames. And she turned from me, and sunk onto the ground once more, her head flopping haphazardly onto the grass, the smoke creating a gray mist around her.

She was an enormous stone curled up on the land. I shuffled across the smoldering line and once again walked up to her face. Her eyes were open, but looking out at nothing, at a point beyond me and beyond the world. I sat next to her head, my sail drooped back in truce. We sat in silence for a while, watching the stars.

"So you're not a dinosaur," I offered.

She coughed out a laugh and a puff of smoke escaped from her nostrils and floated up towards the moon. "No," she replied. "I'm a dragon."

Upon hearing the word, the comments from Dodo and Lion rushed back to me. "Well, you have to admit we look a lot alike. Others have even said so."

She nodded ever so slightly, in a sure-why-not sort of fashion, still looking through me and the stars.

"So why did you say I'm not the last of my kind?"

Her eyes blinked, then focused on me and her shoulders drooped. She sighed and looked off in the distance again.

"A great war made me the last dragon. Our enemies were small but ruthless and insisted we were conquests despite our rather peaceful nature. For years we fought but our numbers dwindled. We knew going into that last battle that it would be the final battle." Her eyes met mine again. "You never forget that feeling. Striding into a day knowing you won't see the end of it." She turned away again and shook her head. The colors flashed in my mind and I clawed idly at the dirt.

"Then just as you did, I arrived here. At that time, I was the largest creature to wash up on the beach. I recognized almost no one, I looked like no one and I felt entirely alone. Probably kinda how you felt this morning. Or right now. I'm sure Dodo has filled you in on how time works, or rather doesn't work on this island. We're never hungry or thirsty and we never age."

Dodo had left that part out, but she was right. I realized that even though I had been here all day, walking, swimming, and climbing that I had never wanted or needed anything to sustain me. And I didn't now, either.

"Immortality might seem like a blessing, and perhaps on the world we came from it would have been, but for all of us who have seen our species, our friends, our families, our—" she swallowed, "our children die, it's…" The end of her sentence hung there, and the emotion of the silence that followed finished it better than any words ever could. I stared hard at her with concrete understanding, my chest pulsing, trying to push back the colors and faces from flooding my mind.

She met my eyes and held them and for the first time, someone else knew and shared the empty space in my soul. I was under her spell. I hung on her every word and willed myself not to cry.

"I'm not a dinosaur. You're not a dragon. No, none of us are the same species. But what creatures have something more in common than us? We don't all have feathers or stripes or swim or—"

"Blow fire?"

"Ha, or that. But we all share one big thing. We're bonded by an indescribable tragedy no one else could ever fully understand if they haven't been through it firsthand. We're not related, but we can relate to each other in a deeper way than any others can. We're a family – a species of devastating memories and unfathomable loss. We're the last, but we're not the last of our kind." She attempted a soothing grin, her needle teeth bared. "This island is full of our kind."

Moments after Dragon had stopped speaking, I was still comprehending her words and unknowingly tearing up when a blue bird with a round, black beak and bright yellow chest flew overhead and landed in front of us. It breathed heavily and swallowed.

"Why Parrot, what brings you here?" Dragon said, in a friendly tone.

"Dragon!" he said, then looked at me curiously. "You! Come quick!" He exhaled quickly again. "It's the new arrival." Without another word, Parrot took off the way he came.

Dragon looked concerned and I immediately jumped onto her back. We soared back to the shore I had washed up on only hours before.

It was dawn when we reached the shore. An unruly mob had formed. Creatures of every kind were arguing with one another. Dodo stood in the midst of the madness, trying desperately to get everyone's attention. "Please! Please!" he kept shouting.

"I say we kill it!" shouted a gray, leathery-skinned animal with a fat horn sitting on the end of his snout. He was in tears. More shouts erupted at this.

I recognized Heath Hen, sitting atop the grey animal sounding her support.

"An eye for an eye!" she yelled, her feathers ruffled and her stance defiant.

"We can't just kill the last of a species," begged Dodo.

A rotund, black and white furry animal with two round ears shouted back, "That's what *it* did!"

"And are *we* no better?" sounded a large, black-furred animal as he beat his bald chest with one of his hands. His black eyes glared seriously under his heavy brow.

Then I saw him. The new animal. He struggled to his feet and everyone went silent. Dragon's breath, a pulsing warm breeze, hitched and stopped. All was still. I stared at his face and saw myself in his eyes. Only this morning I had carried the same emotions as him. I still carried some of them now. I looked around at the expressions of the crowd, puzzled. Aren't we one big family? Isn't that what Dragon's little speech had been about? The new creature stood with his feet at the edge of the shore, the small waves lapping up to him. All the creatures stood still. I crawled down off Dragon's back and headed toward him. Dragon nipped at my tail and I turned around. She pleaded at me with her eyes, but I frowned at her hypocrisy and continued on.

The animals parted as I made my way toward him, and I could feel every eye following me. As I came closer, the new creature instinctively moved away from me. Ah, the usual reaction. I smiled at him, but my teeth scared him even more and he stumbled backwards into the water. In apology, I retreated a step back from him. No one else moved. What is going on? I looked back again at the mob, my eyes hopping from face to face, every single one staring at the new last thing. What sort of welcome committee was this? I looked at Dodo with a confused and helpless expression. His face was drooped, eyes staring at the ground, avoiding mine. Seconds later, he looked up at me in sad acceptance. I didn't understand. Dodo waddled up next to me, not taking his eyes off his feet. He sighed and with strained amiability, finally spoke to the new creature. His tone was unenthusiastic, a memorized and standard greeting.

"Welcome to the Island of Last Things. You are the last of your species. We too share painful memories like the ones you, no doubt, possess." A distant voice from the crowd cried "Murderer!" I looked back fleetingly to see if I could catch who.

Dodo paused for a moment, unsure how to continue, and tapped his left foot upon the ground. "But." He stopped tapping and looked up, intensely locking eyes with the new arrival. "Make no mistake. We do *not* carry the guilt that will weigh heavily on you for having to spend eternity with us. In that, you remain alone." Then to himself, so only I and the newcomer could hear: "I feared this day would come." Dodo looked at me, then back at the new arrival, then at his own two feet again, and in a monotone, hollow voice said: "Welcome, human."

"The Butcher Buccaneer of Brighton Bay" by Rob Walker

Psycho Killer in the Ocean

The man in the blood-spattered pirate costume was tired. He was especially exhausted now that he found himself hanging upside down in a fisherman's net. Blood was flowing to his head and the glow-in-the-dark skull mask affixed to his face didn't breathe. For months he had been scaring townies and high school students from Brighton Bay in hopes that he could lower the area's property value. He thought that if people were scared, local business owners would have no choice but to sell and he, Lester Wilkins, visionary real estate developer, would swoop in and snap it up cheap. In five years, give or take, the dilapidated boardwalk would be a hip waterfront neighborhood, in which financially flush young idiots would spend tens of thousands each month to be close to organic coffee shops and artisanal mustache barbers.

But the people didn't scare. The Butcher Buccaneer of Brighton Bay had actually made the area *more* desirable. The Brighton Bay

Boardwalk was on the verge of financial collapse but with the rumors of a ghost haunting the area, businesses had seen an unexpected boost. "Madame Cleota's Ghost Tours" was the first cottage industry to spring up around spectral sailors, and the people came in droves. Then the Discovery Channel sent those "Spirit Hunter" dopes to Brighton Bay for their show. The morons didn't find anything of course, but with that single broadcast, the area gained national attention. Then there were t-shirt shops and ghost pirate themed tiki bars. Business was booming all thanks to his ill-conceived real estate scam and the $30-dollar pirate costume he bought online.

He hadn't planned on killing anyone, not at first. He had been under the boardwalk, half in the bag, contemplating his financial ruin when they saw him and started laughing.

"Are you the ghost pirate?" one of them tittered.

"He looks like a homeless guy in a cheap costume," said a tall, young man in a Brighton Bay Buccaneers jersey.

"Can we get a picture?" said the young woman flipping out her phone.

That was the final insult. He was supposed to be an up-and-coming developer and now here he was, in a frilly lace cravat, reduced to taking selfies with college kids.

"It wasn't supposed to be like this." He muttered to himself behind his glow-in-the-dark skull mask. They thought he was getting ready for a photograph when he beheaded the tall young man and ran the other one through. The girl attempted to run and call for help, but tripped and with one swipe, was silenced.

"Heels? On the beach?" he thought to himself, before he blacked out.

The next morning, it was all over the front page of the Brighton Bay Crow's Nest.

Someone had uncovered the cell phone and a blurry image of a skeleton pirate standing over the corpse of a young coed was the image they pulled. Suddenly, the Ghost Pirate was dangerous, and the coroner had three dead bodies prove it. Everyone was terrified, but Lester Wilkins couldn't have been more pleased. He had found the missing ingredient to his plan, murder.

Glorious, grisly murder. The first three had been a fluke, just a couple of drunk kids out for a night of bar-hopping. He had to work harder for the others.

There was the elderly couple that owned the candle making store "Let There Be Light."

He left them floating in a vat of candle wax. Then there was a divorced man on vacation; he had to break into the hotel for that one. He was sure to lock the door, to make it appear as though the ghost could walk through walls. As the body count was mounting, tourists were emptying out and he saw his plan coming to fruition. Sure, he felt a little bad about the murders, but he saw these acts as minor, moral kerfuffles that could be tolerated and forgotten about once he owned Brighton Bay.

"You can't tell me that Steve Jobs never did anything bad on his way to turning Apple into a household brand," he would think aloud as he prepared for his nightly activities. "No successful person in this country has ever achieved greatness without drowning a cheerleader in the ocean or beheading a retired postal worker in a photo booth...for example."

He had planned on just a few more bodies and then he was sure that Brighton Bay would be his. He just hadn't anticipated those friggin' kids and their damn dog.

For the final stage of his business plan, he had secretly boarded a ferry called the Brighton Beauty in hopes of killing everyone on board. It would be horrible, no doubt about it, but a coup de grace is exactly what he needed to push his plan over the top and a flying Dutchman busting into Brighton Pier with a crew of dead bodies onboard would make a hell of a picture for the evening edition. He should have noticed how empty the ferry was at the time, but he assumed it was because the scourge of the Ghost Pirate was taking hold. So, when he approached the young, ginger-haired college student gazing out into the bay, he didn't suspect a trap. Least of all a spring-loaded fisherman's net. As he raised his saber above his head, hoping to cleave the young woman in two, he heard a young man yell, "Now!" It was a blur after that.

As he hung there, surrounded by a scrum of smiling teens brandishing cameras and magnifying glasses flanked by a growling mastiff, it donned on Lester Wilkins that things may have gotten a tad out of hand. He learned later, that while he was stalking victims, an after-school club of teenagers had been tracking his movements. They contacted local law enforcement and laid the perfect trap. "The Mystery of the Butcher Buccaneer of Brighton Bay," as the papers called it, was a jewel in the crown for the young detectives. As a matter of fact, they unmasked him there on the deck of the ferry in front of a crowd of eager reporters, relieved Brighton Bay residents and celebrity actor Don Knotts, who was in attendance to cut the ribbon on the new ghost-themed wax museum. Lester Wilkins didn't fancy himself a killer, he was a just a real estate guy who had run out of options. It was a good plan though, and he might've gotten away with it, too.

"A Sudden Odd Feeling" by Mike Cervantes

Dinosaur in the Triassic

It is said that life on Earth began approximately 300 million years ago, a cosmically large sum, but a drop in the bucket compared to the 13.82 billion years there even was a universe. Then there's the 201 million years which made the genesis of every five-year-old future scientist's favorite time period: the Triassic. The turning point of the Mesozoic era wherein all species of life; be they amphibious, reptile, mammal, or aquatic; were established in the firmament of life on this planet. It came to be our amazement that the largest species of the era happened to be the reptiles; who first found themselves the size of the most fabled Tyrannosaurus Rex in this era, and the widest representation of terrible lizards—whether they were carnivorous, plant-eating, or lake dwelling—wandered the early planet in life's first intricate ballet beneath the Earth's firmament.

It came to be, at some specific point in this already miraculous era, that one eternally famed species, that Tyrannosaurus Rex, stood upon a pillar-like rock on the outskirts of the vast and uncharted forest, surveying what we romanticize to be his kingdom, looking outward into chaos, order, the past, present, the future and the like, when it was overcome by this sudden odd feeling. It basked in it, allowing it to overcome it, as it stood among the rocks, and occasionally brought its shoulder to a nearby tree to give it a nice, firm scratching. There it lingered for a considerable amount of time, when another T-Rex emerged from the same brush an incalculable amount of time later and began to speak.

"Heya Shep."

"Heya Lou."

"What'cha doin'?"

"I'm not too sure, Lou." The T-Rex paused to rub its shoulder on the tree again. "I just had this sudden, frustrating thought."

"It's about the brachiosaurs, isn't it? The way they just sit in the middle of the water hole, where it might be too deep for us to just tromp in there and bite 'em, since we don't know if it's that deep. Not to mention the fact that they…y'know. Pee in there? The crocodiles live down there too, just swimmin' in the brachiosaurs' toilet. And they're all so smug…just sitting in that pond all day with their necks curved, like they're posing for a picture."

"What the hell is a picture?" asked Shep.

"I dunno," Lou twisted its large, heavy, head a bit sideways. "Well, maybe…you've seen the small furry things, right? Sometimes they'll hold a piece of crap in their forelegs, and then smear it all over a rock, right? Maybe that's a picture."

"Maybe, but I don't think this is about the Brachiosaurs."

"Well what is it about then? You know, you make me worry when you get like this…."

"Sorry. I was just thinking…well…Do you ever kind of wish that something…exciting would happen?"

"What's exciting?"

"I dunno," Shep looked up, where a Pteranodon flew past their vision. Shep tried to lift up its neck and bite it, but he just couldn't reach. "Well…you know when the rock rolled off the hill and smacked that ankylosaur, and they both rolled down, and then the rock smacked into the water and scared out the crocodiles, so they ran to the shore across the itchy bushes, and then they were irate and twitchy for weeks?"

"Yeah?"

"I think that's exciting. That doesn't happen every day. But today happens every day, and that makes me feel down."

"So, it's just that today is the same as a few other days that you're feeling this way?" Lou craned its neck back. "Maaaaaybe...if I were to roll a rock down the hill. Would that make you feel better?"

"I don't think so, what are your odds of hitting an ankylosaur?"

"Pretty good, I say. I've been practicing! Now, here we go! Heave-ho!"

"No no no, don't..." Shep took a moment to bump its head across Lou's chest, just to keep its attention. "I think if that would happen again, that wouldn't be exciting anymore, I'm talking about...REAL excitement?"

"Well, how do you make...REAL excitement?"

"I don't think you can. Just try to follow me on this Lou: What if...this feeling isn't about me?"

"Well if your feelings aren't about you, then who are they about?"

"I dunno." Shep was silent for a moment. It looked down at his toes and counted them, having found a long time ago that it was impossible to count its fingers. "I mean, do you remember that time we found that egg on the hill, and I smashed it, and we never knew where it came from or who it belonged to? And didn't you tell me you felt bad that happened?"

"Too right," Lou gave a nod. "Afterwards we couldn't eat it."

"Okay, okay, so...follow me along with this: what if there are things out there...that we just can't eat?"

"That's crazy," Lou chuffed. "You're talking crazy."

"Well, think about it: what are we standing on right now?"

"A hill."

"Can we eat the hill?"

"No, and I don't think I'd even want to. If I ate the hill, where would I stand?"

"Exactly, and what about this big blue thing that's around us all the time?"

"The sky?"

"I think that's what it is…Well, do you ever remember eating that?"

"I don't think so," Lou took a moment and snapped the sky with its teeth, and then it swallowed. The sky didn't seem to be a food. But they tried it again, and after two or three tries, Shep tried it too. And they both stood on this rock, snapping at the air for a moment.

"I can't do it, it's like it's not there."

"But it is there, it's the sky, we named it and everything. And it's not the same as eating the hill. If we bit the hill our teeth would hurt. But if we bite the sky, it doesn't die, and our teeth don't hurt. So, how are we supposed to know we're supposed to eat it or not? It doesn't even play by the rules."

"I hadn't thought about it that way before." Lou bowed its body to the left, scratching its shoulder on a tree that was of the same type, but a different distance from Shep's. "So, what you're trying to say…is that there are some things that don't exist for us to either eat, or get hurt on, and that makes you upset?"

"I think so," Shep hung its head a bit as he said it. "For a while, I thought that being a big ol' T-Rex and being able to stomp around and ram into rocks and eat everything in sight was the best thing in the whole world, but now I have to think, that there's a whole other pile of stuff that we can't do, just because we're T-Rexes."

"Oh come on, Shep, name one thing we can't do."

"Well, for example," Shep took a pause to reach up again with his neck at another passing Pteranodon. "We can't do that."

"We can have all the Pteranodons you want, Shep, you just need to wait until it's evening and they're nesting…"

"No, I mean, Pteranodons are ON the sky. We're not on the sky."

"Well, I mean, it's because they have those great big skin-covered arms. We only have these little tiny, shrimpy arms. That's simple science."

"What's science?"

"I dunno," Lou paused to flap its tiny arms up and down really quick. "Well do you remember that one night when the sky got mad and made that flash. Then the flash turned red and landed in that nest of the tiny, furry things. Then we went over and ate them, and they were extra good?"

"Yeah."

"I think that's science."

"I see. But I still have to wonder. Right now, we can't be on the sky like the Pteranodons. Are we ever going to get to?"

"Get to be on the sky? That'd be neat: we could totally walk right on top of the brachiosaurs and pee on them. That'll show 'em who's boss!"

"I think it'd just be swell to be up there."

"Are you kidding, Shep? All those guys eat are worms and seaweed. I wouldn't want to eat just worms and seaweed. I'm a T-Rex. I can eat anything I set my cat-sized mind to."

"What's a cat?"

"You know those small furry things who scream a lot and pick on all the other small furry things? Those are cats."

"Oh."

"And one time I heard Barry say he saw a T-Rex crack his head open, and inside was a pink squishy thing the size of a cat."

"What does that have to do with anything?"

Lou paused to scratch his shoulder on the tree. "I dunno, I forgot. So anyway, I don't think you have to worry too much about this. They're Pteranodons, and you're a T-Rex, we all just do what we're supposed to do. Maybe you can't be on the sky, but you sure as hell can eat everything."

"Except the hill and the sky."

"But you can eat enough things. That has to count for something doesn't it?"

"It does, but there's still something else I've been thinking."

"There's something else…okay there's ALWAYS something else," Lou heaved, his tiny arms drooping down in the center of his massive chest. "What is it this time, Shep?"

"I mean, here we are, somewhere vaguely in the middle of this whole book…"

"What's a book?"

"I dunno," Shep leaned over and scratched itself for an especially long time. "Okay, you remember when that raptor got its claws in an armadillo and sliced it in half? Then all the guts and the junk it just ate spilled all over and it smelled like hell, and it took the whole thing, skin and all, and splattered it on top of a big flat rock. Then it took another big flat rock and slapped it on top of it, and it went totally flat. Then the raptor stood there looking all smug and proud?"

"Yeah?"

"I think that's a book."

"Okay, so go on…"

"So here we are, all scrambled up and smashed in between two rocks, and besides the fact we're not even alive at that point, we're just this side show for the amusement of just one weirdo: Raptor. But even that's not the worst of it. Suppose there is just you, me, this hill and that sky: we're just two T-Rexes living where we're supposed to live, doing what we're supposed to do, and there's got to be tons of stuff still out there that somehow have more value than we do."

"Things like what, Shep?"

"Well, suppose there are things like…sharks, and aliens, and babies and keytarists, and aliens, and clowns, and imaginary friends, and murderers, and hydras, and clowns…"

Lou shook its head around in a very bewildered way, "Okay, you've completely lost me."

"Sorry. I'm just trying to say is…just how big is all of this? There's got to be more out there besides this hill, and those Pteranodons, and those jerky brachiosaurs, and it won't take long before we get clobbered by some great big rock and we're not going to see it all."

"Okay, okay, okay." Lou waved its arms back and forth and collided its head with Shep's chest to calm it down. "I think you're going a bit too far in all of this. I can't keep myself around if you keep on going like this."

"Why not, Lou?"

"Well, I remember this one time, you wandered into the den one day and you said to me, 'Lou, I have this sudden odd feeling.' Then you lay on top of me, and hopping up and down like crazy, then a little while later, my belly got really big. Then I laid that egg. Then after a while, that little tiny T-Rex burst out of the shell?"

"Yeah?"

"Then I ate it?"

"Uh-huh."

"That's what happens when you take these things too far. I need you to be just a little bit okay with how things are. Otherwise, we can't make things like that happen. Who cares if we can't fly like our food can? Or that we can't pee on the brachiosaurs. We can still walk around and eat just about everything that's not the hill or the sky, and I tell you: that ain't so bad."

"Yeah, I think you're right, Lou," Shep cooed fondly, closing its eyes and softly bumping noses with Lou. At last they made the choice to turn around and climb back up the hill.

"Where are you going?"

"Back to the den, I think it's a better idea for me to keep my sudden odd feelings up there from now on."

"Well, maybe. But I wouldn't mind having one in front of the brachiosaurs, just once, to see the look on their faces."

And so, these two tyrannosaurs went back to their den. Sadly, there isn't a more expedited way to tell the rest of this story: suffice it to say brachiosaurs peed on things, furry mammals crapped on their paws and smeared them on rocks, raptors crushed armadillos between large rocks. Inevitably as a direct and meaningful parallel to all these actions, the modern world happened. Civilizations rose and fell, our intellectual minds, which are, for the most part, much larger than that of a cat, developed to invent realms of possibilities far greater than anything our dominant predecessors could ever have imagined.

It is said, that evolution of the dinosaur species was inevitably brought to our modern age intact. The once powerful reptilian species that populated the planet are now considered to be the ancestors of several avian species, including chickens, ostriches, and parakeets. Their compact size, their greater species adaptability, and, for many species, their ability to take to the skies, has ensured their place as a vastly more enduring species in the modern age.

And it just so happened that in this wonderful modern age, two parakeets were sitting on a wooden post in their birdcage…

"The Atavist" by E. Godhand
Psycho Killer in the Triassic

It was dark when Reika got home. The bus was late again. That was the third time this week and frankly she was getting annoyed. A man had stepped in front of it as it pulled up, and they needed time to clean him out of the grill. Though it was always some version of dark nowadays, even when the sun was up, so it shouldn't have mattered to her much except this meant more time in a world where men preferred to walk in front of buses instead of playing in the peaceful world of Arcadia. The news alert on her phone suggested it was another case of the smog blocking vision, but no one believed that. Not anymore.

Her little apartment wasn't much brighter. As a pharmacist, she could have splurged for the room with a window (a view was extra), and maybe more room than a raised bed above a microwave and sink. But that would be all her rent for the month, and entire families made do with this much space, so she counted herself lucky. Besides, her sister, the doctor and favorite, had a window and most days she saw white fog. Only the top floors could afford to see above the heavy clouds.

Reika removed her mask, a cloth tied around the lower half of her face, and reminded herself to change the charcoal filter soon. She climbed up into her bunk and emptied her purse onto the covers. The real reason she didn't have a nicer place, if she was honest with herself, was that she needed the money for the latest expansion of Arcadia.

The Fall had happened so quickly, and there was nowhere left to retreat except the worlds that humanity made.

The virtual reality was her second home. Or her first, if you actually counted her play time. She turned the case of hardware over in her hands and read the pitch on the back:

The first of many explorations of life in the Mesozoic era, experience a world of fire and ice! The Great Extinction left 95% of the biosphere dead. Start on the beaches of Pangea and work your way in. Will you and your tribe become the dominant life form, merely survive, or succumb to the dangers of the dinosaurs?

Below the text was a map of Pangea. It looked like a man bent over smoking a pipe. She loaded the game into her machine and put on her goggles. She laid down on the bed with her arms stretched out and waited for the game to load.

The main server of Arcadia was a lush virtual wilderness. It started as a hiking simulator to explore what once were the National Forests.

But once the players figured out how to modify it to build villagers and grow crops, it expanded into a refuge where people could learn new skills, solve quests, explore mines, make friends, or just sit and enjoy the sun on their faces and the sounds of a creek babbling through a green forest.

Reika's tribe, The Deadfall, so named for the tree line in the distance of a quaint village in the valley shadowed by the mountains, was on a peaceful PVE server where players couldn't attack one another. That didn't eliminate disputes, mind you, but the Council was reasonable, and one member even knew a Moderator. There, she was the local Apothecary and had a cottage with an herb garden. There, she could nourish something and watch it grow, then salvage it to make poultices and teas and rolled pills that healed those around her. Seeing the suffering leave their face as her medicine kicked in made it all worth it. She had planned on making sweet bread after grinding the rind of a citron with the poppy seeds, but the expansion came first.

She left a tribe-wide message for everyone that she'd be unavailable for the time being, and who else was going to try the expansion?

No hits. She sighed, then heard the download finish with a happy tone. Finally.

A screen popped up to choose where to load on the map. She picked the southwest corner of Pangea, a warm temperate zone near what would be modern-day Argentina. The freezing tundra at the poles and the deserts between the Tropic of Cancer and the Tropic of Capricorn seemed a bit much for a starting zone.

...Loading...
...Loading...
...Loading...

She was in.

Reika loaded onto the beach, soaked from the salt ocean that lapped at her toes and dusted with thick sand that scratched everything not covered by her modest bandeau and loincloth.

With a gasp, she forced her eyes open and pushed herself to her feet. Once she had her bearings, she twirled in place to take in this new world. Mosses covered broken boulders along the beach, ferns scattered the hillside in between trees of larger ferns. The forest beyond was filled with conifers: pine trees and firs and spruces, until the tree line of the Andes mountains in the distance cut off all life. A lystrosaurus wandered by, a pug-nosed creature no taller than two feet high that waddled on four legs and snuffled at the various plant life.

Reika smiled and wiggled in excitement. She would need to gather beach wood and rocks for a fire. There would be long branches she could use to make a conical shelter and side it with stripped leaves from the fern trees. First, she'd need a spear. She walked until she found a suitable stick and sat down to sharpen a rock for a point.

She had just finished wrapping the spearhead with twine when she spotted another player tag approaching. *BitterPoussin*. Reika hopped to her feet and waved.

Something was coming towards her. Before she could blink a second time, the other player's spear lodged itself through her chest. The game screen faded to black as naturally as if she had fallen asleep.

Wait, had she logged onto the player vs player server by accident? She pulled up the server list when it asked if she wanted to respawn. There were only PVP servers for this expansion.

No one had ever killed her before in Arcadia. That was the whole appeal of it. No one had ever made an attempt in her village. Bears and wolves were scary, but they were only mythical creatures. People were real. There were people on the other end of these avatars.

And a person just stabbed her through the heart without a second thought.

Reika tore off the headgear and let her eyes adjust to the darkness of her room. Deep breaths. In and out. She was alive here. It was cold and quiet, but it was safe. Well, except for her neighbors shouting again. But they never bothered her. She groaned and used her phone to illuminate the game box. "PVP Experience." How did she not notice this sooner? Seriously? What game allowed for a death simulation outside of the military training programs? She used her phone to check the website forums, which said given the recent feedback at launch, eventually they'd consider a making private servers or PVE servers.

Well. She could always go back to her village.

She clicked her headgear back into place and selected the original Arcadia. No one was online. She could make the lemon poppy bread, but there was no one to eat it with. She could tend her plants, but they were all watered. She groaned and kicked the front door of her floral painted cottage. Great, now she could repair the durability on it. This was stupid. She bought the game, she was going to play it.

Reika logged back into Pangea. There was always going to be someone bigger, faster, or stronger, but that didn't mean that they were necessarily going to survive. There were still promises of dinosaurs and if she stayed hidden, maybe the dinosaurs would keep Bitter busy.

She selected another spawn point, further north on the beach. The sand, the waves, the heat of the sun on her bare skin, all of it came back, but none of the supplies she gathered, and not the spear she crafted. She started over with nothing. She dove into a bush and waited.

An eoraptor walked by, a creature that came up to her knees and had a long body and tail and scales. It squawked at her like the chickens from her neighbor's coop and blinked round, yellow eyes at her. Reika eased her way out of the bush and reached out a hand. It gave her another 'bawk' and sniffed her hand. She smiled and trailed her fingers down its rough, sunny scales. At least she made a friend this time.

The tiny eoraptor leaned its head back and let out a honk louder than she expected. Several friends came out of the bushes and sprinted on stubby three-toed claws towards her with furious squawking. The yellow one snapped tight onto her hand with needle-like teeth. Pulling was futile. She landed her fist into its head repeatedly until it released. She gripped the proto-bird by the neck and flicked it around her wrist to snap the spine.

Now Reika had everyone's attention. She chucked the corpse far down the beach and ran.

A delta to a small river caught her attention. The water would hide her scent. She scrambled up the limbs of a gingko tree, just like the last trees that grew in the city, and hid among the green fans of leaves. Her breath came in ragged gasps as she took in her situation. She hadn't learned to make anything but a spear yet, and she'd die a thousand times before she learned how to fight the dinosaurs or even what was safe to eat. There had to be options. She tapped a button behind her right ear to pull up the menu. Import save! Yes, she could still have her old skills from the main game.

She glanced around her. The gingko tree had nuts which, while edible, contained fruit that smelled like the city bus and had a cheesy texture. She often sold the extract of leaves to treat blood and memory disorders, so maybe it'd help. If she could make a mortar and pestle. But actually touching the flesh with her bare hands, she risked getting blisters on her skin. It was toxic. She was hungry. Running at such a low level used up so much of her food meter she needed to replace it, or starve. She gathered a bunch and realized she had nowhere to store them. No fiber or hide to make a bag or clothing. She scarfed them down, barely taking time to crack open the shell, and tried to imagine them as tasting like a delicate green plum.

The horsetails along the riverbank below would work for her hand's wound. If she could grind them, that is. Definitely didn't want to eat the mess, however, no matter how hungry she was. It would act as a diuretic and she'd dehydrate, and she was already thirsty. The river was below. She could try to drink there and hope nothing upstream was dead or relieving itself. Or anything hungry downstream.

Reika peered below her. The eoraptor pack was gone. Instead, a peaceful pisanosaurus, a fluffy feathered version of the eoraptor with stubby arms, munched a fern by the bank. An herbivore. Finally. Another herbivore, this one on four legs with armored plates on its back and tail, wandered under her tree. An aetosaur. It paused by the water to drink. The sun bored through the gingko leaves to Reika. She could feel herself burning, even in the shade. The air was thin here and she'd likely dehydrate by the end of the day. Her body wasn't adapted like the birds and reptiles. Modern versions excreted a paste of uric acid instead of pissing out all their water like mammals. And this was the humid climate. It'd get worse the further north she went. She'd have to make a flask out of hide, if she could even kill something first. The air was so dry to breathe she could feel herself shriveling into a husk. Stupid glandless lizards. Stupid birds with air sacs.

In fact, it felt hard to breathe at all. She was more winded than she would've ever been in Arcadia. She pulled up her HUD and noted the oxygen was half of what it was in Arcadia. It'd get worse the higher elevation she went. She noted the volcano at the center of the map where the end game content waited, and that it was in the middle of a desert. No way. No way would anyone make it there. She couldn't even cross the Andes Mountains at this rate. This felt like breathing at 9,000 ft above sea level and she was right on the beach.

Water. Right. Focus, Reika. You have to survive. What else is there?

No sooner had Reika lowered one foot off the branch to hop down to the ground, the fluffy chicken looking pisanosaurus was snatched up by a giant crocodile taller than Reika. It wailed then disappeared under the water. Her heart protested in her chest and beat on her ribs to escape. Reika quieted it with a deep, shaky breath and dropped to the jungle floor. This was her chance. It was distracted. Run. *Run.*

She broke the tree line into a plain dotted with more ferns. To her surprise, it started to snow. No, not snow - ash. She wanted water, she'd get water, but the rain would be acidic with this much lye in the air. The volcano must do this periodically. One part of the world had to ruin the rest, didn't it? Lystrosaurus, the pug-nosed creature she first met on the beach, likely survived by burrowing underground. She should follow suit soon. The mountains would have caves she could hide in.

In the distance she spotted a familiar gamertag. Bitter was back, this time hopefully hunting for something other than low-level players to pick off. She hadn't seen Reika yet. The only trees to climb this time were ferns. She hid behind a bush and waited for her to pass. At least stealth still worked in this DLC.

The woman wore leather armor scaled with bony plates and draped a multi-stranded necklace of pearls across her chest. No, not pearls. Teeth. Trophies. She had painted her skin in intricate symbols with red dye or blood, Reika wasn't sure which. She could try to get the jump on

E. Godhand

her if she made a spear. Bitter's tag had a new designation behind her: Hydra Tribe. So she wasn't alone anymore.

A pounding in the dirt caught her attention. A Herrerasaurus, a carnivore shoulder high but meters long, stomped towards the higher-level player with hooked rows of teeth visible. Reika could let the dinosaur take care of this problem for her. It wouldn't need the gear, just the flesh. A tiny hopeful smile spread across her lips.

Bitter stood her ground and whistled. The dinosaur stopped in front of her, breathing out large nostrils into her face. The woman bared her teeth in a grin and lifted a saddle she had made from the spoils of her hunt. She mounted the tame creature and rode north.

Reika was not going to mess with an apex predator. Nope. She was going to stay right there in her fern and try not to shit herself. Back to plan A: run, and find a cave. Bury herself in the dirt to hide before someone bigger and stronger did it for her. She scurried away from bush to bush like the fragile, weak mammal she felt herself to be until she found a small break in the rocks. When it was survival of the fittest sometimes that meant whomever could fit into the tiny hole. Night was falling fast. She needed somewhere hidden, somewhere safe, somewhere warm. She had the presence of mind to grab a handful of horsetails and fern branches for her hand later. It was starting to throb from the eoraptor bite.

She was going to regret the gingko fruit in the morning, but at least she wasn't starving. A fire seemed less than prudent. She didn't have enough wood, and the crack in the rock seemed no more than that. She'd suffocate before she ever woke to realize her mistake. That's assuming a predator didn't see her fire first. Once inside, it was bigger than she expected, with wet walls and dripping stalactites. She settled on the damp floor underneath one and weaved the fern leaves into a basket to collect the droplets. It wouldn't hold watertight, but it might be enough to get her something to drink. She ground the horsetail leaves on the rocks, wet the poultice, and wrapped her hand. Morning would be better. It had to be.

Reika woke sometime during the night to something warm and furry lying in her arms and licking her skin. She cracked an eye open and, in the weak moonlight through the break in rock, spotted a tiny adelobasileus cuddling her. It was a precious thing, like a giant shrew, and was delicately grooming the wound on her hand. Reika smiled and stroked its head.

"We mammals have to stick together, right?" she whispered to it.

Its tongue tickled. No, everything tickled. She sat up in alarm and felt the need to brush herself down. Spiders, millipedes, beetles, all sorts of insects were crawling over her in the dark. She hadn't made a friend; it was helping itself to the buffet her wound had made her. Her other hand was covered in open weeping blisters from the gingko nuts.

Her food and water meters blinked at her in green and blue, respectively. Her health was low, too, an angry red bar nearly empty. Infection, said the debuff on her HUD. She should've felt cold in the night air, but she was strangely warm. No wonder she was lit up like a beacon to everything around her. She drank what little water had collected in the fern basket and made her way to the entrance.

The moonlight illuminated a piece of writing on the wall. *Et in Arcadia ego*, it said. Even I am in Arcadia.

Well no shit, thought Reika. *Everyone was. What a stupid Easter egg from the designers.* She leaned closer, smashing a centipede head under foot and crunching into the body for nutrition. She ran her fingers over the lettering. No, this was fresh. And black, like blood in moonlight. Like the paint on Bitter. She needed to go.

No sooner had she scrambled out of the cave on her hands and knees, did she see bare feet and leather shin guards waiting for her outside. She glanced up and recognized the pearly necklace, the gamertag. A hand with a multi-headed snake tattooed into the palm reached for her. Her hit point meter was too low, and all lights went out.

Instead of a loading screen, she was left in darkness. She didn't die, not yet. She lost consciousness.

When Reika woke, it was in a bamboo cage with her wrists bound in front of her with twine. Someone was drawing blood from her arm. Her meters were full again, somehow. She was soaking wet and freezing, her teeth chattering to the point of pain. But that wasn't her biggest concern. Everything was labeled in red tags to show she was in enemy territory. This was the Hydra Tribe camp. How had they built this in one day? How organized was their tribe? The expansion had only come out today. Hooded silhouettes whispered by a distant fire and pulled her attention. She leaned against the bars and pretended to sleep still.

"You better act right. I don't care if you hunted it, the meat belongs to the tribe," said a man's voice. It was higher than she expected. He was young.

"It's my claim," said a woman, her voice as smoky as the bonfire at the center of camp. "I'm willing to share, but you can't just take credit for it."

"I am Alpha of this pack, and if you're going to stay in, you're going to play by my rules. Do you want to go back outside the walls?"

Bitter, as she recognized the tag now, mumbled something unintelligible.

"Go on. Continue to speak. See where that lands you," said the Alpha. "Now whose meat is it? The tribe's, right?"

"The tribe's," echoed Bitter weakly.

"Good. Now go collect her. I think she's awake."

A cold sweat dripped down Reika's spine. She got the feeling Bitter wasn't going to eat her in a way she'd enjoy. This wasn't what the developers meant by PVP, right? There were lines of decency. She gnawed on the rope that bound her wrists. There had to be a way to get free.

Bitter knelt in front of the cage. In the firelight, Reika could see she now covered the lower half of her face in a brown muslin cloth, and the top half was speckled in red from a fresh kill. She said nothing and reached in to the cage to coax her with one long, curled finger. She wasn't asking. Reika steadied herself with a deep breath and leaned forward.

"You want out, precious?" whispered Bitter.

"You *murdered* me," hissed Reika.

"You had a spear. What was I to think?"

"You abducted me!"

"You would've died on your own. I saved you."

Reika twisted her wrists to loosen the ropes. "Then what's this?"

"...Precautions," said Bitter, a smile spread behind her mask. "And the blood?"

"Testing. Enough questions." Bitter reached in and jerked Reika closer so that only the bars separated their faces. "Do you know what I'm asking you? We're the newest members of the tribe."

Reika knew exactly what she was saying. They could be the only members. The hard work had already been done. The rest of the tribe would start over with nothing on the beach, while they'd have the fortified base with all the food, water, and herbs. A blacksmith quarters all the tamed dinosaurs. Cages for those willing to remain and work. Sure, the other members would still belong. But they couldn't get in if the doors were locked. And it wouldn't matter if they built a new door behind it.

The taller player stroked a cold hand down Reika's sweaty, dusted face and eyed her up and down. "Now, you want to tell me how you burned your hand? I checked your character profile. You were quite high level, weren't you? What else can you do with herbs? The dose makes the poison and all. It'd really help the tribe for us to know the difference."

Her breath tasted of raw meat even through the mask. Reika closed her eyes and leaned away. Bitter forced her back with a firm grip on her chin.

"Well?"

Reika kept her gaze. "What's your position in the tribe?"

"I'm the best hunter but only chick. Of course, they made me the cook."

"I see," said Reika, her stare not wavering. "Well, gingko nuts are edible, but the flesh is toxic to skin. It's easy to mistake it for plum when eating it. Horsetail is useful for healing wounds, but it will dehydrate you quickly if you ingest it. Clubmoss is said to be good for esteem and making you feel stronger, but too much will make you empty from both ends. And the spores act like flash powder and will ignite a whole room in flame. So, you'll have to be careful when gathering these supplies. You know. For the tribe."

Bitter lightly slapped her cheek and grinned. "Good girl. You may be useful after all." She turned to leave. Reika grabbed her hand and held it tight between her healed palms. For her efforts she came face to face with a sharpened stone knife pointed between her eyes. Bitter raised her eyebrows and stared her down. She trailed the tip of the knife along the bridge of Reika's nose, then narrowed her eyes and cut the ropes.

"Come on then. We'll go make breakfast. You can earn your place."

Reika's suspicions were confirmed when Bitter left her independent to help prepare the food. She expected a leather collar or shackles around her ankles, but none came. Instead, the kitchen was neat, albeit primitive, and stocked with meats stewing in a large pot on a bonfire and racks of dinosaur ribs dry brining from the rafters. Bitter motioned her to the attached hut where unorganized piles of flora littered the dirt ground.

"See what you can do with that, won't you?"

Of course. Here was gingko nut that could be pressed into a cold, sweet juice. When ground fine, they wouldn't know she left the skin on. There was horsetail, which when boiled could make a fine extract to add to the drink. And the clubmoss. A fine vegetable to add to the stew, and the men should eat their vegetables, shouldn't they? For their health. She'd save the powder in little jars. For later.

"Sure thing," said Reika. She tossed a haphazard salute and set to work. She was tired of being prey. She wanted to play the game, so, she was going to play to win. There were only about twenty men standing in her way.

At sunrise, the men guarding on night shift came down for breakfast, and those who worked in the day woke to eat. Reika and Bitter had sent the stew and barrel of juice for the tribe to the dining hall. They stayed back to clean up together. Bitter snuck another piece of meat and wiped the blood off her mouth with her sleeve.

"Good work. That should last them——"

A man, pale and trembling, threw himself against the open-door frame and reached out for Reika.

"H-healer, we need——"

He collapsed in the dirt. The red of his HP bar, the blue of his hydration meter, the green of his stamina, all depleted. Behind him, the tribes' meters depleted as well. The higher levels, who were permitted to eat first, were knocked to a quarter of their bars. The newer members were passed unconscious over their plates. The Alpha, standing at the end of the table, drew a long spear from his back and used it to hold himself upright as he hobbled towards the two women.

Bitter blanched and hid behind the wall. She glanced from the remaining flesh in her hand to Reika.

"What did you do?" she mouthed.

"Just what you asked," answered Reika. She fingered the tiny jars of clubmoss powder in the new pouch Bitter had leant her. Her other hand curled around the handle of a stone butcher's knife.

"What are you talking about?" said Bitter. "I only asked what skills you had, not to do...this." She noted the knife and froze. "What's that for?"

Reika inspected the blade. It was dull. They better hope the first blow killed them.

"Don't put this on me. I didn't ask for this. I don't want this," said Bitter. "I just wanted to play a game with my friends."

Reika didn't say a word and marched past Bitter, stepping on the body of the unconscious man in the doorway. The first body she came to, she dragged by the leg into the first of many cages. She did the same with the next, and the next. The Alpha was close enough now he could throw his spear and hit her. She could see his figure stalking behind the flames of the bonfire they ate around. He reared back, weapon poised to strike her. She could tolerate that. Start over with nothing again on the beach.

Or.

She palmed two jars of the clubmoss powder and tossed one into the fire as the spear hurled towards her. The flames sparked high in sharp yellow spikes, hot enough and bright enough for him to shield his eyes. The second jar hit his side and shattered. The Alpha screamed as the flare consumed him, drowning him in shallow fire. It wouldn't stick, of course, but she didn't need it to. She needed him distracted while she collected his spear out of the sand and returned it to him through his chest. He still showed a sliver of red on his health meter. With him skewered like an adelobasileus on a spit, she twisted and threw his body into the fire. He died screaming as she kicked him off the shaft. It'd be some time before he respawned and made his way back to the tribe's base.

The higher-level players were on her with axes and chains. She kept them at bay with the spear as they surrounded her. In one organized call, they charged her. Reika knocked an axe away and brought the spear down on his neck. She spun it around and jabbed towards a man who flailed towards her with his chain. The metal links wrapped around the shaft, but were futile to prevent it from piercing his gut. Blood dripped down the chain and redirected it away from her grip. The next man took an armored spear to the side of his knees, as did the next. Both fell to the ground. Their own axes severed their heads from their bodies once Reika got a hold of them. A third ran into her spear. He ran into her spear six times. She pierced his head on the stick and planted it in the freshly made mud. Some company to talk to. She was soaked in slick gore and out of breath, but victorious. All that was left was to cripple the legs of the men waking in the cages and hang them out to dry on the barricades of the fort if they wouldn't obey. Perhaps they'd even attract more dinosaurs for Bitter to tame if she hung them by their entrails. Seeing their own corpse greeting them at the door might deter them from reclaiming the fort. She didn't even want their base. But this was more fun than collecting plants.

Bitter had finally left the shack once it quieted down. She surveyed the carnage with her hands open in front of her, trembling and slowly curling into fists.

"Why?" she begged.

She wanted an answer. Any answer. Reika didn't have one that would satisfy her. It was fun. She wanted to see if she could. That was how the game was played, right? If one user could take down a whole tribe, they should learn to play better. *Get good, noobs.*

Bitter came to the charred, black remains of the Alpha still crackling in the fire and the head of her comrade on the spear. She took his cheeks in her hands and pulled him off. She gently set his head by the fire and kicked the spear into her hand. She pointed it at Reika.

"You don't regret it at all?"

Reika watched her carefully and tightened her grip on her new axes. She glanced down to one and raised it. "I regret not killing you sooner,"

"Oh, go shit yourself, you piece of fu—" Her words caught in her throat as Reika's axe landed in her chest. Her health bar sunk to half. Bitter yanked the axe out of her breast with one fluid jerk and whistled.

Reika tilted her head and lifted the other axe. She froze when wood splintered in the distance. The ground quacked with rhythmic, crashing footsteps. She looked over her shoulder, axe raised, but a deep, rumbling growl made her duck.

The herrerasaurus was slinking towards her. Stalking, hunting.

Bitter sprinted for Reika and snatched her by the throat. She chucked her over her hip and let her body bounce off the ground in front of the dinosaur. The herrerasaurus paused over her with hooked claws clutching her arms, and breathed hot, wet, putrid air over Reika. She could try to run. She would die tired. She stared at teeth as long as her hands. The dinosaur rumbled at her again, a vocalization she didn't so much hear as felt vibrate down her spine and freeze her with primal fear.

Bitter's boots crunched the dirt beside her. With one snap of her fingers, the carnivore obeyed and snatched Reika up in its jaw. Everything went black.

The beach materialized underneath her once more. Her weapons and armor and herbs were gone, and again she was left with nothing more than the clothes on her back. She rolled her neck and listened for the squawking of the eoraptors nearby. Hearing nothing, she turned around and spotted several men holding wet, bloody spears in one hand and eoraptor carcasses in the other. They tossed one at her feet and stepped forward silently.

She pulled up the menu and logged off.

...Disconnecting...

Reika took her helmet off and let out a sigh. Sweat soaked her hair and chilled her spine in the cold, dark apartment. A giggle festered in her and bubbled its way out into a hearty laugh. That was the most fun she'd had in a long time. She couldn't wait to play again.

"All for a Loaf of Bread" by H.L. Huner
Alien in Space

Funny thing is I don't feel like a condemned man. Despite the glare of the yellow star burning my retinas, the pull of death hasn't quite slapped me into awareness yet. I don't think I'm going to die. I should feel guilty for my crime, but I don't. I guess that means this isn't a story about regret.

I was supposed to be herding the prisoners into camp. Those Lian scum, the race we've been fighting for over a thousand years. Of course, we fought with them. After all, how can a species with only two arms be considered worthwhile? How can a species that lives in smog and desert and heat be superior? Compared to us, they are weak, deserving of elimination. Our people need to expand, and they are mere obstacles in our path. I remember standing there, all four arms gripping weapons, daring someone to try something. I was itching for a fight. But the fight I got wasn't the one I wanted.

We were on my home planet, rubble from the war smoldering at our feet. My mossy skin burned at the sensation of the heat. No matter how much water I drank, my skin still felt dry. The war had shifted the temperature of my home dramatically. With bombs bombarding our marshland every few hours, it was no surprise most of it had burned. The Lian's assault on our home has brought it to ruin. Lush greenery was now twisted, ashen remnants. This whole war was their fault. I hated them for it. Hated them for existing. At least, I've only ever been ordered to hate them.

I shift my weight against my ship's restraints. Today, my ship feels cramped; normally I can stretch for miles. Maybe I'm afraid; the star is getting bigger in my view field. I feel like I'm starting to drown in the light from it. Or maybe it's the memory of what happened that day that is making me uncomfortable.

That Lian prisoner's face is burned into my brain. I remember him running towards me; loaf of bread tucked under his left arm. He looked scraggly, even for his species. His clothes were ripped and torn and his fleshy, grey feet were bare. I could see them bleeding blue from across the courtyard. Ash and smoke smudged his face, but I could still see the ocean eyes beneath. I'll say this for the Lian: they have enviable eyes. A pair of guards chased him as I aimed my gun, ready to take him out before he could evade capture. And then he did it. Handed off the bread to a war orphan. A little girl. Only she wasn't a Lian. No, she was of my species. A stranger to this Lian criminal. Something inside me shifted. Or perhaps it awoke. My fingers froze. Not a single one of my four hands could pull the trigger. My eyes locked with the Lian's as he hurried past. He flashed a smile of gratitude that stuttered my double hearts. And then he was gone, vanished into the rubble of a broken city.

Immediately I was brought before my commanding officer. I couldn't offer up an excuse. I couldn't even bring myself to apologize. My commanding officer beat me until my green insides stained the ground. Screamed curses at my crumpled up form. "Who do you think you are, defying orders?"

"It was not my intent to freeze. I did not think it would lead to his escape."

"Who told you to think? You are a soldier, you point and shoot. Anything else is treason."

"But what if we are wrong? That man helped a war orphan, a child of our species. Is that not deserving of respect? Of gratitude?"

"He is the enemy! He is the one responsible for our misery, for this war. He made that child an orphan. And even if he hadn't, that war orphan should be proud her parents died honorable deaths for the cause. His assistance only adds insult to injury. We should not feel gratitude at his pathetic attempts to cleanse his soul."

"Shouldn't we strive to be better though? Is war really the only way?"

"Enough of this nonsense! Will you follow orders soldier and leave behind this momentary lapse in judgement? Or will you continue to betray your brothers and sisters in arms?"

I met the gazes of my comrades. None of them looked at me without shame, without malice. Once, I had felt a connection to them. They were my allies, my blood, my everything. But now, looking into their disappointment, I felt nothing. No remorse, no sadness. No reason to admit that letting that prisoner go was wrong. It didn't feel wrong. For the first time it felt like I was doing something worthwhile.

"Maybe I am tired of fighting."

"You are a soldier, and I fear a poor one at that. Feeling tired is not a luxury you get to have. You have disobeyed orders for the final time." He turned his back on me. "Prepare him for execution."

I was stripped of rank, denied a ceremonial burial. Instead, my ship would be launched into the heart of a star where I would be incinerated instantly. I was labeled a traitor. Betrayer.

They aren't wrong. I am a traitor. But I can't bring myself to care. Over and over and over I replay that moment. As if one of these times it will change, and I'll fire my gun. As if one of those times I'll do what I was told. But the memory remains as it always was. I know that if I was standing there now, I'd do the same thing. I'd hesitate one more time. Because that's the thing about the past. No matter the regrets, it always plays out the same.

Maybe the doubt isn't new. Maybe it's always been there. Looking back on it, I suppose this isn't the first time I've questioned orders. Never have I questioned so outright before. Normally it's just a tugging at my gut, telling me that something is wrong. Until now, I've ignored it—writing it off as battle jitters. But it was so much more than that. I lost hope in my people, in my commanding officers. I think that thief restored that hope somewhere else. Somewhere good, that used to be lost in a sea of cannon fire and smoke.

I wonder what happened to that prisoner. Funny, that I should be worried about him when my demise is so imminent. Maybe death makes you compassionate. Or maybe it just makes you stupid.

I wish I could pace. Waiting for death is making me antsy. I suppose that's the point of this though. Make me uncomfortable on my way to the afterlife. Assuming I even get in. Maybe my soul will be trapped in that star forever, a punishment for turning my back on my people. I wonder what it'd be like, to finish existence as a star. Would it be more fulfilling? To sit and watch the planets turn around you? To watch species destroy themselves while you stretch on forever?

Alarms on my console are going off now. The shielding can't fight off the radiation much longer. I brace myself. A flash of light and then….

My ship stops. Mere moments from death it halts, once more my double hearts stutter. Slowly, something pulls my ship away from the star, out of the gravitational pull. It isn't me. My commanding officer destroyed my control panel. I crane my neck looking out the view panel. A Lian ship towers above me. I'm caught in a tractor beam. Great. I escaped the star only to be eaten by my enemy. How thrilling.

I'm pulled into their ship with all the sensation of being swallowed whole. The airlock opens without ceremony. I brace myself for a brawl, but my skin is dried out from the heat of the star, making me feel weak. I stand no chance to fight.

It's him. The Lian who got me into this mess. I'd recall those eyes anywhere. He smiles and offers a grey hand towards me. An invitation that I don't know how to interpret. "Hello, friend."

"Why did you save me?" I don't like how dry my voice sounds. It makes me seem afraid. I'm not afraid. Well, maybe just a little.

This close I can see intricate circles etched into his grey cheek, just below his eye. I wondered if they're tribal marking of some sort. Whatever they are, they're pretty. I wonder if the Lian females have them, too. Odd, I'd never noticed them before. "You saved my life. It's only right I save yours."

"You're my enemy, though. You should be glad to be rid of me. One less to slaughter."

His black eyebrow rose and his hand dropped, as if he knew I wouldn't shake it. "I could say the same of you. Despite orders, you didn't kill me when I stole that loaf of bread. So why didn't you pull the trigger?"

"I saw you give the bread to the little girl. That's why I spared you."

"Why should my giving an orphan bread matter?"

I look around their ship. It looks simple, metal and ordinary. Nothing threating about it. In fact, if I didn't know otherwise, I might mistake it for one of ours. Maybe that was why I feel so relaxed, so at home here. Maybe that's why I feel compelled to talk to this mysterious alien. "I don't know, but it does. Why'd you do it?"

"What, you mean why'd I steal the bread? Or why'd I give it to the child?

"Both."

He moves to stand next to the view panel, stars outlining his silhouette. "I don't like seeing the innocent in peril, no matter what species they are. This war has caused enough damage. I won't let an orphan starve in the street. Not when they've already lost so much. Haven't you ever wanted to make a difference? To be more than the destruction we leave behind? That's why I did it, and I'm sure that's why you didn't pull the trigger that day, either."

"I follow orders."

He laughs; a sound that startles me. I didn't know his people could do that. They are cold-hearted and cruel. Monsters aren't supposed to laugh. "So you say. But I've seen your soul, I know what you are."

"What am I then?"

"An ally."

I couldn't help the snort of derision that slipped out, "Really? What makes you say that? My people have tried to kill yours for eons. I hate you. And you hate me, that's how this works."

He smiles wider. It comes off as callous, leaving me questioning if I could trust him or not. I want to. At least...I think I do. "Maybe it's time for the war to end. Maybe it's time for peace. And I think you can help me do that."

I regard him with curiosity. He looks like the other Lian I had seen, but he carries himself with a different sort of weight. It wasn't the weight of a warrior, not really, but of something similar. "Who are you?"

"My name is Jai. I'm the crown prince of the Lian. I want to save my people. I want to save yours, too. We don't have to keep fighting."

"I'm a killer. I can't change overnight, no matter how pretty your words sound."

"You don't have to be what your superiors tell you to be. You've proven that much already. Our people can be beautiful together if we can move forward from the past. If we can forgive mistakes and see beyond the hatred."

"I can't trust you. You're the enemy." But the hesitation in my voice proves I don't exactly think that way anymore.

"Maybe. I don't expect results like the snap of fingers. Peace takes time. You aren't the first of your kind I've asked for help. Many have accepted. Others have not. In the end what I want doesn't matter. All that matters is what you want."

"But...what if I don't know what I want?"

"I think you do know what you want; otherwise you wouldn't be standing here talking to me. Besides, I can guarantee you don't want to die. So why don't I give you some options? Option one: I put you back in your ship, send you back towards that little star of yours. We pretend this conversation never happened and you die as a betrayer of your people. You die unceremoniously, as if nothing leading up to this moment mattered. You die as your superiors wanted."

"What's option two?"

"Option two: you come with me. You and I bridge the gap between our people and change history. We end the war and you are hailed as a hero by your people." He held out his hand. This was an invitation that I could understand. "You forget the lies you've been told and you look into things yourself. You become more than just a soldier, more than a puppet. You become what you were always supposed to be."

I look at him, weighing my options. I don't want to die, he is right about that. But can I really listen to those doubts that had been pulling at the back of my mind? Can I really take his hand, forget about the hatred that is supposed to be boiling in my heart? Can everything truly change because of one loaf of bread and a thief unashamed? My hands should have been shaking. I should have been scared. I should have wanted to fall back on my military training and kill all of them. But I don't. All I feel is calm. All I feel is certainty.

"Alright. Where do we begin?"

"Fluffles" by David Munson
Clown in Space

The ship's lights were out; the air was cold but fresh. Clearly the life support systems were still functioning. Waving his hand in front of his face, Fluffles could barely see the white gloves that covered his hands.

"Fluffles you buffoon, why didn't you plug in the harness last night? Now here we are, no light and, no doubt, low batteries," he said angrily to himself.

His cherry red nose lifted slightly as irritation crossed his face.

"Oh, shut up you! I did plug in the stupid harness, despite the fact that it was your turn to plug it in," Fluffles grumbled.

Feeling around the backside of his suspenders, his gloved finger came across the switch. It made a light click as he depressed it, and suddenly there were several bright lights illuminating the hallway from his clothing. His toes were an arrangement of blue and purple. Up his legs, to his chest, and down his arms were bright orange and reds. There were also several brighter white lights he could toggle on and off from a controller on his wrist. The brighter white lights were set about his heavy-set frame in patterns.

"See you old fool, plenty of power. No thanks to you, that is," Fluffles said as he admired his bright arms.

Looking around, the hallway was plain, barren even. The floor and walls were a shiny steel that gave Fluffles an eerie feeling. The lights from his clothes reflected off the walls like mirrors. Gazing at himself he struck a pose—hair was perfect, eyes bright, his nose was nothing short of spectacular. His smile, however, faded as he noticed one of his nipples was out. He fumbled with the light for just a moment shaking and pinching it until he happened to look up to the wall again. Instantly he covered his unlit nipple and his eyes opened wide in shock.

"It's not what it looks like you, creeper!" Fluffles shouted at the wall. "Get your jollies someplace else."

"Don't shout at me!" he shouted back. "I was in this wall first, move on if you don't want me seeing you."

Fluffles looked down and flicked his nipple one last time, there was a slight shutter and just like that, the light was back on.

"Humph, I am done here anyway," he grumbled to himself. Now, with all of his lights on, he began to make his way down the hallway. Looking back and forth from one wall to the next, the bright colors blurred slightly as he walked. With his smile slowly returning to his face, he reached into his pocket and pulled out his earbuds. After placing them in his ears, and making certain that he had them well seated, he turned on the music. Instantly his eyes rolled up slightly and closed. He then began moving and swaying to the beat.

"I was struck by lightning."

He began to sing as he walked down the hallway.

"Walking down the street, I was hit by something bam hum. It's a dead man's party. Who could ask for more?"

His moves became more exaggerated as he continued singing.

"Don't run away, it's only me. Fluffles, I love this song!" he shouted. The lights on his arms blurred as he danced down the hallway. Suddenly the song stopped, and he was snapped back into reality. His smile faded to a frown of disappointment. Looking around with his frustration building, he noticed a door. His head began to slowly bob from side to side as the next song came on, the smile slowly returning. Scanning the door with his eyes he discovered a series of buttons. He added his hands and shoulders into his dance. He considered his options carefully, then with a deliberate quiet, he closed his eyes and, without breaking rhythm, he stuck his fingers out until they found a button. The curiosity surrounding his decision was instantly satiated as he felt a firm satisfying click. As he opened his eyes, he found the door opening. With his lips set in an arrogant grin, he began to overemphasize his head movements.

"Ya, that's right! No door can keep the great Fluffles out!"

He burst through the door, his entire body falling back into his rhythm. The new room was large and open. There were several large screens above control panels filled with buttons, knobs, and switches. One of the screens was filled with all kinds of letters and symbols, none of which were anything he had ever seen before. He did notice that several of the symbols on the screen had corresponding symbols on a few of the buttons. His lips slowly formed a frown as he considered his options. He raised his hands up on either side of his shoulders.

"Well, what do we do now?" Fluffles asked out loud.

"Nope, this one is all on you, I opened the door," he replied.

"Did not, besides even if you did, I got the lights on."

"What does that have to do with anything?" Fluffles demanded. "Quit wasting time and clown up!"

Grunting, he reached down and pushed a button that reminded him of men falling, clearly the funniest of all the buttons he had to choose from. As soon as he felt that now familiar and satisfying click, the darkened room was suddenly illuminated with a series of bright, flashing red lights. All the screens lit up with similar red lights and an entire new set of letters and symbols. Instantly panicking, Fluffles stopped dancing and his eyes opened and darted between the screens and buttons wildly. Unable to make a quick decision, he reached for a button that was also illuminated in red. Just as he was about to depress the button, a loud alarm sounded from just behind him. Fluffles screamed and fell forward slightly, his hand slamming into a long lever that was propelled forward. Instantly, there was a low-sounding tone that resonated through the room. The screens and lights around the room were changed into a bright green. From far beneath him, Fluffles could hear a deep, grinding followed by a series of loud bangs. The room fell silent for just a moment.

"Fluffles what did you do?" He demanded.

Almost as if in answer to the question, the floor began to vibrate as the grinding returned. His heartbeat slowed as he began to feel the pressure. The ship began to stretch out before him, and he could feel his body being pulled and stretched almost to his utter breaking point. Just as he felt he could take no more, there was a deafening *bong* sound and the ship lurched forward, sending poor Fluffles flying backwards. His body resembling a flailing rag doll; he was flung into a railing that knocked the wind from his lungs.

"Fluffles, help me!" he screamed out into the expanse.

Straining with his might, he pulled himself up and his eyes widened in wonder. Just as the realization of what he was seeing struck him, a wave of exhaustion fell upon him and his eyes closed as he fell to the floor, covered only by the darkness as it again filled the room.

"To Be Your Friend" by Thomas A. Fowler

Imaginary Friend in Space

My last friend jettisoned from the ship. Their corpse released from the shuttle to reduce weight. Never in the logs of potential scenarios did I think I'd have to launch each of my six crewmembers out of the ship after they'd died. I sat alone, watching out the vast window at the collapsing star. The Captain's body floated like he'd eventually reach it.

I thought of the Captain's soul, free from his body and able to float around in space however he felt. He'd probably remain with his own body, at least for a while, eager to see what happened by passing through a star. Since he was now a gas or spiritual cloud or something, he could do it without care.

Lenara wasn't far behind him, headed for a galaxy cluster. Anthony next, he was floating up from the ship. Made sense for the tiny little bastard. Carmella was fourth, floating as if she were dancing. Then Patty also made their way toward the star. Even in death, Patty followed the Captain, which was the perfect end. Finally, my best and last friend, Jordan.

He was the first to die, sacrificing himself so Carmella could get back on board when everything went to shit. It was his M.O. to help others to the point of never thinking of himself. It finally caught up to him in the biggest way possible. He got depressed a lot on our mission, never feeling like he was doing enough while giving everything he had, often until there was nothing left to care for his own heart.

I tapped on the glass, my finger pointed toward Jordan's body. I didn't know why I did it, maybe in hope he'd see me or hear me still reaching out to him from the afterlife. I couldn't tell. I was so tired and beaten at this point, how could I even tell what I was feeling?

The communications panel pinged. A signal from home. I was grateful, I needed something to take me away from watching the crew, Jordan most of all, drift away from me forever. I pulled up the communications deck.

Please confirm complete reduction of extraneous weight.

They kept using that term: extraneous weight. They were fucking people. The bucket seats, observation gear we never got to use, all the equipment I dumped first, sure, was extraneous weight. But my friends? The people I'd spent two years trying to reach another galaxy with? Guess they didn't want to use the term "bodies" or something to spare my feelings or make a personal connection. But in doing so, they made it all that much worse. I replied.

All equipment jettisoned. Crew members have been sent to rest in space. Nothing more to lose, next would be food, water, or a system I need to live.

It always took several minutes to relay back from Earth. I returned to the port-side window. The Captain was hard to make out now, his shape getting smaller and smaller. Then, the craziest thing: Jordan had somehow collided and got caught up with Carmella. The two twirled around in space, floating locked together.

"No shit," I said. "You two crazy kids. You could be dancing forever together."

The two spun, sent into the spiraling motion by their impact. They became smaller, too. The Captain now looked like a white, little Tic Tac, headed for the collapsing star with Patty in pursuit.

Another ping. I floated back to the communications panel.

Burn engines as long as you can at full capacity. The faster you can launch, the better your odds of getting home. Rations will be quartered to ensure you don't starve or die of dehydration. Power is sustainable so filtration systems will filter urine for more drinking water. Not the glamorous life of an astronaut you envisioned, but we are hopeful you can survive the return journey.

I hated what I read. Astronauts don't "hope." That's the word they use when they don't have a real solution but have to remain optimistic. Astronauts don't cross their fingers hoping things work out. They solve problems. When a message talks about being "hopeful" I can survive the return journey, it means my odds are gutter shit at best.

Putting my long, black hair behind me, I tighten the hair tie, frustrated at the loose strands in zero gravity brushing my face. I respond back.

Beginning burn in two minutes. Thank you for all the help in finding a way home.

It wouldn't help anyone to be doubtful I'd survive. Just kept it quick to move on. I'd asked for two minutes, not because I had to prep the ship, the burn was ready at any moment. Would take me twenty seconds. I needed a minute more to say goodbye.

Looking out, I couldn't see the Captain anymore. The rest were small, little, white Tic Tacs, flying to their respective resting place. I only focused on the two Tic Tacs twirling together in the void of space. I watched as Jordan and Carmella continued to spin, without gravity they'd dance like that until some external force stopped them.

There was a part of me that wished I wasn't so stubborn, that I insisted on fighting to the end. The part of me wanted to jettison myself toward Jordan, join him and Carmella so we could spin through space as friends forever. It wasn't in my nature, nor any astronaut's nature. I knew if he were in my place, he'd say, "Have a nice trip and keep fighting, my friend." Or tell me I shouldn't worry, as I left, he'd call me the most beautiful shooting star he'd ever seen. He always found ways to compliment me and lift me up, even though we knew we'd never been together as anything other than friends.

"Safe journeys, my friends," I said to the six, lost crew members. Looking at Jordan, specifically, I called out to him. "I'll always remember you."

Closing my brown eyes, I brought my fingers to my lips, kissing them, then put them to the glass, hoping that Jordan's soul could feel my wish to have him around as my best friend, as the one person who got me more than anyone else in the world— or the galaxy, for that matter.

Sitting at the pilot's helm, I tightened the straps, making sure I wouldn't get thrown off the chair once I burned the engines. I turned on the video log to provide an update one last time before attempting the burn.

"This is astronaut Paige McCaslin. Providing a video log moments before performing my final burn to hopefully reach Earth." I said "hopefully" with a sardonic bite to it. "I've jettisoned every last piece of spare equipment I could to lighten the ship. I was even ordered to jettison the deceased crew members. I'm sad they've left, but think they'd appreciate their final resting place will be somewhere no human has ever been."

Turning the switches to prepare the engines, they whirred as they spun to life. The sound of increasing power echoed from the back of the ship.

"Seeing them floating toward stars and galaxy clusters, I wondered what's happened to their souls. If there is a heaven, does it exist in space? Or if so, do they pop up in heaven immediately or is there a return journey for the soul to reach it?"

I brought the side and dorsal flaps in to minimize resistance. Guidance was aligned to reach Earth so steering wouldn't help, only slow down the trajectory.

"Anyways, the thoughts going through the mind of the last survivor *The Xia II*. Beginning my final engine burn until fuel runs out. Then it's six months of survival on solar batteries. With the collapsing star nearby giving off some final bursts of light, they had a full charge and plenty of time to run all major systems. This is Paige McCaslin of *The Xia II*. Signing off."

I didn't wait long after switching off the video log. I threw the switch for the engines. The ship rattled for a moment. Then the steady push intensified as the engines increased in thrust. I checked the straps, they weren't going anywhere but it didn't hurt to adjust one more time. As the engine roar amplified, I heard something crash behind me. I turned around and couldn't see anything disturbed. A small container floated in the ship, flying back as the ship accelerated. The food was all in a storage unit. I hadn't taken any out. Maybe there'd been one left out, but that didn't make sense. I did inventory so Houston could tell me how to ration for the trip. I couldn't figure out how it went from the storage unit to free-floating within the ship.

There was nothing I could about it for now, the food container wouldn't go anywhere that'd cause problems. I'd just pick it up once the engine burn stopped in about an hour.

"You wanna split some Sesame Chicken?"

A small creature popped up to my right, extending the small container.

"Jesus!" I swung my arm out, slapping the creature.

It was an auto-response. The little shit asked me so loud, and I thought I was alone. I turned around, seeing the small creature struggling on the floor. It shook its green head back and forth, a silver metal helmet, too large for its own head, shaking almost independently in the zero gravity. The creature brought up its four arms, steadying the helmet.

"That was a bit uncalled for," the creature said.

"You scared the shit out of me," I replied.

"Do you need to change then?" it asked.

"What?"

"Do you need to change? Since I scared the shit out of you?" it asked, tilting its head to the side like a dog unsure if its master had a treat or not. The helmet listed to the right with it, but rotated slower since it had space to spare and didn't fit properly.

"What? No, it's a saying. It just means you made me feel really scared for a moment. How did you get on board? No, better question first: why are you on board?" I asked. "Should I be worried?"

My stomach was feeling unsettled. As the force of the ship continued to increase during the engine burn, the G force pushed, rattling my digestive system. Looking backwards wasn't helping either. I looked straight ahead, finding a star to focus on and did some heavy breathing.

"I can answer them all: You let me on, I'm here to be your friend, and no," the creature said.

It walked up the ship and sat in the co-pilot's chair. It patted its four hands on its legs in a rhythm, humming a tune to itself. "What do you want to do?"

"Huh?" I asked. "I didn't let you on. Wait, what did you ask me? I can't hear you over all this noise."

"What do you want to do? I'm here to be your friend, might as well have some fun while we're flying." The creature made a small fist, and playfully jabbed me in the shoulder.

"Ah!" I retreated my shoulder. "I can't do anything."

"Can't do anything?" it asked.

"Not right now, if I unbuckle myself from this seat, I'll go flying into the back and crash, break some bones, gravity doesn't seem to affect you the way it does to me," I said. "So if I'm doing anything, it's focusing on not puking because the G force is getting intense."

"I bet it won't," it replied. "If you unbuckle yourself."

"I don't know how your species responds to gravity and force, but humans definitely can't take this, I'm having a hard enough time just not puking right noooooooghughw…" I brought my hand to my mouth. No. It's not happening. I stopped talking to the creature, closed my eyes and kept breathing.

"Whatcha doing?" it asked.

"Trying to breathe, relax my stomach," I said. "Please stop talking just for a minute."

After only three breaths, I could feel my stomach start to settle. The engines still fired at full steam, so the unease lingered. But I at least had the chance to center myself, avoid my stomach retching to the point that I'd have to clean the deck once the engine burn finished. I strongly inhaled through my nose, then felt the damned creature jump on my lap.

"Ah, what the hell are you doing?" I pushed it. With its four arms, it retaliated, playing with me as it reached for the straps.

"I'm letting you out, freeing you." It clapped with two of its hands, the other two continued to clutch at the safety latches.

"No, don't. I'll fall back, it could literally kill me," I said.

"It won't. I bet your stomach will feel better too," it replied.

"I guaran-fucking-tee it won't." I swatted one arm, only for three more to come at me. "It's making it worse right now because I'm thinking about falling and vomiting."

He got to the clasps, the straps fell off me. But I didn't fly off the seat. The straps slid off my shoulders with ease, and I floated through the air without any G force. I hated to admit, but my stomach felt better.

"What's happening? Did the engine cut out?" I asked, floating toward the controls.

"No," it replied.

"How is this happening?" I asked.

"I told you, I'm here to be your friend, Paige. So, I made it easier for you to deal with this all," it replied, shrugging. "I'll do whatever works."

"Thank you, I don't get how you could do this, but I'm grateful," I said.

Floating toward the back of the ship, sure enough the engines were burning bright and hot, firing at full capacity. I smiled, but it faded once I realized something. "I didn't tell you my name was Paige."

"I know you didn't. But I know it," it smiled. "I'm supposed to, I'm here to be your friend, after all."

There was something familiar about its smile. It was an oddly reminiscent feeling, one I felt not all that long ago before the mission went south.

"What's your name?" I asked.

It smiled. "Jordan."

"Shut the fuck up."

"Why?" it replied.

"What's your name?" I asked again.

"I told you, Jordan."

"Fuck you." I pointed my finger in a rage.

"Hey, ouch, why?" He brought his hands to his chest, surprised and scoffing at the vulgarity and anger.

"Your name can't be Jordan," I said.

Was that why the smile was so familiar? It made no sense. The odds of an alien creature arriving in my ship and having the same name as my recently dead best friend. It made no sense.

"Say 'it made no sense' one more time while you have a conversation with the alien creature, Paige," I said to myself.

"Why would you do that?" Jordan asked.

"No, I was talking to myself. It doesn't concern you," I replied.

"Well, it kind of does. If the situation doesn't make sense, that means I don't make sense." It grabbed a handle by the barracks. Holding on to a pole used to pull yourself into bed, Jordan started doing pushups on the bar, his legs floating in space. He went back and forth.

"What about this does make sense? I'm curious," I said.

"It makes sense that I'm here," he responded.

"Oh yeah?" I said.

"Yeah," he said.

"Why?"

"Because you needed a friend, so I'm here," he replied.

I floated in the ship. Looking around, I tried to look for a sign, a clue as to how this creature got in, how it arrived. Nothing. Every scan of the ship gave no indication anything was amiss. Yet here was a tiny alien, hanging on to a barracks pole and swinging around without a care.

"What do you do?" I asked.

"How's that?" he replied.

"What do you do? If you're here to help me, what can you do?" I asked.

"I can't really do anything," Jordan said.

"You made my stomach feel better, make it so the G forces didn't make me sick," I responded.

"Ah, I can't do anything to change your life, I can only be here as your friend." Jordan let go of the pole. He brought up a leg and kicked it against the wall. "It's a weird, funny line."

"But you did change my life, you made it so I could withstand an insane amount of Gs, calm my stomach. Yet the engines are still going." I pointed back at the engines.

"All I did was help you to realize you weren't feeling the effects," Jordan replied. "The rest fell in to place because of you. Your response to me, your friend."

"I don't get this," I said.

"You don't have to. There'll come a time you will," he replied. "In the meantime, what do you want to do?"

"I'm hungry," I said. "It's been one thing after another I haven't had a chance to sit down."

"Rest, the engine burn will end when it ends, can't stop it now. You're burning until the fuel runs out to get going as fast as you can.

Sleep, I'll keep an eye out, not literally, another one of those phrases. I'll also work on dinner. It'll be ready once you wake up," Jordan said.

"Thank you," I said, headed for the barracks. "But what about you?"

"I'll be fine," he replied.

I put my head on my pillow, putting on the straps to avoid me floating off. I felt like I should be thinking about my friends, about the road of survival ahead. But I'd fought enough. I closed my eyes, giving in to the sleep I so desperately needed.

I woke to a quiet ship. There was calm music, nothing else. The engines had stopped. Getting out of the barracks, I looked at the front of the ship. I don't know why I thought I'd be able to tell if I was still headed for Earth from just looking, but it was an instinctive action. I floated up, checking the navigation computer. Still Earthbound. The engines gave out six hours ago. Six hours? When I went to sleep, it was expected to last only another hour at best. Had I really slept seven hours straight with no disruption? I had missed messages from Houston.

Showing engine burn has stopped. Trajectory to Earth still aligned. Please provide status to confirm you're reading the same.

They signed out, then checked in every twenty-two minutes. The messages increased in panicked tone, each one a little more frenetic than the last. I typed back to calm them down.

Sorry, fell asleep. Navigation is on point, burn was successful. Speed is better than anticipated.

I started to type why I was able to sleep, but realized I had no idea where Jordan was. I looked back, nothing. Pushing off the floor, I floated through the ship, using the walls to control my flight through the cabin of the ship. "Jordan?"

Looking out the back, it was a darker picture. The engines were dead. A few streaks of residual matter permeated off the ends, sifting out into space as the last remnants of burned fuel entered the void.

"I went with the Sesame Chicken," Jordan shouted.

I spun around, he was in the middle of the ship. A table sat in the center, two chairs, and full plates of food. Not rehydrated portions, but real, restaurant-quality Sesame Chicken.

"Where were you?" I asked, floating toward him and the table.

"Making this real," he replied.

"It doesn't seem real." I sat.

"That doesn't matter, what matters is I'm here to help, to be your friend." He handed me a fork and spoon. It was real cutlery, not the standard-issue, light utensils we had on the ship.

"It's because it isn't real, is it?" I asked.

"Eat, enjoy this," he said.

I took a bite and groaned. "This is the best Sesame Chicken I've ever fucking tasted."

"I knew you'd like it," Jordan replied.

We ate. He told me to communicate with Houston again while he cleaned up. Afterwards, we played. Jordan curled into a ball and I threw him across the ship. He mimicked the sound of a shooting star, flying across the open universe. Using his large, metallic helmet, he let his head hit the wall of the ship. The protective helmet dinged as metal clashed with metal. Jordan flung his arms and legs out, recreating an explosion. We swapped sides, using his four arms to grab on to me as I tucked my knees to my chest and wrapped my arms tightly. He launched me, I slid down the long corridor of the ship, only I didn't let my head collide at the end. I brought up my arms, slowed the impact and flailed my legs like the fiery aftermath of the impact. We played a few board games I didn't even know we had aboard the ship, the first day of my long trip home proved to be a blast.

I heard the *ping* from Houston. Going up to the controls, I sat in the pilot seat; Jordan settled next to me in the other chair.

Trajectory danger close. Redirect battery power to engines immediately.

I looked out, there was nothing in the ship's way. There were a few stars in the distance, but they were so far from me they were nothing to worry about.

Please advise, no danger imminent. What are you reading?

An orange and teal flash of light passed through the cabin. First, the warm, orange surged through, illuminating *The Xia II* in a warm glow, followed by the cool swirls of teal. It made the ship look for a moment as if it were submerged in tropical ocean waters. The surges of light disappeared.

Nothing was amiss. I waited for the response from Houston, nothing. The orange and teal flashes of light came again. Then a periodic beeping started. It wasn't the *ping* from Houston, but the rising sound of the ship alarms. But they never started quiet and increased in volume. They were built to go full steam from the beginning. Then, as the alarms reached full volume, the orange and teal light flashed by again. It was the light of the collapsing star I'd left. The ship was in a dead spin.

My stomach felt uneasy again. Looking over at the co-pilot's seat, Jordan wasn't there.

"Jordan?" I looked around, nothing. He was nowhere inside the ship.

Grabbing the controls, I tried firing the engines. The batteries were exhausted, no fuel left. I'd imagined it all. Every moment. My head felt light from the decreasing oxygen in the ship. Every system was failing or had failed. The ship spiraled toward the collapsing star. *The Xia II* was destined never to make it. Soon the gravity of the collapsing star would take over and pull me into it.

I could barely keep from tumbling around inside the ship. The gravity changed with the spinning course and as the collapsing star increased its pull, things became more sporadic. The momentum of the ship and the gravity of the star were at war with one another. I crashed into the ceiling, then used the top supports to pull myself over to the spacewalkers. Stepping inside the suit, I sent a final message. I pulled up the audio transmission link.

"Houston, this is Paige McCaslin of *The Xia II*. All systems are inoperable. Ship is headed for a collapsing star. I'm evacuating in a spacewalker...uh...suit Tango-Eleven-Fifteen."

I scanned the ship one more time, no sign of Jordan. "Jordan?"

Pressing the release button, the mechanical lift pulled the spacewalker suit back toward the release pod. Another swirl of orange and teal pushed through the ship as the ship spiraled out of control. The mechanical lift rocked side to side as the gravitational pull jolted the ship.

"Please lock onto coordinates and send rescue." I pushed the release.

My suit flew back and out from the lift. Drifting in space, the front end of the ship swung around, headed right for me. As it spun, I engaged the guidance controls, pushing down to get underneath the ship, that way I could monitor it until it was far enough away and not at risk of getting pummeled by my own ship.

The guidance systems hissed, pushing me down to avoid the nose of *The Xia II.* Through the front window of the ship, I saw Jordan. He was on the control panel, waving with a huge grin on his face.

"Jordan!" I shouted. "Jordan you have to get out!"

The Xia II's front nose kept spinning, turning away from me. It kept going toward the collapsing star.

"Jordan!"

I used the guidance system to push back toward the ship. Its tail-end faced me now. I had no rightly idea how I'd grab hold of the lift to get myself back in, but I had to try. I had to try to save at least one friend now.

"Where you going?" Jordan asked.

He landed on my shoulder, using his four arms to cling to the guidance system on the back of the suit.

"Jordan," I sighed and stopped flying toward the ship. "I didn't think you were on board still. Otherwise, I would've brought you out with me."

"Well, I'm here now," he replied.

"I...I didn't think you were real," I said.

"I was real in your heart, which is where it matters most, it makes me more real than you may think. Wouldn't you say?" Jordan asked.

"Guess so," I said.

A *ping* from Houston. "Paige, this is Houston. Well, it's me, Flight Director Paulson. We've surveyed the area. Closest ship can reach you is 96 days away, that's with the ship burning full speed the entire trip and you flying right for them exhausting your systems, no power to respond to anything that may occur."

"I don't have any food or water," I said out loud, even though communications channel wasn't open. "I've got a tenth of that time for rescue, maybe a few days more, if I'm lucky."

I watched the collapsing star swallow *The Xia II*. The ship's engines pulled in first, panels flying off the hull piece by piece. The body of the ship then burst into flame and disappeared as it evaporated from the dense energy, swallowing it whole.

Jordan patted my shoulder, he tried to say something a few times, but couldn't think of the words. "Can you radio aliens?"

"You'd be able to answer that question better than me," I said, grabbing his hand with mine. The immense glove covered his entire hand and part of his forearm. "Humans haven't found alien lifeforms yet."

"You found me, I'm pretty alien," he replied.

"Except you're all in my head," I said. "But at this point, I'm open to anything because…well…yeah…this seems like it."

"That'd be a cool way to go, though. 'Paige McCaslin, astronaut, last surviving member of her crew. First human to discover alien lifeforms," Jordan said. "We could take a picture, send it to Earth to show them."

"Would you show up in it?" I asked.

"Let's find out," Jordan said.

"Yeah, fuck it. Let's take a space selfie before I open my visor or fly into the sun or something," I said. Using the hydraulic arm, I removed the shoulder camera and turned it toward us. "Let's wave."

The two of us waved together. Jordan had two of his arms up, flailing about in glee. As I looked at the screen on the camera, he was absent. He was real to me, but it ended there.

"Well, Houston's going to get some very odd footage of me talking to myself and a confusing last few images," I said.

"Who's Houston?" he asked.

"Not a person, it's a place. It's where our control center on Earth is." I put the camera back on my shoulder. Whatever I decided to do, I'll still transmit the signal automatically, may as well see if my death can provide some knowledge about the area. We didn't get to our destination or fulfil any primary objectives, so something from the mission to benefit Earth would be nice.

"Can you fly there?" Jordan asked.

"Earth? I could technically navigate my suit to fly there, but I'd be dead long before I ever got there." I added, "Entering the planet in a spacewalker suit wouldn't work too well, either. I'd burn up going through the atmosphere. It'd look kinda cool."

"There's one option you maybe haven't thought of yet," Jordan said.

"What's that?" I asked. "To survive? Not seeing many options here, bud."

"No, I can't really help you there, this is a pretty unwinnable situation." Jordan patted my shoulder again. "I'm sorry about that, but there's a destination you haven't thought about yet."

"I'm open to suggestions, hate to say this but I'm thinking my best option is flying toward that collapsing star there, end this quick," I said.

"Fly to your friend," Jordan suggested.

"What do you mean?" I asked.

Jordan pointed out toward the sky, at an oddly specific destination, as if he knew where I should go.

"You let your crew go from the ship before I found you, one of them was your best friend, yes?" he asked.

"Yeah, he ended up flying with Carmella, who was also a dear friend of mine, and a great crewmate," I said.

"Find them, be with them," he suggested. "Then your last act will be with your friends."

"But it's been so long," I said.

"It's been less time than you think, our time on the ship largely happened only between us, but physical time as you know it has not altered but for a few minutes after you started the burn. The engines went out fast," Jordan said. "Find your friend."

"Their coordinates are active, I can lock on with the spacewalker, find them in less than an hour." I entered their location into my navigation on the suit controls.

"Then you should go," Jordan said.

"I think it's the only way I'd feel peaceful...now," I said.

The spacewalker suit turned, beginning navigation. As I floated, I felt two of Jordan's hands let go of my suit. His feet flew freely in the open gravity. He patted my shoulders one more time.

"Wait, what are you doing?" I asked.

"I was here to be your friend, now that you're finding them, it's time," he said. "Now go find me, I'll be waiting."

"What? Are you actually Jordan?" I stopped the navigation system, turning my suit. "Is this you after death? What's happening?"

As I spun, I saw two tiny Tic Tac looking shapes, twirling in space getting closer. Pivoting fully around, the last of creature Jordan's four arms let go of me. He adjusted his big helmet, hugged me one last time, then pushed off, waving his four arms all at once.

"When you find him, you'll be with me, too." A big, stupid grin across his face as he flailed his arms around. He did a backstroke, swimming through space.

"Jordan!" I tried reaching out to him. I looked back, grabbing the hydraulic arm to reach out to him. I turned back around to retrieve him, bring him back to me. "Jordan?"

All that was behind me was the collapsing star and the infinite of space. I floated, still in the seas of the galaxy. I looked around, seeing galaxy clusters, star after star. The creature Jordan had gone again, no explanation. After a moment more, I turned back toward Carmella and human Jordan.

My friends spun in their infinite dance. I turned the navigation back on to reach them. I grabbed their hands, putting them in mine. The three of us spun in infinite space. I floated with them for a while, enjoying the slow turn. I hummed a song, something I didn't even know, just made it up as I went. Then I reached down to the controls, getting ready to raise my visor.

As I pressed it, another creature of a very different kind appeared behind Carmella. She smiled; two, solid huge eyes batted at me; a wide smile revealing a huge set of sharp teeth. She crawled over human Carmella, extended her arms, and took my hands in hers.

"Carmella?" I asked.

"Hi, buddy," she replied. Her long, purple tails had flaps between them, letting her rise into space and twirl about in a graceful dance. "I hoped you'd join us."

"You always had such great moves," I said.

"I can teach you," creature Carmella said, flapping her tails and returning to me.

Another hand grabbed mine. Well, four hands grabbed mine. A tiny, green creature with a large, ill-fitting metal helmet reached out to Carmella. The three of us spun in a circle. I felt my body changing, skin turning an oceanic teal, becoming a beautiful fish to swim through the ocean of our galaxy.

"Jordan?" I said, feeling his hands tighten their grip.

The creature smiled, joining me and Carmella in our adventures ahead through space. As we flew through the vast open, he smiled. "You really are the most beautiful shooting star I've ever seen."

"Worst Laid Plans" by Thomas A. Fowler

Kaiju in Space

Clarita couldn't bring herself to turn on the auto-pilot. Aboard *The Vanda*, she piloted the ship, next to her captain. The ship moved slowly, a hefty tow in the loading bay caused departure and initial thrust to hit well below anticipated propulsion rates. They didn't calculate for the stowaways that came with their main cargo.

As they passed the moon, Clarita tapped her near-maroon lips. She rolled her jaw left and right in a nervous tick, staring out the window of the pilot's quarters. To their left was their sister ship, *The Taira*. It flew a bit faster, which wasn't a surprise, considering the lighter cargo. Behind *The Taira,* its shape cast a shadow over the moon.

Their radio fired to life. "*Vanda*, this is *Taira*. Come back."

Clarita looked over at Steven, her captain. He extended an open palm toward the radio, welcoming her to take the comm. She flipped the main switch. "*Taira*, this is *Vanda*. We are receiving. What's up, Xia?"

"I've got enough momentum. I don't need to slingshot. Propulsion is on target," Xia replied.

"Copy that," Clarita replied. "We're dragging more weight than we thought, need to go around the moon, burn thrusters, and let the momentum build make up for what we lost in launch. You okay arriving first?"

"Yes. We're showing targets are over 250 kilos from our landing zone, so we can let our cargo loose, let her figure out Mars' gravity before the fight," Xia said. "We'll wait for you. Noticed your ass was dragging."

"Copy," Clarita said. "Uploading new flight path and trajectory. If it changes after the thruster burn, we'll update you and Houston."

"Catch you on the flip side of Mars, bestie," Xia closed out.

"Don't get started without us," Clarita replied. "*Vanda* out."

"*Taira* ending transmission."

Ahead of her ship, *The Taira* continued straight, passing the moon. As it progressed toward Mars, the ship's thrusters became all Clarita could make out.

"Permission to burn thrusters, Captain Martin," Clarita said.

"Permission granted," he replied.

"Houston, this is *Vanda*. Preparing to burn thrusters," Clarita said.

"Roger, *Vanda*. Set burn for 3 minutes, 46 seconds at 86% capacity, beginning at coordinates being sent by Guidance now," the head of Flight Ops said.

"Thank you, Propulsion and Flight Ops. Thank you, Guidance," Clarita replied.

She plugged in the coordinates for the burn. They'd reach the dark side of the moon, then engage thrusters as they neared its end, returning to the light. Then, the thrusters would accelerate them around the moon's gravity and create a slingshot effect to speed up their ship toward Mars.

The window went dark, revealing only the stars residing in far-off galaxies. Clarita pulled up the cargo monitors. All seemed well, but her gut still didn't feel that way. The cargo crew kept their monitoring in top shape. There was no guessing, which lined up; space didn't allow for guesswork.

"Thrusters engaging," Steven said.

The Vanda's engines fired up as they reached the end of the dark side of the moon. As they turned, Earth came back into view. She could barely make out the edge of Asia. Its curves slipping down toward Australia and New Zealand. She watched Earth for the final time, nervous as the ship turned around the moon. She could feel her stomach rumbling from the increase in Gs. She kept her eyes on her home planet as long as she could.

"You okay, Cortez?" Steven asked.

"Yes, Captain Martin," she replied. Clarita shook her head. Her training at NASA was all about learning the warning signs of a mission. She didn't know why she hesitated to speak up. "No, sir."

"What's on your mind?" he asked.

"You don't find this premise is a bit 'doomed from the start?'" Clarita asked. "The odds of a return journey appear pretty slim."

"We knew the deal when we signed up," he replied.

"We signed up for interplanetary exploration and cultural exchange with the Martians," Clarita said. "At no point did I sign up for this."

"The Martians asked for our help, we're giving them help," he replied.

Vanda officially passed the moon. It faced the open vastness of the Milky Way. The thrusters burned for a few more seconds, then stopped.

"Why did we have to take it on this way?" Clarita asked. "Our ship is equipped for the fight. I don't like that we're lugging a kaiju in our cargo bay." She heard herself out loud. "Did not expect to say those words in my lifetime."

"We're outmatched when it comes to the size and strength of the Martian monsters, bringing Soritan and Mordera gives us the advantage," the Captain said. "We need that. Our two ships can morph into fighting robot monsters, and each one is towing an ancient Earth kaiju known for defending us, in an attempt to help the Martians with their destructive kaiju…seems pretty straight forward to me," he replied.

"You're hearing yourself say these things out loud, right?" Clarita said. "The variables. What happens if Soritan wakes up? He'll tear this ship apart because he won't understand what's happening. Not to mention the parasites, grime, and dust he's carrying in his fur. All that crap was the extra weight that slowed down our launch."

"Look, has Soritan caused some damage? Destroyed some cities in the past? Yes. Has he, generally speaking, helped us? Yes," Steven said.

"But that's the point, he's been hostile at times. And humans have been collateral damage more times than I can count," Clarita said. "Our ship is built to fight, but our armor is external, our structure isn't great for an internal thrashing by a kaiju."

"We have three times the supplies to keep Soritan sedated for the trip here and back," Steven said.

"That long of a sedation won't cause problems? Grogginess? Disorientation? Further complicate his acclimation to Mars and its gravity?" Clarita asked.

"You're overthinking it. Soritan was asleep for thousands of years before humans accidentally woke him because of global warming, and he was ready to fight then," Steven said. "You get to pilot a robot fighter in a kaiju battle on Mars. Stop worrying about it."

Their journey continued. The Earth and moon went from discernable shapes to small specs of light far behind them. Weeks went by, yet Clarita's intuition continued to tell her this wasn't going to end well. Somehow, *The Vanda* and *Taira* were on a one-way trip. The question became: would they make it to Mars, or be destroyed during the flight?

The day before their arrival, the details of Mars began to take shape. No longer a spec to aim for, the large mountains in shades of red and orange revealed the craters from various impacts throughout the years and dust storms moving about.

Clarita could also see *The Taira* not far ahead.

"Is that you riding my ass, bestie?" Xia radioed.

"Yeah, you wanna speed it up?" Clarita replied. "We've got some giant monsters to fight, in case you forgot!"

"You get much closer I'll slam on my brakes, make you rear-end me." Xia replied. "Insurance claims are always on my side."

"Except our conversations are recorded, so you just gave the game away," she said. "Your claim won't hold up in court one bit!"

Clarita brought up the security monitor in the cargo bay. Soritan remained asleep. His scruffy fur floated in zero gravity, bottom two teeth protruded from his mouth. Long snout and wide nostrils huffed in a deep rest. Its three, long claws on each of its four feet rolled about calmly as he dreamed.

"You got me," Xia said.

Clarita stared at the kaiju, its long tail had extra fur. No gravity made it look like the tail had seen the worst case of static electricity you'd ever seen. Every strand stuck up and out.

"Clarita?" Xia radioed. "*Vanda,* this is *Taira.* Are you receiving?"

"Yes, this is *Vanda,* still receiving," Clarita responded. "Sorry, still feel uneasy about this."

"It's a risk," Xia said. "What are you most concerned about?"

"Honestly, it's not the battle on Mars. It's having a kaiju on board during the flight," Clarita said. "We're this close, I'm thinking of talking to Biology, seeing if we can increase the sedative for entry."

"That's not a bad idea," Xia said. "How far are the targets from our landing zones? Are they still running around all buddy-buddy?"

"I'll check. Hold, please." Clarita pulled up satellite imagery.

"You going to start up some elevator music?" Xia replied.

Clarita pulled up the last satellite images sent to them from Houston. She turned her attention back to the radio and sang for a moment, "The girl from Ipanema, she does the stuff…"

"Don't know the lyrics?" Xia asked.

"After 'the girl from Ipanema?'" Clarita radioed. "Not a word."

She laughed. Looking through the satellite imagery, she identified the Martian kaiju's location, then punched the numbers in and checked them against the landing zones.

"They were at 113 kilos from our landing zone. Satellite scan was four hours, 13 mikes ago," Clarita said.

"Shit, they keep getting closer," Xia said.

"To be fair, Biology did a great job calculating their eventual spot based on behavior," Clarita said.

"Too damned good," Xia replied. "We're going to land right on top of them."

"I'm going to talk to Biology, see what we can do about our kaiju cargo," Clarita said. "Did not expect to say those words in my lifetime."

"Copy, catch you on the Mars side, bestie," Xia radioed.

Clarita looked at the monsters, one stood well over 20 meters. The other wasn't tall, but long. A snake-like creature, it was only about 7 meters tall, but spanned a good 35 meters long, some sort of stinger at the end of its tail added a few more. Her cargo, Soritan, was only 12 meters from head to tail. *The Vanda* stood 14 meters after converting to fighting form, *Taira* was a stockier transformation at 13 meters, but packed the heavier weaponry, weighing 3 more tons than her, hence why they had Mordera in their cargo. A lighter, lizard-esque flyer, Mordera had a wingspan of 24 meters, but she weighed nothing. Her body was only 8 meters from ass to beak. Her bones were hollow to allow flight so she would have to strike and fly, strike and fly to hold up against these Martian kaiju.

Clarita asked for Steven to join the conference call with Biology. Xia joined from *The Taira,* along with her co-pilot, Dave.

"We're landing tomorrow morning, but we're feeling some concern on our end about entry through the Martian atmosphere," Steven said. "Is there any chance we could increase sedatives to make sure Mordera and Soritan don't wake up on our descent?"

"Do we have new satellite readings on our targets?" Katherine, the Flight Director at NASA, asked.

"Yes," the imagery team radioed in. "Biology's projections were accurate on their destination, problem is they're moving faster than expected. We're at less than 70 kilometers from the landing zone."

"That puts them at less than 50 kilos by the time *Vanda* and *Taira* attempt entry," Propulsion reported.

"And our ships will be like bright, shiny beacons to the targets, they'll likely walk right toward us," Xia said.

"Can we burn thrusters to reach our secondary landing zones?" Katherine asked.

"If so, our targets will reach the Martian establishment before we can intercept," Propulsion replied.

"So, to repeat our choices: further sedate our cargo and land at the secondary LZ but know the Martians will be under attack by the time we can get there. Other option is we land at the primary LZ ready to fight," Katherine iterated.

"Or land at the primary with standard sedation, *Vanda* and *Taira* crews start the fight. Soritan and Mordera join when they wake up," Biology radioed.

"That sounds less than optimal," Steve said.

"I know my preference, but I'm not the one piloting the mechs in the fight. Captains?" Katherine asked.

"We promised to help the Martians, I say we help the Martians," Xia said. "I vote we land at the primary ready to go."

"Captain Martin?" Katherine asked.

"Agreed," Steven replied.

"All right. Houston, I want options on the table in the next two hours on ways to give our team time," Katherine said. "Diversion, earlier cargo deployment, anything to give more time because right now it seems everyone's going to be in a fight before we even land. And we don't yet know what these two Martian monsters are capable of."

Two hours and seven minutes later they had their plan. Houston diverted all satellite attention to scanning the target locations and paths. It didn't give them good news. They'd be within 20 kilometers of one another by the time they'd land, within blatant sight of one another. The destructive habits of the Martian kaiju meant once they were within range of one another that was it, it was a fight until one side was dead.

"At the earliest stage, we fire a few diversionary missiles, hoping the targets follow those before they see the ships entering the atmosphere. We know you requested further sedation of our cargo. I know this will be the last thing you want to hear but we're going to start waking them up ahead of schedule," Katherine said. "Drop the cargo at maximum height, let the parachutes glide them down while *Vanda* and *Taira* land, transform, then we're ready to go. This isn't ideal but with landing procedures already in place, we need to make a choice with the circumstances we're given."

No one said anything. Everyone knew the fight was coming, but its arrival left a new aura in the air.

"Teams?" Katherine checked.

"Roger that, Director," Steven said.

"Roger that, Director," Xia added.

"All right, missile coordinates are inbound, correct?" Katherine asked.

"Moments away," Guidance radioed.

"And local satellites have been deployed and put into orbit by *The Vanda*, so we're going to get our first good look at these kaiju. I'm sorry this isn't panning out how we planned, but you four are the best pilots NASA has, you have an artillery no army has ever had at their disposal, and you'll hopefully be helped by two of the strongest kaiju to ever defend Earth."

"Let's hope they can defend us and Mars as well," Clarita added.

"Amen to that," Katherine said.

The two ships approached Mars. Clarita manned her station next to Steven. The duo prepped for landing. Bringing up the monitor, the cargo bay staffed hustled. Biologists moved about the area, prepping syringes the size of two humans to wake Soritan up. Engineers checked the cargo parachutes and launch systems, readying for deployment.

"Houston, this is *The Vanda*. Permission for landing," Steven said.

The radio remained quiet for a beat. Steven and Clarita looked at one another, wondering why the reason for the delay.

"Permission granted," Control radioed. "*Vanda*, you are clear for landing. Godspeed."

"Take us down," Steven said.

"Copy that," Clarita said.

The Vanda rumbled. The ship turned with its thrusters facing down toward the planet surface. The pilot deck looked straight up at the stars. The ship lowered down.

"*Taira,* beginning descent, right behind you, *Vanda*," Xia replied.

Clarita felt the base of her pilot's seat shake. The atmospheric entry sent the ship shaking. Clarita checked her monitors again. Soritan was alone in the cargo bay. Nothing to change course now. In minutes he'd start to wake. They'd deploy the cargo hold, parachutes would release and his descent to the surface would parallel theirs. He'd fought alongside *The Vanda* when the Atlantians tried to invade Earth. Clarita only prayed he'd recognize the ship, despite its modifications for this new battle. They'd fought together before. Mordera had a rockier history, defending its eggs from Earthlings, although humans never went for them, she thought they did. However, when Mordera needed help, we came. We'd have to hope she recalled the kind gesture.

The ship rattled, atmospheric entry rattling them. Soritan remained asleep. But Clarita saw it: a single spasm of its claws. The three, long claws scraped against the metal surface of the ship floor. Then they rested back down, slowly descending back to the floor as Soritan continued to rest. The entire cabin rumbled. Through the noise, she could hear their Flight Director chime in.

"Both ships, deploy your missiles," Katherine said.

"Weapons, you are free," Steven said. "Fire missile."

"Bay 17, missile's away," Weapons radioed.

A click echoed up the ship. The release of the bay door and rocket loosening from *The Vanda*.

"Houston, this is *The Vanda*," Clarita radioed. "Missile deployed."

They waited a moment, then brought up the ship's external cameras. Using them, they scanned the surface. Below, the two Martian kaiju made a straight line for the missile as it impacted the sand. A dust cloud rose up from it.

The bigger kaiju; a red, hard-shelled, monster with long pinchers on its arms webbed feet; lead the charge toward the spot of the missile impact.

"Weapons, line up another missile for the same impact spot," Clarita ordered. "They're both headed right for the impact so let's give them a welcome present."

"Copy that," Weapons replied.

"Fire when ready," Clarita said.

"Bay 16, missile's away," Weapons said.

"Watch for impact," Steven said.

"No time," Clarita pointed to the monitor.

Soritan was waking up. The ship shuddered, feeling the creature stirring their ship.

"Cargo, release the payload now!" Steven ordered.

Soritan stood. His hair no longer floating from zero gravity, it drooped down toward the ship surface as Mars' gravity took hold. He roared, a series of quick outbursts like a whale making a call in short reverberations that could be heard over the engines and their entrance through the atmosphere. The crew hightailed it to the exit doors.

"Checking for missile impact," Clarita looked at the monitors.

Both monsters on the planet surface stirred, orange and red dust from Mars' surface floated around after the impact. The two kaiju shook the impact off, then looked around for their attackers.

"Anything?" Steven said.

"They appear disoriented, no contusions or visual injuries apparent," Clarita said. "They aren't moving either."

"Copy that. Weapons, deploy missiles on target location," Steven ordered.

Missile after missile fired from *The Vanda* and *Taira*. The red and orange sand of Mars exploded like a dusted mushroom cloud. The creatures flailed about. All Clarita could make out were limbs swinging and broad, shadowed shapes of their targets.

The final stage of atmospheric entry caused the ship to rumble. The deep echoes throughout *The Vanda* forced them to focus on landing, not their enemies for the time. Even so, Clarita still watched the monitor, watching Soritan closely. Its three claws jolted against the floor again. Its head shifted to the other side, pressing against it consistently to try to break the seal of the outer walls. It wouldn't be long before it went into a total fit; they'd need every second they could get. This fight would start before they landed.

"Prepare cargo bay for final separation and deployment," Steven said.

Clarita flipped the switches.

"Mayday, mayday, *Taira* is under attack," Xia radioed.

Clarita checked the monitors on the Martian kaiju. The dust cloud was still settling, but among it were two shadows. No projectiles came from the dust cloud. Nothing from the surface fought upward toward either ship.

"What's attacking them, then?" Steven asked.

Clarita looked out their window to the left. *The Taira* descended as if perfectly normal. Then it jerked to the side at the bottom of the ship. Another. It was being torn apart from the inside. Mordera was awake.

"Deploy cargo, now!" Xia ordered.

The cargo bay dispatched.

"We have to do the same, Clarita," Steven said.

"We're 5,000 meters from minimum calculated safe distance," Clarita said.

"He can deal with it," Steven said. "You were right to be concerned, let's focus on the enemy at hand."

"Good luck, buddy." Clarita released the cargo bay. The hydraulic release hissed and Soritan woke up fast. "We'll see you down there."

To their left, they heard something crash and break apart. The cargo hold was destroyed by Mordera. The winged kaiju made a huge call to celebrate her freedom. Then she looked over at her captor, *The Taira.*

"Shit, they're not going to help us," Clarita said. "We're done. We just doubled our enemy count."

"Unless they see there's a bigger threat," Steven said.

"Enemy of my enemy," Clarita said. "Let's piss off some Martian monsters. Weapons, aim guns at our primary targets. Open fire."

The plasma guns opened up. Below the Martian dust had finally calmed, all but the dust kicked up by the kaiju. The missiles didn't cause anything but some concussive damage. It was better than nothing, but it meant their exteriors had hard, protective traits.

"Come on, Mordera," Clarita said.

The winged kaiju clawed at *The Taira* as it descended. They had to land before transforming to fighting robotic form. For now, they had to try to line up their guns and fire back. The kaiju floated back, cawing at the ship. *The Taira* followed Clarita's signal and fired on the Martain kaiju instead, hoping she'd follow the trail of plasma fire and take aim at the two targets below. She looked down at the Martian kaiju, roared, but turned right back toward *The Taira.* Her massive wings kicked back, letting her slide down toward the ship's engines.

"No, no," Clarita said. "Weapons. Port side. Aim your fire at Mordera. Stop her from getting to *Taira's* engines."

The Taira turned its guns too. The flying kaiju roared as the plasma slammed into her torso. She cawed one more time, then collapsed her wings. Bringing her wings to her torso caused her body to fall at an angle, she aimed her claws at the starboard engine.

"Can't fire without risking hitting *The Taira,* Captain," the Weapons team reported.

Mordera's claws ripped against the engine. The engine fired off a few last sputters of power in desperation. Then smoke. Mordera swung around and headed after the Martian kaiju. *The Taira* veered hard to the side, its nose leaning toward the planet surface.

"*Taira,* going down," Xia radioed.

The ship's exterior began fluttering. Pieces of its protective shell shed from the hull. Its inner frameworks exposed. The layers between *The Taira* crew and the exposed Martian atmosphere lessened by the second.

"All crew evacuate," Xia ordered.

"Open up our landing gear," Steven told Clarita. "There's nothing we can do from here to help them."

Clarita opened the landing gear. She held the flap on the control panel for the ship to convert to its robotic fighting form, readying it for the second they landed to begin transformation.

"We'll scan readouts after the battle, pickup any survivors," Steven said. "Let's make sure we're able to by landing safely first."

Clarita looked to her left again, seeing her friend's ship falling apart. Small shuttles evacuated from the main hull.

"Xia, eject." Clarita said.

"Negative, still have crew evacuating. I'm going to keep it as stable as I can until everyone's off," Xia replied. "Catch you on the Mars side, bestie."

Clarita tightened her grip on the controls, steadying their own landing. She looked over one last time, *The Taira* was on its side, quickly veering and soon would be completely upside down. She didn't see the ejector seats fire from the pilot's quarters.

"Eject," Clarita whispered. "Eject."

"We are landing," Steven said. "Are you ready?"

"Yes, sir," she replied.

"I'm sorry, Clarita," Steven said.

"Me too," she replied. "Thank you, Steve."

The Taira fell apart. The nose tore from the main hull. As it did, a tear went through the right side, shredding the ship into three parts. Clarita couldn't look out her pilot's window.

Checking the monitors, the two Martian kaiju issued threats to Mordera. They called out. Their bodies consumed almost the entire view on the monitor, despite several meters away. One had a huge, red shell and singular pinchers on its front feet, its back feet had four smaller claws, the primary stabilizers that allowed it to stand as a biped or hop down and use its front pinchers as a quadruped.

"I'm calling the one on the left 'Red,'" Clarita said.

The other was long but wasn't built like a snake. Its torso was thicker. The tail forked into four stingers. Along the body, dozens of small feet wriggled to push its elongated body. At the front, six eyes gave it a wide field of vison. Four incisors extended from its mouth, inside its mouth were hundreds of serrated teeth to tear apart flesh and enemies. It was the largest, nastiest millipede she'd ever seen or would ever see.

"Other one I'm calling 'Millie,'" Clarita said. "All units, we're calling Targets 1 and 2 Red and Millie, respectively."

"I know Mordera tore *The Taira* apart, she'll get what she deserves, but remain focused on Red and Millie," Steven said. "She isn't coming after us, so let's see if she can realize we're not trying to hurt her."

"Does she deserve it, though?" Clarita asked. "We took her from Earth without her consent, she's just lashing out against a perceived predator."

"That was your best friend in the captain's seat," Steven said.

"Who completed her orders as she was given them," Clarita replied. "I told you these orders were doomed to fail, Captain Martin."

The Vanda's engines slowed. The ship landed calmly on the Martian surface. Red continued to threaten Mordera, swinging its pinchers up at the flying kaiju. Millie had other ideas. Drawn by the flames on the engine and dust kicked up, its dozens of feet pattered over the surface, making its way over to them.

"Begin conversion," Steven ordered.

"Beginning conversion," Clarita said.

"Weapons, let loose, see if we can scare this thing off for a second, we need it," Steven said.

The plasma guns fired in rapid succession. The whir of the ship firing to life signaled the transformation start. Two sides of the ship pulled out from the main hull, rotating on a gimbal. The side-splits divided in two each, creating the four limbs of the robot form. The leg pieces moved down, as the arms spun up the ship to lock into the "shoulder joint." The captain's quarters rotated from straight up, to parallel the ground. The head of *The Vanda* took shape.

Millie was not deterred by the plasma guns. It would dart to the right in response to a shot, but then curve its long body around to continue forward, charging after them.

"How long?" Steven asked.

"Twenty seconds," Clarita said.

The plasma guns had to stop firing, their positioning changed, drawing them up toward the arms or embedding in the "chest" of the robot.

"Fire our engines," Clarita said. "Give it a quick burst, see if it creates a dust cloud so it can't see us."

"Engines, engage thrusters as much as you can without taking off," Steven ordered.

The roar of the engines joined the hydraulic movement of the robotic pieces clicking and clanging together. Dust surrounded them. The cloud swirled up and out, creating a cloak for them for a few moments.

"Ten seconds," Clarita said.

A piece clicked together to create the rotating knee joint. Then, the whir of the central engines slowed as the robot stood upright, nearly ready to fight.

Millie turned to its left, then to its right, and made out the shadow through the dust cloud. It charged.

"Five," Clarita said.

The kaiju lifted the front part of its torso, ready to wrap around them.

"Four."

"Brace for impact," Steven added.

"Three."

Millie slammed its body against *The Vanda*. Rather than attack immediately with its front incisors, it used its feet to climb around and up.

"Two." Clarita radioed, "Weapons, be at the ready!"

Millie drove its incisors into the hull of the transformed robot. Sparks flew in the pilot's seat. The entire ship shuddered in an unstable collapse. The legs hadn't engaged without the final power-up finishing. *The Vanda* fell backward, a 14-meter tall tower pummeling toward the ground.

"Brace, brace!" Steven shouted.

The hull of the converted *Vanda* tumbled against a rock formation. Millie withdrew her incisors, then unwrapped her body to get the piece underneath the robot freed. It clawed its way toward the pilot area, ready to go for "the head."

"Weapons, let loose," Steven said.

The guns in the torso fired, but the arms couldn't move without finishing the sequence. Millie took a few shots, but quickly spiraled away from the fixed positions on the torso.

"You were right," Steven said. "Bringing earth monsters along with ships that converted into a fighting robot to battle Martian kaiju was a bad idea."

As Millie brought its head up, ready to slam its incisors down on the pilot area, there came a massive roar. Something pulled at Millie's body. It suddenly flew off *The Vanda's* hull and away from everything.

"Finish conversion," Steven said.

Clarita fixed a broken piece on the panel, then turned it to restart the conversion. "One."

The Vanda stood, the legs pushing up from the ground. Its arms aimed out but kept from firing. Clarita could see Mordera pecking at Red. Millie rolled over a rocky ridge. In front of the ridge, Soritan roared at the kaiju. Red took notice as the millipede-like kaiju retreated for a moment. Soritan roared again, begging for Red to come at him. Red welcomed the challenge. The two charged after one another, screaming massive threats. The dust of Mars flew about. As they charged, Mordera flew in from the back. She extended her claws, swiping at the neck and head of Red. As she did, Soritan jumped into the air, bringing its three claws down on Red.

Clarita looked over by the ridge. Millie crawled around the rocks, trying to sneak up on Soritan from behind. "Captain."

"I see it. Weapons, open up on starboard side, target Millie," Steven ordered.

The Vanda, now fully formed and able to move, kicked its legs into motion. The tank-like treads on the bottom of its feet ground against the rocks and ridges of Mars. The heavy thuds on the surface didn't rattle

Millie at all. It continued toward them, the stingers on its tail swiped back, readying to attack.

Plasma guns fired, but did little. Millie jolted slightly a few times, but its path didn't waiver. Millie bit into *Vanda's* leg. The hydraulics on the ankle joint stopped as one of its incisors serrated the hydraulic line to provide pressure for the rotation. Millie did not let go. Its teeth ground against the leg. Clarita brought up the right hand of her robot kaiju.

"Weapons, when I swing down, unleash the starboard arm artillery, anything we can use," she ordered.

The right arm came down jabbing against Millie's torso. The plasma guns fired. They finally did some damage. Green blood splattered up from Millie's segments on its body. In response, it released the leg, then crawled up *Vanda's* body. The massive weight of a 35-meter-long monster clinging to it caused the robot to stumble. As the right leg planted, the ankle wouldn't move. Clarita brought both arms up, using them to push against the ridge and stop from falling completely.

"Guidance, have we lost the right leg?" Steven asked.

"Ankle joint has lost hydraulics, we can't rotate it," Guidance reported back.

"Then we're fighting with a limp," Steven said.

Clarita struggled to bring *Vanda* to its feet. The robot kaiju couldn't fight the weight of Millie as it continued to wrap around them and climb on. It settled on their back, bringing its incisors down on the back. Its body twirled around the torso, tail near the hips. The stingers on the tail stabbed the hips. Warning alarms blared throughout the control panel.

"If we've got a weapon that can hit this thing, fire it. Otherwise this is going to be a short fight," Clarita said.

The gunners never let up their fire. One of Millie's stingers blew off. Green blood and clear poisonous-plasma spewed from the severed stinger. Clarita brought *The Vanda's* left arm back, elbowing Millie's head. Clarita spun the elbow joint to bring the hand around to its back. The hand grabbed one of the incisors, yanking it out. Millie retreated, unspooling and falling back behind the ridge again.

Clarita brought *The Vanda* back to its feet. The right ankle wouldn't move. Several of the guns had been damaged, and one of the stabilizers on the left shoulder had been ripped apart by Millie's incisors. Clarita compensated by moving the left leg out, stomping down firmly.

She surveyed the kaiju battle against Red. Mordera was on the ground. Her wings flapped up and down as she lay on her back, unable to get back up. Soritan and Red threw blow after blow at one another. They exhaustively punched at the other.

"No clear shot," Clarita said.

As she said it, the back gunners opened up. "Incoming!"

Clarita didn't have enough time to swing *Vanda* around before Millie crawled onto their back again, slapping its body against the back torso. *The Vanda* collapsed. Falling to the ground, Clarita felt the sharp jab of her shoulder harnesses dug into her suit. Her head snapped forward, then back, whiplashed by the impact.

She swung the arms back again, pivoting at the elbow to move the robot's hands back to try to lift Millie off their body. The hands clutched at the incisors. Clarita used the grip to twist Millie's head. It flailed its body, trying to free itself from their grip.

"Mordera, I hate you, you shit. But get over here," Clarita said.

The flying kaiju rolled over one of its wings to get off her back. She flapped her wings, gaining momentum in the air. As she flew, she clawed at Red's skull quickly, distracting it enough to give Soritan a moment to retaliate. Then Mordera swooped down, grabbing Millie's tail. She flew straight away from *Vanda*. Her flight stretched the kaiju. Clarita kept *The Vanda's* grip tight on the incisors.

Seeing the millipede stretched out from mouth to stinger, Soritan planted his front legs, then kicked up onto Red's jaw. The feet cracked the kaiju's jaw. Red shook its head as it fell back in a daze.

Soritan planted its rear legs, twisted the claws into the soil, and leapt forward toward Millie. He dug his front claws into the underbelly, then bit into it with its teeth. Soritan shot himself forward so violently, that his body rolled over top of Millie, hind legs flying toward the air as it tumbled over the kaiju. But he didn't relent his claws or teeth, he kept them dug in. Millie's body spun from the momentum. Soritan's shoulders and back landed on the Mars ground. It sent Millie crashing on top of Vanda and flung Mordera to the ground. Not losing a second, Mordera adjusted her grip on the stingers, flew again, and pulled at Millie's tail to keep the body stretched.

Clarita dug the left leg of the robot into the ground, pushing *The Vanda* back to pull at Millie's head. The millipede kaiju now looked like an arrow—the body was stretched so taught and straight. Soritan stood, pushing its claws out as it bit into the body. The claws ripped through the kaiju, tearing Millie into three pieces, the tail, the head, and whatever shreds remained in the middle.

Clarita threw her portion of Millie's body to the ground, rolled over, and used the arms to push *The Vanda* up. The robot stood, Mordera and Soritan staring at it in curiosity. Clarita pointed the machine's hand toward Red, who stirred back up. Blood dripped from its broken jaw, it still made a strong, threatening bellow toward the group.

"Come on, guys," Clarita said. "Don't charge me. Help me out."

Soritan turned toward Red, then roared. Mordera let out a call and flew into the air. *The Vanda* readied its weapons. The three of them charged as one. The outer edges of Red's shell began to glow. A deep rumble stirred within its torso.

"I don't know what Red's brewing, and I don't want to find out," Clarita said. "Weapons, open up."

As their plasma guns let loose, Red fought through the pain of opening its fractured jaw, and fired an energy beam toward them. Red fired at Mordera first, she flew away from the beam, but Red pivoted to pursue. The beam hit one of her wings, bringing Mordera down; she tried to stabilize her descent. Red moved the beam down and over, hitting Soritan next.

"Brace," Steven said.

"Port side arm, cease fire!" Clarita swung the left arm up, using it to shield *The Vanda's* main torso and hull.

Red's energy beam slammed into the arm. The metal limb crashed against the hull. With the right ankle out, Clarita dug the foot in to hold them upright.

"Go." Clarita begged for Soritan and Mordera to help. "I can take this."

Red continued to fire its energy beam into *The Vanda*, clearly targeting the robot kaiju as its primary threat. The beam caused the robot's forearm to dramatically increase in heat.

"Evacuate port side arm," Steven said.

Clarita looked to her right, Soritan stumbled to get up. Mordera fought through pain and gained her traction in the air. She swooped down toward Red, clawing at its back. Her talons couldn't get through the shell-like covering on its back. Red swung one of its pointed arms up, swatting at the kaiju like a bat. It was enough to get Red to stop firing its beam.

"We're no longer taking damage, stop evacuation?" Weapons asked.

"Negative, damage is non-recoverable," Steven said.

"That means we're not going home," Clarita said.

"We don't know that for sure," Steven replied. "Finish this. Pilot us like we have everything to lose."

Clarita used the window of Mordera swiping at Red to move in. She used the left arm to punch down. The metal did nothing to Red's shell. Soritan ran into the side, it did nothing. The protective hull of the Martian kaiju was too thick.

"Let's see what you've got underneath then," Clarita said. "Starboard side arm, get ready to unleash everything on my command."

Clarita piloted *The Vanda* to reach under Red. She dug the feet against rocks behind her and lifted. The kaiju wouldn't turn. It slammed its feet against the ground. Soritan ran over to join *The Vanda*. The two lifted, still not enough. They could get the shell and right legs off the ground, but not enough to flip Red over.

Mordera flew down, clawing at the side of the shell. She flew back, reaching at the shell to help push Red over. Red fired its energy beam again. *The Vanda's* right shoulder took a nasty hit. Clarita swung the robot's torso back under the Martian kaiju and pushed. It was enough to get it higher up. Mordera did another pull as Red's energy beam turned and hit her directly.

Mordera's wings collapsed, she let out a dying cry as the energy beam went from cutting her wings apart to directly impacting her beak and head. Mordera kept her grip, pulling Red onto its back as its dying motion. Red's torso tumbled over.

Soritan and *The Vanda* both punched at Red's limbs, keeping it from planting its arms or legs onto the planet surface to turn back over. Clarita piloted the robot to sit on top of Red, using the left arm to pin Red's head back. It fired its energy beam anyway, hoping the force would free it somehow or hit one of its attackers. Soritan dug its three

119

claws into Red's underbelly. As it did, Clarita lined up the right arm with the neck and chest of Red.

"Fire it all!" She ordered.

The guns unleased. Plasma fire rammed into the kaiju's throat. Red swung one of its pinchers up, breaking *The Vanda's* left arm from its socket. The back leg broke free and kicked Soritan away. With free legs, it swung its legs back and up, slamming against the right leg of *Vanda.* The right leg buckled at the hip joint.

Clarita let *The Vanda* fall, it collapsed onto Red, keeping it pinned down.

"Torso guns, prepare to fire," Clarita said.

"No! It's direct range, it'll destroy the cannon systems, god knows what else," Steven said.

"It's that or Red tears us apart, he's already taken out two limbs, care to lose more?" Clarita asked.

The Captain hesitated, knowing what such intense damage would do to *The Vanda.*

"Captain, we're not going home," Clarita said. "At least not in this ship."

"Torso guns, fire," Steven ordered.

The entire hull rocked about as the guns fired with zero space between the end of the barrels and Red's underbelly. The concussive impacts broke two of the guns instantaneously. Red swung its pincher up, pulling at the right arm. More torso guns broke. The weapons on the right arm crumbled under the pressure of the pincher.

"Down to our last torso gun," Weapons reported.

"Don't stop, it's weakening!" Steven said.

The whir of the firing gun sizzled to a stop. They'd lost every last one of their guns. Clarita swung the left leg, trying to knee Red in the gut, the last act of a dying robot.

"All units, immediate evacuation," Steven ordered. "Abandon ship."

"I'm keeping us in the fight as long as we can," Clarita said.

"And I'm fighting with you," Steven said.

Clarita kept kneeing the torso. Red pinched at the hull.

"Losing guidance," Clarita said.

"Central engine penetrated, running at 30 percent," Steven replied.

The leg slowed. Clarita swung it around to try to pin Red down as the evacuation shuttles started taking off. One of the pinchers went into the side. The main engine fell apart in an explosion of fire and shrapnel.

"It's been an honor, Captain Martin," Clarita said.

"The honor has been having you as my pilot," Steven replied. "You put up a hell of a fight."

Red removed its pincher. It brought both arms out wide, preparing for the final blow. From behind, a shadow flew over them. Soritan leapt from behind. His claws extended, he swung down to stab Red in its skull. Red, seeing the incoming kaiju, swung its pinchers up. They stabbed Soritan's chest as he drove his claws into Red's skull. The skull caved in. Soritan collapsed onto *The Vanda* and Red's body. The top of the protective hull buckled. Clarita and Steven raised their arms, protecting their head and neck.

After a deafening cry of victory from Soritan, the kaiju rested, passing peacefully. Then there was silence. The fight was over. Clarita and Steven lowered their arms, realizing they hadn't been crushed from Soritan falling on top of them.

"Holy shit," Clarita said.

"Evacuate," Steven said. "We'll celebrate after we aren't in a broken robot about to fall apart."

They followed a few stragglers on *The Vanda* into the evacuation area, putting on exosuits. Getting out, they surveyed the damage, all four kaiju lay dead, some in pieces. But their Earth-based kaiju, Soritan and Mordera, looked as if they were sleeping their most peaceful sleep. It was a deserved rest, they'd been fighting other kaiju and humans for decades.

"Thank you," Clarita said.

Everyone stood in silence for a few minutes. They helped their wounded as they formulated their next move.

"The Martian city isn't too far, we can walk," Clarita said. "We saved their entire planet, so think they'll accommodate us until rescue can arrive."

"Not a bad idea," their radio sparked up.

"Xia?" Clarita asked.

"I'm coming to you with *The Taira* survivors, bestie." Xia waved from far off on the horizon. "Told you I'd catch you on the Mars side."

"Which I know is a play on 'catch you on the flip side,' but it's so corny," Clarita said. "But I wouldn't have it any other way, bestie. Now that we don't have to worry about the kaiju, let's go ask for some help from the Martians." She shook her head, smiling. "Did not expect to say those words in my lifetime."

"Damn It All to Hell" by Jason Henry Evans

Robot Assassin in Space

Year: 759 Common Galactic Year
System: Emira Asteroid Belt, New Damascus
Ship: Republican Fleet Ship Emissary

Smuggler hunting can be pretty boring. There's a lot of long-range scanning, a lot of stop and processing of digital manifests, and even less ship inspection. On the rare occasion a fight actually breaks out, it ends pretty fast. That's what the Orbital Marines are for, after all. The crew of the RFS *Emissary* were surprised this afternoon when all of the above happened.

People are always smuggling something. If it isn't contraband, like guns to would-be freedom fighters, then it's alcohol to worlds aligned to the Caliphate. Sometimes people are so petty, they smuggle stuff in just because they don't want to pay the tariffs or duties or some other petty tax. Unfortunately, that was not the case today.

Fucking slavers.

Humans make up the majority of the republic, but there are a couple of alien species that have been given– no, have earned – citizen status within the Republic. The Hairne are one of them. With their lithe bodies and pale blue skin, the freaks on every planet will pay top fees to sleep with the Hairne.

Once the Orbital Marines discovered the 57 unsanitary cryogenic crates filled with Hairne, it was on. Surprisingly, it didn't go well for the Orbital Marines.

"What's their distance?"

"Ten million klicks, Skipper," replied the helmsman.

The captain turned to the Orbital Marine in olive draft. "Your men ready, captain?"

Captain Strode nodded, jaw clinched.

"Skipper," began the helmsman. "Projections have them headed to the Emira Asteroid Belt."

The captain raised an eyebrow. Asteroid belts were notoriously dangerous places to hide. It wasn't the large rocks that you worried about, it was the little ones. Thousands of them that slipped in between shield frequencies and peppered your hull. Eventually, your ablative armor cracked and fell off, exposing the tender hull underneath to more damage.

"I don't give a damn. Continue pursuit speed," said the ship's captain.

The Emissary increased speed to keep up with the smugglers.

"Entering the Emira Asteroid Belt, Captain." The helmsman raised the ship's shields. Immediately, the tapping of a thousand tiny pebbles, like a spring rain on a rickety barn, echoed off the hull of the Emissary. "Asteroid, forward port," said the Helmsman.

"Initiate active defenses," said the captain.

On the hull of the ship, a dozen automatic plasma cannons sprung to life and began to fire against computer selected targets.

"Large object starboard. Too big for the guns," said the helmsman.

"Evasive action," said the captain.

The ship turned port – hard. Bridge crews had to hang on to their stations. Some buckled themselves to their chairs.

"Status of the smugglers," asked the captain.

The helmsman brushed brown hair out of his eyes. "Accelerating." Alarms on his console lit up. "Asteroid, 12 o'clock." Without even asking, he made the Emissary dive beneath the ship.

"Skipper, we're losing them," said the marine. "Let me take the skiffs. They're more maneuverable than the frigate. We can get through."

The captain nodded. "Your marines may launch when ready."

"Alright, devil dogs. You know the drill," barked a large, black man. He couldn't even be bothered to remove his smoking cigar while he spoke. "We will liberate our fellow citizens, the Hearne. We will extinguish all resistance to legitimate Republican authority. We will do it with *panache*."

"*OOHRAH!*"

The marines, forty of them, checked their light gear in the hanger bay of the skiffs. Light chatter buoyed spirits. A slender man with a single gold bar walked into bay.

"ATTENTION ON DECK!" Barked a marine.

Everybody stopped and stood at attention.

"At ease, marines. Gunny Boone, can I talk to you?" asked the lieutenant.

"Yes sir!" Gunny Boone ran to the lieutenant. "How can I help, lieutenant Ritchey?"

The lieutenant leaned in. "I just spoke with the captain. We leave in twenty. Wrap it up, Gunny."

Gunny Boone nodded. "Consider it wrapped."

Lieutenant Ritchey turned towards the door. "Alright you Half-Witted Xather Suckling mates. Get to it! We are burning daylight! Move! Move! Move!"

The packing sped up. Soon every orbital marine was in their space suit and shouldering a plasma rifle.

"We don't have all day, ladies. Board the skiffs. You know the drill. Move it! Move It! Move it!"

Gunny Boone looked at his data pad. He checked and double checked as every Orbital Marine found their place before launching.

"Gunny," said Lieutenant Ritchey. "I'll be in the command skiff."

Gunny Boone nodded.

The whine of ion engines cranked up. The three transport vessels began to levitate. Taped warnings reminded fleet personal that the atmosphere would be sucked out of the bay so the floor could open, and the ships drop.

"Marine Skiffs, you are cleared for launch," said the helmsman.

Ten hours. In a skiff. Ten hours surfing asteroids and looking for smugglers. The adrenaline of the afternoon gave way to boredom. Gunny Boone sighed. "Do another sweep, pilot."

"Aye, aye, Gunny."

Gunny Boone got on the commlink. "This is skiff 441. Skiff 437, do you copy?"

"This is 437, we copy."

Gunny Boone sighed. "Anything caught in the net?"

"Negative, gunny. How about you? – copy."

"A big nothing – copy."

Gunny Boone wiped the sweat from his forehead. His chest tightened. The low, dark ceilings loomed over his thoughts. Where were these bastards? How could they have disappeared? If the smugglers had been destroyed in the asteroid field, there would have been debris. But there was no clue. Gunny Boone got back on the commlink. "Skiff 437, I –"

"I got something."

"Copy that?" asked Gunny Boone.

"Hey. Hey, I got something." The exuberance in the man's voice spread to the other ships. "This is – uh, Skiff 419. We got an energy wake."

Gunny Boone jumped in. "What's your position? We'll support."

"521 by 89 –" the transmission was garbled. "We're . . ."

"Breaking up, 419. Can you repeat? Copy."

"Under Attack . . . taking evasive action." Static interrupted the transmission.

Gunny Boone tapped the pilot's shoulder. "Take us over there."

"I can't, Gunny, he didn't finish relaying coordinates," replied the pilot.

"How hard is it to guess? Pick a number to end the coordinates. Once there, we'll scan the other sections, okay?" Gunny took a deep breath.

The pilot checked his navigation computer. "I've always liked the number seven." He pushed more buttons. The skiff accelerated forward.

It was a relatively short trip. "Well," said the pilot. "We're here."

Gunny Boone looked around the view panel. "The asteroid field is unusually clear around here. I wonder why?" No large asteroids obscured their vision. As Gunny Boone peered into the void of the asteroid belt, something sparkled and caught his eye in the distance. "What is that?"

"A star, I guess."

"I don't think so, pilot. It's too faint. Scan it."

The pilot began the scan. "No heat source, so its light is reflected." He read more data. "It's a dwarf planet." The pilot smiled. "How much do you wanna bet our pirates went there, Gunny?"

A good question. A dwarf planet would explain why this area was clear of large asteroids – they were being drawn to the dwarf. But Boone's marines had been out there almost eleven hours. He got on the commlink. "Skiff 437, I think we have something."

Gunny Boone's skiff made contact with Lieutenant Ritchey's in the void of the asteroid belt. They flew together towards the dim, twinkling light. The pilot of Gunny Boone's skiff read some statistics.

"Well, it is a dwarf planet. It's hydrostatic. Its diameter is about twenty-seven thousand kilometers. It's even got two – no – three satellites." The pilot looked down at his instruments. "Wait. I don't understand these readings."

Gunny Boone leaned in to look at the instruments, too. "What do you see?"

"That's no moon." The pilot looked up. "That's a space station."

Gunny Boone peered into the view screen as they flew closer. Slowly, the planet came into view. It was brown and tan, with ribbons of black blotching its surface. A small, polar ice cap at its top crowned the dwarf planet with white.

"There's the first satellite," said the pilot. He pointed towards a large asteroid to the port of the skiff, some twenty klicks wide. "There's the second satellite," said the pilot. In the distance, a small rock, no more than four kilometers wide, danced in the darkness of space. "And there, is the space station."

Gunny Boone couldn't believe it. Above this tiny dwarf of a planet was a space station, orbiting its southern hemisphere. "Can you scan for an energy source?"

"Yeah. It's got a nuclear reactor. I'm reading controlled radiation."

Gunny Boone scratched his chin. "Does it have a transponder signal?"

The pilot manipulated his instruments. "No, Gunny. There's no transponder signal."

"Do a hard reboot of her systems," Gunny Boone said.

"Huh?"

"That's a Republican orbital platform. You should be able to broadcast a general signal to the station which will reboot the computer systems. It's a failsafe, in case of emergency. Check your manual." Gunny Boone pointed to the computer port.

The pilot scoured the computer screen, scanning file after file. Suddenly he stopped, mumbled to himself, and chuckled. He looked at gunny Boone. "Son of a bitch, Boone. You're right."

The gunnery sergeant smirked. "That's why I make the big bucks."

The pilot typed furiously into his data-board. "Ok. Sending signal . . ." the pilot dramatically pushed a button on his counsel. "Now." He waited a minute. Off in the distance the space station spiraled along as it always did. Then, suddenly, lights came on. The lower levels, then the middle, then the top levels. Finally, as the skiff came closer, the lights illuminating the name of the station turned on.

"Well would you look at that," said the pilot.

"You got a transponder signal now?" asked gunny Boone.

The pilot looked down on his screen. "It's definitely a Republic station. It's also a Fleet station. Um, Space Station Theta."

"Anything in the database?" asked gunny Boone.

"Nope. But ours is limited. The Emissary would have a larger database, though." The pilot manipulated the controls. "We should be getting within its docking beams –"

Bright, flashing lights erupted from the space station.

"What the hell." Gunny Boone leaned forward. "That smuggler. She was docked. Is that smoke?"

"There's another ship, too." The pilot read data coming from the navigational computer, hot and fast. "It ain't docked, gunny. It's orbiting the space station." He scanned his data again. "Holy shit."

"That's a Xather ship."

"What?" stuttered Gunny Boone. "Has it locked on us?"

The pilot shook his head. "It's not active. I get no reactor signature." He looked at his scanners again. "But that smuggler. She's abandoning ship. We got'em now."

Gunny Boone got on the commlink. "Sir, do you read this? Over."

"I do. We're going to commandeer Fleet property by landing on that station and we're going to get those pirates. Over."

"Roger that, sir." Gunny Boone turned to the other orbital marines in the skiff. "Lock and load. We're going in hot."

The ships increased speed. Gunny Boone could feel the g-forces and decided to sit down. "Strap yourself in, put your helmets on." Boone watched as every orbital marine followed directions.

The skiff shuddered.

"Station docking beams have a lock. We should be there in three minutes," said the pilot.

"Checklist," Gunny Boone barked. "Rifle. Helmet patch. Extra battery. Commlink." Each time gunny Boone spoke the orbital marines physically checked their gear. "War is hell. It is a particular hell in space. A stray cut, a crack in your helmet, and you will die slowly. Take care of your equipment and it will take care of you."

The pilot flipped a switch. Flashing red and yellow lights flooded the cabin. "Docking with station in three . . . two . . . one." The ship shuddered. It was followed by a loud hissing sound. The flashing red and yellow lights switched to a bright, static green. The back of the skiff opened up.

"GO YOU DEVIL DOGS, GO!" barked gunny Boone.

Orbital marines in space suits poured out of the skiff onto the landing bay, plasma rifles charged and ready. Moments later Skiff 437 landed and supported Gunny Boone's men and women.

"Clear," said one of the forward marines.

The other marines moved along as a port at the back of the bay opened up. Lt. Ritchey spoke to gunny Boone. "We need computers coded. Security footage. We have an advantage here, this being a Fleet station."

Gunny Boone nodded. "Yes, sir. My thoughts exactly." He turned to the other marines. "Dornbusch, Manifold, Kelly. Find a terminal. Get security up and running. There should be counter-measures in case of assault."

"Aye, aye, gunny," said Corporal Dornbusch. He took charge of the other two.

Gunny Boone moved forward with his men. Down one corridor, then another. They moved swiftly, efficiently. The layout of the station was the same as a thousand other research bases run by the Republic Fleet. But why was this one here? Did it break orbit from New Damascus? Go adrift? Gunny Boone tried not to be morbid – especially since they could go into combat at any moment – but he had another nagging question. If this was an accident. He would expect to find bodies. But there were none. Did they evacuate safely?

"Gunny, this is Dornbusch. Copy."

"Talk to me, Dornbusch."

"We found a console. It's running a really old OS. But we've got access to security cameras. It looks like the smugglers are on level six," said Cpl. Dornbusch.

Gunny Boone nodded unconsciously. "Launch the defense protocols. That will save us some steps."

"Yeah, about that. This system is odd. Under defensive systems, it gives two protocols, an A and a B, but A is not responding."

Gunny Boone furrowed his brow and scratched his head. "Huh? I don't know, launch protocol B, marine."

"But Gunny –"

"Crap on a comet, son. Just get it done." Gunny Boone was done with talking.

"Aye, aye Gunny."

The lights dimmed where the marines stood and hid. A heavy humming vibrated through the bulkheads and into the feet of the orbital marines.

"What the hell?" said one orbital marine.

"Great gas giants." Replied another.

Suddenly, the lights stopped flickering and the humming stopped.

"I guess we're good to go?" asked Cpl. Dornbusch.

Boone nodded. "Let's earn a bonus."

The orbital marines went up three levels on turbo lifts. "Gunny," said Cpl. Dornbusch. "We've got movement on Level 4. Heat signatures, too. Security cameras are offline in some places, but we got plasma scorches, explosions. Looks like there was a battle here."

Gunny Boone rubbed his forehead. "With who?"

The corporal shrugged.

"Shit. Alright. Squad: put your heads on a swivel. We got to check this out." He called on his commlink. "Lt. Ritchey, Sir. We got heat signatures and movement on level four. We're going to check it out. Copy."

The lieutenant's voice crackled over the commlink. "Copy that, Gunny. We've got movement on level four as well. Happy hunting," said the lieutenant.

Gunny Boone pushed the turbo lift keypad to go up one more level. He turned to his squad. "Short bursts. Watch your rifles for overheating." He spied his men. All too young, as far as Boone was concerned. "And breathe."

He could see the fear on some of their faces. The sweat glistening from their foreheads. The dilated pupils and shallow breathing. The trembling. Gunny Boone held his rifle point in the air. With his left hand he started a silent countdown for his men.

Five.

Four.

Three.

Two.

One.

The turbo lift doors opened to the smell of acrid smoke and burning. Burning plastic, burning cloth and burning flesh.

"MOVE."

Orbital marines crashed the hallway from the turbo lift, in either directions.

"Visibility compromised," said one marine.

"What the hell happened here?" asked another.

"Cut the chatter, marines." Gunny Boone entered the hallway. "Secure the passage ways." He motioned for Cpl. Dornbusch to go left while he went right.

"Gunny, we got drones over here — and bodies," said Lt. Cpl. Manifold.

"I'm coming, Manifold. Hang on. Dornbusch, get the filters on this tub to work overtime. Clear the air. Copy."

"Gotcha, Gunny. Copy," said Cpl. Dornbusch.

Boone moved twenty meters down the hall, amid thick, gray smoke. Where the corridor veered both left and right, three marines took defensive positions while a third stood over four bodies. Boone looked at the corpses, in garish space suits, clutching plasma pistols and rifles. "Whatcha find, Manifold?"

"Pirates." He pointed his rifle at the corpses. "They haven't been dead long."

"Guesses on the cause of death?"

"Plasma fire — no doubt," said Lt. Cpl. Manifold.

"Any injured or dead marines?"

Manifold shook his head. He then took a data pad out and handed it to Boone. "Check this out."

Boone took the pad and pressed play. Video of the passageway showed three cautious pirates, guns drawn, peering down the corridor

Gunny Boone now stood in. Suddenly there was an explosion and automatic fire. Smoke filled the corridor. The last thing Boone saw were pirates dropping to the ground, whimpering. He handed the data pad back. "Who ambushed them?"

Manifold shrugged again. "I don't think it was us."

"Of course, it was us. We —"

The sound of engines kicking into high gear interrupted the conversation. The smoke swirled and dissipated in front of the marines. "Air scrubbers on line, Gunny," said Cpl. Dornbusch over the commlink.

"Anything interesting over your way?" asked Gunny Boone.

"Nothing, boss."

Gunny Boone got on the commlink. "Lieutenant, sir."

"Copy that."

"Did you send anybody to reconnoiter level four?"

"No. Why?"

That was odd. "We got dead pirates down here. If you didn't send anybody to level four —"

An explosion went off over the commlink.

"Sir? SIR?"

The line filled with alternating static, plasma fire, explosions and screaming. "HELP."

"Sir? Sir?" Boone had to think. "EVERYBODY, back on the turbo lift!"

The marines raced aboard as Gunny Boone counted men. He got in last and pressed buttons. "Let me go first, spread out left, then right. Find cover. Whoever hitting us knows the station." He looked around at his wide-eyed orbital marines. "Keep your head on a swivel."

They all nodded.

The lift doors opened to screams and streaks of light.

Gunny Boone leapt out of the turbo lift and almost tripped on a dead marine. Others partially hid behind door jams, trying to return fire. Every flash of green laser fire was accompanied by screams of terror.

"MY LEG!"

"OH GOD!"

"Move to your right," Gunny Boone barked.

His men ran out, dived for cover in abandoned offices and laboratories. What was shooting them? The fire seemed to come from everywhere.

A black streak passed by a T-section of hallway, unseen by others because of the smoke of burning plastic.

"Find cover, lead others to safety," Gunny Boone said. He took a deep breath and charged forward, into smoke and debris.

"Where you going, Gunny?" called one of the orbital marines.

Smoke from burning and smoldering plastic burned Gunny Boone's eyes and choked his throat.

"Help," someone called out weakly.

Gunny Boone moved through the smoke. The whine of turbo lasers spitting death echoed off the walls. Boone dropped to the floor. More cries for help wafted through the smoke. Boone crawled forward to a downed orbital marine. Her back moved slowly, rhythmically. "Hey, marine, talk to me," Gunny Boone whispered.

"Ugh . . ."

Gunny Boone turned her over on her back.

Her right eye scanned the ceiling as she took shallow breaths. Her left eye was melted into her cheek bone. Suddenly she recognized Boone, clutched his arm, exhaled and died.

Boone clinched his teeth. Gently, he laid her down and shut her remaining eye.

What the fuck was going on?

The whirl of hover drone engines got louder. Suddenly green streaks peppered the floor around him. Boone grabbed the dead marine and covered himself with her.

Laser fire peppered her corpse.

Boone tried to hide, but laser fire grazed his legs.

He tried to adjust the dead marine's body. On her hip was a holster. Boone pulled the pistol and returned fire.

The smoke thinned and Boone saw a small, black orb, floating in the sky, shooting in all directions.

He fired again, but the drone seemed to absorb the shot. "What the hell?"

Red streaks of laser zoomed past the drone, hitting ceiling and wall around it. The orb moved away from Boone, into the direction of the fire.

Then it exploded. The whine of its engines dying down as it rolled on the floor.

"Hey Gunny, you alright?"

Boone sighed. "Manifold, is that you?" He rolled the dead marine off of his body and stood. A smoldering ball of metal and plastic smoked and beeped before two marines.

"What the fuck is going on, Gunny?" asked Manifold.

"I have no idea."

Gunny Boone let a medic look at his ankles and feet. "You got lucky. Some grazing, but nothing serious. You can walk in about twenty minutes."

"Thanks, Doc."

Cpl. Dornbusch waited to talk to Gunny Boone, rifle slung over his shoulder.

"Report, Corporal."

"This was a slaughter, Gunny. We have ten dead, including the lieutenant; six in critical and four seriously hurt." Dornbusch wiped the sweat from his brow.

"The ones that can talk. What did they say?" asked Gunny Boone.

"Drones. Drones happened."

"How is that even possible? We've got noting that powerful in the Fleet."

Dornbusch nodded in agreement. "I know, Gunny, I know. But they said drones came down a hallway and spat fire. Half of them were dead before they could take the safety latches off their weapons."

"How many attacked them? Ten? Twenty?"

Dornbusch sighed and looked heavenward.

"How many, Corporal?"

"Three."

Gunny Boone jumped up. "You mean three drones put down a squad of orbital marines?"

"That's what I mean, Gunny."

Gunny Boone sighed. He wanted those slavers, but the situation had changed. "Well fuck this. We are evacuating."

"What about the pirates? What about the Hairne?" asked the medic.

"If those pirates have tech like this, then saving the Hairne is a suicide mission. We need to evac, NOW." Gunny Boone waited for other arguments. None came. "Let's move out. Load the skiffs with the wounded first, then the dead."

Marines moved with just a look. God, did Gunny Boone love these men & women, but they were at half their fighting strength. If they stayed, their chances of survival went down with every hour. He couldn't bear to see any more of them injured or killed.

The critically wounded were moved to the skiffs first. Then the dead were moved into the bay.

"Manifold, download this station's data core, Fleet intelligence will want to know about this place," Gunny Boone said.

"On it, Gunny."

Suddenly an explosion went off in the docking bay. Orbital marines ran to help.

Two, black drones flew out of the bay, firing in every direction. Orbital marines fell like heavy snow onto the deck.

Manifold returned fire in the hallway and got shot in the shoulder.

Other marines, one by one, fell as the drones spread out and surgically butchered Gunny Boone's marines.

"What do we do, Gunny?"

"Help!"

"My leg. My leg."

"Fallback! Into the rooms, marines!" Boone ushered people into the makeshift medic bay. Only three marines made it into the medic bay. "Get down, on the ground," Gunny Boone barked, and moved on to the next room—a lab.

Four marines joined Gunny Boone in the lab. A young woman, not even twenty, rushed in as the door shut. The five survivors awaited Boone's next command.

"Short the lock," Gunny Boone shouted.

Manifold tapped a keypad by the door. A green light turned red. Suddenly he pulled his blaster pistol and shot the panel. Satisfied, he turned to Boone. "Lock shorted."

Another marine screamed.

A drone stopped in front of one of the large windows that lined the room. It sent a series of blue pulses of light through the entire room.

Boone raised his hand to the other marines, who froze in place.

The drone stopped its scan and fired a burst of laser fire at the glass.

It bounced off.

Gunny Boone sighed.

The drone shot another blast that also bounced off, harmlessly.

"Thank the stars for transparent aluminum," said one of the marines.

"Don't count your blessings yet." One of the other marines pointed. "Look."

The two other floating robots aligned themselves with the first drone. Together they shot a unified beam of blue light, pinpointed on the same spot.

"Do you smell that?" Manifold asked.

Gunny Boone crawled to the far side of the room. "Everyone, check your weapons." He turned a table over on its side. "Get any cover you can."

Suddenly, a large crash distracted them.

"Hey jarheads, get over here if living is something you like doing." A low cabinet door opened with a protruding hand that motioned them to follow. "We're running out of time, assholes."

Gunny Boone looked at the window, then the hand. "Let's move marines."

The smell of burning aluminum permeated the air as the four marines crawled into the cabinet.

The drones continued to burn a circular hole into the transparent aluminum.

Two marines were through.

The hole was now a semi-circle.

Another marine crawled through the opening.

The hole was three quarters complete.

"Get in there, kid." Boone rushed the woman in.

The cut aluminum slowly turned red.

The final marine crawled through the cabinet.

Boone took some string out and tied it to the cabinet latch before crawling in. He heard the aluminum hit the ground as he followed the others in the cabinet. The last thing he did was pull the string and close the cabinet door. He prayed the killer drones wouldn't follow.

Gunny Boone crawled along an electrical conduit and air duct in silence for some time. To him, it felt like a hundred years, but was obviously shorter. The conduit was as cold as death when he entered it. It made sense though. Humans rarely got into these spaces – that's what robots were for – so why design them with heating elements?

There was also no light except the occasional access panel that blinked green and red lights. As they continued, the conduit warmed considerably with their carbon dioxide and adrenalin fueled sweating. Surprisingly, no one spoke. Were his marines in shock? Were they scared or just happy to still be alive?

Light flooded the conduit. Light and cooking smells. Slowly the marines exited the conduit.

A pale hand covered in rings appeared before Gunny Boone. "There you go, soldier."

Boone took the hand out of the conduit.

It was once a storage area. Piles of old crates and boxes lay strewn all over a large area. Four, wildly dressed men and women stood looking at Gunny Boone and his marines. A fifth person, only a child, moved smoking food around in a skillet.

Gunny looked at the man who helped him up. His hair was wild, long and unkempt, in strands of black, green and purple. His gold-capped teeth sparkled as the man smiled.

"We're not soldiers. We are marines," Gunny Boone said.

"My mistake, *marine.*" The man bowed.

"Why are we helping these pigs?" asked one of the women.

"Now, now, Lisbeth," began the man. "We need them." He turned to look at Boone. "As I am sure they are aware they need us."

"What in the name of an exploding gas giant is going on?" Boone adjusted his weight to his left foot and cocked his head.

The man with the wild hair spoke. "I am captain Throm, of the ship *Carnival*."

"You're the captain of that pirate ship we were following?" asked Gunny Boone.

"He's the cook, on the pirate ship you were chasing," said another woman.

Throm wagged a finger at the woman. "Tut. Tut. I was given a promotion at sea, as it were, Bernice."

"You mean everyone else is dead, Throm," Bernice said.

"Bernice, where are your manners?" Throm turned to Gunny Boone. "Allow me to introduce my intrepid crew. The wiry lady is Lisbeth. Bernice you've met, she's our engineer. The tall fellow is Alfie. The dirty little fellow with the lazy eye, that's Brett."

"Who's the girl?" asked Manifold.

"The little one cooking? That's Comet. She's not much of a talker but she's a really good cook. Taught her all she knows." Throm smiled broadly.

"Thank you for saving us," Gunny Boone began. "We were goners if–"

"This isn't a fucking humanitarian mission," Bernice interrupted. "Can you get us out of here?"

"You're the ones with the ship, lady. *Can you get us out of here?*" asked the female marine.

"Stow it, marine," Gunny Boone said. "Who are you, anyways? You're not one of mine."

"I'm PFC Arcy. Just transferred in, Gunny."

"Well, stow it, Pfc. I've got figuring to do."

PFC Arcy shut her mouth and found a crate to sit on.

Gunny Boone turned back to Throm. "I'm Boone. That there is Manifold. This is Hercules Sanchez. We just call him Herc. Over there is Torchy. This is Sgt. Smith. He's our medic, so we just call him 'Doc.'" Boone took a seat on a crate. "So what in hell is going on?"

"We thought you knew. Didn't you reboot the station's systems and send the drones?" asked Bernice, who wiped grime from her forehead under her long, brown bangs.

The other marines looked at Boone.

The gunnery sergeant's breathing shallowed. Had he done all of this? He sighed. "Yeah, that was my order."

"You SON OF A BITCH!" Brett lunged at Boone. He was stopped by Alfie and Lisbeth. "You killed my wife." Brett struggled a bit before collapsing in tears.

Herc took his helmet off. "How many did you lose?"

"Thirteen. Including his wife, Comet's mom, and our entire command crew," replied Alfie.

"Is this Republic justice?" asked Brett between sobs.

Boone was tired of the theatrics. "I'm real sorry for your loss, son, but those killer robots hit us, too."

"That's right, Brett. We've all lost someone," Lisbeth said.

"What is this place?" asked Arcy.

Brett sat down on a crate, held by Lisbeth.

Alfie turned to Arcy, arms raised. "This? This is a floating laboratory, abandoned by the Republic decades ago. It's one of the dirty little secrets your 'grand republic' wants kept off the grid and hidden in secret."

"You're bullshitting," said Manifold.

"Am I? I'd take you to a data terminal, but right now those murder bots are preventing a grand tour. You saw the Xather ship orbiting the station, didn't you?"

"Yea, we did." Arcy took her helmet off.

"Do you think we could capture a maggot ship? No. It's been here for decades," Alfie said.

"Look, I don't–"

A general argument broke out among pirates and orbital marines.

"THAT'S ENOUGH!" Boone erupted.

Everyone stopped. The only sound was the sizzling of food in the background.

"I'm not here to discuss any of that. It's all above my paygrade. All I know is that we have to detach ourselves from this space station, pronto. And THAT is only going to happen if we work together."

For the next four hours they ate, talked, and got to know one another. The pirates were from all over known space. A bunch of downtrodden outcasts who found themselves smuggling and stealing for a living. The fact that they were slavers didn't really matter to them. As far as they were concerned, they were all slaves to a Republic that had abandoned them.

"So this is what we do," Gunny Boone began. "First, we get to a data terminal, and check the security feed. We need to see if there are pockets of survivors anywhere else on the station."

"Agreed," said Alfie.

"Next, we bring them here." Boone turned to Bernice. "Can you fire up the engines of that pirate ship of yours?"

She nodded.

"Then we try to get to your ship."

"What happens after?" asked Brett, knowing that escaping was just part of their problems.

Boone looked around. Tension filled the room. "Look, I'm liberating your cargo. Pure and simple. If you want to get on life pods and get out before we dock with a Fleet vessel, that's on you. But you're not taking the Hairne to market. That is final."

"You fucking Jarheads and–"

"BRETT," hollered Lisbeth. "Now is not the time."

"I agree," said Throm. "How about we leave this discussion for another time, like when those killer bots aren't actively trying to murder us?"

"Agreed," said Lisbeth.

"Agreed," said Manifold and Herc.

"Throm, I want you two of your guys to go with Arcy and Doc, and Herc. They'll find a data port and get schematics, look for survivors," Boone said.

Throm nodded. "You can have Alfie and Lisbeth. Can I have Manifold? He can help Bernice re-establish a link with our ship. Maybe even get her to dock?"

"Agreed," nodded Boone.

"What do the rest of us do?" asked Brett.

"Stay here," said Boone.

"How do we communicate?" asked Alfie.

"We don't. We have to stay radio silent or else those murder bots might find us." Boone checked his rifle's battery meter. He then put his helmet on.

"Where are you going, Gunny?" asked Arcy.

"Me? I'm going back to reconnoiter that scene of the crime. See if I can't find a way to get to the skiffs and set the auto-distress beacon."

Throm pulled at the large, flowing, leather duster he wore to reveal a blaster pistol at his hip. "Want some company?"

Boone shrugged.

Throm chuckled at the marine and opened the electrical conduit and went in.

The two crawled on their hands and knees in the cold and dark, intermittently lit by beeping lights on access panels. They reached the original lab rather quickly. After Throm exited the conduit, Boone came up behind them.

The lab smelled of ozone and burnt aluminum. Both men knew to be quiet. They were taking a chance that the drones were no longer there. Or, were at least inactive. The wrong sound could change that.

Boone stood and peered out the window. Dead orbital marines littered the hallway. Their blood splattered against the walls.

Boone ground his teeth.

Throm took out a tool from his belt to work on the door control panel. Sparks flew and smoke rose as he worked. Finally, the door slid open.

Boone was impressed.

The two walked around and over the dead in silence. Boone couldn't stand to look down. These were his friends and colleagues. His brothers and sisters.

They moved some fifteen meters before they got to the landing bay.

"Sweet star clusters," Boone whispered.

Dead. They were all dead. Another twelve marines. The injured and the medics to tend to them. Butchered.

Tears welled in his eyes. Boone touched the panel to open the hatch.

Throm grabbed his wrist before he could and pointed.

There was a drone hovering lazily above the skiffs, waiting to jump into action.

Boone pointed backwards and Throm nodded. Gingerly, they both made it back to the laboratory.

"OK. So the beacon is out," said Throm. "That's okay. If we can get to our ship, we'll be fine."

"What is going on here?" Boone asked.

"I don't follow."

"The old-style space station. Orbiting a dwarf planet. With drones I've never seen before? And, an old Xather ship in close orbit around, too?" Boone pulled his pistol. "You're not telling me everything."

Throm put his hands up. "I don't know anything."

"Don't lie to me."

"Honestly." Throm's voice was raised, but he lowered it. "Honestly, I don't know. I've been with this crew for about two years. This was just one of half a dozen hideouts. Kept the station power on low, stayed for two, maybe three weeks at a time. Maybe twice a year."

"No one asked about how weird this place was? The maggot ship in orbit?"

Throm was sweating now. "Look, these guys once hid in the low orbit of a sun's corona to avoid the Fleet. They were crazy. An abandoned station was *the least crazy thing they did.*"

Throm had a point.

"What ab–"

Plasma fire and a woman's screams echoed from another corridor.

Boone looked at Throm, then touched the door sensor to open it.

Another scream, this time from a man.

Boone ran with his rifle in his arms. He turned one corridor, then another. In front of him stood Herc, leaning against a wall, clutching his chest. "Herc, what happened?" Boone ran to him.

"Arcy . . ." Herc collapsed on the ground.

The smell of melting plastic permeated the air. Streaks of green lasers flashed in the distance. Suddenly Arcy appeared, face flush, running towards Boone. "Help," she cried out.

Boone aimed his rifle past her and fired as a drone turned the corner.

The drone sparked and tilted backwards, but didn't fall. Suddenly, it unleashed a torrent of green laser fire at Boone.

He shot again. And again.

Arcy ran past Boone.

His shot hit the drone. Sparks and smoke came from it.

This thing wasn't going down like the previous one. This one was tough. Boone turned and ran. He almost hit Throm as he followed Arcy.

"I thought we were going this way?" Throm asked.

"Changed our minds!" barked Boone.

The three headed down the corridor.

"NO," cried Boone. "Go to the turbo lift. They won't expect that."

Arcy made a beeline for the turbo lift as green laser fire peppered the walls, floor, and corpses.

Arcy pushed the button and pulled her pistol.

Boone leapt over dead marines and made it to the door as the lift opened. "Come on Throm!"

The pirate ran, but slipped in coagulated blood.

"NO." Boone fired his rifle, hitting the drone at least twice.

Throm scrambled to get up, but slipped again.

"Forget him, Gunny. He'll be dead soon, anyways."

"No. We work together," Gunny Boone barked.

The doors to the hangar bay opened up and the second drone came out.

Throm scrambled on all fours, then ran to the elevator as the doors shut. He collapsed on the floor, covered in blood.

"What happened?" asked Gunny Boone.

Arcy sucked in breath as she spoke. "Got ambushed by drones. I'm sorry. Lisbeth, Herc, Doc, Alfie. They're all dead." She bent down to breathe.

Gunny Boone sighed. In a matter of seconds, they lost a third of their strength.

"Where are we going?" asked Throm between hard breaths.

"To the command deck. I got questions."

"But shouldn't we check in with Bernice and Manifold?" Arcy asked.

"In time. I got questions."

"But–"

"Shut your yap, marine. THAT'S an order." Boone glared at Arcy. The girl clinched her teeth, looked down, and was silent.

The command center was on the top-most level of the space station. When the doors opened, a fine layer of dust covered everything. The command consuls, the commander's chair, even the table and chairs in the conference room.

Boone stepped out first. "Throm, get the air scrubbers working in here. It smells awful," Boone said. "Arcy, see if you can't get the automated distress beacon up and running."

The two nodded and got to work.

Boone sat in the command chair and worked some buttons. 3D displays popped up before his eyes.

"What are you doing?" asked Arcy.

"Just checking things out," Boone replied.

He looked through the commander's logs, the station registry, and other docs.

The station was over a hundred years old. Yet basic command codes still worked. Codes no pirates should have been privy to.

Suddenly, fans turned on and the whine of air circulators hummed into action.

"Thanks Throm," said Gunny Boone.

Throm just nodded.

Boone went through dozens of files on the computer's core. "Defense protocol Theta?" He pushed the link. "Operation Pandora?"

Red lights began to blink in the command room. The 3D images vanished before he could read them.

"What's happening?"

"Gunny, I think you triggered something when you went into that Theta file." Arcy frantically pushed buttons, trying to turn the alarms off. Then she stopped. "No," she whispered.

Boone ran to the window. The pirate ship moved closer to the station. "They did it, she's docking."

"But Gunny, the defense systems have been activated," said Arcy.

Heavy laser cannons spat green lightening at the ship. First the pirate vessel shimmied, then wobbled, before blowing up. The command deck shuttered at the explosion. Bits of debris hit the transparent aluminum screens.

"We'd better be going," said Throm.

"Yeah," said Gunny Boone. "I agree."

They raced to the turbo lift as more debris battered the hull. Alarms went off.

"What is that?" asked Throm.

"Hull breach alert," said Boone as the turbo lift doors closed.

The lift rocked and shimmied as it went down.

"What do we do now?" asked Arcy.

"Hell if I know?" Boone shook his head in disgust.

The turbo lift went down a deck below where the pirate survivors hid. Boone, Arcy and Throm took conduits up one deck, in hopes it would throw the drones off. When they arrived, the other survivors sat, crestfallen.

"What happened?" asked Throm.

Bernice sat on an open crate, crying. Brett consoled her.

"Bernice, what happened?"

The pirate woman looked up, face reddened. "The station's defense mechanisms all of a sudden turned on. Our ship took a pounding, then exploded. We ran away from the data station, afraid of a hull breech. But, we were slow. Hull breech sirens went off. We . . . we . . ." her words trailed off.

Manifold continued. "We made it to a safe corridor before the bulkheads came down to seal the breach. But then we saw a drone. We ran and ran. We didn't even try to fire on it. We turned a corner and there was Torchy. He laid down cover fire so we could get away."

Bernice's cries turned to sobs.

Gunny Boone clinched his fist. Another orbital marine gone.

Brett asked about the others, but Boone couldn't bring himself to tell of their deaths, so Arcy did.

"That's it," Brett said. "We're all dead."

"Knock it off," Boone said.

"Why? What's wrong with the truth?" Brett got up to confront Boone.

Arcy pulled her pistol on the man.

"Arcy, that's not necessary. Put the pistol away," Boone said.

"What's one less pirate trash?" Arcy's face was calm, cool.

Brett's eyes widened. His jaw slacked.

"Arcy, put that pistol away. THAT is an order." Boone put his hand on the barrel and slowly lowered it.

No one spoke for some time.

"What about those skiffs. Can you pilot one, Gunny Boone?" Bernice asked.

Boone nodded. "Yeah, but we'll need a diversion."

The group devised a plan. Boone and Arcy would create a diversion on the same deck as the skiffs. This would draw away the drones. The others would make it to the skiff and wait until they got back.

"No offense, but what if you don't make it?" Manifold asked.

"Then set the automatic beacon. The skiffs are pretty tough. You should be able to survive a while until the Fleet arrives."

The two crews looked at each other.

"It will work. It has to work," Boone said.

They got some sleep. No more than a few hours, but it helped Boone. When he awoke, the others were sleeping – except Arcy. She sat, cleaning her rifle in perfect silence, with only a sliver of light catching the glow in her eyes. "You up, Gunny?"

"Yeah. Sleep was nice."

"I bet."

"Did you get any?" Gunny Boone asked.

"Yeah. But, you know, I'm excited. So I got up and cleaned my weapon."

Arcy had the stuff to make an exceptional marine. Protect your tools and your tools will protect you. That's what the Corps always taught.

"Come on, marine. We got work to do."

Boone woke Manifold and told him they were going to get ready. The other marine understood. "Good luck, Gunny."

The two crawled through the electrical conduit back to the original laboratory. No drones patrolled the area. They moved into the hallway and down a corridor into another lab. There they found a small table that they moved out into a T hallway to give them some cover.

"This plan doesn't have much of a chance of working, Gunny."

"I know that. But if we can make a diversion, the others can get into the skiff. That'll be enough." Gunny Boone scratched his curly, black hair.

"But what about us?"

Boone smiled. "Don't worry, I've always got something up my sleeve." He looked at the girl. Lean build. Beautiful blue eyes and short, blond hair. She was perfect. "My watch says they should be moving through the conduit now. So we should start."

Arcy nodded.

Gunny Boone fired three shots at the ceiling. "Any minute now."

A drone came down from the direction of the hangar bay. As soon the hovering robot saw the two, it began shooting.

Boone dropped behind the table, hoping it would protect him.

"Gunny, another drone," Arcy said with ice in her voice.

Boone looked past her right shoulder and saw it coming. He opened fired.

It returned fire, hitting the ground around them.

Boone pushed Arcy down and fired over her head, hitting the drone again.

It smoked and lost altitude.

Boone shot it again.

The floating robot exploded, its innards thrown all over the hallway.

Arcy popped up and shot the first drone multiple times with her rifle.

It exploded, sending hot shards of steel and plastic everywhere.

"Gunny. I think that's it." Arcy got up.

"Wait a minute." Boone checked his watch.

"But Gunny, if we hurry, we can still catch them. Still escape."

"We're not doing anything of the sort, Arcy."

"What are you talking about?"

Gunny Boone sat the table upright and sat on it. "What did you say? 'He'll be dead soon, anyways,' when you ran to the lift?"

"Gunny we don't –"

"You know, I've seen men and women die for thirty years. But I'm a grizzled vet. What are you, twenty? Not one tear for your fallen comrades. Your voice didn't break once."

Arcy cocked her head.

"And when we were on the bridge, I was so sure I didn't trip any security protocols. Yet, there were those flashing lights and system crash."

Arcy said nothing.

"The kicker was when I woke up. The glow in your eyes as the artificial light hit them. That was the kicker." Gunny Boone put his rifle on the table next to him. "These drones. They weren't here to protect the station. They were here to protect you. You are Defense Protocol B. Some kind of advanced AI war machine, I would guess."

"I can't let you tell anyone. I am sorry." Arcy raised her rifle.

"Oh, I know. That's why I changed the times table before we left." Gunny Boone looked at his watch. "They should be gone by now." He smiled. "And, oh, you can forget using the second skiff. Manifold set that to–"

An explosion made the station shutter.

"Ah, there it goes now." Boone held on to the table as the station rocked. "So did you take a uniform off of a dead marine?"

Arcy nodded.

"What were you going to do?"

"Fulfill my programing, thanks to you. Without your hard re-boot, I would have never come online." Arcy smiled. "Thank you."

Gunny Boone sighed. "Well, damn it all to Hell. I think we're even."

Explosions went off in some far-off corner of the ship. The lights flickered, then went out. It would be over soon. Gunny Boone thought of his friends.

"Propulsion" by Thomas A. Fowler
Dinosaur in Space

The egg holding me was misshapen. Rather than an oblong form with a narrowed top, I rested inside a perfect sphere. I shouldn't be able to see through the egg either. Yet I knew the process of growing inside an egg; I'd been born once already. Have I died? Is this my rebirth? The bubbling, blue liquid I rested in made it nearly impossible to see anything outside my rounded chamber. I could only see the vague silhouettes of creatures.

The voice of those odd creatures echoed throughout the space beyond my egg; muffled calls of varying inflections between them, nothing said to me. Beyond these creatures, I made out the shadow of a small opening. All I could see beyond the entrance was a black sky and the glow of a few vibrant stars far beyond us. The stars moved slowly by the small opening. This vessel was moving. I tried to understand the odd creatures. They were small, stood on two legs. They did not share my long neck, nor did they sport tails for balance. Their center of gravity must occur some other way. Their presence felt unnatural, as if a gap in the lives of earth's creatures had been closed.

My entire life felt unnatural. I felt a beckoning for large trees, green sweeping landscapes. Yet all I have ever seen are chambers and eggs to hold me in and apart from the world I longed to explore. I accepted these places as I was fed, kept from predators, and given a calm place to sleep. Yet the wild was where I belonged.

Two of the odd creatures walked closer. Their voices became clearer. The chamber still muffled their words. I looked down at them. They were small beasts, I could step on one and still have room to spare on the bottom of my foot. The two seemed to be arguing while looking at me. I felt out of place, as if one of them didn't want my presence, nor the presence of the spheres that surrounded me.

My long neck turned, cheek rubbing against the rounded container surface as I pushed unnaturally down. I wanted to see them better. I couldn't tell who they were. As I kicked my legs up, trying to flip inside the egg, I recognized one of the odd creatures. He was the one who fed me, washed me. He'd periodically stick me with a long, silver stick full of liquid that stung, but I felt healthy afterwards. I did not recognize the other.

The bubbles were less vigorous at the base of my round chamber. They expanded as they rose to the top. As a result, I could see out of my chamber better. I realized the size of the space I was in. I wasn't the only one in a cylindrical egg. There were hundreds, no, thousands of them. Each one housed an animal, many of them creatures from my time. I recognized several others from my feeding chambers back when I could still see ground. We were all being moved together. Everyone was asleep, even others of my own kind. I could not understand my purpose, yet I knew worrying would get me nowhere. I rested my eyes as the trip continued.

The black sky outside of the window turned orange. Fire, like a volcano, shone outside of the tiny opening. The vessel rumbled. I felt only mild tremors nestled inside the bubbling liquid, which absorbed much of the impact and with my egg mounted firmly against the side walls of this mobile vessel. The orange glow outside of the small opening changed. It turned red, a fiery blaze. It faded away. In its place came a blue sky outside. It was like the view I saw when there was ground beneath my feet. Far off, outside the window, were green trees and lush hills. It was the utopia I recalled from a vague memory of my kind, memories of a past life. The vessel stopped in a large, open pasture. The hills were covered with vibrant flowers, much bigger than the kind I'd ever seen in my past enclosure, before this moving vessel, before this trip through the skies. The trees were taller than me, something I hadn't witnessed before. I felt a slight shake in my egg. My stomach settled for the first time, the vessel had stopped moving. The shake came as the view from the small opening settled, we'd stopped in the wide-open pasture.

I heard a click; a rounded scoop settled in below my sphere. My egg began to move. I kicked against the clear shell. It did not give. That wasn't how I remembered eggs working. I remembered darkness, kicking, and then the silver room where I was raised. This egg didn't surrender. I bellowed. Bubbles escaped my mouth; my cries garbled and disappeared in the liquid of this sphere. Other containers like mine moved ahead and behind me. We were moving in a straight line. Looking forward, I saw something. We were headed for the green pasture.

Ahead of me, another creature, like my own appearance, reached the exit. The cylindrical egg drained its liquid. Then the container rose from the ground. My own ran in a panic from the egg toward the green pasture. The bubbles below me began to swell. They were vigorous, raging. I couldn't see a thing outside of this cylinder. The liquid dropped.

A loud click. The sound echoed inside the sphere without the liquid to muffle the noises within the shell. I raised my head and took in a strong breath of air. The liquid dropped until all that was left were dripping remnants falling from my body. The blue residue trickled off my neck, chin, and tail. The egg lifted. I blinked. My eyes itched from the liquid. I pivoted my neck, rubbing my eyes against my massive frame. Dozens of the tiny, odd, two-legged creatures stood below me. They pointed out toward the pasture. I looked out, there were dozens of creatures. Many were my own kind; others were similar, but separate. One had three, pointed horns on its head; others had a club tail; and some adorned plates from their back hide. Then there were the long necked, biggest creatures, four legs stomping about. I stepped outside of my chamber. My foot hit the strong, silver surface I grew up in for the first few steps. Then, my foot rested onto the green pasture. The soft dirt caved from my weight. Blades of grass curled in as my foot sunk the earth below me. I'd never felt something so different, so calming. I looked out at the trees not far from the pasture. Their massive leaves were like the food I was given, but it was there for the taking. No more would I have to wait for one of the two-legged creatures to give them to me.

We settled into herds, as we all ate plants. Periodically, the odd creatures would come and take one of us. I believed they used us for meat. Their visits were rare; we weighed a lot. The odd creatures didn't take more than they could use. But I would see bones the size of a creature from the herd being used for a shelter for the odd creatures. They appeared to use us for a vital resource, yet left us to live on our own, otherwise. With massive bones and lots of meat, we were the right option to bring to this new place, far from where I used to call my home. I curved my neck up, biting on a nearby tree. Being free in the open air made the plants taste all that much better. It felt like the home I yearned for; yet something about it was fresh and new.

"Fool's Gold" by TJ Valour
Psycho Killer in Space

I steel myself and step inside the lift. Compared to the other lifts I've used since my arrival to the Sorjana Space Station, this one is luxurious. A Plogrun male in a three-piece, pink suit leans against the back wall. The bright color of the suit is garish against his mustard-color skin. He straightens as the doors close behind me.

"What floor, sir?" he asks with the elongated vowels and growling speech of his species.

"The lounge please."

His gaze flicks to me, and with a black claw he enters a series of numbers on the lift's key pad.

I face the viewport. The exterior hull turns into a blur of movement as we rocket upwards toward the First Class section. The butterflies in my gut all take flight at once and it has nothing to do with the movement and everything to do with my destination.

"Who are you to play god?" the Plogrun asks.

I turn toward him, not sure if he actually spoke to me or is just thinking aloud. "Excuse me?"

"Only gods and demons deal in death. You are neither, and *she's* not the former."

Understanding dawns and a bolt of anger scorches up my spine.

This alien thinks he has some right to judge me and the decisions that brought me here. I painstakingly weighed every viable option with my family, and this was the best option *for us*. It is my right as a citizen of the Galactic Republic to choose to end my suffering, to terminate my intolerable existence. I may be young by human standards, but to live every day with a million piranhas inside my body, consuming my life in excruciating bites from the inside out...is an existence I wouldn't wish on my worst enemy.

The Plogrun stares at me for a long second. "If you have a brain cell in that small, round skull, now is the last chance you'll have to use it."

I open my mouth to speak, but the lift doors open. Deciding to be the better sentient being, I exit the lift.

A low growl escapes him and I glance over my shoulder.

His eyes narrow and his nostrils flare out repeatedly as if I'm the one who's done something offensive. "It's a meat market she runs—not a charity." He switches into his native tongue, and I only understand bits of what follows. Several swear words mixed in with something roughly translated to hell and damnation.

The lift door closes before I can retort.

I inhale a deep breath through my nose and release it through my mouth to calm down. The Plogruns are known for their religious beliefs, all five-hundred plus sects of them, but they're also known for their civil approach to others. Otherwise, their species would invariably be in a never-ending religious war.

"Zealot," I mutter. *A meat market.* Give me a break. Leera provides the opportunity for individuals to control their life's end with some dignity.

Yet the lingering remnants of his accusation weave through my brain and herald a sharp pain in my abdomen. It jabs up my sternum to imbed in my lungs. I double over and use the wall adjacent to the lift as support. My vision dims and my thoughts fizzle and grow fuzzy. Tremors start in my hands and move up my arms until my whole body shakes. The medication that I used to take muffled the worst of it, but the attacks lasted hours. Now the meds are out of my system and the attacks are far more powerful, but pass in minutes.

The attack ends and I'm left a pathetic, quivering mess. Beads of cold sweat trickle from my temples and down my back, causing my clothes to stick against my skin. My right cheek, shoulder, and upper chest are pressed into the textured fabric of the wall hard enough to leave swirl impressions on my jaundiced skin. I gasp in a lungful of air and right myself. The floor and walls around me remain stationary, which is always a good sign.

After another minute, I'm well enough to move.

I adjust my tie and round a slight corner to approach the maître d' stand of the Sorjana Space Station's exclusive lounge. Before this morning, my keycard wouldn't even have allowed me on the lift that delivered me up here. The maître d', a striking Imdaali male, blinks at me with his four, obsidian eyes. My reflection is distorted in their multi-faceted depths but none-the-less identifiable. My new suit hangs off my thin frame, even though I've owned it less than two weeks. The suit provides me a costume to fit seamlessly into this part of the station. Unfortunately, the expression on my face blatantly announces otherwise. I appear as dazed and confused as the maître d' no doubt thinks I am. A sheen of sweat still coats my skin and my pallor likely resembles an unripe Dávorit lemon.

"Do you have a reservation, human?"

Human. The word sounds like a term for something slimy scraped off the bottom of a shoe, and it reminds me exactly how far from my home world I am.

I clear my throat. "I'm Theo Gromm."

The maître d' blinks again before switching his attention to the subtly glowing podium he stands behind. A second later his angular shoulders straighten, and his black eyes fix on me. This time, the weight of his attention feels like an iron band constricting around my chest.

He now knows who I am meeting and what that means. The righteous anger and confidence I felt in the lift seems like eons ago. I breathe the recycled air and slip my sweating palms in my pockets.

"You're expected. Please follow me, sir." With an incline of his head, the Imdaali turns smoothly on his heel.

I follow him down a hallway flickering with firelight even though there are no fireplaces or candles. The sound of falling water acts as a subtle texture against the soft romantic music playing through unseen speakers. Plush carpet in a dark blue veined in gold mutes the ever increasing sounds of conversation and the tinkling of dinnerware.

The lounge clearly caters to and accommodates countless species of alien. A wall of water separates a large portion of the tiered entertaining space. I can just make out several bulbous shapes with tentacles on the other side. Another portion of the lounge is decorated with a riot of vibrant flora. Millions of blooms wrap the pendant lighting and sheets of leafy vines create a sense of intimacy around several sitting areas. Humidity and the sweetness of the nectar wafts across my skin as we pass.

We continue up a flight of stairs and enter a section that fits what I envisioned when I'd accepted this meeting place. Floor to ceiling viewports showcase the surrounding planets and stars. Crystalline lamps shed light on white chairs and polished tables the color of pitch. The surround is at odds to the rotten meat smell hanging in the air.

In a booth sequestered in a small inlet off the main space is the single occupied table. And Leera is sitting at it.

She looks exactly like the image attached to the contract, but my blood still turns to ice in my veins. Every second thought that I have had over the last six months comes roaring back to the surface of my mind.

I don't know what the maitre d' says as he leaves. I'm positive he spoke, I saw his lips move, but the buzzing in my ears drowns out everything.

Leera's eyes meet mine from across the room and instead of panic I feel instant calm. Just like the advertisement that drew me to her agency from the beginning. Everything about her draws me like a moth to a flame. The ambient noise of the lounge returns and the off-putting stench is pulled away on a current of fresh air. I walk toward her with sure steps. Her full lips kick up at the corners at my approach.

She stands and holds out her hand toward me. I never have been able to figure out what alien species she belongs to, but whatever Leera is, she is lovely—beyond worldly beauty—and she steals my breath. Her skin is luminous porcelain. Long, dark hair frames her heart-shaped face. Her ears are long and elfin except from the narrow earlobe are two, almost delicate, appendages that dangle like glowing earrings. She has humanoid shaped eyes and they are edged with long, feathery lashes, but instead of a round pupil hers are elongated like a cat's or some other night-stalking predator. In my mind, I know that Leera is the predator her sharp eyes indicate, but I don't care. I am willing to give myself over to her. It's the best thing I can do for myself and my family.

I reach her, but instead of shaking hands, she intertwines her fingers with my own and guides me to the seat across from her at the table. Her skin is cooler than mine but not unpleasantly so.

Her shimmering sheath dress compliments her pale skin and green eyes. It also shows off her ample cleavage.

"Would you like a drink?" she asks. The question a purr. Her voice is so much more sensual in person than on the Vid-feed.

I swallow and nod.

Leera, with the hand not holding mine, taps a command into the creation stand built into the wall. "A Hetu stout? Or something lighter?"

"The stout is fine." I'd been too nervous to eat anything since breakfast and my favorite beverage will provide calories and energy.

My beer appears a moment later. I pull it toward me and take a deep swallow. The wispy smokiness, bitter chocolate and dark licorice flavors from my home planet lick over my tongue. And for a second, I'm back there, the nightmare of the past few years falling away.

She squeezes my hand once before releasing me in order to fold her hands on the table.

"When was your last injection?" Leera asks. Her eyes soft, empathetic.

"Two weeks ago."

A small incline of her head. "And your family?"

I take another drink of my beer. "They were encouraging about this trip. It's been a hard last few years for everyone."

"Of course." She reaches down to a bag near her feet and places a tablet between us. "The finalized contract." Leera holds my gaze and my heart beat goes into triple-time. "Only you can make this choice, and it's utterly within your rights as a sentient being." She pushes the tablet until it's directly in front of me.

"I understand." I scan the contract, reading over every detail for the hundredth time. The payment to my family's accounts, the disposition of my body. I will be sent back to Hetu for internment in our family plot. Any organs viable for medical study or donation will be procured and donated accordingly.

"When will I be able to make my call?"

Leera sets down the tall, opaque glass that she's been sipping from. "As soon as we're done here. Your funds will be transferred during that time, should you wish to confirm that those you love have received it prior to the event."

The event. She means when she will kill me.

I glance up before signing my name. I'm not sure what makes me ask, maybe curiosity, but I want to know more about who and what she is. How she does what she does to survive.

"How many clients have you had like this?"

She tilts her head to the side, studying me. Her predator eyes seem to glow for the briefest of moments.

"Legally, you will be my seven hundred and thirtieth. As you well know, the Senate did not always favor my kind, or the symbiosis we offer other species."

I watch the movement of Leera's tongue as she licks her bottom lip. Then her words sink in. So many. She is obviously older than her appearance implies. Leera looks only a few years older than me, maybe twenty to twenty-five in human years. If that were accurate, she would have to have killed twenty-nine beings every year since her birth, which is asinine.

The red-gold emblem she wears on her breast catches the light. However attractive, the broach's coloring isn't for appearances, it's an outward symbol of nonalignment and diplomatic immunity. Anything she does while openly wearing that can't be held against her in a planetary court. She is held only to the laws and regulations of the Galactic Senate. Another failsafe for her, us, and what we're doing.

Of course, it's perfectly legal because we—me, my family, and Leera's company—have followed every guideline and process put in place for these very circumstances. Yet there is a reason why her company is based on a space station so far from my world. There remain plenty of beings whose beliefs are archaic or whose thoughts are closed-minded. Like the alien in the lift. They don't understand and why should they? They haven't stood in my shoes, lived a half-life due to a crippling, incurable disease.

As if conjured by my thoughts, the tell-tale prickles start in my lungs. I pull a black handkerchief out of my breast pocket and hold it to my lips as I turn my head and cough. It's a deep, wet-rattling sound and the dark cloth is burnished with my blood when I pull it away. Leera watches me, as I carefully fold it and slip it away.

She has never been anything less than professional. I did my research and Leera, her agency, are the best. Every reference I found was another rave review of the kindness, compassion, and skill that Leera and her company extended to their family during a time of grief and loss. Those experiences are why I'm here.

Toying with my beer bottle, I stare into her exotic face. "Will it hurt?" The question seems silly and juvenile as soon as I say it aloud.

"Only if you want it to. Theo, you control it all. Every action I take will be because you have indicated your desire." Leera tips her chin toward the tablet displaying our contract. "Whatever you stipulate will be hard boundaries, and I never have, nor would I ever, cross them."

I scroll my finger over the screen of the tablet. It flares green and a pop-up box appears. *Theo Gromm, identity confirmed.*

They processed my voice tones, blood type, finger and footprints, and complete body composition at the physical exam two months ago. My identity has been confirmed eight-ways to Sunday since my arrival on the Sorjana Space Station too. At my check-in upon arrival and again when granting me the extended clearance earlier today.

"Does what I select change the effect for you?"

Leera smiles endearingly at me, and it shows her brilliant white and sharp teeth. "How would it, sweet Theo? The end result is always the same, no matter the path taken."

I shrug. I don't know what I thought she would say. My family's words about expecting human rationale from an alien species flash in my mind. After going over the brochure with my baby sister Twyla, she had turned to me and said, "It's all so clinical." A shake of her head. "At least you know the emotional part of it, the gratification, the pleasure, isn't why they feed on people's life force…"

My conversation with my sister, and other confirmations since, made me feel better about the whole situation and my choice to go through with this. My family and I will not support an entity or organization that gets their jollies by hurting, destroying, and ultimately murdering people.

A feeling of peace replaces the trepidation I felt leading up to this meeting. Calmness descends in my brain where apprehension and fear have lived for so long, I'd forgotten there is an alternative. Leera's company will take care of everything, end my suffering, pay off the debt I still owe the medical treatment facilities, and provide my family enough to move on after my death with some stability. Leera and her agency are not some black market subterfuge, they are everything they claim to be and exactly what I need and want. No more pain, just peace.

I place both of my thumbs over the signature squares and an instant of heat washes over the skin there.

This time the pop-up box has swirly font. *Thank You. Signature accepted.* I take a final sip of my beer and leave another swallow or two in the bottle. The dregs mixed in with the last bit of liquid would sour the entire experience.

Leera takes the tablet off the table and puts it back into her bag. She picks up her bag and rises from her chair. I follow suit. Standing she is nearly a foot taller than me. Her company must have some arrangement with the lounge because she doesn't leave any payment. We just get up and walk out through a side door.

The door opens into a wide hallway. The flooring is a gray stone and the walls a cream color so seamless I can't tell where the walls end and the ceiling begins. We arrive at a steel door at the end of the hall. Leera types a long string of characters into the key pad and the door slides open. Nothing about this second hallway is beautiful or welcoming. It's sterile, stark cold, and smells like disinfectant. A shiver goes through my body at the drop in temperature.

Leera glances at me. "This way Theo, the waiting room is just around the corner."

The waiting room turns out to be the reality of the first picture on their brochure. Polished chrome, softly glowing white floor panels, and plush, organically shaped sofas interspersed with luxury dispenser stations. Galactic specialty liquors, epicurean foods, and the finest of recreational substances. Whatever I want I can have in my last minutes of life.

A small shelf next to the door holds two, small vials, one blue and one yellow. Leera removes the blue one and holds it out to me. "Take this now to relax, and once you have concluded your affairs—" She nods toward a computer terminal on the far side of the room. "Drink the yellow one and push the call button." She indicates a red button on the other side of the door from the vials.

I take the blue vial and throw it back like a shot of Tragon Whiskey. Except, unlike the Tragon, it doesn't burn all the way to my gut. It goes down like water and leaves no residual taste in my mouth. Odd.

Leera takes the empty vial and turns to go. "If there is anything you need, press the call button."

The door shuts behind her. I wander around the space twice, trying to decide what to do first. I cue up the computer and type in my mother's code but don't press send. I'm not ready yet.

I order my last meal. It consists of some of the most expensive delicacies from the surrounding star systems: Kywak coffee, one-hundred-year-old black pearl caviar, and Gorjanii steak so perfectly cooked it melts on my tongue. The average price for just a cup of the Kywak coffee is more than two months of my prior rent. I relish every sip and allow my taste buds to savor every bite of food.

For dessert I order and eat a Luminae truffle. I wash it down with a small glass of milk from my home world before I sit down in front of the computer. I contemplate ordering another truffle, but decide against it. I'm too full to appreciate the flavor, and it's time. Squaring my shoulders, I send in the call.

A chime sounds a second later and my mother's face shimmers into focus on the vid screen.

"Theo!" she exclaims, her fingertips brushing over the lens as if to touch my face. "My beautiful boy." Her blue eyes are the mirror image of my sister's and they swim with unshed tears. "You made it okay?"

I nod. "The trip went smoothly and everything has gone really well."

My sister's voice comes from off camera. "Tell him we got the deposit and it's cleared." Her normally strong voice is sullen. She wanted to come with me.

"Did you hear Twy? The money came through."

"Yes." I swallow and glance away from the screen. In my periphery, I can see my sister come to stand by my mom. Tears are streaming unchecked down her cheeks. I force my attention back to my family. I have to say this. "Mom, Twy…"

The tightness is back in my chest. My eyes water but I blink it away. I'm the strong one. This is me controlling my destiny. "I'm sorry I can't say good bye in person, but you know how much I love you." Mom dashes away a stray tear and Twy bites her lip. "I'm so blessed to have been your son, your brother. Take care of each other." I try and give them a megawatt smile, but it feels flatter than I intend. "I love you." I can't bring myself to actually say good bye.

"I'll miss you with my every breath, Theo. I'm so proud of you, honey," Mom says as she dabs her eye.

"I'll take care of Mom. Thank you for what you're doing for us." Twyla bites her lip but isn't done. "There was another case, just like yours, on Vhallis II. I heard from the hospital that she decided to do what you did but the company was a total sham. Her family never got the full payment and instead of giving her body to medical research and those that need it, they sold every bone and organ off to the highest bidder—" Her voice drops. "—A carnivore and outlaw who is wanted on five planets."

There's red on my mother's cheeks when Twy finishes. She glares at my sister before looking back at me. "Don't listen to your sister's gossip, Theo. We've already got the full payment without any issues. We trust your choice."

The moment I told my mother how much my death could bring, she was against it. She didn't want me to martyr myself for her. Since my father's death and her accident, she hasn't been able to work steadily. Mom would never accept a handout though, and it took both Twy and I to finally get her consent to this. I need to do this for her, for them, it's my duty as the eldest child. The deposit they received from Leera would afford them the necessities for the next twenty years if they managed it well.

"Leera and her company's history speak for itself, Twy. They've been nothing but professional and I've not seen or heard anything to indicate otherwise." Even as the words leave my mouth, I'm reminded of the Plogrun in the lift, the doubts, the tiny minutiae that made me pause along this route. "But I promise if anything feels off, I'll back out."

163

"Promise, Theo?" Twyla asks and the hope in her voice is a dagger in my heart. "They could still find a cure. You could have a full life…"

"I swear. You read the contract with me, you know there's a clause in there for second thoughts." I taste iron in my mouth, and I swallow back some blood. I must have bit my cheek or tongue. "I doubt I'll back out Twy, this is what I want." This is the only thing I can do to provide for them and stop the pain, control my last moments.

A small, teary smile from my sister. "I love you, Theo."

"I love you, too," I say.

My mother strokes the screen again and then blows me a kiss. "Good bye, son. You have all my love."

I shut off the transmission before my tears escape down my cheeks.

I'm not sure how long I let myself cry, but by the time I'm done, my stomach hurts and my eyes are swollen. Whatever the person Twyla heard about experienced; it isn't my problem. Leera isn't who they went through. And yes, maybe there are some shady money-grabbing dirt bags in Leera's industry, but it's not so different than any other business or trade. There are better and worse options, companies with integrity and those without.

My choice is the right one. My family needs this and only a fool would choose to experience the slow, sordid death that awaits me otherwise. I move to the door, but instead of drinking from the vial I push the red button. Leera can answer my last questions before I drink it. It's in the contract and it'll give me a final peace of mind.

I don't even have time to sit down before the door opens and Leera appears.

She's not in her dress any longer but some sort of white lab-type coat. Her eyes appear even more luminous and her lips are stained a brilliant red in the bright light. The smile she gives me turns her from beautiful to stunning. The clamp of sadness around my heart eases a fraction. What I am doing is the right thing. On her lapel is the diplomatic immunity emblem.

Leera glances at the remaining vial and back at me. A frown mars her features.

"Just a quick question…" I clear my throat and taste copper again. "My sister wanted me to ask because she'd heard rumors about people doing this with bad results…"

Leera tilts her head to the side, waiting. I soldier on, my words fast and running together, "Lack of payments to the family and the donations not being handled legitimately." I shrug. Knowing this is a silly thing to bring up at this point.

"Your family received the full amount already, yes?" she asks and holds out her hand. I take it, nodding.

Her eyes capture mine and I'm entranced by their shimmering depths. There are so many colors in her eyes, so many shades of green and even some yellow. It reminds me of a forest coming awake in spring.

"Theo, no matter the path one takes the outcome is always the same," Leera purrs and leans closer to me. I can see each tantalizing eyelash. She doesn't blink and I'm once again drawn into the depths of her gaze. So lovely. So enthralling—

The remaining vial is in my hand. I don't remember grabbing it, but I need to drink it. I swallow the yellow liquid in one gulp. It's an odd, citrus taste and my limbs feel heavy almost as soon as it hits my stomach.

"This way, Theo." Leera pulls me gently out of the waiting room.

Was there something I had asked her? I can't remember and it seems irrelevant now. Peace is finally within my grasp.

We walk across the hall and into a typical hospital room. Monitoring equipment is connected to an angled bed at its center. There is no other furniture. A mirror runs the length of the room on one side. Leera sees my interest. "The physicians who will be handling your organ and tissue donation are on the other side. They must observe in order to act in the necessary moment."

She squeezes my hand. "Take a seat."

I sit on the bed and the angle of the back becomes more pronounced like a chair. My arms fall to the armrests. It's very comfortable. I roll my shoulders and settle back into the plush fabric.

My eyes are drawn back to the one-way mirror. As I stare at the chrome surface, it shifts. Rainbow ripples replace the mirror and for a moment, I swear I can see through them into the room beyond. Aliens stand ready with preservation cases marked as biohazard. Not one of them is wearing a lab coat or any personal protective equipment.

My head lolls forward. The polished floor, cracks and splits beneath me. A deafening roar resonates in my ears. Lava flows inches below my feet. I can feel the heat through the soles of my shoes. Sulfur burns my nostrils and sour eggs coat my throat.

"Leeeera..." I slur out, try to scream, but my tongue is swollen and uncooperative.

She tilts up my chin. Bright predator eyes meet mine. "What you are feeling is a compromise between me and the harvesters. I need your fear and they need your organs, tissue, and skin in the best possible shape for auction."

No. No. No...that isn't how it supposed to work. Medical donations go to save lives, help with research.

I see a flash of fangs as Leera smiles down at me. "The drugs you so willingly consumed will keep your body relaxed as if in sleep, but you won't be sleeping, Theo. You will be very much awake as you experience the nightmare of your end."

Terror floods my system and red washes over my iris. I scream and thrash, but no sound comes out of my mouth and my body doesn't so much as twitch. Panic settles into my bones, into my every thought as I realize the horrific mistake I've made.

My baby sister was right.

The gullibility of humanity is quite convenient. It's in my nature to stalk, wait, and enjoy the kill. But why expend the time and energy for all of that lead up, when those eager to die will come straight to my lair?

I acknowledge the team of harvesters on the other side of the mirror to begin the countdown. Resale capability and taste, so I'm told, have a direct correlation to the speed of collection upon last breath. Which is why we'll keep Theo's body functional as long as possible, he'll remain medically alive throughout my feed and into the harvest. Once I'm through feasting on sweet Theo's fear and have sucked his soul dry, the vultures will come in and take everything else. Every viable scrap of tissue and organ will be stabilized and prepared to be shipped out. At least the cost of working with such vermin covers the inconvenience. A measly bit of flesh and bone pays handsomely in certain circles in the galaxy. Well enough for my business to flourish.

Death is a lucrative business and now that the Senate has accepted *our right* to partake in it…

I allow the other side of me to come out and play.

The lights flicker once then dim. My vision remains clear, but the room is no longer the garish gray. It's swathed in beautiful shadow.

A hiss escapes my mouth as my jaw unhinges to free the two rows of my tapered fangs. The skin over my face stretches and contracts. My nostrils shrink and the black spines of my gender protrude along my brow and cheek bones. A shudder resonates through my bones at the freedom. My tongue flicks out, tasting, honing in on the delicious taste of my prey.

The faint green glow from my eyes casts an eerie light onto his face. Theo's eyes widen and the sweetness of fear licks the air. His mouth drops open in a soundless scream that sends sparks of life into my veins. The human's eyelids droop close and flutter for a moment before slowly opening again. His pupils are so dilated they resemble black holes bouncing around inside his sclera. Whatever hallucination the drugs are currently showing him has him terrified. The delicious mess of his horror is ambrosia to my parched body.

I caress the softness of Theo's throat, scraping my claws up to his jaw. I allow them to bite into the skin enough to taste the renewed spike of fear in the air. It mingles with the richness of human blood. I turn his head to the side. The whites of his eyes grow impossibly larger and another wave of fear washes over me. I savor its fleeting caress. I wonder if he's too far lost into his mind to know I'm smiling.

My tongue flicks out to stroke his cheek, touch his ear. Every sluggish beat of his heart is a siren song I feel like an electric pulse against me. My fangs ache. The human's terror ratchets up impossibly higher. It peaks as my fangs sink into his flesh. Luscious heat fills my mouth. Energy floods my body as I consume everything that I can.

It's over in seconds. The heart monitor ceases beeping, forcing me to pull away.

I haven't even wiped my mouth before the harvesters rush in the room. Dabbing gently at the corner of my bottom lip with the underside of my lab coat I leave. Sated for the moment, but my hunger is never ceasing.

My body reverts to my luring form, mostly non-threatening in appearance and considered striking by many a species. Now, instead of a necessary decoy, my visually appealing facade is just a bonus when conducting business.

Clarence is waiting in the hall, his ugly pink suit revolting against his yellow skin. "Your next appointment is in two hours. A Quvorkian female down on love. Her matched partner backed out of their union after seeing her image."

I grin. The women often have so much more emotion to give at the end. "Excellent. The zealot card won't work for her, her kind aren't open to religious or spiritual views. Tastefully remind her of why she chose to come here. She's a disgrace of her race. She's obviously ugly, worthless, and unintelligent."

"And if she resists? Changes her mind?"

I show him my teeth. "The outcome will be the same."

"Scratchers" by Jason Kent
Alien in an Alternate Future

They came on August 6, 1887. We didn't stand a chance.

I'm not sure how many people were there to see the first ships land. All we have are stories passed from one survivor to another. I guess the eye witnesses were too busy staying alive to write a book. I understand. Surviving in The Wastes is a full-time job.

I raised binoculars to my eyes and studied the alien machine chewing its way across the countryside. From what I've heard, the Pyxis didn't bring these huge machines with them. They took what they needed from humanity and started building. They haven't stopped since. Scratchers, like the smoke belching monster I was trailing, provided all the raw materials the aliens needed to construct their tower cities and even more mining machines. I wasn't sure how much more Earth could take. I wasn't sure if humanity could survive if we didn't do something to stop them.

Two, quick whistles caught my attention. My hunting partner, Axle, motioned me forward. I'd been covering his advance from a low ridge covered with thorny bushes. I pushed through, ignoring the scratches and tears I was getting. We'd been watching for any signs of Pyxis guards. After days of observation, it was time to strike.

Axle and I came from a long line of fighters—stretching back to the invasion, nearly a hundred and thirty years. Like our predecessors, we have had mixed success. The scratchers and other alien machines we often went up against were nearly indestructible. We've slowed them down now and then, but never managed to stop one completely. And the Pyxis themselves? Who knows? They spend their time in their unbelievably tall towers, looking down on us with the alien equivalent of indifference. They haven't bothered sending out anything more than a few drones to fight with us since my grandfather's time. Either they don't have ground troops anymore or think we aren't worth the trouble to come after. Hopefully, Axle and I can change their minds this time.

The grinding noise from the scratcher grew painfully loud as I got closer. I stopped, crouched behind a rock, and plugged my ears with cotton. It wasn't perfect, but it would keep me from going deaf. On the move again, I hit the boundary of the mining operation. Scratchers moved on giant tracks while carving out a trench nearly a quarter mile wide and forty feet deep. I'd seen them used to clear out an area by digging back and forth over an area determined by their controllers. Trenches got deeper and deeper, leaving nothing but the waste material behind. Heavy conveyor belts stretched from the side of the machines, dumping the scratcher's waste into long hills. From what I could tell, nothing was able to grow in the mine tailings, thus, The Wastes. A century plus of such destruction was a long time; long enough to turn most of our once-green planet into what amounted to one, big, strip mine. The scratcher Axle and I were going after seemed to have a new goal in mind. I looked back on the straight line of waste left in the machine's wake. For whatever purpose, the Pyxis were sending this beast straight for my home in what left of Philadelphia. Yes, scratchers were loud, evil smelling, and nearly impossible to stop. Still, we'd be sent to do the impossible.

Right.

"We doing this, Trip?" Axle shouted as he dove for cover behind the same rock. Axle and I had grown up scratching what existence we could amid the ruins of civilization. There was no one better to have with you on a suicide mission.

"Can't turn back now," I replied loudly and pointed to a ladder hanging down between the third and fourth sets of steel treads. "That's our way inside."

Axle put his battered rifle to his shoulder and stared through the scope, studying the scratcher. He shook his head as he let the glasses drop. "One wrong move and we're ground rat meat!"

"I've done this before, remember?" No need to tell Axle I'd nearly messed my jump up to a ladder just like this during my last attempt to disable one of these monsters. And yes, those treads do look terrifying when you're staring at them from two feet away, hanging by one hand.

"There's got to be another way," Axle grumbled. He moved his rifle from bow to stern. He stopped when his sights reached the top of the machine. "If only we could get on top."

"Not likely," I laughed bitterly. This close to the scratcher I had to tilt my head far back to see the source of the billowing smoke casting a pall over everything within a mile of our location. I knew from studying scratchers there would be a landing pad just in front of the first smokestack. The aliens rarely used ground transportation. They preferred traveling in self-powered fliers to avoid having to get their feet dirty.

"A bloke can dream, can't he?"

"We go in through one of the lower maintenance hatches or we leave."

"This thing will have chewed through Independence Hall by tomorrow!" He said with a shake of his head. Of all the structures in the city, the Hall had remained standing. It was a miracle which many of us took as a sign we were meant to overcome our adversaries. Maybe the Pyxis had found this out somehow, and decided to scrub it from the face of the Earth. One more monument of hope would be gone.

"Then I suggest we keep moving!" I rose and started across the hillock of waste material. For a machine designed to chew through so many yards of rock, the ruined buildings and streets of the dump we called home would prove to be no obstacle. The churning metal teeth would gobble up everything and everyone I'd ever known. Axle and I were the only hope to save our friends.

The thirty-foot mound of tailings provided little traction for my heavy boots. I was forced to scramble up the steep slope on all fours. Even then, my hands and feet sunk deeply into the dusty silt. Whether from the processing the pulverized rock had gone through, or some chemical reaction the waste had been subjected to, the loose material was uncomfortably warm. I reached the top of the hill and began the long slide down the far side. Choking dust filled my lungs. I tried breathing through my noise and cursed that I'd forgotten to pull up my face mask when I'd stopped to plug my ears. Axle landed by my side with his face fully covered in dark goggles and filter. I jerked the googles down from my forehead and slipped the filter into place over my mouth and nose. I hoped not too much of the junk I'd sucked in settled permanently in my lungs.

The noise of the vehicle was almost unbearably loud as we ran alongside the clanking treads. The sheer scale of the scratcher up close made me doubt our plans. I knew we could stop the machine, we'd done it before, but this time we needed to be sure it was damaged beyond repair. Hopefully Axle and I had learned enough from our previous attacks to place the explosives where they would do the most damage. We passed a gigantic drive wheel. I felt our time running short as each revolution of the rusted, steel gear moved the scratcher all the closer to the only home I'd ever known.

Not today. I felt a grin spread across my dirty face at the thought. This particular roving hunk of destruction was about to meet its match. I gritted my teeth and pushed forward. The heavy pack thumped against my back with each pounding step. My grin widened as I imagined the damage the explosives I was carrying were going to cause.

The ground was nearly as treacherous as the hill we'd scrambled over. It was like trying to dash across a freshly tilled field. With an effort, I remained upright and finally overtook the leading edge of the grinding tracks.

I spotted our goal. There was no time to think. The bottom rung of the ladder was suddenly right in front of me. I took one more running stride then launched myself sideways directly in the path of the clattering tread. I managed to grab the second rung from the bottom with both hands. The knowledge that any mistakes would cause me to fall onto the ground and be crushed by untold tons of steel keenly focused my attention. I reached for the next rung and hauled myself up, hand over hand, until I could get a foot on the ladder as well. I slipped once and experienced a second of pure terror before I got my footing back. I quickly scrambled higher to make room for my partner.

I looked down just in time to see Axle make the same crazy leap. He was taller than me, so his legs didn't have to move quite as fast as mine to keep up the machine. Axle made the sideways jump and grab look easy. He pulled himself up and slapped my boot. "Keep moving, Trip!"

The treads ground noisily beside me. No need to tell me twice. Thirty-three rungs latter, I was face to face with a rusted hatch. I was sure no self-respecting Pyxis would ever allow any surface in one of their glittering towers to get into such a condition. There probably hadn't been anyone on this ladder or even through this door since it was built and then unleashed upon the planet. I had to give it to the blood-suckers, they knew how to build things to last. There had probably been no need for a maintenance visit in all the years this beast had been churning through the dirt.

I reached up and grabbed the handle. It wouldn't budge. I didn't expect it would, but the attempt was worth a shot. Even the Pyxis understand the concept of a door lock. Fortunately, I was prepared for this. I reached into a vest pouch and pulled out a compact, brass object. I pressed the activator switch set into the smooth, upper surface and six, spindly legs sprang out of the bottom of the device. I opened the access panel protecting the door controls and attached the lock pick to the keypad. The device detected the keys and went to work punching codes with blinding speed. I'd used this clockwork device on similar doors before. The pick was smart, in its own way, and got quicker with each use. The Pyxis door was open in less than thirty seconds. I looked at the code and shook my head. These aliens may have been geniuses at building things, but that didn't mean they were all that smart; the code was the same as the last scratcher I'd snuck aboard.

The inside of the machine was even louder than the outside. The roar of the engine and the thunder of rocks being crushed together contributed to the insane racket.

"Where do we plant the charges?" Axle shouted. He had to lean close to be sure I heard him. I'd been inside more scratchers than him, which made me the expert on their layout.

"Up!" I jerked my thumb at the ceiling of the dimly lit corridor. The machine's ore processing was done in the lowest levels of the massive vehicle. Multiple engines drove the treads from the upper levels.

Without waiting for a response, I plunged into the heart of the beast. Luckily for both of us, I'd spent hours exploring another scratcher—memorizing the layout before deciding where to try my explosives. My attempts to detonate the power core had not been successful during that trip. I had another idea I wanted to try.

We made it to the portside engine compartment without much trouble. We kept our rifles out but we didn't need them. As far as I could tell, the entire machine was running itself. Someone had tried to tell me the aliens could control these things from far away using some form of wireless telephone, but I was still a little fuzzy on how that was possible. I shouldn't be surprised. The Pyxis came from another world, they were sure to have technology we hadn't even dreamed of yet.

I dropped my heavy pack on the metal floor with a thud. A series of thick gears and greased drive shafts spun at fantastic speeds right next to the walkway. There was a protective covering over the works made of a clear, smooth material—like glass. It was sturdy, but I was pretty sure it wouldn't be able to withstand the blast from the TNT Axle and I had planned to set off.

"This the place?" Axle yelled in my ear. He started to shrug off his pack.

I pointed at a narrow catwalk over which spanned the open interior of the machine. Below, rock crushers, smelters, and sorting machines churned. Foul-smelling fumes floated up from the factory levels, wreathing the walkway in noxious smoke.

Axle pulled his filter down and shouted, "Over there? Are you crazy?!" He was brave, but I could tell being inside the alien vehicle was getting to him. I slapped my friend on the shoulder and gave him a reassuring smile.

I removed my filter so Axle could understand me. "We'll stop them cold! Each side is driven by one of these engines," I explained loudly. "We need to take out both transmissions to stop this thing!" I wasn't sure how much of this Axle could hear over the racket. Enough must have made it through because he nodded and started off over the catwalk. I got busy setting my charge next to the gear box, as much of a soft spot as I could find in the bowels of the scratcher. I pulled out the timer and stared at it for a moment. I wondered briefly how many packs of TNT it would take to breach the main power plant. The scratcher didn't run on coal. In fact, no one could tell me what the Pyxis used for power. Whatever was behind that thick casing in the next room, it provided more heat than all the steam engines ever built before the aliens arrived. If only I could get to it…

The change in pitch for the engines was the first indication something was wrong. All around me the sounds of the machine changed. The grating of the drill grew louder as the engines went into overdrive. Thousands of moving parts screeched louder than ever before. The giant transmission next to me protested and grated against one another as the machine shifted into lower gear. The scratcher jerked and started moving slower. Whatever the drill face had come up against, I hoped it gave the machine indigestion.

I checked to be sure the timer on my bomb was still active and looked over to see how Axle was doing. He was nearly to the far side of the catwalk. I stood up and glanced around, wondering what else I could break while I waited.

The sound of steel grinding against hard rock as joined by a deep groan was building in intensity. Something under tremendous pressure exploded. I grabbed the nearest railing and held on tight as the scratcher lurched violently all around me. There was definitely something obstructing the machine's path. I shuffled away from the gear box, afraid I'd get pulled under the spinning shaft should I slip. Axle's shout of surprise was nearly drowned out by the tortured sounds the scratcher was making. I looked toward the catwalk but a fresh wave of smoke gushed upwards and blocked everything from view.

"Crap…" I staggered towards Axle. "Hang on!"

I reached the edge of the catwalk and the smoke cleared for just an instant. My heart froze when I saw Axle hanging onto a piece of broken railing. Below him, a molten river of metal was casting a red-orange glow over everything. Our eyes met for an instant.

The machine lurched again, throwing me from my feet. Axle lost his grip and fell into a fresh cloud of roiling cloud of smoke.

"Trip!" Axle's scream was swallowed by the screech of steel as it reached its breaking point. The dense smoke made my eyes water but I couldn't look away. Finally, I caught a glimpse of the empty catwalk.

Axle. Gone.

The dark realization I'd lost my friend was followed quickly by the thought he'd had a huge pack of explosives strapped to his back. Not good. I pushed myself up and staggered away from the damaged catwalk. I only made it as far as the spot where I'd left my pack before the charges Axle was carrying exploded. The shockwave tossed forward as if I was a tumbleweed out on the Wastes. I'm not sure what it was I slammed into. It didn't really matter. I blacked out.

My head was killing me when I woke up. I immediately tried to get up but stopped when the throbbing pain brought a cloud of darkness over my vision. The last thing I needed right now was to pass out again. I squeezed my eyes closed against the dizziness and swallowed down the bile rising in my throat. It was nearly a minute before I felt like I could look around without blacking out or throwing up. The sight of the mangled metal of the catwalk at the end of the corridor gave me a kick in the gut. I was nearly sick again as the memory of Axle's last moment played across my mind.

I was breathing hard by the time I got to my hands and knees. I was staring at my hands when I realized there was only the slightest vibration from nearby engines in standby mode and nothing from the drill to be felt through the floor plates. Whatever Axle's explosives had damaged, it was enough to bring the scratcher to a stop. My momentary elation at the thought was quickly replaced by fear. If the machine had stopped, there would soon be aliens swooping in from the sky to find out why.

Surging off the floor, I turned to check on the explosives I'd planted. I wasn't sure how long I'd been out. I could have minutes or seconds before the blast blew me to pieces along with everything else in the engine compartment. My head spun, forcing me to grab a hand rail for balance. My vision was blurry as I turned managed to squint at my pack. I took an unsteady step forward, intending to reset the timer. All I needed was a few minutes to get clear.

I took one more step before I realized I was not alone in the corridor. Someone was standing next to my pack of explosives.

Pyxis!

I fumbled for my rifle. All I managed to do was get tangled up in the strap as I struggled to bring the weapon to bear.

"Do not raise your weapon." The sound of the alien's voice startled me. I let go of my rifle, letting it dangle at my side, and raised my hands slowly.

My first impression of the Pyxis? He wasn't what I was expecting. The alien was no taller than me and possessed a nearly identical build. If it wasn't for the all black eyes and small, bony ridges instead of hair, I would have mistaken him for human.

"You can talk…" I knew I sounded like an idiot even as I spoke. I stopped myself, afraid I'd make an even bigger fool of myself if I kept babbling. I knew if I was going to survive, I needed to catalog the dangers I faced. First, the gun aimed at me was small but I had no doubts about the lethality of the compact, black device. You didn't take over an entire world without bringing along with you the most deadly toys. Second, the Pyxis could be trained in hand-to-hand combat. I couldn't remember any stories about humans fighting directly with the aliens, but that didn't mean much. There was a lot about these guys we simply did not know. My mind whirled as I judged the distance between the Pyxis and me. The equation didn't work out in my favor. The alien had the upper hand with a weapon pointing unerringly at my chest. Finally, there was my bomb. I glanced down at the satchel and my heart sank. The timer was missing. I saw it an instant later in the alien's grip, loose wires dangling.

The Pyxis caught my stare and held up the timer. His eyes flicked toward the device. "Primitive, but effective." He swung his disconcerting gaze back to me. "You wished to disable our machine?"

"Well, yeah." Yup. My wit was truly shining now.

"Why?"

The puzzled look on the alien's face gave me pause. Could an advanced race of beings truly be so thick? My anger built as I thought of Axle falling to his death. My mouth twisted into a snarl. "Because your *machine* is about to destroy my home!" I bit off the word 'machine'. "And I'm tired of watching your scratchers lay waste to my planet!"

"Scratchers?" The Pyxis tilted his head and considered me for a long moment. "Ah, yes. Your slang nomenclature for the autonomous mining systems."

"Do you even realize how many humans this thing is about to murder?!"

"It is as I suspected then."

When he didn't elaborate, I spat, "What did you suspect?"

"That the ruins we were heading for are inhabited."

"Of course they're inhabited! It's the only place we have left for miles in any direction!"

"You must understand, the resources harvested will provide—"

"Resources?!" I jabbed my finger in the direction of the city. "Those are people out there!"

"You misunderstand me. I am not advocating the destruction of your…homes."

This turn of the conversation surprised me. "Then why are you here?"

"To find you."

"Me?" I'd always thought humans were beneath notice of the invaders. Now one of them was telling me they were looking for me.

"Well, not you exactly. But someone like you. I have been seeking humans willing to take action against my kind."

My ego took a dive. The Pyxis was looking for any human. It could have been me who bit the dust and Axle having this conversation for all this alien cared.

"You wanted to find someone … to attack your own people?" I said slowly. I wondered if there might some misunderstanding due to some misinterpretation.

"Yes."

"Huh." This day was really not going how I'd imagined it would. Forgetting about the gun still aimed at me, I scratched the stubble on my chin. "Care to tell me why?"

"I have come to believe we have done wrong by your species."

"So, when you said you suspected the ruins were inhabited, you were…"

"I was concerned for your well-being, not annoyed by your presence. Most of my kind would simply have ordered the machine to continue its path with no thought to what might happen to the native inhabitants. I wish to … alter their thinking."

"What did you have in mind?" I asked carefully. I wondered what his angle might be.

"A partnership." He lowered his gun. Not a smart move for someone facing a feral human. But, the action did back up what he was saying.

"To do what?" He had my attention now. As far as I knew, the only thing the Pyxis wanted were Earth's resources. They'd never shown the least bit of interest in humanity, even when they first arrived.

"I cannot stand by any longer while my people destroy this world and all of its inhabitants."

"You're a little late," I said and laughed bitterly. "There's not a whole lot left."

"Perhaps not. I've conducted a survey and discovered multiple pockets of your kind." He gave me a shrewd look. "It seems humans are extremely hard to wipe out. I've even found humans living in areas believed to have been … cleared."

"Sorry if we're giving you guys a hard time." I smiled at the thought of the Pyxis leaders throwing up their hands in frustration thanks to us humans.

"On the contrary. You have proven to me you deserve the chance to take back your world."

"You want to partner up with me? With a human?

"Yes."

"How are we supposed to fight back? We can barely make a dent in your machines!" I gestured at the timer still in the Pyxis hand.

The alien looked at the timer then tossed it carelessly on top of the pack of explosives. "That can be changed."

"I like where this is going!" I rubbed by hands together then offered one to the Pyxis. "I'm Trip. Do you have a name?"

The Pyxis stared at my hand for a few seconds before he reached out and shook it. He tilted his head fractionally forward. "I am Lev."

"Where do you want to start, Lev?"

"Here," the Pyxis gestured around the engine compartment. "Do you know why we mine your planet? Many of the same resources can be found on the asteroids or moons found throughout your star system."

"Because you like the scenery?"

Lev's mouth twitched up in a ghost of a smile. "Something like that. My people would be forced to live in spacecraft if we spent our days tracking down comets and such."

"But here, you can live in your towers with real air." I finished the alien's thought.

"At the expense of the planetary ecology, unfortunately."

"I've noticed." I said, my tone as dry as the deserts the Pyxis had created across the globe.

"You can change that!" The alien insisted and stepped close. In his growing excitement, he'd forgotten we were enemies.

I resisted the urge to lash out and break the alien's neck. If what he was saying was true, I figured it probably wasn't the best idea to kill humanity's last hope to break free from the alien overlords stripping our planet to the bone. Something changed in me as I stared into his face. Before today, I'd faced a future filled with nothing but a struggle for survival. All I could hope for was to stay alive long enough to see the next generation enter the world. Thanks to this Pyxis, I was catching my first glimpse of a new future. Something … better.

I slammed the door closed on this glimmer of sunshine. Hope was something you learned to not rely on out here. Still, I couldn't shake the question. What if?

"What exactly did you have in mind?" I asked

"Humanity reclaiming its place in the world … and maybe the stars," the alien replied. "I think we can convince my leaders to give humans their planet back. If we can show them humans are an equal species worthy of consideration." He looked around at the machinery crowding the walkway then back at me. "But first, we need to be sure your home is safe."

After a quick trip to the mysterious power generator, we took Lev's flier and flew to a nearby hill to take in the results of our handiwork.

The sight of the scratcher blowing to bits brought a grim smile to my face. I watched as smoking chunks of steel flew into the sky and patter down on the barren ground in every direction.

"Beautiful," I said as the smoke continued to pour from the ruined husk. I turned to my new conspirator. "That's more than I could have hoped for. Two questions though: what kind of explosive was that and where can I get my hands on some more?" The device Lev had slapped against the shielding of the core was laughably small. If I hadn't seen the results of setting it off on my own, I'm not sure I would have believed it was bomb at all.

"I can get you more of these devices," Lev said. As usual, the Pyxis' face was inscrutable. He locked his alien eyes with mine. "This is just the beginning."

I wondered again what was going on in his mind. His offer of help against his own kind was nearly too good to be true. In my experience, that usually meant I was being played. Still, I couldn't help but go along. If the offer of help was genuine, I couldn't afford to walk away. I wouldn't be able to live with myself and I wasn't sure how long anyone else would last if humanity didn't do something drastic. I looked from the alien to the scratcher wreckage and considered his words. I vowed to take action then, no matter who I had to tag up with. I was going to do something drastic.

"We must go. The controllers will send out drones to ascertain the cause of their interrupted signal. They will most likely assume this," he made a sweeping gesture over the smoking remains, "was an accident, not an attack."

"Should buy us some time," I agreed. If Axle and I had managed to complete our mission, the aliens would have been able to detect our handiwork. With the device the alien had brought along, all evidence Axle and I had been here had been obliterated. To the controllers, it would look like the main power supply had malfunctioned. Although we've tried, no one had been able to breach a core until now. Of all the technology brought from the stars, the cores were the most powerful and mysterious. They were heavily shielded, not to mention huge. Even if we captured one, there'd be no way to move and hide a core until we could figure out how it worked. I hadn't managed to capture a trophy for humanity, but I was feeling pretty good about blowing one of them to heaven.

I followed Lev back to his flyer. It was a sleek affair with room for two up front and cargo behind our seats. I figured I could cram six fighters in the hold. With our new friend, his flier, and powerful explosives, I figured we could cause a lot of damage.

We took off and flew off in the direction the scratcher had been following. Independence Hall jutted up into the sky, defiant of the wasteland crouching upon the battered outskirts of the old city. I had Lev put down just outside of the ruins. I figured landing on the square next to Chestnut Street would not be good for the health of the alien. Or me, come to think about it. More than likely we would both have been killed on sight before I had a chance to explain.

"I can only wait here a short while." Lev eyed the crumbling brick walls. "I must return to the tower soon." An attacker could easily open fire before he could take off again. I wasn't sure if the flier was bullet proof. Maybe Lev was wondering the same thing.

"Understood." I jumped down the leaned back into the cab. "I'll fire two shots in the air when I've convinced the others."

He nodded and hit a button to close the door. I turned and jogged between the broken walls. I found Madam Currie along with a crowd of townsfolk and other fighters waiting for me when I reached the steps of the Hall. Looking over my shoulder, I could see they'd come out to look at the column of smoke rising from the scratcher we'd destroyed.

One of the fighters, a big man named Slate, leveled his rifle in my direction when I stepped around a corner. I knew he would be able to identify me, even from a distance, as he was wearing his amplification goggles. Slate lowered his rifle and strode in my direction. I walked forward to meet him.

"Was that you and Axle's doing?" Slate gestured at the smoke drifting along with the wind. He flicked a glance behind me then narrowed his eyes. "And where is Axle? How'd you manage to get back here so fast, Trip?"

I could see his hands tighten around his rifle. I raised my hands in a peaceful gesture. "Axle didn't make it, Slate. I'm sorry." Axle and Slate were tight. I knew he would take the loss badly. Still, we didn't have time to mourn right now. "There's something I need to tell Currie. You'll want to hear it as well."

Slate forced down the anger. Hopefully, he would be able to make good use of that soon. We walked back to the crowd gathered by the Hall. I nodded respectfully at our town's leader. Madam Currie nodded back.

"Trip. What have you to report?"

"Ma'am. I think we have a chance to take the fight to the Pyxis." I provided a quick summary of the raid, including Axle's valiant sacrifice to bring the scratcher to a halt. I left out the part about getting knocked unconscious and skipped ahead to meeting Lev. There were gasps when I revealed it was the Pyxis who had ultimately destroyed the scratcher.

"He wants to help humans fight so we can negotiate a truce from a position of strength," I finished.

A young fighter named Clutch exploded, "Why should we trust him?! The Pyxis destroyed our world! Killed millions!"

I shrugged. The reaction was to be expected. In fact, I was wondering the same thing. "Maybe because he's tired of watching them destroy our world and kill millions of people."

"Why does he need us?" Slate asked, his tone deadly calm.

"He can't carry out the plan without help."

"So, he's got no friends," Slate snorted.

"I get the feeling he can't really trust any of the other Pyxis," I replied. "He's been looking for human help for some time."

"So, he came to us to bring down a tower, commit mass murder," Slate surmised. He shook his head. "Can't do it."

The crowd fell silent and I felt my chance to recruit help slipping away. Slate was right. I knew as much. If we went and killed a million aliens, were we really any different than them? Then again, we weren't the ones trashing their home planet.

"You're right," I admitted slowly. "You're absolutely right." I took in the surprised looks from those gathered around me. "But you're also very wrong." I pointed past the ruined buildings to the smoke rising from the burning scratcher. "We'll lose our homes. Yes, we stopped them for today. But, if we know anything about these beings, they are thorough. They'll be back. And we'll be killed or forced to move. I can't say when this will happen. But I am positive it will."

"We'll fight!" Clutch shouted.

"I know, you will. But I'm not going to wait around for another scratcher to come this way. Or worse, an attack if they figure out where Axle and I came from." I locked eyes with Slate. "What Axle died for."

"They'll never stop hunting for us if you manage to do this." Madam Currie noted solemnly. "The result of your action may simply be to bring about an earlier death."

"Then we keep hitting them," I urged. "Until they leave us alone! The only thing we can do to save ourselves is to show we can lay waste to their cities as they have done to ours. They won't have a choice. They'll be forced to negotiate and stop destroying our planet."

"What you're asking is very dangerous," Madam Currie said slowly. "I cannot condone this course of action."

"I'm going," Slate announced. He strode forward and stood beside me and glared at the others, daring them to argue with him. And just like that, the momentum had shifted back to my argument. I pressed forward.

"There will be a minimum of casualties," I explained. "They use fliers to move around the tower. Once we hit the base, there should be time for most of the population to get airborne." I grinned savagely. "Let's see how they like being relocated."

"If you do this," Madam Currie asked, "what next?"

"We offer to negotiate. We'll stop our attacks if they leave the planet surface."

"And if they won't negotiate?"

"We strike more of their machines," I said, deadly serious now. "And there are plenty of other towers for us to choose from."

"Let's do this," Slate said. "What choice have they left us?"

Madam Currie sighed. "This will the death of many."

"Better to die a man than a rat," Slate said, repeating a common fighter refrain.

I raised my rifle and fired two rounds into the air. The flyer was over our heads a moment later. The sight incited panic. People hustled for cover. Some things are too well ingrained to be overcome after the short speech I'd given. I covered my eyes against the grit thrown up by the landing vanes.

The engines shut down and Lev emerged. He didn't raise his hand in greeting or offer any words of encouragement. Instead, he gave me a hard look and asked, "You were successful?"

I looked at Slate then behind me where five other fighters had assembled. Everyone else except Madam Currie had vanished into the ruins. Slate and the three men and two women all wore grim expressions. Of everyone I knew, they'd been furthest out into the Wastes than the other townspeople. I think they wanted to fight partly because they knew there was nowhere else to go and partly because we'd been watching the aliens take our world from us a piece at a time for our entire lives. I turned back to Lev.

"We want to punch those tower-dwelling punks in the nose." I smiled then added, "No offense."

"I understand the sentiment fully."

I motioned toward the flier and the others approached warily. They stood well back as the alien tapped on a glowing device strapped to his forearm. The cargo door opened for them as if by magic. When they saw there were no enemy soldiers waiting for them, they piled inside.

When I started to follow, Madam Currie laid her frail hand on my arm. "Come back to us."

I looked into her aged face and forced a grin onto my face. "I mean to, ma'am."

Madam Currie returned the smile and backed away from the flier. When I dropped into the second front seat, I found her staring at me through the cab windows. She raised her hand. I wondered if I'd ever see her others again.

"The matriarch will be fine," Lev said as he powered up the engines.

"Can you know that for sure?" He lifted off and I lost sight of Madam Currie in the swirl of dust we kicked up.

"Because my people will soon have too much to worry about to think about reprisals."

We flew in silence. If Lev was having any second thoughts about the betrayal he was about to engage in, he showed no outward signs. If it been me, I'd have been a mess. I leaned forward as the spire of the Pyxis tower came into view. From this distance, it was a hazy outline dividing the sky. I had to strain against my harness and crane my neck to catch a glimpse of the top. The tower was huge.

"What exactly did you have in mind?" I asked. I glanced at the fighters I'd talked into coming with me. They were checking weapons and looking out the small windows trying to catch a glimpse of our target.

"We will land in the lower levels and destroy the power plant."

"Simple and direct. Won't there be guards?"

"A few," Lev admitted. "I trust your colleagues will be able to handle them. There have been no attacks on any of our cities in more than twenty cycles. The guards will not be on high alert."

"If you say so." Despite the reassurance, my heart was racing. What made me think I would succeed where other attackers had failed? I considered what Lev had been able to do to the scratcher and smiled grimly. If nothing else, we were going to give the Pyxis tower-dwellers quite a show.

The tower just kept getting bigger. I'd seen it once before from afar during a long-range patrol. There were dozens of these structures scattered over the planet but his was the closest one to Philadelphia. It was impressive. Nearly a half-mile across at the base and stretching up into the clouds, more than a mile high, the tower terminated in a series of launch platforms where the Pyxis would take off for space. During my earlier visit, I'd watched through binoculars as a stream of transports carried the spoils of our planet upward. What the Pyxis were building above the sky, I couldn't guess. If this attack went as planned, perhaps there would be a chance to take the fight to the ships above.

For now though, the tower had to be my focus. The opening bolstered my renewed fight against the invaders.

Getting into the tower with the flyer was unbelievably easy. The ground access was heavily guarded and protected by thick, steel doors. The upper levels were wide open. The Pyxis had no fear of an air attack because we humans did not possess the technology to build fliers.

We entered a hanger. There were a few other fliers parked around the landing pad but no other Pyxis were in sight.

Lev quickly led the way out of the hanger and through a maze of corridors and ramps until we found ourselves outside what he called the Power Center. He opened a satchel he'd brought from the flier and handed out more of the explosive devices I'd seen him use in the scratcher.

"What exactly are these?" I asked as I turned one over in my hand.

"Explosives specially designed to cut through heavy shielding using a directed charge. They need to be place around the perimeter of the power generator." Lev held up his arm. The device strapped to his wrist glowed with its own light. "I can detonate the charges with this."

"Let's get moving then," Clutch urged. His eyes were wide as he looked one way and then the other. "The sooner we're away from here the better!"

"I'll take a team and head counter-clockwise along the south wall," Slate said. He looked at me. "Go with your friend there and take care of the north side." Slate got the others moving and headed off. Lev placed the first charge then headed down the curving passageway.

We placed all but one charge before we were spotted.

The guards called out something in their own language. Clutch shot down the Pyxis before I could turn around. The other guard opened fire. I dove for cover and aimed my rifle around the corner. The Pyxis guard was swinging his blaster my way. He didn't make it. I fired and he went down.

Clutch was dead and Lev had been hit. I hurried over to Lev and knelt by his side. The alien was looking at me with his unreadable black eyes. He said something I didn't catch.

"What is it, Lev?" I leaned close, hoping no other armed Pyxis would chose this moment to make an appearance.

Lev swallowed. "It's up to you now." He peeled the control device from his wrist and pressed it into my hand. He stopped breathing.

I looked at the display unit. Knowing there was no time, I slapped it against my wrist, picked up Lev's pack and headed back to meet up with Slate and the others.

Slate nearly shot me when I rounded the last corner.

"It's me!"

Slate lowered his rifle. "God, Trip! You almost found a new permanent home in this tower." His eyes narrowed. "Where's Clutch?"

I shook my head. "Gone. So's Lev."

"How are we going to blow this thing?" Slate hissed.

I held up my arm. "I think I can figure this out." I started running back toward the flier. Slate caught up with me.

"I sure hope so."

Slate and Blade shot the next pair of surprised guards we met. We made it to the hanger before a weird-sounding alarm activated. Pyxis dashed into the hanger as we scrambled into Lev's flier.

"Fire over their heads!" I ordered over the wailing alarm. I put my hands on the controls and, to my surprise, the engines started up. I imitated the motions I'd seen Lev make earlier and pulled back on the control stick.

The flier leapt into the air accompanied by a chorus of complaints from the fighters in the back.

"Sorry!" I slewed sideways, anxious to get out into open air before I slammed into a wall. I overcompensated and scraped along the floor before we shot out into open space in an experience which was both exhilarating and terrifying. I shouted to Slate, "Take the controls!"

"What!?" Slate yelled but grabbed at the second stick in front of him. I held up the control device and studied the glowing pictures on the display. I could read a little Pyxis thanks to my grandmother. Lord knows where she learned to read the alien script. I found what I was looking for and did not hesitate.

"Here goes nothing!" I jabbed my finger against the device. I wasn't sure how much pressure these things needed to activate. Now was not the time to be gentle. The picture flashed the alien word for 'received'.

"You done over there?!" Slate shouted.

"I hope—" The explosion blossomed all around the base of the tower. I grabbed the controls and pulled back. We shot higher into the sky. Outside, flame and smoke was pouring from the structure.

"It's not falling!" Slate growled. "Fall!"

As if the Pyxis tower could hear Slate, it began to settle lower while tilting to one side. All up and down the city spire, fliers were taking to the air.

Slate pounded me on the shoulder and whooped, "She's going down!" Similar cheers went up from the others.

We were miles away by the time the tower finally hit the ground. It crumpled and sent up a choking cloud of dust. More explosions erupted, adding to the chaos.

Slate sat back in his seat, a huge grin plastered across his face. "That…was a good start."

"When to do we go again?" I turned to find Blade holding up two more packs identical to the one Lev had carried.

"Are those…" I began.

Blade pulled out an explosive device. "They sure are."

I turned back to my flying, my mind already picking out the next Pyxis target. Time to take back our planet. Time to take back our home.

"Gag Order" by Heather Crowley
Clown in an Alternate Future

The alarm always sounds at 6 a.m., regardless of whether or not we are ready for it. Some have latched onto the lifestyle and jump out of bed the second that racket comes out of the overhead speakers.

Others, like me, lay in bed for a moment wondering how our lives could have possibly gone to shit so quickly.

Then, like the lifeless robots we've become, we each get out of bed, dress, and pull our sheets straight.

I sneeze, then so does the girl who sleeps one bed over. Our glance at each other is brief and grim as we stand at attention near the foot of our beds.

The sergeant walks slowly up and down the center aisle. He stops every so often to inspect the quality of bed-making or the shine on someone's shoes.

Terrence, the boy who sleeps directly across the aisle from me, has broken out in a visible sweat. It drips down his baby-soft face, and he blinks furiously to keep the salt from getting into his eyes.

I groan inwardly, and the girl next to me fidgets with her fingernails.

What have you done, Terrence? We both think it. We all know that we can commit only so many offenses before being thrown into solitary. The boy is hanging by a thread here.

"I smell fear," the gruff sergeant growls as he approaches Terrence.

The man stares the boy down for only a moment, enough to cause him panic, before he begins to rip the blankets and sheets from the bed.

Sarge flips the mattress from the bedframe, and there lies the incriminating evidence. Sergeant stands to his full height, proud of himself for knowing the boy would be caught. "What do we have here? Just couldn't part with your wig, I see." He holds up a royal blue wig with wild curls.

Terrence sputters and whimpers. He knows this is the end for him. He tries to hold it together as he is escorted from the barracks by two, armed guards.

Sergeant stays behind and looks over this part of his domain, enjoying the fresh wave of fear he's pushed on all of us.

"Anyone else want to show me their paraphernalia before I find it myself? Might go easy on you…" He turns on his heels, lips still puckered in the silent word, and waits for someone to come forward.

No one does. No one ever does, because everyone knows that he will not go easier; the result is the same whether we admit to it or not.

"Alright, you're all dismissed for breakfast."

We know he will go through our things while we're eating and out jogging laps.

We stand in line silently. The group around me is always silent, but there are more boisterous prisoners ahead that seem to be happy with their current situation.

The girl who sleeps in the bed beside mine also sits beside me during meals and runs beside me during physical training. We've barely said a word to each other, but she's always there, and I'm not sure why. I've never been curious enough to ask.

"Where's Terrence?" grunts the man across from me. Phillips has been here longer than any of us, and his bitter attitude outshines the rest of ours. Surviving thirty years in a camp like this will do that to a person.

No one speaks, and everyone else stares down at their food, so Phillips repeats himself more aggressively.

"Sent to the pit," I finally answer him after I shove a forkful of tasteless biscuits and gravy into my mouth. It amazes me that something so simple can be so bland.

Phillips doesn't seem phased as he scrapes his food around his tray. "Knew that kid was gonna get solitary." He glances up at me with his loaded fork suspended between the tray and his mouth. "Think he'll survive?" he asks, then empties his fork.

I shrug, but I don't think so. None of us do. Hardly anyone survives.

"I know he won't," Phillips continues before he swallows. He eats loud, his lips smacking like a bovine's. I watch the half-chewed food roll around in his mouth as he talks, and some of it oozes into the corners of his lips. He doesn't wipe it away. "The kid's been doomed from the start, thinkin' he could keep that photograph. *Then* they find his juggling gear in his suitcase the first day he's here. He had it comin'. What'd they find this time?"

"A blue wig," says the girl beside me.

Phillips snorts and leers at her. I think he meant to smile, but it doesn't come across that way. "A blue wig, huh? Nice and curly? Ain't that a bummer? Are *you* packin' anything illegal, cutie pie?" he asks her.

I suddenly don't like his tone, and the girl is back to silently shaking her head and staring at her food.

Phillips looks up at me. "Quiet lil' thing."

"She's been that way since she came in." It's not much of a defense, but I feel the urge to say something for her.

Five minutes until the hour's up, so we wolf down the rest of our food, drop the trays off where the inmates on "good behavior" are allowed to wash and handle the dishes for a very small pay, and head out to the yard.

"I don't want to see any stragglers today!" shouts the instructor. He used to be an inmate here, too, and apparently did so well and liked it so much that they gave him a full-time position.

He blows his whistle, and we're off down the red, infield gravel mix that lines the yard just inside of the electric, barb-wired fence.

The girl jogs beside me and pulls ahead a few times. I like that she runs with me because she's in much better shape and I find myself trying to keep up with her. I run a little faster, and I think I see a hint of a grin on her lips as she pulls even farther ahead. She wants to make this a game.

I fall behind, not just to catch my breath, but to get her to fall back as well. She won't go too far ahead without me; that much I know. Soon enough, she glances over her shoulder, and the people around her speed by as she slows down until I can catch up.

"Come on, Winthrop!" the instructor yells at her. "I know you can do better!"

I stop playing and run to my full potential, which pulls a giggle from her when I pass her by.

Next, panting and wary, we make our way to the showers. They don't segregate here, so armed guards stand at both main entrances and at the entrances of the showers, as well.

Most of us keep our eyes to ourselves and, once we're finished, we split into groups. Some get rec time while the rest of us go to group therapy. The girl comes with me.

"So glad you could all make it!" the therapist exclaims with excitement. She is a little over the top, but she means well so I continue attending.

"How are we all doing today?"

No one answers her; it always takes a great deal of coaxing to get the first person to speak up.

She sits in her metal folding chair, and her smile becomes painted as she glances around the circle to realize that no one is going to answer her. I have a great amount of respect and sympathy for the woman; she never loses her motivation.

She clears her throat and flips through her pad of paper. "Well, I did hear that Terrence was sent to solitary. Does anyway want to talk about that? I know a few of you were in his barracks." She looks directly at me, because I'm usually the first one to speak up anyway.

I sigh as if I'm weighed down by what had happened. The truth is that I'm saddened, I really liked Terrence and all of his innocence, but I'm not burdened by his demise. He wasn't my responsibility. No one here is.

"I was there," I tell her. "He slept across from me."

"I'm so sorry to hear it," she says sincerely.

I shrug. "He knew the rules, but he broke them anyway. No clown paraphernalia, not even a red ball or a bowling pin, and he had several things in his possession that he knew he couldn't have."

She hesitates when I pause. "And how do you feel about that, Josh?" she asks me.

"I feel sad that it happened, because I liked him, but fair's fair. He chose to become a clown, knowing the stigma that went along with it and knowing the risks. He knew he might end up here. Then he kept his wig and his props knowing that he might get thrown into solitary. He's a risk taker, and those kinds of people don't survive here. It's a fact of life."

She nods slowly in agreement. "Does anyone else have a thought?"

A girl with dark hair and thick eyeliner speaks up from across the circle. "I think it's bullshit." She's slouched in her chair and looks as though she were dragged to this optional gathering.

"What part of it is bullshit, Cassandra?"

"I think it's bullshit that our society has become so consumed by their fear of us that they have to herd us all together and imprison us in these…these work camps. I think it's bullshit that we aren't allowed to have any sign of our past lives here. I mean…Terrence got in trouble for a photo. *A photo*. The rest of us are allowed to have pictures of our families, why can't he have a photo that reminds him of his happiest moments?"

The therapist tilts her head in thought. "Well, I would assume it is because the photograph was of himself dressed a clown, and things like that are forbidden here."

Cassandra scoffs and waves off the logic as if it doesn't, or shouldn't, apply.

Secretly, I agree with her. Terrence should not have received a citation for that photograph. It wasn't even in color.

"Anyone else?" she asks. No one speaks up, so she moves on. "Great. Other than that, how is everyone doing? Are we all fitting in okay?"

We nod mechanically.

"How about you?" she turns her attention to the silent girl beside me. "How are you holding up here, Jada?"

She curls into herself and looks around the room, alarmed that she is now in the middle ring. If she could pull her head into her chest cavity like a turtle, she would have.

"'M fine," she squeaks.

"Tell me about your time here so far," the therapist prods. "Are you dealing with the day-to-day routine okay?"

Jada nods.

"How do you feel about being here, Jada?"

She looks at me to help her, and I don't know why because I can't. I only give her a small, encouraging smile.

Then, she glances over at Cassandra who is watching, amused by the exchange. "I...I think I agree with her. I don't think we all belong here. Or any of us. I don't think it's fair to punish all of us for the act of the few."

I stare at her, stunned. I've never heard so many words come out of her mouth at once.

Cassandra smirks. "I knew I couldn't be the only one. I wasn't even a real clown, you know? I just painted my face and went to ICP cover band concerts. None of the original members are even alive anymore! Good thing they didn't have to see what our world has come to."

A dark boy across the room perks up. He has always been soft spoken, sweet, and often hung around Terrence. "You are into ICP, too?" he asks her.

"Hell yeah, bro. They raided one of the concerts and got most of us, but we aren't even real clowns! We weren't entertaining anybody; it was just face paint."

"The name has 'clown' in it..." pipes up another man to my left.

Cassandra goes red in the face, and the therapist interjects before she can cut him down. "Alright! I think that's plenty for today. We can further discuss the ethics and treatment during tomorrow's session."

We stand, fold our chairs, and stack them neatly in the corner of the room.

When we head out for rec time Jada is by my side, but then Cassandra is by hers.

"So, you don't think we all deserve to be here either," she says. A smile is stuck to her face and she hops around to face Jada and me.

Jada glances up at me sheepishly. I don't know what to tell her. I don't know why she's so attached to me.

"No, I don't," is all she says.

For some reason that pleases Cassandra and she bounces back around to walk forward by her side. "I think I have some people you should meet. Come by barrack twelve before curfew." She gives me a hardened glance before saying, "And don't bring your friend along."

Jada stops in the middle of the courtyard to watch Cassandra run off to a group who welcomes her with fist-bumps and pats on the back.

"I don't want to go to barrack twelve," she tells me. She looks up at me, "Not without you."

I scoff and ask a little too harshly, "Why not?"

She's taken aback, realizing that I don't feel the same connection to her as she does to me.

Guilt tears at my gut when I see the hurt written on her face. I don't know why she's attached to me, but I realize I don't want her attached to anyone else.

Before I can apologize, she runs back into the building.

I don't see Jada for the rest of the day. Usually she's back sitting in her bed as dusk falls, writing in her journal, but she's not there. I feel a void without her. Her steady presence beside me for two months has apparently made me dependent on her as well.

I lay on my pillow with an arm behind my head and glance over at her empty bed, then at the empty one across the aisle. What a day.

I slip into sleep without realizing, and I hear Jada come quietly to bed just before the lights are turned out for curfew, but I'm too far under to react and ask where she's been.

The next morning, Jada and I stand at attention during inspections. She doesn't look at me, doesn't fidget, doesn't do anything except run ahead and disappear into the crowd once we are dismissed for breakfast.

I sit with Phillips, and he immediately notices her absence.

"What, she get sent to solitary, too?" he asks, incredulous.

I shake my head and spy her at another table, silent like always, but this time with Cassandra and her loud group. They aren't like the others who are happy to be here, but they are loud and obnoxious like rebels who want to bring down The Ringmaster. Revolutionists. It's unnerving to see quiet, little innocent Jada sitting among them.

"Where is she?"

"She got tired of you scoping her out every morning. Decided to hang with another group."

She doesn't run with me during training; in fact, she laps me several times. She doesn't sit with me at therapy either. I don't see her *or* Cassandra in therapy.

"Where's your friend?" the therapist asks sweetly as we set up.

I shrug. "We aren't really friends."

She smiles warmly. "She's been glued to your side for months. I find it hard to believe that you aren't friends."

I want to snap at her, but she's too cheerful. It's almost be like kicking a well-behaved dog who wants nothing but to be a good boy.

Once we are settled and the new people have introduced themselves, she refreshes everyone on what happened to Terrence.

"We had some that thought he may have deserved what he got, and others felt it was unfair." She turns to me. Of course, she turns to me. "Josh, can you expand on what you said yesterday?"

I lean forward and take a large breath. I didn't want to have to talk today, but it will earn me points toward good behavior, so I suck it up.

"I actually agree with Cassandra on the photograph issue. I don't think he should have been reprimanded for that."

"But the wig?"

I contemplate it for a moment. "If he hadn't gotten a citation for the photograph, then the wig wouldn't have condemned him to solitary, and he might have nothing else to incriminate himself with. Or he would have been smart enough to dispose of it. So…maybe he didn't deserve solitary. But he did mess around with fate."

"Can I ask you something, Josh?" she says delicately.

I raise my eyebrow. It's not like I have any place to be.

"What are your thoughts on these work camps? Do you believe that every clown deserves to be here? Or do you lean more toward Jada's philosophy yesterday when she said that the actions of a few should not condemn everyone?"

I scratch at my chin. I haven't shaven in several days and stubble pokes at my fingertips. "I think that America is a great country, and we need to do what we can to make our citizens feel safe…"

"You make us sound like the damned army," Phillips coughs from the right side of the room.

I'd been so distracted by Jada and Cassandra's absence that I hadn't noticed Phillips sitting there. He never comes to therapy.

"That's not exactly what I mean," I continue. "America has always been terrified by clowns. Portrayed as evil cultists and serial killers on television and in movies…not only portrayed, but there have been *actual* serial killers that were employed as clowns."

"One. There was one," someone interjects.

"There was Gacy in the old days, and then just a few years ago there was Ingrid Jaime. A decade before that, Shawn Nielsen was caught with several, live children in his basement and a truck-full of dead ones buried on his hundred-acre tree farm. All three were employed as child entertainers and dressed as clowns." My argument is valid, and they all know it. They stare at me as if they're seeing me for the first time. "Not to mention the cult started by Joel Smith that went around killing any political extremist, conservative *or* liberal. They had followers from all over and terrorized the entire country…"

"They weren't actually clowns," someone interrupts.

"They dressed like us," I snap. "Look," I turn my attention back to the therapist who is enthralled with my speech. "I did the research before I became one, to know what I was getting myself into. I did the research so I wouldn't repeat their mistakes. If any of you have watched the news during rec time, they now theorize that choosing to be a clown unhinges people; that dressing so ridiculously and putting so much paint on the face somehow alters the human chemistry to this horrible…" I struggle to come up with the correct terminology, "…rapey, killer mind-set."

"And how do you feel about the public's opinion on that?"

"I dressed as a clown and put on face paint every day for five years before they brought me in. I was an entertainer on the underground. I'd go into a party, usually for the wealthy, dressed like a regular man, change in one of their many bedrooms, entertain, then change back into my street clothes and leave with my brief case. Not once in those five years did I feel the urge to kill anyone or take anyone's child."

"Maybe it takes more than five years…" someone commented.

"Ingrid was only employed for three. She killed twenty children in that time," I inform the smart-ass.

"So let me ask you again, Josh. Do you believe that we all deserve to be here because of what those people have done?" the therapist re-calibrates the conversation.

I chew on that for a moment. "I think so, yes. Even though I've never done anything wrong, our world is changing. Our society as a whole is terrified of clowns, of what others like us have done in the past. It creates a black market for children's entertainment, and we get paid a hell of a lot more. I was a millionaire before I got caught. So…yeah. I feel like if you get caught doing something illegal, whether you feel like it should even *be* illegal in the first place or not, you should be thrown into a camp."

Some glare at me. Others avoid looking at me. Now I've done it.

I go out to the yard and Jada is sitting on the bleachers with Cassandra and her gang of rebels. She is silent as usual, staring down at her own feet. She looks up at me briefly and either squints or glares, I can't really tell from here, and looks back down.

I want to go and tell her that I'm sorry, but her new friends surround her and look overly protective, so I walk the other way toward the weight benches.

That night I toss and turn, restless in my bed while the lights are on. I've never been so open in therapy before, and I hate that I went all day without quiet Jada by my side.

I'm relieved when it's curfew, because she has no choice but to sleep in the bed next to mine, and her presence calms me. More than anything, I actually miss the smell of her. They don't allow perfumes here, but the scent of her sweat mixed with her cucumber deodorant is unique to her.

I'm not sure what time it is when someone shakes me awake. It's dark, I can't see details of who stands above me, but her gentle touch and the outline of her hair up in a messy bun tells me, undoubtedly, that it's Jada trying to wake me.

She crouches to my level beside my bed. "We don't have much time," she whispers into my ear. "Come with me."

Slipping on my shoes as quietly as I can, I follow her to the barrack door.

"We can't leave," I hiss at her.

She pushes the door open defiantly, grabs my arm, and pulls me out into the night.

We traipse across the lawn, over the winding sidewalks, and to barrack twelve.

"No way," I tell her immediately.

She looks at me wide-eyed, and I almost crumble. "Trust me. Please?"

My eyes lock with hers, and then I do crumble. She sees it and pulls me into the barrack.

A candle is lit in the middle of the room, low and out of sight of the windows. A group huddles around it, whispering as we approach.

Cassandra notices us first, and her face contorts to anger. "I thought I told you 'no!'"

"We can trust him!" Jada tells her. Her hand is still wrapped around my arm. The way she tugs me against her side tells me that she missed me today, too.

Cassandra gives her a disapproving glance and lowers herself back into the circle. "Well, I guess we have no choice now. Either you're in, or you're dead," she tells me. "Got it?"

I don't agree or disagree. "What exactly are we 'in' to?" I ask.

Jada's hand slides into my own, and she laces our fingers together. I give her a gentle squeeze, and she squeezes back.

Cassandra sees our exchange and looks sick, but she continues as if she hasn't just witnessed something disgusting. "We're staging a revolt."

I look around the circle and raise my eyebrow.

She sees my doubt and expounds. "Not just us, jerk wad. We have support from the do-gooders like yourself, and the reformed clowns who got out by denouncing everything they are."

"They didn't get out just by…" I begin.

She stands suddenly, blistering angry and red-faced. "THE POINT is that they can't do this to us!"

Several in the circle shush her. We don't want to get the attention of the guards, or, god forbid, the Sergeant.

"And how do you plan to revolt? What are you going to do once you get out?"

She smiles slyly. "All of us in this room have enough good-behavior points to get out, if only we renounce everything we are and wear a tracking chip. When we get out, we have the support of the clowns on the outside, and we are going to try to convince the world that we're not all bad."

"How?"

"I don't know yet!" she hisses. "All I know is that it is totally inhumane to lock us up for something so stupid. I've never even heard of anyone being treated like this before! Have you?" She looks around the circle as if daring someone to challenge her intelligence.

I struggle to keep in a laugh. How young and naïve she is; all of them are really.

"Actually, it has happened before, in the old days. When Japan bombed our naval base, we put our own citizens of Japanese descent into work camps."

"*Again*, unfair because our supposed 'great' country was afraid that *all* Japanese people were going to do something rash. Just because a few took out our base."

I ignore her, only because it was a fair point. "In that same war, a man named Adolph Hitler gathered people of descent that he didn't like and shipped them off to death camps. *Death* camps," I reiterate. "He and his blind followers killed *millions* of people for being born the way they were, for things completely out of their control. Hair, eye, and skin color, mental retardation…"

Cassandra's skin had faded to a pale green.

"It's in the history books. Didn't any of you go to school?" I ask.

They all look shocked. Even Jada's hand had stiffened in mine.

"Point is…" Cassandra begins weakly, "They were all wrong. Weren't they?"

I nod.

"They're wrong now. Let's show them that they are."

"How are you going to show them?"

She puts her hands on her hips and considers the question. "It'll have to be a peaceful demonstration."

"Those always go over well." No one catches my sarcasm.

"Are you in?" she asks. "Or will we have to throw you into the pit?" She crosses her arms and waits for my answer.

I don't really have a choice. I certainly don't want to leave Jada alone with this group.

"I'm in. What's the plan?"

"Confessionals are tomorrow. If we all renounce our ways, they'll inject us with a tracker and we'll be out of here by tomorrow morning."

Jada and I walk quietly back to our own barracks. I like the way her hand feels in mine. It's small, warm, and comforting, like a foam nose.

As we near the pit in the center of campus, we hear a pitiful moan.

Jada whimpers and clings to me. I hold my hand against her free ear, and we hurry past. I don't want to think about what kind of state Terrence is in right now. He must be almost dead. I want to throw him food and water, but getting caught doing so would lose all of the good-behavior points I've racked up.

We reach our barrack undetected, and we both slide beneath our respective covers, pondering what tomorrow will bring. I don't know about Jada, but I'm also thinking about Terrence and the horror of what he must be going through in that pit. It's been almost three days. No one has survived longer than that.

Morning brings a fresh view on things. The sun burns a little brighter, the sky is a little bluer…even the clouds over head seem a little fluffier than usual. The grass is greener, and the birds are happier. The food tastes better.

Jada is smiling. It's muted, but she's doing it. Even when Phillips comments on her sudden reappearance beside me.

"Musta' done her a favor," he comments, then makes a lewd gesture. We ignore him, and I squeeze her hand under the table.

Instead of running after breakfast, we line up for confessions. We all have to do it, and it takes all day, but luckily Jada and I, and the rebels, get into line pretty early. We don't have to wait long to be seen.

The confessions remind me of my mother's church that I grew up in. A man of God usually sat in one side of a wooden box, and I always sat on the other. There was a wall with a small screen between us so that we could talk, but it was supposed to be anonymous.

It was almost exactly like that now.

"Forgive me Father, for I have sinned," I begin, and chuckle. The man on the other side is not amused.

"What is it you want to confess?"

I drop my smile and clear my throat. "I want to confess that I was a black market clown for five years. Other than that, I never did anything illegal. I made a lot of money though, and then I lost it to the government when they arrested me."

Silence.

"Um, I'd also like to renounce my past and anything to do with the lifestyle."

The man on the other side shifted. "Alright. You'll have to give me your name so the warden can review your case."

"Joshua Leyton."

"Thank you, Joshua. You are free to go."

I leave the box, and the air seems crisper than it had been moments before.

I give Jada the thumbs up and watch her go into the confessional box.

Our day progresses. Today's schedule is all recreation due to confessions, but about mid-day my name is called over the loudspeaker and I'm brought to the warden's office.

He's a big, bald man, and it looks as though he never leaves his large desk chair. "So you've renounced your past life," he observes as he looks through my file. "Says here you were a black market clown for five years."

I nod.

"Did you do anything else? Hurt anyone? Kill anyone?" He gives me a skeptical over his glasses.

"No sir, I never did anything of that. Just made a boat load of money." My fingers fidget together in my lap.

He sits back in his chair with more of a grunt than a sigh. "Well, I don't see why you can't reintegrate into society. You'll have a tracking chip, and there's nothin' here indicating that you'll be a menace to society. I'll have a chat with the therapist and as long as she clears you, you'll be free by nightfall."

My heart skips a beat. I can't leave without Jada. Will they even take us to the same place?

"Thank you, sir," I tell him, and leave.

I join the rebel group out in the yard, but Jada is called in with the Warden next.

"How'd it go?" Cassandra asks excitedly.

202

"It was fine…he said I'm not a 'menace' so I'll probably be free to go by tonight."

Her eyes sparkle, and the group continues to daydream about what life on the outside might be like. What is it like to be gainfully employed? To live with no past, no family, no history?

The rest are interviewed, and a few are turned down immediately for reintegration. Cassandra sympathizes with them, telling them to keep racking up the good behavior points and to find us when they are able to leave.

Several hours before curfew, they round up those of us eligible for reintegration. They give us a packet, a hundred dollars, and put us on a yellow bus.

"Ya'll are goin' to Lubbock, Texas. It's the nearest town with a drop-off point," the warden wheezes. He's still out of breath from coming down the walkway. "You'll be injected with trackers on the way, an' we'll keep an eye on ya'. Good luck."

The bus pulls away from the camp, and excitement ricochets through me. Jada glances at me, her eyes lit with the same feeling, and she squeezes my hand. She does that a lot now, and I prefer it to talking, anyway.

She bounces a little in her seat as the camp slides away behind us. She can hardly contain herself.

I smile and watch her. Maybe we can start a life together. We aren't allowed to go to our hometowns or contact our family. They will know if we do, and we'll be taken back to the work camp. Half of the people there used to be out on good behavior, but they were brought back due to contact with past loved ones.

I don't have anyone to contact. My wife left me as soon as she found out what I'd been doing and that was three years before I was taken.

Jada leans her head on my shoulder and gives a deep, heavy sigh. Her eyelids flutter a moment, and then close as the last of the sunset darkens to black.

I lay my head on hers, and soon we've both slipped into a world of exciting dreams.

The bus jolts to a stop, and I lift my head too quickly. My neck is stiff, and I'm pretty sure I pull a muscle as a few vertebrae in my neck crack and pop.

Jada is already gazing out of the window, standing up to get a better view of our surroundings from her seat.

We can see the very first hints of a sunrise slipping over the eastern horizon.

We file off of the bus and it drives away, leaving us at a convenience store in the middle of a Podunk town.

"Now what?" a man asks. I don't know him, only a handful of us made it out. Me, Jada, Cassandra, and two of her closest friends.

Cassandra glances around as a gust of wind kicks some dirt up and throws it at us. She squints against it, and her face screws up into a grimace. "Not sure. We each have a hundred bucks, right? I'll use fifteen of mine for a burner phone. I'll call my guy."

No one questions her. It must be one of the reformed clown contacts she'd been talking about.

She disappears into the store, then emerges with a phone and five bottles of water. She walks some distance away with the phone to her ear and none of us can make out what she's saying.

"He'll be here in a few hours. We should get something to eat," she reports when she comes back.

We sit down at the café inside the convenience store. Jada leans against me, yawns, and fades in and out as we wait. Several shady characters come through the store, but none of them stop long enough to cause trouble. The man behind the counter looks like he's had a few trouble makers in his day, anyway. He is not someone I'd want to tangle with.

"He's here," Cassandra announces several hours later. The sun has risen and warms our faces as we walk out to find a black, fifteen passenger van parked nearest the entrance. All of the windows, except the front driver and passenger, are painted over.

A gaunt man with wiry, sandy hair sits in the driver's seat with an overtly large amount of chew in his bottom lip. He spits at my feet as we gather around his open window, and I notice a party-hat tattooed on his neck.

"Y'all with Cassy?" he drawls.

We nod in unison, and Jada latches to my side. I slide my arm around her and hold her close so that she knows she's safe.

Cassandra opens the sliding door, and, at first we think we're to file in, but instead she reaches into the back of the van. There are no seats, only boxes of all shapes and sizes. She flips several open, and shuts them again, growling in frustration until she sees what she wants.

Both of her friends drop their jaws at what she presents us. Even Jada lets go of me to better observe the firearm that Cassandra wields.

I swallow my anxiety. This is not looking like a peaceful protest.

"What do we need automatic weapons for?" I ask. My stomach suddenly squirms and twists its self into nauseating knots.

She ignores me. "We've got grenades, too, and rifles. Pick what you want," she tells us.

"What for?" I ask again.

To my horror, Jada disappears into the van and sorts through the weaponry.

Cassandra finally turns to me with the AK slung across her back. "I lied to you, okay jerk-wad? There's not a peaceful protest. My buddy Niles here got us some weapons," she smiles and sticks her head through his window to give him a long kiss on the lips.

"You owe me, baby," he tells her.

She throws him a flattering, flirtatious grin. "Oh I know, don't you worry." She turns her attention back to me. "We're going back to that hell hole and gunnin' it down. You can come with, or you can disappear quietly. Up to you."

My blood runs cold and my nerves deaden. This can't be what's really going down, I must still be dreaming. Jada would never agree to this...or would she? I don't actually know her. All I know about her is that I like her beside me. We've never held a conversation, never talked about anything deep.

When she reappears with two grenades and a 9mm, my whole world is turned upside down. She handles the weapons so naturally, but it seems out of place. She's so quiet, so reserved how can this be?

I look at her and her stare back at me is hard and cold. "Are you with us?" she asks.

"No!" I exclaim. "No way in hell am I going to go and kill all of those...those people..." Panic begins to set in, and I have to sit down.

Jada sits beside me. She tries to hold my hand but I don't let her. "I thought you were different," I tell her.

"I'm sorry," she tells me quietly. "I couldn't tell you what they really had planned, but I wanted to get you out of there before they did it. You mean so much to me..."

"Do I?" I ask her desperately.

She closes her mouth and doesn't answer. "You should go," she urges me. "Run as far as you can."

I grind my teeth. "Come with me." It comes out like a terse command, but it doesn't faze her.

"Work camps are wrong. My ancestors were some of those you talked about after Pearl Harbor. They lost everything. I can't let this country do it again, it's not fair."

I swallow my panic, my anxiety, and my pride, and I face her. I push her silky black hair behind her ear and cup her cheek in my hand. She leans gratefully into it. "You do what you have to do," I tell her. "And then you come find me if you survive."

I kiss her forehead, and Cassandra, who now wears a pale pink wig and has slapped large, red circles of paint on her face, yells at her to join them.

She kisses my cheek, squeezes my hand, and they disappear before I can tell her goodbye.

By the following morning, I've hitchhiked my way to a truck stop. I've used their facilities, and a full plate of bacon and eggs sit before me. I've really missed food like this.

The nightly news is on and there is an announcement bulletin. I've speared my first bite, but it falls back onto the plate as my jaw drops.

"...four gunmen entered the campus with semi-automatic rifles and military grade weapons," the news anchor informs grimly. "It seems like the targets were all of the employees of the work camp, and the gunmen had, ironically, just been released on good behavior. They entered the campus with painted faces and colorful wigs. Several inmates were caught and killed in the crossfire. None of those employed, including the Warden, survived. The National Guard was called in and all four of the gunmen were sniped and killed on sight."

It's a good thing I'm sitting. My world is spinning, and my stomach tries to wretch, but there is nothing in it to bring up.

Jada was my last hope at companionship. No one will want to be with me knowing what I've done for a living and where I've been for the last seven years.

Now she's dead.

I'm all alone.

"To Your Own Self, Be True" by Jason Henry Evans

Imaginary Friend in an Alternate Future

My name is Elena. Or, I think it is. I'm really not sure. I'll get back to you later about that. It all started when I woke up in the hospital a couple of days ago. Yeah. I think that's a good place to start.

I woke up, burns on my face and hands, tube going up my nose. I remember being woozy.

"Doctor, she's awake." The voice was familiar. A rich baritone voice that brought me comfort.

A tall man with high cheek bones and a lab coat examined me. "You're lucky. Your injuries could have been much worse. You have minor burns on your left cheek, a sprained left shoulder, and contusions all over your body." His accent was heavy, but I couldn't place it.

"What happened?"

"That new particle machine overheated and blew up," said the first voice.

208

The fog in my mind began to lift. I worked in a lab – at a university. I'm a doctoral student at the California Technical Institute – Cal Tech, for short. I study nuclear physics.

"Doctor, I have a major headache," I said.

"Probably a minor concussion. You'll be fine. Just rest." What was that accent? I couldn't place it.

"Was anybody else hurt?" I asked.

"No," said the baritone voice.

I look up to see warm, brown eyes and luxurious black hair. "Eric." I smile.

"Hi baby. You worried us for a while." Eric smiled at me and a warmth that comes from my stomach flooded my body.

The doctor made notes on a chart. "We'll observe you overnight, then release you in the morning."

"Thank you, doctor." I smiled at the stern man in the lab coat.

Eric squeezed my hand. "Get some rest, dear. I've got to study."

I'm released the next day. Eric comes to pick me up. We met first year of graduate school and dated since then. He's a biologist, I'm a nuclear physicist. I mean, I will be once I graduate.

Eric took me back to my apartment; a drab, grey building across the street from the university. I have an urge to watch television, but forgot I don't have one. I spend a lot of time in bed.

Elena. Elena! Listen! I need your help!

The alarm goes off. 7 a.m. on a Thursday morning. I've slept and moped around this dreary place for two days. Time to get back to work.

I walk across the street and through the maze of buildings and manicured lawns. The nuclear physics lab is seven stories tall and white, with the school logo and the seal of California on the front. One of the windows – the one with scorch marks – has workmen dutifully painting over the damage.

"Elaina!"

"Oh, hi Ivana."

"We were so happy you weren't hurt badly. Are you feeling better?"

"Only my pride." I force a smile on my face.

"Well, the lab got cleaned up, but it's not open yet. You know the cops were asking questions, right?" Ivana asks.

"Oh, good grief." I roll my eyes in exasperation.

Ivana's eyes widen and the color leaves her face. "Be careful, Elaina."

We exchange pleasantries and I get back to my office and the laboratory.

The damage, thankfully, was minor. I don't really remember what happened. I do remember getting shocked and people screaming. I remember the smell of smoke. But that doesn't matter anymore. Time to get back to work.

My office was small by any standard. I have a desk, a map of the periodic tables, some pictures of friends, and a computer.

The phone rings. "Elena Richardson's office?"

"Ms. Richardson, Dean Cranston would like to speak with you. Please come immediately." The dean's secretary betrays no emotions.

"I'll be right there," I reply, then hang up.

When I get to the dean's office, I get ushered inside. Waiting for me is my mentor, Dr. Andropov; a police officer; and Dean Cranston.

"Good morning, Ms. Richardson. We are so happy to see you are feeling better. Would you please take a seat?" The dean's smile belies the worry on his face. Beads of sweat dangle from the top of his balding head.

I sit

"Dr. Andropov, you know. This is Lt. Colonel Henry Clay from the California Secret Police."

The colonel stands and takes my hand. "A pleasure."

I smile in reply.

The dean coughs. "The colonel just has some questions for you. Merely a formality."

If this is a formality, why does the dean look like he's going to shit himself?

"Please, recall the events of that day," Colonel Clay says.

So, I do what I'm told. Four hours later, the colonel stops questioning me.

"Well, that should just about wrap it up. Thank you, Ms. Richardson, Dr. Andropov. We can never be too careful with state secrets."

"Does anybody know when we will receive a new machine?" I blurt out.

The color leaves the dean's face. His eyes widen.

Colonel Clay raises an eyebrow. "You'll have to discuss that with the department of science. This is not my expertise." The colonel smiles at me, stands and leaves.

Once gone, Dean Cranston sighs. "Elena, that was reckless."

"I asked a simple question."

"You were pushy, arrogant."

Dr. Andropov agrees. "Yes, you must really be careful. Science is politically important now. That could change."

"Science is always important, Dr. Andropov."

My mentor smirks at me. He knows how to push my buttons. The dean, on the other hand, looks close to a heart attack.

Dr. Andropov looks at his watch and changes the subject. "It's almost time for the university-wide lecture. We must go."

I'm grateful for the change of subject.

My mentor, Dr. Andropov, and I walked in silence to the new, open air, small stadium. The line moved quickly – everyone is used to lines these days.

As we got to our seats in the science section, the band started up the national anthem.

We placed our hands over our hearts to the hymn, *Sons of California*, and watched the Bear Flag Republic raise solemnly.

"Good Afternoon, faculty and students of Cal Tech," thundered the loudspeaker. "Please be seated as our presentation begins."

I hated Republic Day. Another waste of my time. But, the law was the law.

"Twenty-Seven years ago, the Capitalist Criminals launched a devastating attack on the peaceful people of the Soviet Union . . ."

They always started like this.

". . . but what the evil mastermind of the world-wide capitalist empire did not realize was that their entire edifice would crumble before the might of the combined strengths of the proletariat. Soon, the decadent capitals of imperialism and capitalism, Washington D.C &

*New York City, would burn in the righteous fire of nuclear retaliation .
. ."*

A story, I'm sure, every man & woman here could recite from
memory.

*". . . soon the people of California would rise up and join their
brothers around the world and join the revolution. This is why the
People's Republic of California is great! This is why California earned
its status among brother nations and emerged from the wreckage of the
decadent United States to become the premiere power in the Pacific
Rim and brother nation to the Soviet Union. All HAIL CALIFORNIA!"*

I got a call from my mom when I got home. "Honey, how are you
doing?"

"I'm fine, mom."

"We were so worried when we heard about the accident. Are you
sure you're okay?"

"Just some bruises and some redness. How are things in Tucson?"

Silence followed. "We're fine dear."

"Did you get the extra ration cards?"

"Yes, Elena. Thank you."

I hung up soon afterwards. I knew things were bad. I also knew the
cops were listening, so further talk would just make it worse. Besides I
had friends to go out with. I met Eric at a local bar – Lucky Baldwin's.
He greeted me with a gentle hug and kiss. "I won't break, you know." I
jabbed him in the ribs.

"Just making sure. Come on, the gang awaits." Eric led me into the
back and up the stairs to the private loft above the bar. Some friends
greeted us with cheers of delight: Becky and her boyfriend Karl, my lab
mate Amy, along with Eric's neighbor, Susan.

Amy hugged me tightly. "I'm so sorry I wasn't there," she
whispered in my ear.

"It's alright. I got a little banged up, Amy." I hugged her back.

We have squatted in this dank bar since we got to graduate school. Holding Amy, I glanced at the pictures on the wall. A lot of them had Eric, Amy, and me in them, but there was one photo with a woman I couldn't place. The picture was black & white. She wore a wry smile with her arms folded across her chest.

Amy pulled away from me and stared quizzically. I stared past her at the picture.

"Elena."

Who was that woman?

"ELENA."

Eric took my gently took my arm. "Do you want some schnapps?"

"Huh? Yes."

We drank, talked about old professors and potential jobs. We teased Eric a lot, too. I tried not to talk about work, but slipped into it a couple of times.

"Did you guys hear?" asked Becky.

Amy answered, "What, Becky?"

"The news says the Freedom Party rigged the election in the Republic of Texas. That Aaron Ritchey will be their new president." Becky sipped her schnapps.

"Oh Becky, why do you have to ruin things with politics?" asked Amy.

"I heard that President Martinez in Denver is going to sign a non-aggression pact with Texas," said Susan. "All over immigration and trade."

"Come on guys," Karl said. "We were having a good time."

"But the Rocky Mountain Republic is already on good terms with Mexico. If they draw Texas in their orbit, we're screwed." Becky drained her glass.

Eric huffed. "Texas and Mexico, *allies?* Yeah, right."

Becky tried to reply. "But if –"

"This was fun guys, but I've got to go home. Lab reopens tomorrow." I got up to go, hugged everyone and left. I glanced one last time at that picture.

Elena! Elena! Can you hear me? Elena. I need your help. Only you can fix this. Elena, the answers are in the lab. Elena? The lab. Only you can help me!

I woke up, covered in sweat. Eric snored softly by my side. His hand draped across my body. I had the urge to pee, so I snuck under his arm and used the bathroom. I couldn't sleep though. So, I went to the computer.

Access to the information network is highly regulated in the People's Republic of California, but, as a scientist, I am allowed.

I go to the history section and read about the glorious revolution. How American jets routinely went into Soviet air space and were recalled as an act of hyper capitalist aggression. How on August 13th, 1985 an American jet dropped a payload of bombs on Vladivostok. The Soviets retaliated and knocked out Washington, D.C. and New York.

The U.S. surrendered after her communication grid stopped working. Her entire arsenal of nuclear weapons unresponsive. The surrender took place in Philadelphia that November. Both coasts were occupied, and civil war broke out soon, afterwards. I knew this story. Every child growing up in California knows this story. Why did I need to read about it?

History was dry. Just scanning over the words made my eye lids droop. I stumbled back to bed and next to Eric. It was good to feel his warmth, to smell his scent. The bruises still covered my body, so sex was out. A girl could dream though, and I drifted to sleep with the thought of making love to him. I dreamt of his weight on top of me, the smell of his clean body, the feel of his rhythm joining with mine.

Elena, Elena. I'm in trouble. The world is in trouble. Only you can fix it.

What? Who are you? What do you want?

Elena. It's me, Cynthia. You know what to do. You must know what to do.

"Elena." Eric called to me.

I woke up, trembling.

"Are you alright, honey?"

"I think so. Bad dream." I shivered.

"You're cold." Eric took the blankets, piled at our feet, and covered me.

I looked into his eyes. "I'm fine," I said. I nuzzled closer to him. I kissed his neck and chest. "I want you," I said between kisses. My hand fingered his abdomen. "I need you."

He kissed me. Softly, slowly working his mouth around my ear. When we finished our lovemaking, I slept sound until morning.

I had no other dreams that night. I have had sexual dreams before, but never one that changed like last night. One minute I'm in Eric's arms, the next some woman calls me. Weird.

Golden rays of sunshine coupled with the smells of coffee resurrected me. We spoke about our day ahead and when we would see each other again. He kissed me gently.

I got to the lab where technicians finished repairing the machine that shorted and led to my accident.

"Ah, Elena. I'm glad to see you here. We should be able to resume our experiments shortly." Dr. Andropov smiled. "Coffee?"

"No, thank you. Do we know what happened yet?"

"Best guess? A power surge. Electricity can be fickle, you know. We'll run some tests later, but for now we must continue re-checking our equations." Dr. Andropov marched to the white board.

"Yes, doctor. Of course. I'll check my notes in my office," I said.

He nodded and I left for my office. I daydreamed all along the way.

"Excuse me."

I stumbled into a man. "Please, forgive me."

"It happens," he said.

"Wait, aren't you Professor Sanders? The historian?"

His eyes lit up. "Yes. Yes, I am. I'm surprised anyone would know me in the nuclear physics department."

"You're a celebrity, professor. Every year you're interviewed on California Day."

"Well, yes. A celebrity is a benefit – or a curse."

"Do you have some time? I'd love to ask a few questions."

The professor raised an eyebrow and smiled. "Alright."

Professor Sanders was the foremost authority on the People's Revolution, as it was called. A short man of Afro-Californian decent, the professor had published countless papers on the war that followed the brief nuclear exchange.

We went into my office. I made coffee and we chatted. He talked about the attack on Vladivostok, the retaliation on New York, and the civil war that followed. We talked for over an hour.

"Of course, the early stages of the conflict were farcical. The habits of obedience were ingrained in the proletariat of North America to support the bourgeois." He spoke in perfect Marxist language.

"Professor, what about the original attack? What happened to the pilot? The plane?" I asked.

"No one knows. After the war, the old American Air Force flight plans showed some sort of malfunction, then communication black out. Of course, these records were probably forged to make the capitalists look innocent," Professor Sanders said.

"Why didn't the Americans retaliate against New York and Washington, DC? Why not a full-scale attack?" I stirred cream into my coffee as I questioned him.

He smirked. "Shoddy equipment. The capitalists had convinced the world that market economies made better equipment. Yet their ICBMs faltered. Their radar crashed. They couldn't even get messages to their submarines weeks later."

"Professor, could you email me a list of published articles I could read? I am fascinated about this time period."

"Of course! I would be happy to." The small man got up from his seat. "You know, I have never met a physicist with such a curiosity about history before. This has been a wonderful chat."

Professor Sanders left me with many questions, but I had no time to ponder. I got on my computer to recalculate my equations. All afternoon I went over each number. By the end, I was sure we did nothing wrong.

There was only one way to be certain.

I returned to the lab at six that evening. Everyone but first year graduate students were gone. "You students can go. Take the rest of the evening off."

The three men looked at each other. One shrugged, grabbed his notebook and left. The other two followed.

Finally alone, I lifted the tarp on the machine.

The machine's original purpose, as explained by Dr. Andropov, was to study Cherenkov radiation. You know, the blue glow a reactor makes when it's submerged in water? That's Cherenkov radiation. Theoretically, it should exist in other places, as well. The purpose of the machine was to discover other sources of that radiation. But something went wrong.

I checked all the fuses. I checked the relays and the connectors. I checked every wire and every tube. "What went wrong?" I said aloud.

"I don't know? Maybe it just doesn't like you?" Eric leaned on the door frame, arms folded. "I thought we were meeting for dinner?"

"I'm sorry, sweetie. Something about this bothers me. I have to test it."

"Did you get permission from Dr. Andropov? You know how these Russians get about protocol." He moved closer to me.

"I just want to turn it on, make some observations. It won't take more than an hour."

Outside, the sounds of chanting started. It was soft at first, but grew in volume. I turned to look outside.

"What's that all about?" I asked.

"President Schwarzenegger announced he broke off diplomatic relations with the People's Republic of Texas over allegations of electoral improprieties."

The air left my lungs. "What?" I stammered. "That will surely force Texas into action."

"I know. President Martinez of the Rocky Mountain Republic has already denounced the move and asked to mediate."

"Huh! She's just trying to make herself look good at California's expense." This news bothered me. My family was in Tucson. If fighting broke out, they would be in danger. But I couldn't think about this now. I had work to do. "Look. I can't think about politics right now. I have to study this machine."

"You're serious about this, aren't you?" Eric cocked his head and narrowed his eyes on me.

I nodded.

"Alright. Let me help. I'll monitor its functions while you take notes." Eric smiled.

"This is why I love you."

He grabbed a technician's lab coat and a pair of goggles. "What does this thing do, anyways?"

"It finds Cherenkov radiation."

"Interesting. I read a paper that said Cherenkov radiation might be found in the wake of a tachyon particles."

"I have no time for theoretical physics, Eric. Okay. Flip the switch."

A loud hum reverberated through the lab. I could feel the vibrations ten feet away. We went over a check list. The lights flicked.

"Starting at 2000 mega joules."

I started to take notes.

"4000 mega joules."

The hum's pitched increased. Everything was working.

"6000 mega joules. 8000 mega joules."

"The scanner. Look at the scanner, Eric!"

"What is the meaning of this?" Dr. Andropov burst in.

"Doctor, please. I'm only taking notes. We will be done soon," I begged.

"There was no authorization." Dr. Andropov turned to Eric. "Shut that machine down, now!"

"We're almost done, doctor. Please," Eric said.

"Bah!" Dr. Andropov thundered over to the machine.

Sparks flew. Arcs of electricity flared out from the machine. More arcs roared upward, blackening the ceiling. Then it happened.

"Can you hear that?" I asked.

Dr. Andropov stood, eyes fixed above the machine. "Look."

Electricity danced and popped overhead. Smoke escaped the machine, first in small tuffs. A loud crack. The overhead lights failed. A crack of sound came from the machine. Dr. Andropov and Eric dove to the floor as smoke filled the room.

Then it happened.

Arcs of electricity shot out from the machine and formed an irregular circle of energy. Inside that circle a clear, night sky came into view.

"What . . . is . . . this?" Dr. Andropov muttered.

A large arc flared out from the machine. I flew backwards.

Two arcs of electricity formed a circle above the machine. Inside the circle was another sky. No. It was the inside of a plane. We were viewing things from the pilot's point of view.

"I'm having trouble. Repeat, I am having trouble. Systems shutting down." The pilot didn't panic. He went through a number of protocols. "I'm flying dead stick here."

I looked down to see the instrument panel and made a mental note.

Elena. Elena. It's me, Cynthia.
Who?
You almost did it, Elena. Try again.
Who are you? Why are you talking to me?
Tachyons, Elena. You're covered in them. They're inside of you.
What?
One more time. Try one more time.

I woke up with a splitting head ache. My bones ached.

"Elena, can you hear me?"

A bright light invaded my eye. Then a click and it was gone.

"She's developed a concussion," the voice said.

"Where . . . where am I?"

"You're at St. Luke's medical center," said another voice.

I opened my eyes to see a black woman in a lab coat. Behind her were two men dressed in olive, drab uniforms with gold buttons and black caps.

"You are Dr. Elena Collins?" The soldier flipped through some papers in a notebook.

"I'm not a doctor. I won't be done for another year or two," I said.

The soldier raised an eyebrow at me. "Academic humility. That's new." He scribbled some notes. "What happened at the lab that night the machine was turned on again?"

"I – I don't know. Things are fuzzy."

"It is imperative we find out, Ms. Collins."

"Where is Eric? Where is Dr. Andropov?" I asked.

"Just answer the questions, please."

"The radiation machine was tested. We took notes. Sparks came out of it. An arc of electricity hit me. That's all I remember."

The soldier continued to scribble notes. He didn't look up. "Who authorized its activation?"

"What?" I didn't quite understand his question.

The soldier looked up at me. "Listen to me, Ms. Collins. I understand your head might be foggy, but this is very serious. Who authorized the activation of the machine?"

The soldier's eyes were a piercing blue-green. I noticed the condor insignia on his collar. He was secret police. I was in trouble.

"I did. I authorized it. I wanted to make some observations."

The soldier scribbled more notes.

"Where is Dr. Andropov? He can tell you I've worked on this project for years."

The soldier turned to his colleague and nodded. The other soldier took out handcuffs and cuffed me to my gurney.

"Ms. Collins you are under arrest for crimes against the state. You will also be charged with reckless endangerment, wasting state resources, and manslaughter."

"What?"

"Dr. Andropov is dead." He said it the way other men would tell you about the weather. Both men began to walk out.

"Eric. What about Eric?"

"Eric is in critical condition with electrical burns."

This was my fault. All my fault. One man was dead. I will always be responsible for that. But Eric, my sweet Eric. I never should have involved him. I cried until the nurse came.

"Oh sweetie. It will be alright. Here, take this for the pain." She handed me some pills.

I refused them.

"Well, how about some television?" She took the remote from a side table. The TV blared on and she adjusted the sound.

"President Schwarzenegger has denounced the incursion of Mexican jets into California's air space. He says any attempts to disrupt the sovereign borders of California will be met with force. Meanwhile, contested Texan President Aaron Ritchey says skirmishes

on the Texas-California border must end. He also says other powers have recognized his election and President Schwarzenegger must do so as well."

"How long was I out?"

"Two days," said the nurse.

"Can you give me something to sleep? I don't feel well."

The nurse nodded and came back with some pills.

I cried myself to sleep, thinking of Eric and Dr. Andropov. I thought of my family possibly caught on the front lines of a Texas-Californian war, or a Mexican-Californian war. It was all too much.

And then there was Cynthia. Who was Cynthia? Was I imagining it? This time she said something about tachyons.

What was I rambling about? I was in serious trouble. I looked at the handcuff tying me to the gurney. Even if I could figure out what was going on, I couldn't do anything about.

While I slept, I didn't dream of Cynthia. I dreamt of that pilot.

"I'm flying dead stick, here," he said. That meant the instruments weren't responding. What could make that happen? What would make the instruments stop working? Think Elena, you're a scientist.

Computers sometimes fry because of an electrical charge. An electro-magnetic pulse can knock out circuits from televisions, personal computers & radios. But military craft have defenses—extra insulation—to prevent that from happening.

These were my thoughts as I drifted off to sleep.

A lawyer came to visit me from the public defender's office. A young woman in a fashionable dress carrying an even more fashionable, satchel bag.

"Hi, my name is Cori, Cori French. These are some serious charges, the worst of which are wasting state resources and manslaughter. But, I need to talk to you about something."

"Yes?"

"The Secret Police went through your personal records, your computer, even your bank statements. They found nothing indicating that you were an enemy agent. However, your family is from Tucson?" Cori's eyes narrowed on me.

"Yeah. I grew up there. Why?" I asked.

Cori pulled something out of her satchel bag. "It says your maternal grandfather emigrated from Denver, after the Second Civil War. That puts you under suspicion for being a sleeper agent."

"What? That's absurd."

"I know. I know. Look." She took my hand in the handcuff. "I don't know if you've been watching the news, but war is pretty likely. The Secret Police would like a show trial and a guilty verdict to make this all go away."

"Guilty? But all I did was take some notes."

"You're in serious trouble here, Elena. I would plead guilty."

I fumed, unable to respond.

"If you plead guilty, you'll get a year in prison – reduced to less than six months."

"But how am I supposed to finish my training?"

Cori looked at me, blankly. "Oh, Elena. You're being expelled. Didn't anybody tell you?"

"What?" I couldn't breathe.

"Are you alright?"

The pretty lawyer called for the nurse, who gave me more pills. This time, I didn't dream at all.

I woke up that evening. Groggy and disoriented, I reached for the nurse button. My bed pan was full.

The nurse came in and switched them out. "Are you hungry?" she asked.

I shook my head no. The nurse left as I drifted back to sleep.

Elena. ELENA!

I opened my eyes. A shimmering vision of a woman hovered before me.

Elena. One more time, Elena. One more time.

"Wha—what do you want with me?" Butterflies danced in my stomach and my heart fluttered.

This world. It isn't real.

The woman furrowed her brow and shook her head.

I mean, it's not supposed to be real. Only you can change things back.

"Why me?"

The other scientists got erased from the timeline. Elena. You are the only one.

"Who are you? Why can't you fix things?"

Elena, I'm stuck between realities. I can't explain it. But of all the people in that room, you are the only one in this reality. Elena, you can stop this. You can prevent this.

"How?"

Search for other pictures, other scenes with the machine. Find us, Elena. Find us.

I woke up in the dead of night. The wall clock said 2 a.m. I didn't know if that woman was real or not. But with Eric in the hospital, Dr. Andropov dead, and the western powers looking to go to war, I wished she was real. I wished that this world was a mistake.

Two days later, my lawyer returned with a woman police officer. "You are to be arraigned today, Elena. It's just a formality, but you need to be there." She carried a garment bag with her. "I went to your place and grabbed some things for you to wear."

"Thank you," I said.

The police officer unlocked my handcuff. I was allowed to take a shower by myself. It was nice to shower and get clean. The burns were minor this time, but ran along my legs and my arms.

I toweled off and changed in front of the officer and my lawyers. I had one chance.

The officer moved to cuff me again.

"Is that really necessary?" asked Cori.

"State polic—" the cop started to say. I grabbed the clean bedpan from my bed and hit her in the head.

The officer staggered. I grabbed her gun from her holster.

"What are you doing?" Cori shrieked.

"Saving the world."

The walk out to my lawyer's car was relatively calm. I took her keys before I let her in on the driver's side, then followed around myself.

"You're a spy, aren't you?" Cori asked.

"No. But I've got nothing to lose." I handed her the keys. "Let's go."

Cori drove us out of the parking lot.

"Take me to Cal Tech," I said.

Cori looked shocked. Just as shocked as when I told her to tie the officer up with my bed sheets and lock her in the bathroom.

The campus wasn't far away.

"Why are you going here? Your office has been sealed. Whatever secrets you have aren't accessible."

"Park and get out of the car *slowly*. I am a desperate woman."

The color left Cori's face as we parked. I took my lawyer by the arm, my pistol neatly in my pocket. Suddenly the alarm bells rang.

"What was that?" Cori asked.

"Campus wide alert. That police officer was probably discovered by the nurse. We're running out of time." We continued our walk to the physics department.

Bewildered students past us, trying to figure out what the alarm was for. It was good cover. We made it inside the physics building.

"Elena?"

It was one of the graduate technicians. His confusion turned to horror once he realized I was there.

I pulled the gun and waved it at Cori. "Don't make any sudden moves, or else she dies."

He stood there mute.

I moved past him and to the laboratory.

"This is where we part ways, counselor."

"You're not going to hurt me?"

I pointed the gun at her. "Just leave."

She ran, screaming down the hall.

The laboratory was covered in police tape. Too bad I had a gun and not a knife. I ripped away the tape and unlocked the door. The machine looked in worse shape than when I left it. Streaks of black soot covered its front panel of diodes and switches. Trails of soot arced up the wall.

I turned it on.

A low hum rumbled through the lab. The lights flickered and the alert siren weakened. Arcs of electricity leapt from the machine repeatedly. The hum was replaced with a whine.

There! I see it! The arcs form a circle above the machine. I see the pilot.

"I'm having trouble. Repeat, I am having trouble. Systems shutting down." The pilot works his way through some protocols.

"No," I blurt out. It's all just replaying again. I can't change it. I slam my hand on the hot console.

"I'm having trouble . . ."

Wait, what just happened?

I grab one of the knobs.

"Going down. I repeat. I'm dead stick."

I turn the knob the other direction.

"I'm having trouble . . ."

It's like a VCR tape. I can control the speed of the events in the past.

Okay, I try another knob.

"STOP!" A cop bursts through the door.

I ignore him.

The sound of more sirens waft into the air.

"What's going on?" I ask.

"Put your hands in the air or I will shoot!"

I grab another knob. The scene above me changes. I can't place it, so I turn again.

BANG.

"That was a warning shot. Put your hands in the air...now!"

I turn around slowly as tears well in my eyes. "I can fix this. I can make it all go away."

"Put your hands in the air." The officer pulls the hammer back on his revolver.

Suddenly the ground trembles. I lose my balance, as does the cop. The lights blow out and people scream. We've just been bombed. I crawl to my feet. The machine still works. I move another knob.

BANG.

A sharp pain strikes my right shoulder, throwing me to the ground. I've been shot.

"Oh my god, Cynthia, you're gross. Just flip the switch."

Wait—that was my voice.

I look up and see this Cynthia woman standing in this lab talking to Eric – and me. I get to my feet, my shoulder hot with pain.

"Now what?" I ask no one in particular. "How do I go back?"

I flip switches, press buttons, turn other knobs. Another round of quakes as another bomb hits. Debris from the ceiling rains down. I smell smoke.

In the distance I hear the roar of jets loom overhead. One more bomb and we're done. Flames shoot out of the machine. I flipped any switch I can find. Then it hits me. *Turn it off.*

A bomb hits the building, throwing me into a cauldron of black chaos.

"Doctor, she's awake." The voice was familiar. A rich baritone voice that brought me comfort.

A tall man with high cheek bones and a lab coat examined me. He points a light in my eye.

"Doc, please."

The doctor steps back. "You're lucky. Your injuries could have been much worse. You have minor burns on your left cheek, a sprained left shoulder, and contusions all over your body." He turns to someone behind me. "Watch her, she might have a concussion."

"Thank you, doctor," says a familiar woman's voice.

I turn to it. There she is, Dr. Cynthia Krakora.

"Do you know me?" she asks.

Through tears I nod, yes.

Cynthia comes to me, takes my hand. She leans in close to whisper. "You brought me back."

I nod and cry. "So, I did it?"

Cynthia smiles at me. "Si, lo hiciste."

"What? This is California, right?"

"Yes, Elena. *El Reino de California.* The King will thank you, once he returns."

I got dizzy again and passed out.

"A Good One" by Thomas A. Fowler
Kaiju in an Alternate Future

I scrolled through Monstreamity, seeing if any new shows were worth watching. After a while, I knew I had to get dinner going for Meg. My phone, a new five-foot wide screen, flashed as I got a new text.

Emerged from the Pacific. There in 10.

As I walked toward the kitchen, I pushed my mane back, letting its tail drape over my shoulder. I gripped my phone with my front paw, holding it between two toes as I walked on all fours. Once in, I stepped back onto my hind legs and texted Meg back.

Sounds good. You okay binging 'Golden Growls?' Can't find anything good.

She replied, *Always!*

Reaching into the fridge, I pulled out two, humpback whales from the freezer. Using my retractable claws, I sliced the humpback whale meat into chunks. Grabbing my oil, I tipped the four-foot bottle toward the sauté pan, adding some salt and taco seasoning. In another pot, I started melting cheese, throwing a container of whole peppers and onions in, figuring a few dozen for each of us should do.

As the cheese melted and whale began to turn a warm brown in the pan, Meg knocked on the door and entered my apartment. A long kaiju, Meg had a huge mouth with hundreds of teeth, her silver hide and fins helped her swim through the ocean, but her four legs that stemmed from her body let her walk on the land and fight humans any time they invaded our city.

"That smells amazeballs, Kimmi!" Meg stood on her hind legs, coiling her tail for extra support as she stood and wrapped her front fins and legs around me.

"Hey, buddy," I replied. "Got some grilled humpback and nachos."

"How are you single?" Meg squeezed me one more time, then dipped one of her fins into the nacho cheese, sampling it.

"Good question, Meg," I replied.

"Not that I have any grounds to judge," Meg said.

"Didn't work out with Shrimai?" I plated some food.

"No, jackass got all aggressive, we ended up fighting in the water. Military showed up, I had to sink three submarines. Three!" Meg raised her fin, it didn't have any points of articulation. She dropped it and raised a foot instead, raising three of her four claws. "And what did he do when the humans showed up?"

"He didn't," I said.

"He left me to fight the humans off by myself." Meg dabbed her fin into the nacho sauce again. "He yelled one warning call, then high-tailed it…literally. He has two tails and he used his high-tail to get out of there faster. The higher tail is the wider one. Asshole couldn't even fire a radioactive beam to slow one down. Kaiju men are the worst."

"The worst!" I pulled the whale from the sauté pan. "If anyone ever needed further evidence sexuality isn't a choice, they just need to look at kaiju men. This isn't what I want in a relationship, either."

"I also don't get what the humans think they're doing, they haven't been able to kill hardly any of us. They need to know when they're beaten," Meg said. "We are living in a kaiju world, and I am a kaiju girl."

"Humans are also the worst. Anyways, 'Golden Growls?'" I asked.

"'Golden Growls!'" she replied.

We brought our plates to the table. I woke my 50-foot plasma screen up again. When it didn't activate, I aggressively smashed the enter button a few more times.

"You're not signed in." Meg pointed at the screen with the flippers on her tail.

"Thank you," I replied.

"Speaking of humans, are you…?" Meg asked. "If you don't want to talk about it…"

"I already told you about it, it's fine." I brought out my mane. "Yeah, should be clear. I found a couple humans about a week ago, but got them combed out, did another hair treatment. That should've taken care of them."

The episode started. The theme song kicked on from the old show. It felt familiar.

"Good, I'm glad. Because of my hide, I can't really get humans. One time they latched on I just went in the ocean, they all fell off and drowned." Meg took a bite of whale.

"So, what? Human bodies were just floating around your place?" I asked, pushing a nacho through my bowl of cheese.

"Ew, what's wrong with you?" Meg swallowed her bite. "I shook them off on the shore, then I ate them."

"You ate them?" I asked.

"Yes, why don't all kaiju do this? They're fatty, salty, full of protein," Meg said. "I don't get the stigma of eating humans. We eat gorillas, cows, elephants, what's so different? They're mammals."

"But humans infect places, for me they get dug into my mane, feed off the small bugs and birds that live in there," I replied.

"Isn't that a risk?" Meg asked.

"Yeah, absolutely, those birds keep the bugs out. The bugs clean my mane. Human infections are dangerous as shit, I could get bacteria, then I'd have to shave my mane." I twisted the end of my mane around, twirling it together.

"No! I mean you'd be able to rock a shaved mane, if you wanted to." Meg took her whale and dumped it on her plate of chips, then added her nacho cheese. "I'm going for it."

"Nice, you do you," I replied. "I like my mane though. Not many rock the mane, female mammalian kaiju anyway. I'd be sad if I had to lose it."

"I would too, just supporting you," Meg said. "So, since you're cleared of humans, you going to go out with Matt again?"

"Think so," I said. "He seemed like a good one. Which has been hard to find. Plus, he didn't judge my mane like that other guy."

"If a guy can't handle a kaiju woman with a mane, he doesn't deserve you. Was the judgy guy a furry kaiju?" Meg asked.

"Lizard-skinned," I said.

"Oh, that's why. Guy couldn't grow any mane, probably doesn't have any frills to push out or anything so he's threatened by you having mane, would make him the 'lesser kaiju.'" She picked up a nacho, with sauce and whale, tackling it all in one massive bite.

"Right?" I replied. "Complete jerk."

"When are you going out?" Meg asked.

"We're figuring it out," I said. "Sometime this weekend."

"Awesome! I'll come over before, do a final check, make sure you're clear." Meg tussled the end of my mane. "Don't want any humans showing up, ruining the night."

"Thanks, Meg," I replied. "You're the best."

"I know. Now let's eat before it gets cold." Meg took a bite, with her mouth full, she blurted out, "Cold whale is the worst!"

"The worst!" I replied. We sat and enjoyed 'The Golden Growls,' while my next date loomed over my head. I hoped humans would stay out of it, their invasions were getting annoying and desperate. I hoped I didn't come across the same.

I siphoned through my mane, praying I wouldn't find a fluke human anywhere. The pads on my right foot tapped the floor of my apartment. The hair between the pads wriggled about as I moved my toes around in a constant nervous rhythm.

Checking my phone, Meg hadn't gotten back to me since her last text. *Hey, guess the humans have a "grudge" against me now because of the sunken submarines. Naval armada's coming after me. Won't be able to check your mane. Sure you're fine. Call me after!*

I tapped the phone, nervous about what to do. I texted Meg.
Need me to help? I can meet you.

Nothing. I checked the news sites, nothing about a naval armada. At this point human attacks were so mundane and accepted, it hardly ever warranted major news stories anymore. I was glad we Kaiju had the capacity to deal with them, but we were over humans. They had their time, now we had ours. We were better for the planet anyways.

I couldn't check the back of my mane. My short arms couldn't reach. I could at least sift through with my claws, if I felt something weird, I'd just pull. Nothing. I called Meg and my friend, Josie.

"Hey, Josie. It's Kimmi."

"Hey, how's it going?" she asked.

"Doing okay, have you heard from Meg? Last I heard she was talking about an armada coming after her because she sunk those three submarines," I said.

"Oh, she's fine. Couple of us are going to help, but she sounded like she didn't need anything," Josie said. "Most of us are going to scare the piss out of the humans. When they hear we charged after them ten-strong we're hoping they'll just leave us the hell alone! We're not asking for much."

"Want me to come meet you?" I asked.

"If you wanted to, it's going to be fun. Humans invented some sort of 'matter redistributor,' think this invention will 'definitely work.' But we should be fine," Josie replied.

"I'll feel better if I do, where is it?" I asked.

"I'll send you a map ping," she replied.

Hanging up, I had one hand in my mane, the other I tapped my phone. My thumbs nervously twitched against the call button as I stared at Matt's number. I dialed. It rang twice. On the third rang I went through the voicemail in my head, lips fluttering as I rehearsed.

Fourth ring. I grabbed my keys and went for the door. A fifth ring, then his voicemail.

"Hi, you've reached Matt, Certified Accountant at Kaiju and Me Finance, please leave a message, and any details I may need to know, including the best way to reach you, after the beep."

It beeped. I exited my apartment and locked the door as I spoke. "Hi, Matt, this is Kimmi. Sorry to do this, but my friend is being attacked by an armada. Bunch of us are getting together to try to scare off the humans for good. I definitely want to meet up, though. So please, know this isn't anything to…"

The voicemail beeped. It stopped recording.

"Dick!" I shouted.

"Hey," my apartment manager said down the hallway.

"Not you, Mr. Gillfand." I waved. "Sorry."

I went back to the voicemail app, rerecording my voicemail. "Hi, Matt, this is Kimmi. Sorry, but my friend is under attack. We're headed to the ocean to scare off the humans. Maybe we could move the date to later tonight or something? Give me a call. It'll take me a few to get there. Talk to you soon. Hopefully. Have a good one. Sorry. Don't know why I said sorry. Anyways, talk soon. Bye."

Hanging up, I felt good, yet nervous. If he wanted to see me again, he'd take the next step. Otherwise, it's a sign. He was cute though, didn't seem to mind my mane either. That was rare.

After a while, I could see the ocean in the distance. The armada was pretty far, it'd take some swimming, but I was up for it as best a mammalian kaiju could be. We weren't known for our speed in the water. A few kaiju stood on the shore, watching. Some recorded the event on their phone. Others were clearly assigned to standing guard, ensuring the armada didn't try to come ashore.

Josie ran toward me. One of the biggest kaiju I'd ever seen, her feet shook the ground, even for us monsters. When we fought the humans to leave us alone, she often took the lead to shake buildings and scare them off. The thuds of her feet made humans tremble. It was great. She was great.

"Hey!" I said.

"Hi, glad you could make it," Josie replied.

"For sure, gotta support Meg," I said.

As we walked down the street toward the shore, my phone vibrated. Pulling it up, Matt was calling.

"Oh, shoot. Can I take this while we walk?" I asked.

"Go for it." Josie motioned toward the phone.

I picked it up. "Hi, Matt?"

"Hi, got your voicemail," he replied.

"Hope that's okay, we can meet later, or find another night that works," I said.

"Well, I'm on the beach, but didn't see you out there," Matt said. "Thought I'd come help you and your friend."

"What? No, it's an armada, you don't have to do that," I said. "Apparently it's a grudge attack."

"Oh, well we better watch out this time, then," Matt said, sarcasm dripping at the human threat. Kaiju, as a whole, were pretty unintimidated at this point. "Do they have some sort of asinine, borderline Rube Goldberg machine that's going to 'definitely take us out this time?'?"

"You know it, you sure you want to do this?" I asked. "Military might flag you."

"I don't care. What are they going to do to us? Seriously?" Matt said. "I'm by the Titan Smoothies & Shakes, does that help at all?"

"You're north of us, I believe," I said.

Josie and I stepped into the water. I only had a couple seconds before I had to hang up and start swimming.

"Oh, you know what? I'm seeing that dumb machine fire in the distance. Meet you there?" he said.

"Yup, we're in the water so I have to let you go," I replied.

"See you there," Matt said.

I hung up, putting my phone away and setting my bag on the beach.

"Who was that?" Josie asked.

We swam, I pulled my mane behind my shoulder so it rested behind me and wouldn't interfere with my paddling. My thick fur and mane weren't meant for the water, but I could make it work.

"Guy I've been on a couple dates with, we're supposed to be meeting for a date," I said. "But helping Meg's more important."

"And he's going to meet you to help fight the humans off?" Josie asked.

I nodded, a smile taking over my face. I tried to focus on the battle ahead. I could hear Meg roar, a few others already with her slashed at a few battleships. A pair of flying kaiju, one like a dragon, the other a three-headed hummingbird with a fifty-foot wingspan, swiped at the jets and helicopters coming after the group.

"Damn, that's nice," Josie said.

"Right?" I said.

We paddled a bit further and came upon our first destroyer. The water was shallow enough we could stand. The two of us roared. Josie had a wide mouth and only four teeth, but her jaw had the power of three kaiju. She bit the tail end of the destroyer. I raised my claws, swinging them down onto the ship. The humans abandoned ship, what ones we didn't destroy immediately.

Two fighter jets came after us. Their missiles impacted, exploding against both me and Josie.

"I can't get to them," Josie said.

"Watch this." I brought my head down, rotating my neck and torso, I got my mane flowing, then cracked my head the other way, sending the mane flying up. It smacked one jet's wings, sending it careening toward the water. The other wobbled from the concussive wave caused by my hair flying by it. The air was enough to cause the engines to sputter. It descended with a failing power supply, just enough to let Josie jump from the water and bite the jet.

It exploded. Pieces of it splashing against the water. Josie and I turned toward the next portion of the fleet.

"Nice whip!" a voice shouted. "Don't know I've ever seen a jet get whipped so hard it crashed into the water." Turning, it was Matt. He made great distance as his six, lanky legs curled through the water with ease. His tall body, capped off with a small, cat-like head and two, massive horns, ebbed through the water. He smiled. "I'm impressed."

"Thanks, for the compliment, and for coming," I said.

"Hey, I'll take any chance to get humans to leave us alone, plus I get to meet your friends," he said. Swiping at a small, frigate ship; it broke in half. Then he extended one arm to Josie. "I'm Matt."

Josie brought up one massive foot, using the round end to nudge his arm. "Name's Josie, appreciate it. Shall we?"

"After you," Matt said, ushering them toward the main armada.

The three of us waded through the water. Joining Meg and a few others, we fought. As a destroyer turned its cannons, I brought one arm up, letting it take the brunt of the shots. Each impact rocked my arm against my torso. Roaring, I swung that same arm down, breaking the destroyer at the bow. The ship tilted down into the water and sank.

To my right, a ship deploying fighter jets had six, lanky legs rise from the water around it. Matt wrapped his limbs around the ship, then lurched it into the water with a single pull.

Seeing the writing on the wall, the ships started to turn. As they fled, we stopped attacking. We were monsters, but we weren't total monsters. In unison, all of us kaiju roared, except Matt. He flailed his limbs, slapping them in the water to create large splashes in the water. I nudged him, looking out to the evacuating fleet. I encouraged him to join the call as we tried once more to give humans a warning to never return. He hesitated, looking almost embarrassed.

"Roar with me." I nudged him again.

"It's not impressive," he warned.

"We're kaiju, anything is impressive to humans," I said.

"Okay," he said.

I smiled. Turning to face the ships, I took in a huge breath, expanding my chest and let out my best roar. Matt did the same, at least in taking a huge breath. But what he let out wasn't a roar. It sounded like a sickly bird squawking. The high-pitched sound pierced my ears. Covering my right ear, I nodded, acknowledging the screech was quite different. His cry stopped, he slapped one more limb against the water, then turned to me.

"I tried to tell you," he said.

"It's not a roar, but it let them know you mean business," I replied. "Ah, that was kinda fun."

"Hell yeah, it was!" Meg shouted. "I was getting so sick of fighting on the shore, I can do it, but..." She raised her fins, awkwardly flailing them around. "You must be Matt?" She extended her fin, needing to use her arms to stay afloat.

Matt extended two of his limbs. He took her fin with one, then wrapped the other around it in a warm welcome. "Yes, you must be Meg?"

"Nice to meet you," Meg said. "Thanks for coming. Hope I didn't ruin anything."

"Of course not, night is young, sun is still out. Why I love summer," Matt said.

I tried to remain calm, but the weight of my soaked mane weighed me down. My paws were wide, but short, not conducive to long periods wading in the water. I was the same in the water as Meg was on land. I could fight, I could move, but not well.

"Anyways, I was thinking we could grab some food," Matt said.

I nodded, smiling and fighting the awkwardness of the swim.

"Should Josie and Meg join us?" Matt asked.

"No," Meg and Josie said in unison.

Meg waved her fin in denial. "We're perfectly fine, no need to tag along. You two have fun. Ah!" She slapped her fin against the water. "Damn humans, they're wading in the water."

"You guys have fun," Josie said.

Meg went to hug me, as she did, she felt my weight pull her down a bit. I used her body to keep me up for a bit of relief.

"Oh, dear god, sweetie," Meg said.

"I know, I'm so tired," I replied.

"It's not far from the shore, you want me to help you?" Meg asked.

"No, I can make it, just needed a second," I replied.

"Thanks for helping, hope they stay away, finally. Humans are the worst," Meg said.

"The worst!" I shouted in reply.

"Good luck. Hope it goes well," Meg said. "I'm going to go nab a sunken submarine."

"For what?" I asked.

"For later." Meg raised her brow a few times. "A shark kaiju can get hers, too, right?"

"You do you, Meg." I let her go and swam for the shore. As we reached the sand, my mane dragged against the ground, hundreds of gallons of water poured from the ends. I paused to grab the ends, twisting it around and squeezing the excess out. As I did, I felt a human holding on. I picked at it, then tossed it to the sand casually, hoping Matt wouldn't notice. They must have been grabbing on in the water, hoping to hitch a ride to the shore. Or had I not gotten rid of them all in the infection? They surely couldn't have held on through the whole fight, must have been survivors from the destroyer I sank. "What do you like to eat?" I asked, turning the focus away from it all.

"I'm not a picky eater, are you in the mood for anything?" he asked.

"I haven't had sushi in a while, there's a nice place not far from here." I nodded toward the north side of the shore.

"Let's do it," he said. We started walking. "It's been a while since I've had decent sushi, there's a place near mine that's not bad, but the choices are a little lim…" He stopped.

I turned toward him. He squinted and encouraged me to turn back the way I was facing by nudging me on the shoulder. "Keep facing that way."

"What is it?" I asked.

"Um, crap." He pinched a few strands of hair in my mane. Pulling something, a few strands stretched out as he pulled back. "Looks like a few humans held on. They're in your mane."

"Oh my god." I brought my paws up to my face, sighing. "I'm so embarrassed."

"Don't be," he said, sifting around my mane. "There were a lot of them in the water. They probably grabbed on to whatever they could. Your mane is long so they could grip those big strands of yours, hold on tight."

"Yeah, are you seeing a lot? I've thought of cutting it," I said.

"No, you shouldn't. Kaiju like you have incredible manes, glad you embraced it," he pulled another. "You should own it."

"Thanks," I smiled. It had been several different dates where the guy either stared at my mane, unsure of what to do about it, or talked about it so distractedly it was obvious they felt awkward seeing it. Then there others that told me mane was meant for male kaiju and it caused problems with how people perceived female kaiju. Those were the same ones that didn't want us fighting the humans. Matt was the first one to just give a compliment as if it were natural and what I should do, and liked that I did.

"You know what?" Matt said. "I'm seeing a few more. There are special combs for this, right?"

"Yeah, I have some," I replied. "I can deal with it."

"Well, there's a store right over there." He pointed. "Let's make a pit stop. We can sit on the beach and watch the sunset while I comb your hair for humans."

"No, you don't have to do that," I said.

"I don't have to do it, I want to do it," Matt said.

"Okay, you want to grab sushi to go? Have it there on the beach, too?" I asked.

"Sunset, beach, sushi, and human combing, couldn't think of anything better," Matt said. "Glad we fought humans together, Kimmi."

"Me too," I replied. As we walked for the store, I nudged him with my head, unable to hold his hand while walking on all fours. He took one of his six limbs and wrapped it around my mane. I'd found a good one.

"Beautiful" by Thomas A. Fowler
Robot Assassin in an Alternate Future

This future had light. The early morning light shone through the module door. The robot assassin stepped out from the module. It was more than the vibrant, morning sun adding warmth to the high clouds. There was stillness about what the robot assassin saw. Large waves crashed into more water. Their rhythm was calm, despite the size of the crests.

The robot couldn't understand the calm nature of the scene around him. He was programmed to prevent this future. It was a future where the oceans rose and consumed all land. He was to remove the hindering targets in power so the people could rise. Yet, there was a certain serenity that came from the people.

Pillars lifted skyscrapers high above the ocean floor. Cities had been constructed on platforms. He paced down the streets. As he moved block to block, the site looked similar to the present he understood, yet there was simplicity to the advancement. Merchants lined the streets; people spoke to one another. They were not staring down at their devices, reliant upon it for social validation. Rather, it seemed their plight in curing the world resurrected something his creator sought: community.

As he crossed another block, the robot turned to look back at his point of origin. Standing in the city center, he could not see the ocean. Had he generated here, he would've never been able to see that the ocean had consumed the planet. The robot paced about, seeing the desalination chambers that hung from the sides of the platform. They fed into a towering pillar. Row after row of vegetables and fruit lined each floor of the tower. Farmers used rope and climbing gear to harvest and tend to their crops. There were fewer buildings, but they rose higher than any skyscraper he knew in the present. Which he realized was now the past. Humanity found a way to rebuild and make a new way of life.

The robot returned to his generation point. This was an accident. The transport module showed an error in the coding. He had seen what the world could become through human error. Through communal learning. This was the future he was made to prevent. This couldn't be, his creator thought the assassination of world leaders would let the people create their own future. Yet, evidently, the people did on their own. The blue skies and vibrant clouds, orange and red with the rays of the sun, were the opposite of the world where he was programmed. There, the world was consumed by grey skies, robbed of conversation, interaction, and concern for others. He opened the control systems for the transport module.

A small girl approached him, her shadow amplified by the sun. She held a cup of juice. Condensation built on the cup. It dripped along her petite fingers.

"Hello," the robot said.

"What is that?" she squinted her dark brown eyes, pointing at the apparatus on his right arm.

"Something I use to get around," the robot tinkered with the code, bringing up the display for time travel. A rotating globe allowed the robot to choose its physical destination. The multiple time displays to adjust when he'd arrive there.

"Like a ship?" she asked.

"Similar," he did not look up.

"Looks fun," she took a sip from her juice.

"Are you not terrified of me?" he asked.

"No, why should I be?" she asked.

"Olivia," her mother called. She walked toward her daughter. "Who's that you're talking to?"

"A robot boy," she replied.

The woman wrapped her arm around her daughter. She pulled her in close.

"It's you," the mother said.

"I apologize. I do not understand your statement." The robot stopped working on the module to establish eye contact.

"Please, wait here," she grabbed her daughter by the hand. She forcibly dragged her along.

"Mom, why are we running from him?" the little girl asked.

The robot returned to the module. He had moments to leave before authorities were likely to converge on him. He tried to connect with the module to understand the programming. His code couldn't connect. He scanned for reasons for the lost connection, the network may have been corrupted. The error was deeper than he thought. He looked around; several people gathered around the module, glaring at his odd, and unknown presence. The mother spoke with an archaic looking old man on a bench. The robot had to leave. The module sparked to life, but he had no idea of the destination. He could end up in any realm with no idea how to return. He had to inform his creator of what he saw. He would have to demand a reset of his system, as sight of his target would trigger his assassination functions. Their firing meant no cognitive problem solving; only unflinching resolve until completion of his assigned task: assassination.

He sat inside the module, about to shut the door and remain hidden until he could solve the problem. He tried configuring only a location jump, going somewhere less crowded to avoid being seen or hunted, but he couldn't stay while the city inhabitants converged on his location. He reached for the controls to close the module doors, but stopped as a grizzled voice spoke to him.

"My friend," the old man sat on a motorized scooter. His hand outreached toward the robot. "My dear friend."

"What is this?" the robot assassin asked.

"You don't remember me, because according to you, we haven't met," the old man said. "You came into my pet store one day. I was just a teenager. You handed me three things. One is a chip to reprogram your module here. Another, this is a chip you are to place in your module so that you'd land here, see the world that could be. When you were programmed, that technology did not exist, humanity had to advance to make it. So now I'm giving them to you so that I can help you in the past."

The old man handed him the chips, they were in a sealed envelope. The robot replaced the chip that existed. The programming allowed him into the system. He looked at the other chip. He'd have to break into the laboratory to ensure he arrived here.

"You mean to say, I reprogrammed my module to land here?" the robot said.

"Yes, so you could see that your mission was not the course of action to be taken," the old man said.

"Thank you," he said. "The third item?"

The little girl pulled the flower from her hair. She lifted her hand as high as it could go, giving him that present.

"So that you know this was the course to take," the old man said.

"Many people must not have survived the ocean uprising," the robot said. "Weren't lives lost?"

"Yes, but far less than the world you were programmed to create," the old man said. "And from what you told me, this life is far greater than the one you made with your assassinations."

The robot took the flower. He stood on the transport module.

"Then there was a version of me that has seen the possibilities of my outcomes, overrode my programming to reach this future instead," the robot assassin said. "What is your name?"

"Ricky," he replied.

"Thank you," the robot assassin said.

The transport module sparked to life. Blue plasma rose from the base, wrapping around his legs like a child holding her mother.

"See you next time," the old man said.

The plasma overtook the robot. The module evaporated. The old man returned to his bench, enjoying juice with his granddaughter.

"Can't believe he showed up," the little girl drank from her juice.

"Now you believe me," he sipped from his cup.

"Yep," she replied. "Still don't believe you about that frog though."

"That's okay," the old man said. "Don't need you to. He was real to me."

He sat content. So many friends had come and gone. Each of them brought him to this moment, on a bench with his daughter and granddaughter, watching the sunrise.

"The Battle Cry of Freedom" by Jason Henry Evans

Dinosaur in an Alternate Future

CRACK.

Those damn rebels fired another shot. That ain't fair. They ain't actually rebels anymore. Riding a horse full bore is hard enough without Confederates after ya. It's really hard when you're black.

My name is Jeremiah, but everyone calls me Brevie.

My horse? His name is Jehoshaphat. He's a good horse, s'far as stallions go. Me? I'd rather have a mare. They run faster. They're also, ahem, less distracted, if you know what I mean. But I digress. You might want to know how I came to this sit-iation. Can't rightly tell, really.

I know I joined up with the Cavalry d'Afrique in Baton Rouge in 1863. That was ten years ago. Saw me some service at Vicksburg. We guarded confiscated cotton in Eastern Tennessee when the word came round what happened at Gettysburg. Apparently, rebel General John Bell Hood split us blue coats on the left in a place called the Wheat

Field, then ran up a hill called Little Round Top. The next day everything went to hell for General Meade. Half the army fled north to Philly, the other half went south to Washington.

We weren't too concerned, 'cause the Mississippi was now a free river! Grant took Vicksburg on the same day Lee forced Mead to retreat. There was talk of invading Georgia, taking Atlanta. Finally ending the war.

Well, that never happened.

The rebels in Pennsylvania were broken, starving men. They sacked Philly, then wintered there. The blue coats were just as broken. A year went by before anything else happened in the east.

Then Lincoln was shot. Lawd that broke my heart. And it just went on and on. No end in sight. About 1869 we got orders to move into Missouri. Some Cherokee rebel named Watie had led an invasion from the Indian Territory. They planned to meet with Quantrille's Raiders and take Columbia. At least, that's what we were told. Probably what happened was someone thought it be a good idea to have colored troops face injuns.

Anyways, we get there winter of '70. Two days after disembarking from the river boats in St. Louis, we rode hard to Springfield, where a mélange of Confederate militia, Cherokee, and guerilla cavalry were about to take the city.

We show up and take our place in the cavalry line. Then on Jan. 22nd, we got orders to charge the left flank, make'em move, ya know? So we charged. That's when they opened up with two Gattling guns. Spraying death on us and every other fool in a blue coat. Things got chaotic, let me tell you.

Now, our colonel, was a proper West Point man. Lt. Colonel Abraham Schwartz. Pennsylvania Dutch, they called him. Good, Godly white folk, understand? Cool as riverboat gambler, he starts giving orders. While the rest of them Yankees were losing their minds, ole Colonel Schwartz calmly got us out of there.

And that was the problem. See, we retreated south and west, into the Indian Territory.

Seemed as long as the rebs was winning, those Cherokee sang Dixie all nice and purdy. So we never got a chance to rest, really. We kept moving, trying to hook up with other Federals, but without any luck.

About six months ago we lost the colonel. Leg wound went bad. Awful fever. His last words to us were "get to Colorado. Make a life for yourselves. Preserve the Union." Colonel promoted a creole sergeant named Napoleon Ruckus brevet major. After he died, Major Ruckus named me *Brevet lieutenant.*

He says, "Jeremiah, you can read good, cantcha?"

I says, "Yup. Pretty good."

"Then I name you Brevet Lieutenant."

"Why?"

"We've got to have our papers strait. Do it all military like. That means reading. I don't care for it. So y'awse got to do."

"Yes, Major." I saluted him and they've called me Brevie, ever sense.

The last year we've been sneaking west, avoiding rebs and Texas rangers. On occasion, we hear stories about how bad it is back East. Don't know who to believe. Hope none of its true.

So you might be asking about the reb's shooting at us? Well, they aren't exactly shooting at all of us, and they ain't exactly rebs. These here Texas rangers. See, we robbed a bank in Amarillo.

Surprised? So were they. Being a Negro is hard. But there is one advantage to being colored in Texas. You're invisible. That is, until, you pull a pistol.

Another shot whizzed by my head.

"Brevie, we ain't got much time."

That was Sargent Cassius. He's a sour man, but deadly with a rifle. We got four other soldiers with us. All of us with tired horses and saddle bags filled with Confederate gold coins.

"What we gonna do, Brevie?"

He was referring to the Canada River. Soon we'd have to cross it, and that's where those rangers would have us.

We can't stop. My revolver is empty, so I can't reload, not at full gallop.

Another bullet whizzes by my head. A light blinds me, momentarily. I grin, then turn sharply into the river. My men follow. The gunshots get closer. We hit the Canada, hard.

"Was this a good idea?" Cassius asks. We've forded a third of the river.

"There was a light. That's gotta be Napoleon with his looking glass," I said.

Sure enough, we get another twenty feet across the river and rifle fire opens up from the trees and the bushes. I looked back to see three, then four rangers fall off their horses. The rest fire from the river bank. We pick off another two or three before they withdraw.

We rode into a thicket of pine to whoops and hollers. Black men in city trousers, workers jeans, and union uniforms come out from among the trees, cheering us. A tall buck, some six feet, with wild hair, like Moses, streaked gray and black, stands up. He took the reins of Jehoshaphat. His name is George, but we call him Grandpa. "That was powoful riding, Brevie. Powoful."

"Thank you, Grandpa. Where the other horses holed up?" I asked.

"We made camp on the other side of this here hill. Napoleon thought you'd need some help."

"Lieutenant, report." That stern voice could only belong to the major. He a brevet too, but don't like being reminded of it. So I don't.

"Yes, sir." I hurried over to a large pine. Major Ruckus was smoking his pipe. Unlike the rest of the men, he kept his uniform spotless. Some of the others call him a house nigger. I tell'em, "He ain't no house nigger, he born free. He a Creole. That's just their way."

The major turned to me with an upturned eyebrow. "Well, Brevie?"

"Went off just like you said, sir. We were completely invisible until we entered the bank. Some old man tried to shoo us out, until he saw the pistol."

"No white folks hurt?"

"No sir, none but the rangers."

Major Ruckus sighed in relief. "I'm glad they ain't many colored people around the panhandle. I'd hate to think they'd get punished for our crimes. Well done, Brevie."

"Sir? Now what?" I ask.

"Well, we hike back over the hill, meet up with the rest. Turn in, get up before dawn tomorrow and head west, into New Mexico territory."

I wiped sweat from my forehead. "And back to the Union."

"Not quite. Frankie brought this in. He scouted south of the river. Found a stage coach rest stop. He took this while he was there." The major handed me a newspaper, about two weeks old. The headline said Confederates re-took Santa Fe.

"Shit."

"Shit is right," the major replied.

"What'll we do?" I ask.

"Nuthin we can do. Can't go back to Amarillo. Can't go north, not yet. Nuthin' there. We got to go west. Get to Santa Fe, get some supplies and make for the pass north to Trinidad."

I smiled. "Sargent Cassius, bring dem saddle bags."

"Yes, sir," Cassius said.

My smile must have been infectious 'cause Major Ruckus smiled, too. "Whadja get, Brevie?"

"Two hundred dollars, mostly in script. But we got sixty of it in gold." Cassius walked into the meeting with three saddle bags about to burst. I opened one and showed the major.

"Who-wee! We can get a whole lot with this. Food, new canteens, horses. The works. Ya'll did good." The major took a puff on his pipe. "Now let's make tracks. The faster we're out of here, the better."

That night I dreamed of Gloria again. She's my wife. Tain't seen her in over a year. Some say the Confederates 'round Atlanta gonna try to move south and west, retake Mobile. If they do, New Orleans will be next. I'm scared what those reb's will do to a colored woman.

In my dream she's wearin' that pretty blue dress, the one with the white lace around the neck. Her eyes twinkle in the afternoon sun, full of tears. I hold her close, one last time before I get on that train. She smiles meekly.

I dream that dream all the time. Lord, do I miss Gloria.

"Brevie. Brevie, wake up." Cassius shakes me out of a deep sleep. "Ya hear dat?" He says.

I listen. A night wind howls in the distance. "I hear the wind."

Cassius grits his teeth and shakes his head. "No, *in the wind*."

I listen again. In the sound of the wind, something lingers. The sound is faint, but baleful. I can't place it, but I don't like. "Cassius, is this why you woke me?"

"No, sir. Time to get up. Sky is already purple. Those Texas rangers will be back. Time to get up and go."

He's right. I gave the order to break camp. By sunrise, all the men were mounted, eating jerky and dried fruit as we got ready to ride.

Three days we rode through desert, sage brush and tumbleweeds. The Lawd was with us though. No sign of Texas Rangers, or the rebels.

We got through some rocky hill country when one of our scouts galloped up.

"Injuns! Injuns!" he hollered.

Sure enough, gun fire followed him. A war party of thirty hot on his tail.

"DO NOT FIRE!" thundered the major.

"Hold your fire," I add.

As the party got closer, we heard their war cries and whelps. I don't know about you, but they sounded like rebel yells, to me.

The injuns got closer, then stopped, about thirty yards away. I guess they realized they were outnumbered. We had 250 on horseback when we got to Missouri. We got about 110 now. Still, that's a lot more than the injuns.

"Major," I ask. "What'll we do?"

"Just wait. We don't provoke them, maybe they don't shoot at us."

"But we can take'em."

The major looked at me like a child who stole something. "Fool. They got about thirty *in this war party.* Do you think that's all the men they have?"

The major had a point.

We waited there maybe ten minutes before the injuns rode away. It was midday and a creek was nearby, so we decided to break for camp. Major soured everyone's mood when he ordered breastworks built. He was right though. Breastworks would protect the camp, in case those injuns came back, which they did.

About sun down, a lone rider carrying a white flag rode about sixty feet from the camp. Major sent me and Cassius to figure out what was what.

"We gonna shoot injuns now?" Cassius asked.

"Hope not."

We rode out.

I thought all injuns wore buckskins and used bows. Not this one. He wore tan work pants and a plaid shirt with a leather vest.

"Who are you?" the injun said.

"We're the 4th colored Cavalry, U.S. Army," I replied. "You speak English."

"The white men arm their slaves now?"

"We ain't no slaves. Most of us free men born. Some used to be slaves. Ain't you seen Union troops before?" I ask.

The man before us cocked his head and furrowed his brow. "You don't fight for white man?"

"Not the ones you refer to."

"You wear blue coats." The injun said.

"Yes sir. The finest uniforms in the Federal army."

His eyes widened underneath his red bandanna. "You are Federals?"

I smiled. "Federal cavalry."

"The elders will want to speak with you."

A baleful, high pitched scream floated softly on the wind. The injun looked around. "You come with me, now."

Cassius and I trotted forward.

"No. Only you."

I turned to Cassius, cock my head back to camp.

"Good, didn't want to go with him, anyways."

I trot forward. "Beggin your pardon, but what nation are you, anyways?"

"Apache."

We travelled for an hour before we arrived in their camp. Strange structures, seven feet high and made of brush and hide, hid the glows of cooking fires. Occasionally, a child stood at the entrance of these homes. We got to a large dwelling, covered in buckskins. Warriors impeded my way at gun point.

"Take your guns off." My host said. Not wanting to die tonight, I obliged.

We went inside where several old men sat around a fire and spoke. My guide started to speak in some language I ain't heard. I stood silent for some time fo' someone spoke to me.

A man, much older than me, with streaks of grey in his hair, spoke first. "Naiche says your men did not fire when we fired upon them. This was wise."

"We want no fightin' with you," I said.

"Are you the Damnyankees, the white men talk about?"

I smiled. "We work with them, yes."

"Why are you here?"

"We are just passing through. Trying to get to Santa Fe, then North to Trinidad, maybe Denver."

"The white men in gray control that place. Will you fight them?"

I shook my head no. "We want no problems. We are tired, sir."

The old man looked around, spoke in his own language. Others replied. It got heated. Then, he looked at me again and spoke. "If the grey coats find out we let you through, it could mean trouble for us."

He had me there. They could get in trouble. How could we work this out, so everyone wins?

"Sir, we want no trouble from anyone. All we want to do is ride through yo land, graze our horses, maybe hunt a little. We'll be gone in a week, maybe two."

"You will take much, like the white man does." The old Apache's eyes narrowed on me.

I smiled. "Then we'll pay for the right. Up front."

"What do you mean, Damnyankee?"

"We have some of the white man's money. We can give you twenty dollars in paper money and ten dollars in gold. Will that be enough?" I didn't really have the right to give up the company's hard-gotten, stolen cash, but I didn't rightly know what to do.

The old Apache spoke in his own language. Others spoke after him. Silence followed before he spoke again. "Twenty gold, forty in paper."

Don't matter you black, white, or red, haggling is haggling.

"12 in gold, 25 in paper," I said.

The Apache scratched his chin. "18 in gold, 30 in paper."

"15 in gold, 30 in paper."

The old man smiled. I guess we had a deal.

Major Ruckus wasn't too happy about the gold, but he saw there wasn't much he could do. I had negotiated a peaceful ride through Apache lands. Their scouts showed us where the good water was, helped us bring down a couple of deer, and even brought us good, root vegetables. Wild onions, celery and carrots, and a whole bunch of edible seeds I had never seen. Dem Apache was good to us.

We rode for about a week through Apache lands, crossed the Canada River again, going west. Things were fine between us. One night though, their scouts told stories about the *Thunderbirds*. Great, flightless birds that would ambush a man and eat'em. That they'd been here, in these hills, since the time when the animals could speak. Those stories were scary, but not as scary as the stories we told.

One day we came through a high meadow and down into a valley. In the middle of that valley was the sleepy old town of Santa Fe.

"Well, I guess this is the end of our journey," I said to our guide, Naiche.

"Be safe, be well, Brevie. We must go, before the grey coats come."

"Thank you, my friend."

Naiche turned his palomino around to ride off, then took my forearm. "Those hills and mountains to the north and west. Ghosts and Thunderbirds rule there. *Be careful.*" His eyes were so earnest, so serious, that it scared me. He let go of my arm, turned and rode off.

We made camp some half mile back from that point, in that meadow. Major wanted me to go with a scouting party to see what the situation was. "Take Cassius, Frankie, and Grandpa," the major said.

We got out of our uniforms. The last thing we needed was to alarm the rebs that a colored cavalry unit was here. We took off or hid most of the horse tacks that could identify us Federal cavalry, too.

The town was small. No more than thirty buildings or so. Some of them looked abandoned. That was to be expected though, 'cause of the occupation. There were few people walking the streets or riding. There were fewer rebs then we expected, too. We tied up our horses at an abandoned house and prayed they'd still be there when we returned.

The middle of town looked deserted. As we walked down the streets, people would gawk at us. I guess they ain't seen many colored folk around here. I was getting nervous when I heard a crash. I looked around to see a woman, about a block away, picking up something in the rode.

"Let's check it out," Cassius said.

"Why not."

"You stupid injun!" an old man howled. "Well, I don't know how you'll pay for a new one. Now get your junk and get."

He was an old man, skinny and pale. The injun – Apache, by the look of it—busied herself with picking some things out of the street. Some great, clay jar had shattered.

"Ma'am, might we be of assistance?" Cassius said, all smooth.

What is he doing? We can't get involved.

The old man turned quick to look at us. He almost fell back in shock. "Where you *niggers* from?"

"Amarillo, Sir," Grandpa said, quick as nuthin. "We teamsters in Texas. And free men. Heard there might be work in Santa Fe."

"Free men, huh? Well, you'd better register with Colonel Ritchey. He don't take to injuns or Mexicans. And he probably won't take to niggers, either."

Now, every inch of my being wanted to shoot that man. Or at least tell him what he could do with his registration. But we spies today. So I doffed my cap and said "Thank you, sir. We'll register right away."

The old man wandered back into his store. Meanwhile, Cassius helped the Apache woman. She, however, didn't want our help.

"I'm fine" she barked.

"Ma'am, let us help," Cassius said.

"I'll manage," was the reply.

That's when I stepped in. "Well, if you won't let us help you, maybe you can help us? We're looking for a furrier. We've got some horses that need lookin' after."

The woman stood up. "You mean a furrier who don't mind helping people like us?"

I nodded.

"Señor Ramos, down the way and to the right. He's a good man. He'll help you." The woman stood and placed the box of items on her right hip, careful not to wrinkle her red skirt too much. "Be careful. That colonel is mean. He's liable to hang you."

"We can take care of ourselves," I say. "But thank you for the information."

We got down to the furrier: an old Mexican, but friendly. We told him about our needs and he agreed to help. Señor Bustos was his name. The man's eyes narrow on something behind us. I turned to see some rebels walking down the street. I turned back to see the look of hate in Señor Bustos' eyes. I know that look well.

I ask one last question, "Señor Bustos, can we keep this, quiet-like? Just between us? We can pay extra?"

Now his eyes narrowed on me. He looked real hard, then nodded. "Come by tomorrow, at dusk."

I nod in agreement.

"Brevie," Grandpa asks as we leave, "when we getting' some victuals?"

"Patience, Grandpa. We'll be back after dusk. We'll bring the horses to get shoed and buy supplies."

Grandpa smiled and nodded.

The sun set and we brought ten horses into town. The furrier spoke while he worked on the first horse. "Take your men and go across the street to get your supplies."

I nodded and took the four with me.

The general store was an old building, made of that there adobe stuff. Inside an old man, hair full of pomade, swept. He wore a black suit with a shopkeeper's white apron waving around his calves with every sweep of the broom.

"Evening," I said.

He looked up, "Close the door."

We did as he asked. "So you are the *Federales*?"

I nodded.

"Claudia," he called out.

A few minutes later, a beautiful Mexican girl comes out. Her white dress floated about her ankles as she walked. "Sí, Papa?"

He gave her instructions in Spanish. She nodded and went to get a large sack of flour.

The shopkeeper and his daughter laid out several large sacks of flour, beans, and corn.

"Everything seems to be in order, so I'll – "

"Well, well, well. What do we have here?"

Lawd, things were goin' so well. I turned and saw three rebels saunter into the store.

"Looky here, we got *niggers* in town. When you boy's get here? And where's your master?" The tall one with the white cowboy hat looked at me.

I removed my hat. "We's just up from Amarillo, sir. We's teamsters. Heard might be work in New Mexico territory."

"Ain't that right? Who's your master, boy?"

I had to think quickly. "Master Ruckus just settled a ranch east of here. Wanted us to get supplies." Would he buy it?

"Woo- Wee! Well would you look at that!" Another rebel called out.

The first one turned to see what was so important. The second rebel, a greasy, skinny man eyed the shopkeeper's daughter, Claudia.

"I do love me some *Mezican señoritas.*"

The tall reb simply forgot I was there and started leering at Claudia.

Claudia shifted her weight from foot to foot. Then the greasy one started to cat call her.

"Señors, please," pleaded the shopkeeper. But the rebels got handsy.

Claudia tried to leave, but the greasy one grabbed her.

That's when it got bad.

Out of the corner of my eye, I see Freddie grab a shovel and hit one in the head.

"What are you doing?" I cry out.

Another rebel pulled his gun, but Grandpa bludgeoned him in the face with a skillet.

The tall one turns around, confused. "What –" he tries to get out, but Lincoln stabs the rebel in the neck with a pitchfork.

In a matter of seconds, it's all over.

The shopkeeper ran to the door, peeked out. "You have to leave, *ahora.*"

"We'll bury the bodies out back."

"No," he said. "There is no time."

"Papa," the girl begins, "they have horses, don't they?"

I nod at her.

"Let them take the *Confederales* with them. It's dark, no one will know."

It's a good plan. Better than what I was thinking. "Alright."

"Do you have a camp?" asked the shopkeeper.

"No. There not from here, papa. I must take them."

"NO. Absolutely not," yells the shopkeeper.

Claudia grabbed her father's hand. "You think I am safe at your side. That you can hide me from danger. Well you can't papa. We are all in danger. So let me play my part. You are a patriot by giving these men supplies. Let me be a patriot by leading them north."

I've never met a woman, black, white, Indian or Mexican, as strong as this señorita was.

"Alright," her father said, reluctantly.

Claudia led us out of Santa Fe and north, into the hills. We buried the rebs in shallow graves under a grove of trees. A few miles north we made camp, 'cause the horses were too tired to ride any more. So we make a fire, and eat some jerky and tortillas Claudia grabbed before leaving. We all sat around the fire, quiet out of weariness.

Claudia looks at me. "You're a long way from home, *Yanquis.*"

"Well, they say 'join the army and you'll have adventure.'"

She chuckled at that.

"Why were you so keen to help black troops?"

"After the Battle of Glorietta Pass, my brother got excited and joined the army."

"Really," I said.

Claudia nodded and smiled. "My father was furious. But, there was nothing he could do."

"Where's your brother at now?" I ask, hopin' he ain't dead.

"I don't know. After Gettysburg, his regiment was called to Kansas. He wrote letters home occasionally. He would even come home on leave. But that was three years ago." Her voice cracked as she talked. "So you see—what is your name?"

"Everyone calls me Brevie."

"You see, Brevie, I must be a patriot. My brother does his part and so must I."

There wasn't much talkin' after that. We finished our food and bunked. But I got that eerie feeling again. Somethin' in the sound of the wind.

I woke up right before dawn. The fire still burned bright. I gazed into the flames until I heard unearthly howls that I still can't describe.

"It's the Thunderbirds. The Apache say the Earth mother put them here to protect these hills. The mother made these hills sacred. The Thunderbirds protect them."

I don't know if it was a peculiar wind, or wolves or what, but I know the sound was terrifying. It continued until dawn. We ate the remaining jerky and tortillas, then get back to our camp.

Boy, were those soldiers happy to see us! Now, I don't know, but it might have been the forty pounds of flour, beans and corn we were carrying, too. I'd like to think it was my sparkling personality.

"Ya'll men did good. Real good," says Major Ruckus. "Let me meet this Mexican woman."

Claudia comes up and gives a sharp salute. This surprised the major. But he returned it.

"Can you get word to your people? We have many more horses need new shoes." Major Ruckus rattles the bag of coins. "We can pay."

"We can't do it in town," Claudia says. "My father has a ranch west of town. Be there in two days. Will have more supplies there. Your men can rest there, too."

"I thank you," Major Ruckus said.

Claudia smiled, got back on her horse and left.

For the next day we try and relax, groom our horses, get some sleep. I assign pickets.

"Brevie! Brevie!" Cassius calls out the next evening.

"What, Cassius?"

Cassius was grey as a ghost, bent over, vomiting. "Sir," he tried to start.

"Easy," I tell him. "I need a canteen!" I call out.

Cassius swallows hard, gains his composure. "Sir. We were . . . doin' picket duty . . . around those shallow graves . . ."

"And?"

"Those rebs . . . dey been *butchered.*"

"What?"

"Butchered, Brevie. Their graves were dug up, parts of 'em all over the area. Torsos with chunks missing." Cassius' eyes showed a fear I hadn't seen since I saw a man get whipped.

I didn't know what to do. I'm sure he was just scared. But of what? Animals can smell a kill, can't they? It could have been bears, or wildcats, or something else. Whatever it was, we didn't have time to figure it out.

Our third day in New Mexico was frightfully cold. A storm came in from the west. We didn't want to call too much attention, so we kept our camp fires low.

About noon that Apache girl shows up in camp, escorted by one of our pickets.

"I'm here to escort you to Señor Bustos' ranch. It's only about half a day's ride. We should get there about dusk."

Major Ruckus looked at me. I nodded.

"Calvary D'Afrique, MOUNT UP!"

We weren't riding our beat nags for an hour before it started raining. First a drizzle, then a hard rain. Thunder and lightning was bad, too. We were tired, sick, sore and wet. The only thing good about that day was the storm drowned out that eerie cry at night.

We got to the ranch. It was on a plain, with a wooded berm to its north. A small barn sat to the south. I looked forward to sleeping on fresh, dry hay.

Major sent scouts ahead to the front door. We saw them go in. We didn't think nuthin' of it. Until the muzzle fire.

Gunfire belched out from the house. Machine gunfire. We had two, shot horses before we knew what was going on.

Then rifle fire came from the barn. Men panicked.

I saw Grandpa fall. Then Major Ruckus died.

I called out "RETREAT," amid the thunder and machine gun rounds. I didn't see where anybody else went. I rode blindly into the storm.

Ten years. Ten years of fighting Johnny Reb. Ten years of showing what us black bucks could do on the battlefield. Now it was all gone.

I sat under a pinon tree, shivering and wet during the storm. Those rebs sent pickets after us, but the storm was so bad it spooked their horses. For a while I just sat under that tree and wept. I stayed there until I heard something cry.

A deep, whiny shriek. Something in pain. Something scared.

Then I heard rustling in the brush. I pulled my revolver out, cocked the hammer. Flashes of lightning shadowed a large figure. Was it those *Thunderbirds* Claudia warned me about?

The sounds got closer. The thunder shook me. I was powerful scared. That Apache girl came through the brush, holding one of our horses. On it was Cassius, unconscious.

I moved to help. Cassius had been shot in the shoulder. It seemed to be a clean wound, though I would know more in morning. We tied the horse up next to mine. The three of us tried to cuddle for warmth. Fitfully, slowly, we fell asleep.

I woke up before dawn again. The storm had slowed to a drizzle. In the distance, that deep, whiny shriek continued and echoed off the hills. I had heard it all night long. My curiosity was killing me, I got up.

"Let it be," the Apache girl said.

I got up anyways. I followed the sound, down the hill and up the other side. I could hear rustling in the brush ahead. Then I heard voices. My heart pounded. I could go back or take the chance of being captured.

The creature's shrieks made up my mind.

I continued through the brush until I got to a clearing. There, was the oddest thing I had ever seen. It was about four feet long, with a lizard-like tail. It had a large beak, like a turkey, but bigger. On its feet were large talons and its arms were covered in bright, fluffy feathers. It looked like a turkey and a peacock had a baby.

It was stuck in a bear trap. It looked at me with fear, but also desperation.

I approached it slowly.

It reared back, as if it wanted to get away. I took another step – and it snapped at me with its beak.

"Whoa fella," I started. "I just want to help."

I don't know what propelled me to go farther, but I did. Maybe because it's whining scared the beejezus out of me. Maybe I pitied the pain it was in. Or maybe I knew what it's like to be shackled and chained.

I launched myself at the release spring. It opened up and the bird was free. It ran down the hill, limping as it went. I sat there, for a moment, proud of letting the... what was that thing, anyways? I hiked back to my pinon tree but heard odd sounds. Damn reb was tracking me. I pulled my pistol to see...

The colorful, flightless bird.

"Go on now, *get!*" I tried to shew it away. It cocked its head at me.

"Go away now, back to your mammy, or whatever you birds have."

It honked at me, like an inquisitive goose. I tried to ignore it, throw things at it. It just kept following me.

"Where did you go, Brevie?" The Apache asked.

The bird bounded in front of me.

"What?" The Apache girl began to tremble. Then she started muttering something in her language.

"You stole it?"

"No! It was hurt, in a trap, I released it."

"It is sacred to my people, Brevie."

"Well then you take it," I said.

"It goes where it wants to go,"

It limped up to the horses, who skittered away and whinnied in dismay.

"Whoa girl . . . boy . . . whatever."

It limped up to me, honked in my face. I wanted to back up, but it did the damndest thing: it nuzzled me. Put its big 'ole head under my chin and rubbed, leaning on me.

"Nice . . . bird."

The thunder cracked in the morning sky and it jumped, sniffed around. All of a sudden, it bound down the hills we was on and ran off.

"What the hell?"

I turned to see Cassius sit up.

"It's a fevah dream, ain't it, Brevie?" Cassius asked.

"The gods favor us," said Imala, the Apache girl.

"Favor, huh?" I huffed. "Why couldn't they favor us last night?" I sat down exhausted, shivering from the cold. "What the hell happened?"

"I don't know," said Imala.

I was too scared to think about it last night. This morning? Too curious about the *Thunderbird.* But it hit me now. "Did those people in town, that grocer and his daughter, did they cross us?"

Imala shook her head. "Those rebs have been harassing the Mexicans and us since they took Santa Fe. No, they couldn't have."

"Then what happened?" I asked.

Imala sighed and rubbed her forehead. "I don't know." She got up from the ground. "I will go into town, see what's happened. Stay here. Rest."

"What if that bird returns? Can we eat it?" Cassius asked a good question.

The look of horror on Imala's face answered the question. She grabbed Cassius' horse and rode out.

That afternoon, the sun peaked from the storm clouds. You'd think rain would be the least of our problems, what with us in a desert and all, but it misted and drizzled all afternoon. I made a fire for warmth. It helped—a little. The problem was we were damp as well as cold.

I checked on Cassius' shoulder. He was lucky the bullet passed through. I prayed he won't take a fever.

By evening, the storm looked like it was just about done. Light rain came down at dusk. Thunder came from somewhere west, which was good. It meant the storm was passing.

Crack.

I look at Cassius.

"Brevie," he says, "taint no thunder. That there was gunfire."

Crack.

I toss my pistol to Cassius and take '66 Winchester from his saddle bag.

Crack.

Followed by the scream of a horse. I don't like this at all.

I hang low, behind some pinons and sage brush, walking towards the gunfire. Soon I hear rebel yells. That damn, rebel yell followed by more gunfire.

In between flashes of lightning, I see Imala, on foot, trying to get away. Behind her some hundred yards are five rebs. They can't follow into the brush, not on horseback. I grind my teeth in anger. Dey could've shot her at any time. *Dey's huntin her.*

I sit behind a rock, resting my muzzle on top of it. Thunder echoes in the distance.

She gets closer.

One of the rebs dismounts, laughing.

I can hear Imala's distress, her heavy breathing. I aim and fire. Dat reb ain't laughing no more. Imala makes it to me, runs past in a panic. No mind. I'm on her heels. We climb back to our makeshift camp.

"What the hell happened?" Cassius asks, pointing my pistol at me.

"Rebs, dat's what."

"They . . . arrested the shopkeeper." Imala panted.

Crack.

Both of us duck.

Crack.

A bullet hits the pinon tree. Bits of bark fly everywhere.

That damn campfire. I start stomping it out, so wee's ain't targets.

Crack.

Another bullet comes by.

"You *darkies throw down them guns.* We ain't gonna hurtcha." This was followed by laughter.

Crack.

The bushes rustled all around us. How did we get surrounded?

Crack.

I got you now, you sonofabitch. I know where that muzzle fire came from. I take a shot and hear a man scream.

"I'll get you, you black monkey."

You'll have to excuse Johnny Reb, he ain't that original with his retorts.

More rustling started in the bushes.

Click.

Shit.

"Alright you black bastards, drop yo weapons," says a man in butternut wearing a cowboy hat.

I comply. So does Cassius.

"You got'em, Sam?" Another voice in the bushes steps out to our right.

"I got'em," Sam says.

More rustling. How many did they bring?

"SAM," yells the first one. We turn to look and the reb is gone. Screaming trails off down the hill.

"Joe? JOE!" Rebel Sam hollers. His eyes dart from us to where his friend was. "How many you here, boy?"

"Just us," I say.

"You lying ni—"

In the distance, more screams. It echoed off the hills followed by begging and more screaming.

The rebel Sam's eyes darted back and forth.

Out of the brush my little friend comes hopping in, squawking.

"What the hell?" says rebel Sam, followed by more screams in the distance.

The bird turns to face rebel Sam and starts to honk at him while it bounces from side to side. Almost like it was protecting me.

Rebel Sam fired at the bird, but missed – the bird was quick.

Just then the reb cries out in pain, leaps forward, and lands awkwardly.

I will never get this moment out of my head. Another bird leaps on the reb's chest and starts pecking at his face. The reb tries to protect himself, tries to fight, but the bird kept pecking.

And this bird? It wasn't four feet tall, like the one I rescued. It was six feet tall, and I don't know how long, what with the night and everything. It had yellow, green, and red feathers running down its neck to all over its body. And it was eating that man.

After a half-dozen pecks, the rebel stopped fighting. The bird, *the Thunderbird,* took a meaty portion out of his chest, like a chicken would catch a worm, tilted its head skyward and swallowed it whole.

"What in the –" Cassius picked up my pistol.

"Cassius, leave it be."

It shrieked something fierce and started to eat some more. Two more came out from the bushes, just as big as the first. One of them made its way towards me. I knew I was a dead man. Then something peculiar happened. The little one, the one I saved. He jumps in my lap, starts nuzzling me and honking at the bigger birds.

The three make their way to me and start sniffing. All of them with bloody beaks.

"What de doin', Brevie?"

"I don't rightly know, Cassius."

"Maybe they just like *white boys*?"

Suddenly one of them turns towards Imala and honks. She pulls something out of a bag on her hip. She offers it to the Thunderbird, head down, like in prayer.

It sniffs it, cocks its head, sniffs it again.

I will admit, at this point I pissed myself.

The Thunderbird ate out of Imala's hand. She prayed in her Apache while the Thunderbird nibbled out of her hand.

Then one of the big ones begins to nuzzle me, like my little friend.

My grandpappy was an itinerant preacher in the Louisiana delta. He used to say *the Lord works in mysterious ways.* Well I'm living proof of that.

The next day, Imala took our horse and round up about thirty survivors. I saw Grandpa die. Lincoln, too. Someone said they found Major Ruckus' body all shot up. That put me in charge, and I had a plan.

"You crazy, Brevie, you know that?" I knew Cassius was feeling better 'cause he was getting ornery.

"Dat may be, but I'ze in charge. Besides, don'tcha wanna get them rebs? Dey can't be that many left. Watcha figure, Imala?"

Imala rubbed the mane of her horse as we rode back into Santa Fe. "I say they have no more than fifty fighting men."

"See, Cassius. We could liberate Santa Fe in the name of the Republic."

Cassius grunted.

I took one last look at the men at my side. Ten years we fought together. Ten years of proving to white men – North and South – dat we was as good as any of dem.

"Ready . . . CHARGE!"

Our bugler had died long ago. So we whupped it up, like the rebs did. We rode into that town like Christ on the judgement day. Imala told us where dem rebs bunked, so we rode down there first. Sure enough, dey didn't think Mexicans and darkies would be brazen enough to attack dem. They scattered like mice.

I sent five men inside. Sure enough, that kindly furrier, the clerk, and his daughter were all tied up in there.

"Gracias," the clerk began.

"No time. Can you ride?"

He nodded 'yes.'

"Good. Just one last thing to do." I rode over to the flag pole and took down the Southern Cross. "Any you rebs can hear me, listen. Dis here Federal Cavalry has officially liberated this town in the name of the Republic. Kindly surrender yourselves or abandon yo posts. If you *seccesh* don't like it, come and get us."

We turned around and trotted north. I was hoping having darkies embarrass them would get their dander up and I was right. We hadn't left town before gunfire echoed from behind.

So we began to ride – hard.

We rode through that northern valley, turning left and right. The crack of pistols and whoops of rebel yells got closer by the minute.

Cassius looked at me worried. I couldn't blame him. They were on us now, no more than thirty yards away.

"NOW!"

Cassius and Imala veered off a dirt path. I prayed dey would be in time. Meanwhile dem rebs were on us hot.

The road north started to climb. Our horses started to tire and the rebs gained on us. It was almost over now. Der rebel yells was fierce. Dey horses screamed. I turned to fire my pistol and saw a Thunderbird leap from behind a pinon tree and take down a reb. It was followed by another one.

Dose crackers weren't doing a rebel yell, dey was screaming in fear.

"Wheel around, boys." We turned and made our stand. My men took fired dey Winchesters, careful not to hit dem Thunderbirds.

We were still outnumbered and dem rebs would figure out quick that you could shoot a Thunderbird like you shoot a horse. So we poured it on.

Imala and Cassius came back with half a dozen more. Imala stood in her saddle, screaming some Apache war cry, while the Thunderbirds honked and waddled back and forth.

We trotted back into town dat afternoon, all boisterous wit our chests puffed out. We sang the Battle Hymn of the Republic down the main thoroughfare, towards the big church in town. People steppen' out of shops and da like.

A group of Mexican boys held half a dozen reb stragglers with rope and guns.

"They tried to get away."

"Much obliged, citizen." Seems like the folks of Santa Fe *liberated themselves.*

One of rebs looked downright ornery. "Who in the name of heaven are you?"

I was feelin' right charitable, so I got off my horse. "I am Brevet Lieutenant Jeremiah Jones of the Louisiana Federal Cavalry D'Afrique. I will take your surrender."

"Surrender?" said the scrawny rebel, "I don't surrender to *niggers*."

Again, with that word. "Well, I could hang you?"

The other rebels gasp. Whispers of "no" float in the crowd.

"You hang us, *boy,* and see what happens when the rest of my men come back." Dat reb had a confident look.

"Oh, dey ain't coming back," Cassius said all nonchalantly-like. "Dey dead. Every last one of them."

The crowd gasped, then cheered.

"Y-you lyin', boy."

"He speaks the truth," yelled Imala. "The *Confederales*, are dead. All of them. Slaughtered in the pass."

The color left that reb's face.

"Now, I am a man of faith, reb. And, I'm feeling charitable. I'm gonna let ya'll go. So start walking south. Get to Albuquerque, or farther. If yo smart, you all will head for Texas, while you at it. But dis here, dis here is Union territory."

The townspeople untied the six rebs. For a moment, they stood there.

I pulled my pistol "I SAID GET!"

They scattered like children.

The people of Santa Fe threw us, what dey called, a *fiesta.* My men found the two, Gatling guns the next day. They would help us defend the town until the end of the war, in '75.

As for the Thunderbirds? Every now and then, I go up into dose hills and camp. I'll play *Rally Round the Flag* on my harmonica, or I'll sing it softly. Sometimes, in the night, I'd like to think they're singing with me. Singing the battle cry of freedom.

"Your Soul, My Soul, We All Fall Down"
by Jennifer Ogden
Psycho Killer in an Alternate Future

One - Reese

Once Logan is unable to navigate any farther over the rocky terrain, he slows our police hover to a stop, shuts off the engine, and we both step out at the base of a mountain. He collects the lantern from the trunk, while I open the back door and feel again for the unconscious girl's frosty breath. *Good, it's still there.* I pull her out, cradling her in my arms.

"Chilly night," comments Logan as he lights the lamp with a spark.

"A bit," I agree, heading toward the tunnel entrance.

"Guess women really don't feel the cold as much." He chuckles at the old wives' tale as he catches up with me.

"Or maybe it's just 'cause you're so old," I joke back.

"Hey now," he protests. "I'm not fifty yet."

As we enter the tunnel, the gas lantern casts our shadows over the cavernous walls carved out of the mountain. Even though it's just the three of us in here, our shadows make it feel crowded.

"Oh, by the way," he starts, "Claire confirmed she's comin' by tonight." Logan's voice echoes through the empty halls.

"Has it really been another week?" My shoulders sag.

"Stop sulking. She's trustworthy. Plus, we need her," Logan reminds me.

"I know. She's just not on my 'fifty favorite people' list, that's all."

"I didn't know you even had fifty favorite people."

I kick at him. "It was a figure of speech."

He smiles. "Detective Lidia Reese, always alone, eh?"

"You got that right." I smile back. "The day you assign me a partner is the day I quit."

He laughs at our familiar back-and-forth.

"Nah, it's not just seeing Claire," I continue. "It's that another week's gone by and I haven't gotten' the asshole who's doing this."

"You will," Logan assures me.

I stay silent.

"Listen, I'm your chief and you have to do what I say, right? And I say you're gonna catch the asshole, so you will."

"Whatever you say *old man*," I tease.

He throws me a smirk, then climbs over a section of difficult, fallen rock, and places the lantern down. "Give her here," he instructs. I hand over Girl 16.

"I'm still pissed they stopped letting us keep them at the hospital." I climb over, grab the lantern, and keep in step with Logan while he carries the girl.

"Yeah, me too. But you know as well as I, they weren't gonna let us keep 'em there for very long. To them, it's a waste of money giving beds to a bunch of girls they can't do anything for."

"They could've kept them warm," I counter.

"Yeah, they could've." We walk in comfortable silence, each lost in our own thoughts. As we close in on the end of our three-mile trek into the bowels of the earth, Logan shifts his hold on the girl. "How old you think she is?"

I look at her face. "Twelve? Thirteen? Just like all the rest I suppose."

We arrive at the last section of debris we need to cross. "You first," he motions, still holding the girl.

The pile of rubble is so high it reaches our necks. I back up a step, then spring forward. With a carefully placed foothold and left-handed grip I pull myself up and jump down the other side. Logan lifts the girl above his head and passes her to me. I receive her and place her gently on the ground. We repeat the process with the lantern.

"Clear?" he asks.

"Clear."

Logan follows the same pattern over the heap and joins me. The boulder that protects the bunker is twice the height and four times as wide as one person. Luckily, it's not very thick, but it still weighs a hundred pounds or so. We position ourselves on one side of it.

"Ready?"

"Ready."

"Push!" Logan instructs and we both give a loud grunt of effort. It moves a few inches. "Again!"

A couple more pushes and we have a hole wide enough for us to shuffle in sideways. Logan grabs the lantern and I carry the girl across the threshold.

The bunker's walls are made of cement and steel. Broken glass litters the floor and dozens of rusted pipes run across the ceiling and down the walls. But it's safe from intruders and that's what matters.

"Can you imagine we used to build bunkers thinking they would protect us from anything? They've always seemed more of a coffin than a haven."

"Minds of the 21st century, huh?" Logan grins. He shares the flame from our gas lantern with several candles we keep spread out down here. Even though the ventilation system remained intact, the heating and electric systems were less fortunate.

"Too bad they couldn't think forward a century or two. More of us might've made it," I remark.

"There's no point arguing about the past, Reese. We have our own troubles to deal with in this century," Logan states, ending the conversation.

I sigh, heading toward the collection of crusty mattresses, moth eaten blankets, and barely alive girls.

I place Girl 16 in-between Girls 14 and 11, trying to make them as warm and comfortable as I can, though that isn't saying much. I stare at them in their trapped state of slumber. The only clear sign they haven't died yet is that their chests still slowly rise and fall. *I still have time. The question is, how much?*

"When did Claire say she'd show?" I ask.

Logan looks at his wrist-com. "In around thirty."

"Might as well do something useful while we wait," I suggest.

So, we spend the next half-hour hunting through some of the deeper corners of the bunker for anything that survived The Great Destruction of 2091.

Forty minutes later, a bang shoots across the still room. I turn and see Claire steadying herself on the entrance boulder, her large medical bag resting clumsily on the ground. "Why does this place..." she takes a deep breath, "need to be so God damn far underground?" she huffs, gasping for air.

"Good evening to you, too," Logan says in greeting.

"I dropped my bag." She says this like an accusation, but I'm unsure who, or what, she's accusing. She takes a step forward and falters slightly.

Logan rushes to help her balance. "Long day?"

"You could say that." She leans against him for support. "Why'd you have to recruit *me* to check up on your mystery girls instead of one of the younger nurses?"

"If it makes you feel any better," I interject, "I ask him that all the time."

She gives me a death glare, but I just ignore it.

"You both know why," Logan scolds.

"Yeah, yeah." She waves a hand dismissively. "I'm trustworthy and know my shit. Well, you know what I don't have? The joints of my youth!" She curls an escaped strand of silver hair behind her ear and checks that the rest of her bun is still intact. "Well, come on, now! Stop dawdling about! I've got patients to check on. Get my bag, idiot, I don't have all day."

I roll my eyes, but retrieve her discarded medical bag. Logan helps Claire kneel next to the tight circle of girls, as I drop her bag next to her. She pulls out a syringe and begins extracting a sample of Girl 16's blood.

"Any useful results from those blood tests?"

"No." She exchanges the full vial of blood for a Body Analyzer and starts to scan for vitals. "The only thing the blood tests reveal are that everything from their liver functions to their potassium levels rest just below average."

The analyzer beeps. She recites their vitals and I record them. They're always the same: 57 heart beats per minute, 95% oxygen, blood pressure 126/79, and a body temperature of 20.1 degrees Celsius. That last one always terrifies me; they're all freezing.

"Any closer to figuring out what's happening to them?" I ask.

"No. Any closer to figuring out *who's* doing this?" Claire counters. I look away.

"That's what I thought. When I have a breakthrough, you'll know about it," she assures me. "Now hush and let me work." Logan helps her shuffle through the unmoving bodies, and I continue to record the data.

We reach the first girl, the one we found two months ago. The analyzer beeps, and I wait for Claire to rattle off the vitals. She doesn't. Instead she restarts the analyzer.

"What's the matter?" Logan inquires, leaning down.

"Quiet!" She shoos him away and keeps focused on the analyzer's screen. When it beeps again, her shoulders slump. "She's dying."

"They're all dying," I reply.

"No idiot," she snaps. "This one's vitals have all dropped since last week. She's on her way out."

"No." I kneel down and place my hand on the girl's forehead. She feels as cold as the others, but no colder. "Are you sure?"

"Unfortunately, yes. I'd say she has less than a week before she dies."

"No," I repeat, staring at the young girl.

For a heartbeat, there's silence.

Then Claire breaks it. "What's happening to these girls is medically impossible. So, pick up the pace and solve this before the rest follow this girl's lead." She returns the equipment to her bag.

"I'm trying!" I stand-up, rigid; my hands balled fists at my side.

Logan helps Claire to her feet. She looks down at the sixteen, unconscious bodies. "I'm sorry," she whispers to them. She focuses back on Logan. "When you find this asshole, make sure to send 'em to hell." She snaps her bag shut and begins shuffling toward the exit.

"Yes, ma'am," Logan says softly to her retreating back.

Logan and I blow out the candles, push the entrance boulder closed, and catch up with Claire.

We emerge from the earth thirty minutes later.

"Work quickly. Your girls don't have much time left," Claire warns.

"We're doing everything we can," Logan assures.

She nods at him, spares a snide glance my way, and then slowly marches to her own hover.

Once she's out of earshot, I remind Logan, "We're not doing everything."

"Not this again." He rolls his neck and returns the lantern to the hover. "Don't start." He snaps the trunk closed.

"Just open one envelope, one calling card. That's it, that's all—"

"Enough! You know the rules as well as I do, Reese. My hands are tied. We have put a request to open them on all sixteen case reports. I have sent an additional fifteen equipment borrow requests for a Gauging Spectrometer to different metros in our area, and some metros in Area 105. None of which have responded."

I slam my palms on the top of our hover. "We should have our own spec."

"I wish we did, but you know we can't afford one."

I brush my hands over my face. "It's not fair."

"No one ever said it was."

Two - Graham

I swing the door to my Gold-Grade hover open and my Oxfords are instantly assaulted by a puddle of muddy drain water. "Ugh." *Why'd I have to get assigned this case?* I shake the wetness from my foot.

As I enter the building, I double-check that my spec is in my blazer pocket, my knife and handcuffs are securely fastened to my belt, and my tie is in a perfect Windsor knot.

Waiting for the elevator takes twice the amount of time it should and when the doors mercifully open on the fifth floor I'm greeted by an underwhelming reception.

A woman with curly, red hair sits behind a cheap, plastic table organizing a mountain of paperwork. She perks up at my approach. "Hello! Welcome to the police department of Area 103's Metro W. What can I do for you today?"

"I'm looking for Chief Logan."

"Sure!" She stands. "Your name?"

"Lieutenant Cody Graham from Area 103's Metro C police department."

The woman freezes in place. "Metro C?"

"Yes."

"Right this way." She quickly, and deftly, walks through waist-high stacks of binders and overflowing boxes of ancient computer parts. I focus on keeping her bouncing red hair in my sight while also not running into anything. I catch up with her as she knocks on a nondescript door. "Chief Logan?"

"In a sec, kay' Jill?" comes a male voice from within.

"Umm… a Lieutenant Cody Graham from our Metro C is here—" she stops mid-sentence due to the sudden cacophony of noise from behind the door. It opens to reveal a man with greying hair.

"Did you say…?" he trails off catching sight of me. "Ah." He straightens his uniform and takes a step outside his office. "Lieutenant." We shake hands.

"Chief Logan," I reply curtly, ending the handshake as soon as could be considered polite.

"To what do I owe the pleasure?" he asks.

"Private matter," I respond, looking pointedly at the receptionist.

"Ah… yes of course." He rubs the back of his neck and looks behind him sheepishly. Even through the crack I can see the mess within. "Working on a big case, you know how it goes." He closes the door and turns to Jill. "Can you let Reese know we're on our way?"

Jill nods and walks off to deliver the message.

"Can I get you anything?" Logan offers. "Water? Coffee?"

"No. I want to get this resolved as quickly as possible."

"Of course, of course." We follow the direction the receptionist disappeared in. Logan stops in front of another nondescript door, this one slightly ajar. "Reese?" He peeks his head in.

"Come on in. Jill gave me the heads up," a woman's voice responds. Logan opens the door fully to reveal an office the size of a broom closet back home. However, unlike the chief's office, which I only got a glimpse of, this one is immaculate. There is a computer-desk, a visitor's chair, a bookshelf, a window, and... not much else. The woman who spoke is sitting behind the computer-desk, her posture informal at best.

"Detective Lidia Reese, this is Lieutenant Cody Graham. Lieutenant Graham, this is Detective Reese."

"Have a seat." Reese gestures to the visitor's chair.

I take a step forward, but don't sit. "I asked to speak in private," I direct to Logan.

He closes the door and responds, "We are."

"Except for me," cuts in Reese. "You're worried about my station, aren't you *Lieutenant* Graham?"

"Yes. I can't be held accountable if you turn destructive with the information I'm about to share."

"Look," Logan starts, rubbing his brow. "Anything you say to me will get to Reese here. She's my right hand and if you have somethin' you need to tell me, she needs to know it, too. You'd be savin' me the trouble of repeatin' it if you just told us both."

My eyes shift from Logan to Reese, still uncertain.

She sighs. "If it'll help...." She suddenly sits straight as an arrow and raises her left forearm to a ninety-degree angle with her palm pointed toward her face, and places her right hand an inch above her heart. In a monotone voice she begins to recite, "I swear to uphold the honors, beliefs, and all that is best for our 1 Nation, 137 Areas, and 2,678 Metros for all the days of my life." She lowers her hands, folding them delicately in her lap.

I sink into the offered chair. *How the hell did she just do that? I didn't think anyone living lower than a Metro K knew that pledge.*

Logan unsuccessfully fights back a snicker. "What was that?"

I answer, "A perfect reciting of the President's Promise Pledge," still gaping at Reese, who is already back to lounging.

Logan controls his snorting, but his smile remains.

"Can we get on with this now?" Reese asks impatiently.

"Yes," I reply, attempting to regain my composure. "Yes, I suppose so." I pull out a data chip and place it in the receiving dock of the computer-desk. Although its grade is much older, the screen inlaid in the top works like the ones from home, just slower.

As the file loads, I begin explaining the case. "An unusual crime was reported last night. Sara Norrington was found unconscious in her bed. After all known awakening methods were attempted, she remained unconscious." The file loads on the screen.

"So, you're interested in the sixteen cases we've filed with the same circumstances," Reese states.

"Sixteen? I knew of only fifteen."

"I just finished the sixteenth report two days ago."

"Ah well.... Regardless, yes, I'm interested in those cases. Particularly in the 'calling cards' left at each crime scene. Your reports describe them as 'envelopes with a red wax seal.' Is that correct?"

"Yes," Logan confirms.

"Our victim, Sara Norrington, didn't have a calling card. It was the only major difference between our two cases. Your request to borrow a Gauging Spectrometer in order to deduce if the envelopes hold anything toxic has not yet been fulfilled, is that also correct?"

"Yes," Reese confirms through gritted teeth.

"Show me the letters," I instruct. "I've brought a spec so I can determine if they're safe to open."

"I'll grab 'em." Logan heads out the door.

Reese leans back silently, shaking her head in disbelief. We wait, the only sound is Reese's fingernails tapping rhythmically against a stained, ceramic, coffee cup. Glancing around her office, I search for something to break the uncomfortable silence with. "Thank you for your help in this matter."

"Of course." Her voice dripping with sarcasm. "We mustn't let one child of wealth be left helpless, so let's use the evidence from the sixteen other girls' crime scenes to help her."

"That's not what I meant."

She continues, disregarding my comment. "How long do you think it would've taken to get someone down here if your Sara Norrington hadn't come down with the same affliction as the sixteen nameless girls down here?"

"I don't know." I remove the spec from my pocket and power it on. I continue, with a sharper edge to my voice. "So, maybe, you should be thankful I'm here now."

"Thankful my ass," she mutters under her breath. Her gaze shifts from me to the spec in my hand, her expression slipping from loathing to longing.

Logan comes back swinging a box in his hands. "Here we go!" he announces. Reese swipes off the screen of her computer-desk and Logan dumps the sixteen sealed envelopes on top of it.

I stand and hover the spec a few inches above the closest envelope. The spec beeps softly while gathering data, then gives a ding to indicate its analyses complete.

"Nothing harmful," I declare after reading the results. "We can open them." In the time it takes me to return the spec to my pocket, Reese has already opened an envelope and begun reading its letter.

"Oh, my God," she repeats over and over again as she reads the letter's contents, her eyes moving faster the longer she reads.

"What? What is it?" asks Logan.

Her whole body shivers. She looks up at Logan, drops the letter, and sprints from the room.

Three - Jackson

I watch from across the street as she finally reads my letter. Good thing I was listening two nights ago and overheard why she hadn't read any of them yet. One trip up to Metro C took care of that problem.

Liddy's grip intensifies as she reads my words of love and devotion. I know when she gets to the end, because her whole body shivers; she remembers me.

I re-read my latest letter.

My Dearest Liddy,

I love you. It's taken longer than I expected, but I'm finally able to tell you. Eighteen years ago, you were ripped from me by your father's actions. When he announced you dead, I nearly died myself. But I realized you couldn't be gone. With a connection like ours, I would have felt your passing.

Before I started searching for you, I vowed to complete the mission you set before me last time we talked. Do you remember? I've done it Liddy, I can do what no other man can: I can hold your soul in my hands.

After completing my mission, I began my search. I found you two months ago waiting on a bench for a public transport to take you home. You were so stunning just sitting there.

A million ways to tell you all I'd done raced through my mind; I couldn't decide which was best. Right then, a young teen girl made a playful screeching noise with her friends. You gave a small, sad smile in the girl's direction and I knew. I knew the best way to show you.

I would protect her, I would protect all of them.

Since then, I've adopted a new mission: to save all the young girls in your city from suffering your same fate.

I hope this gesture is as beautiful to you as you are to me.

Always Yours,
Jackson Raveanie

Four - Reese

I rush to the elevators and press the call button repeatedly. *Why are these things so slow!* I impatiently tap my foot while glaring at the unlit arrow. *Blink. Blink, God damn you!* The light finally comes on and the doors open. "Thank you," I say to the empty air, annoyed at the elevator's lack of urgency.

The elevator doors open on the first floor and I race through the lobby, picking up speed as I hit fresh air. People loitering on the street move out of my way to protect themselves from being barreled into.

I blur out all my surroundings and just run.

So many times I've tried to forget. Tried to push out all memories of my past, the life I used to live, the person I used to be, and the person I wanted to become. But it's never worked. Something always crops back up.

I trip and clumsily fall to my knees. I look up and find I'm in a small graveyard near one of Metro W's churches. I rub my face and try to control my breathing.

The random headstone I've fallen in front of has inscriptions indicating someone long dead and dearly missed. I try to force the memory away, but my own mother's inscription floats to mind.

Here lies Marian Beautishis, wonderful wife and daughter.

My father took me to her grave on my thirteenth birthday; the last day I lived in Metro A. I had just received my womanhood examination, and the next day was going to be my society debut. Father had been hoping I would get a few offers of courtship from wealthy young men.

Standing at my mother's grave, the doctor's diagnosis of 'infertile' hung over us like a black cloud. My father said I'd failed him. All I'd had to do in order to achieve penance for my mother's death was continue his lineage, and I couldn't do it.

After our graveyard visit, father took me to a transportation landing, gave me a one-way ticket to the Lower Metros, told me I wasn't a Beautishis anymore, and left me. I stood there for hours hoping, if I just waited long enough and atoned for my mother's death in childbirth, he'd come back for me.

"Hey." Graham's voice cuts through my trip down memory lane.

"What are you doing here?" I turn my face away, checking the corners of my eyes for tears. When I'm sure they're dry, I grip the random headstone and pull myself up.

"Someone you knew?" He indicates the grave marker.

"No." I brush off a few stray leaves stubbornly clinging to me.

He rises an eyebrow in question. "An odd place to run to—a graveyard."

"I'm aware of that," I respond, walking away.

He matches my pace and we head toward the office.

"I read the letters," Graham states.

"What did the others say?"

"Pretty much the same as the first. Guess he knew you hadn't opened 'em."

"Guess so."

We walk in silence for several minutes. Graham breaks it. "So, are you gonna tell me how you know a Raveanie? They practically own half of Area 103."

I make a noncommittal sound as we enter the building.

"Come on, whoever this Jackson is, your history with him is relevant to our case."

"Our?" I question.

"Yes, *our*."

I hit the button to call the elevator. "We were friends a long time ago."

"What? How?"

"We were neighbors in Metro A, when I was young."

His eyes bulge at the mention of Metro A. "With the Triple P you did up there, I'd figured you grew up in some sort of High Metro, but Metro A? Jesus! What are you doing down here?"

"Wasn't by choice." The light dings and we step in.

"So, what happened?" he presses.

"Not important. What is important is what he said about souls." The elevator doors open, and we head toward my office.

"Why's that? Why would he even use that term, 'souls'?"

"Because the day…" I push open my office door to find Logan in my guest chair. He's studying the sixteen case reports I've made and the one for Sara Norrington on my computer-desk.

He looks up at our entrance. "The run help?"

"Not really." I sit at my desk and take a sip of cold, stale coffee from my ever-present mug.

"Didn't mean to stop your conversation." Logan leans back.

I wave my hand dismissively. "I was just talking about the last time I spoke with Jackson Raveanie." I stare into my coffee. "It was the day before my thirteenth birthday. He asked me 'What do you hope your future husband can do?' and I replied, 'That he's able to hold my soul in his hands.'"

Graham snickers. I stare at him with fire in my eyes. "Sorry," he says, instantly sobering up. "I just didn't peg you as a romantic."

"I'm not," I say deadpan. "That was years ago."

"Ok, ok." Graham puts his hands up in surrender and leans back against a wall.

I go back to staring in my cup. "The tone of his letter... he sounds so... different."

"That was eighteen years ago," Logan states. "Makes sense he's changed."

"I guess." I stand and start to pace as much as I can in my small—and crowded—office.

Logan leans forward, looking at the seventeen reports open on the screen. "Did you say your 'thirteenth birthday'?"

"Yeah, why?"

"Then I think—" he enlarges a few sections of documents. "—I have an idea of how he's picking his victims."

"What? How?" I lean over his shoulders trying to find the pattern he's seeing.

"All sixteen girls we found, which were reported anonymously—"

"Wait," Graham interjects, leaning forward a bit. Logan and I turn to look at him. "What do you mean 'anonymously?'"

"It means," I say, speaking slowly, "That we don't know anything about the victims except what we can see. We don't know their names, we don't know their ages, and we don't know when they were 'put to sleep.'"

"Oh." Graham rests back against the wall.

"As I was saying." Logan turns back to my computer-desk. "All sixteen girls we found are estimated between twelve and thirteen years old, right?"

I nod and he continues.

"Because Sara Norrington, the girl you found—" He indicates Graham. "—was traditionally reported, we have concrete information about her. Get this, she was 'put to sleep' on the eve of her thirteenth birthday."

"Oh, my God." I straighten.

"If Jackson is goin' after girls on the eve of their thirteenth birthday, we might be able to compile a list of possible next victims."

Five - Jackson

"Night, Mom!" the girl calls across her tiny apartment. "Have a good shift!"

"Thanks! Night to you too!" her mother responds, walking out the door.

I watch the young girl through her bedroom window. She smiles, humming a tune while preparing for sleep. I mirror her smile. Thanks to me, she will stay this happy forever. She twirls over the dirty and stained carpet, dancing to her own melody, and climbs into bed.

I continue to wait and watch from my tree nook until her breathing falls into a deep, rhythmic pattern. That's all I need. I climb across one of the tree's sturdy limbs and slide open the window to her second story home. With cat-like stealth, I drop into her room. *If only I could have done this eighteen years ago for Liddy.*

I spray three doses of mist anesthesia into the girl's mouth and wait for the drug to fully enfold her in sleep. After counting to three hundred, I kneel beside her torso, and whisper, "You'll be safe soon."

I select the prepared glass soul vial, which is 25 x 150 mm, from my satchel and unscrew its cap. I reverently attach the funnel into the vial's neck and activate it with a small squeeze. It hums to life in my hands and I feel the warmth growing. I hover my Soul Saving device above the girl's solar plexus and wait. Learning to withstand being stone still for ten minutes was not easy, but I managed it.

Then the best part starts; her soul begins to surface. The first soul orb appears, floating gently out of her. The orbs are as tiny as grains of rice, but perfectly round. Each glow with either a silver or gold light.

I squeeze my device tighter, giving it an extra boost of warmth and power. The first orb, silver this time, is drawn to the warmth radiating from the funnel, flows through it, and into the vial. Soon hundreds of silver and gold orbs follow the first. Twenty minutes pass while the entire soul leaves the girl's body and safely nestles itself into its new home.

With precision and speed, I rotate the device 180 degrees, remove the funnel, and replace the cap on the now full soul vial.

Now safely in my protection, I whisper, "See, I told you," to the girl.

I add the soul vial to my satchel with the seventeen others and place my newest letter on the girl's chest.

I leave the same way I entered.

Six - Reese

As I wait for the elevator, and finish the last of my lunch, my wrist-com chimes. "Hey, Logan. Any improvement on the possible victims list since this morning?"

"Not yet." His voice is rushed. "But meet Graham outside now."

"What, why?" I ask, even though I'm already heading toward the building's doors.

"Another anonymous call just came in."

"Where?" I push open the door and search for Graham's hover.

"187 W. Henerson."

"Got it." I disconnect our line and Graham's hover floats to the edge of the sidewalk. I jump in before he's able to come to a full stop. "Go!"

"Right." He adds acceleration and we pull away.

I input the address into his hover's locating system and minutes later we park outside one of the better tenement buildings in town. Graham and I step out and head toward the main entrance.

"Are you from the police?" A woman with tear stains along her face stumbles up to us in a half-jog.

"Yes," I answer.

"Are you here for the body?"

"Yes."

"I'm so awful." The woman collapses to her knees sobbing at my feet. "I should have just called! I should have just called the instant it happened! My poor Lucy!"

I bend down and lock eyes with the crying woman. "Do you know the girl?"

The woman, still weeping, nods. "She's my daughter! I wanted to call right away, but it's so… we're barley making it… I didn't know if we," she takes a shuddering breath, "If *I* could survive paying any additional fees."

I place my hand on the woman's shoulder. "Someone anonymous tipped us off. If you have any information that might be useful to the case, we would be grateful to hear it, other than that, you have no obligation to us."

"Oh, thank you." She collapses onto my shoulder. "Thank you. Thank you," she continues to repeat.

"You're welcome." I gently push her off me. "Please, show us the body," I request while standing-up.

"Yes, yes, of course, right this way." She stands and hustles toward the building.

"What is she talking about?" asks Graham while we follow the woman.

"What do you mean?"

"She was talking about paying some sort of fee."

I look at him like he's gone mad. "The Crime Bill Law," I say simply, expecting that to clear up his confusion. When it doesn't, I continue, "It was passed four years ago, along with massive budget cuts. The law states if a department doesn't have enough resources to investigate a crime, the victim needs to pay for any investigation fees."

"What?"

"Anyone who calls in a crime needs to pay for it to be solved." We enter the building and head up a flight of stairs. "The only way to avoid the fee is by calling anonymously, but then the police decide whether or not to investigate the crime at all."

"That's crazy," Graham replies. The woman unlocks the door to her apartment and ushers us inside.

"What's even crazier is that you didn't even know it was happening."

"She's in here." The woman opens a door on rusted hinges to reveal her daughter. "It was going to be Lucy's thirteenth birthday." The mother kneels next to her daughter's limp form.

Graham and I share a look. "Thirteen," I whisper so only he can hear. Lucy is displayed like all the others, the only difference being a slight bulge in the envelope resting on her chest. "Mind using your spec?" I look at Graham and indicate the envelope.

He nods and takes out the Gauging Spectrometer from his blazer pocket.

For a minute, the room's only sounds are the beeps of data processing and the mother's soft sniffles. She rubs her daughter's cold hand, presumably attempting to give her warmth. The ding goes off and the spec informs us the substance is safe.

"Have at it," Graham says while returning the spec to his pocket.

"Don't mind if I do." Inside is another letter …and a ring. I unfold the letter and begin to read, Graham doing the same over my shoulder.

286

My Dearest Liddy,

At last you were able to read my letters. Now that you understand what I'm doing you can relax. You know I'm not harming anyone, but protecting them by removing their souls. I promise to protect yours too, Liddy.

I remember you were so nervous for your society debut; just thinking back on it makes me smile. I didn't tell you then, but I was planning to make an offer. Even if you fell flat on your face during the presentation, or stepped on my toes in the dancing segment, I was going to offer. I would court you and then, one day, be your husband. That desire hasn't changed.

It may have taken longer than anticipated, but I have succeeded. And with this ring, I promise to be your husband and protector for all of time.

I love you to the very core of my soul, and will never stop.

Be Mine,
Jackson Raveanie

I'm having trouble breathing. My tight grip has almost torn the paper in half multiple times. I shove the letter, and ring, back into the envelope.

"And I thought his first ones were a bit much," Graham says from behind me.

I need to find Jackson; now, more than ever. If the trail of bodies I've been following is a result of a soul removal device Jackson's created because of me, I have to stop him—no matter the cost.

I calm my breathing and focus on the next step. "We need to move Lucy to the others."

"Move her?" the mother squeaks. "Why?"

"Lucy is not the first victim we've found like this by anonymous calls. We've taken all the others to a safe location away from the city. We need to treat her like all the ones before," I say firmly.

She looks down and, with a bit of resistance, nods. She gives a light kiss on her daughter's forehead, stands, and walks through a doorway, disappearing from view.

I bend and pick Lucy up—the seventeenth girl I've carried like this. Graham and I walk down the flight of stairs and exit the building. While we were inside, the sun had begun its descent in the sky.

My wrist-com chimes when we're halfway to the hover. I try to see who's calling, but carrying Lucy is impairing my view.

"Would you mind?" I turn to Graham and gesture at the girl.

Graham takes Lucy from me and finishes walking to the hover.

I look at the ID and answer my wrist-com, still walking. "Evening, Claire."

"The girl's dead."

I stop dead in my tracks. "What? Are you sure?"

"Do you think this is my first time declaring someone dead? Get down here. I can't carry her worth squat."

"C-carry her?" I'm still trying to absorb the news.

She gives an exaggerated sigh. "To bury her, idiot. Chief's gone to get some shovels, so just get yourself down here to help dig."

"Right, of course. On our—" Claire hangs up before I finish, "...way." I get in Graham's hover in a daze. "We're going here." I input the bunker's coordinates.

He nods and guides the hover in the direction his locating system now indicates.

"The first girl's dead," I say softly.

"What?"

I look out the window. "I said, 'she's dead.'"

Seven - Graham

After following directions for an hour, my headlights illuminate the base of a steep mountain. "Now what?"

"We walk," Reese states without missing a beat. We both step out of my hover. She tosses me a small flashlight and gently picks up Lucy from the backseat.

"What's this for?" I ask holding up the flashlight.

288

"Gets dark in the mountain," she says over her shoulder as she heads toward a tunnel entrance.

I click on the light and follow her in. "If we're heading toward the unconscious girls, why aren't we at a hospital?"

"No room," she replies. "After we discovered the third girl, they said we had to figure something else out. They couldn't justify wasting money for a bunch of kids they couldn't help. So, Logan and I looked through old construction permits and found an abandoned bunker down here."

"So, sixteen unconscious girls are just sleeping in some abandoned bunker?"

"Yes. We needed to keep them somewhere they'd be protected from looters and the like." She pauses at a section of fallen rocks. "Climb over first, then I'll hand you Lucy."

I nod and make the distance in a two-step climb.

"Ready?" she asks.

"Yeah."

She passes me the girl, then hops over with an elegant jump. She retrieves the flashlight, which I'd dropped on the floor, and keeps walking. "Claire, the nurse who's there now," Reese continues, "checks on them once a week. For the past two months it's been just her, Logan, and I trying to solve this."

"Oh," I say softly. Three people stretched thin for so long. In Metro C, we're so overstaffed I barely work a case a month.

We walk in silence for a few more minutes before she announces, "Almost there." In front of us is a landslide of rocks that reaches up to our necks. "I'll go first. Watch my footing and hand placement, ok?"

"Yeah." I tighten my hold on Lucy.

Reese steps back, then gives a small jump, grips a bit of rock, and gracefully pulls herself up and over the incline to land on the other side. She stands, but I can only see her face. "Ok, now pass Lucy and the light, then climb over," she instructs.

I do so, although my attempt to duplicate Reese's smooth movement is less fluid than I'd hoped.

"Not too shabby," Reese says, smiling. Still holding Lucy, she enters the bunker. I lean down and grab the flashlight noticing my Oxfords are completely scuffed. *When did that happen?* I wonder as I trail in after her.

The bunker is a cavernous room made of cement. A scattering of candles enables us to see better than with just the tiny flashlight.

"About time," scorns an elderly female voice. "Took you long enough."

I track the sound of, I assume, Claire's voice. While doing so, my gaze passes over sixteen, cold bodies tucked into a hodgepodge of mattresses and blankets. Claire is sitting in a far corner of the room, her eyes shut and head resting against a wall.

"My God," escapes me in a breath. "They really are… I guess I thought… figure of speech…." My eyes roam the scene before me, my mind not fully able to comprehend it.

Claire's eyes snap open. "Who are you?"

Reese adds Lucy to the pile of mattresses, blankets, and bodies. "This is Lieutenant Graham. He's from our Metro C."

"Metro C, huh? About time you took an interest in these girls. It's not like the help we got is gonna figure this out."

Reese gently folds Lucy in a blanket.

"Chief should be here by now with the shovels," the nurse declares. "I told him not to bother coming back down," she grunts. "You can carry her just fine, right, idiot?" she directs at Reese.

Reese doesn't respond. Instead she simply kneels, tucks her hands under the dead girl's body, rises, and starts walking back toward the sky.

I start to exit the bunker when Claire's yell stops me.

"Hold on boy, help me up! I thought you High Metro boys were supposed to be classy!"

I sigh, but trudge over to help.

The three of us emerge from the tunnel a half hour later.

"Hey!" Logan waves at us. "I thought I'd get started on the diggin'." He holds a shovel out to me. "Care to join?"

I nod in acceptance.

"Well, count me out," says Claire. "I'm going home. I've had enough death for one day." She shuffles into her hover and leaves the three of us to dig alone in the falling darkness.

When we finish digging, Reese, Logan, and I gently lower the body into the ground. Then we pick our shovels back up and cover the nameless girl in earth.

When we finish burying the body, the three of us stand still in the slowly moving breeze, knowing something needs to be said, but none of us knowing exactly what. Quietly, I begin to hum a funeral tune. Logan joins in, and then Reese begins to sing the lyrics.

I dig this grave for the body of a soul
I dig this grave for a beauty to behold
I dig this grave for an ending bitter-sweet
I dig this grave for your immortal sleep

I don't dig this grave for an ending to your soul
I don't know when, but your soul will be reborn
I don't know how, but your story isn't over
I don't know why, but our souls are great immortal

So, I dig this grave for you my sweet
I dig this grave for you to lie in sleep
I dig this grave for your good soul
I dig this grave for you to be at peace

On the final sorrowful note, even the air is motionless out of respect. I grab a nearby stone, use my knife to carve R.I.P., and place it at the head of the grave. I return my knife to my belt, jiggling the handcuffs as I do so.

After several still moments pass, Reese rolls her head back. "I forgot to push the boulder back in place."

"What boulder?" I ask.

"The one Logan pushed aside when he went down with Claire."

"Want help putting it back?" I offer.

They both look at me, stunned.

"What?" I ask.

After a minute of silence, Reese shrugs. "Sure, why not?"

We pass our shovels back to Logan. "Want me to stay...?" he asks.

"Nah. Go home." Reese waves him off. "Maybe one of us can get some quality sleep."

"Ha. That's a dream." He walks toward his hover. "See ya' tomorrow." He starts the engine and pulls away.

Reese and I make the three-mile trek back into the earth and arrive at the bunker's doorway.

"Here it is." Reese begins indicating a location on a very large boulder when she stiffens.

"What's–?" I start.

She quickly shushes me, and peers into the bunker. "Oh, my God," she whispers.

"What? What is it?" I walk behind Reese and stop in place. Standing among the sixteen sleeping girls is a man.

"Is that…?" I trail off.

"Yeah," Reese whispers. "That's him."

Eight - Reese

I'm frozen in place by the scene in front of me: Jackson Raveanie surveying the sixteen girls whose lives he's put in danger as some twisted attempt to court me.

"I'm goin' in," I whisper to Graham.

"What? Are you out of your mind?"

"No," I say over my shoulder. "It's my fault those girls are lying in there dying, instead of at home living their lives."

"No, it's not." He comfortingly places a hand on my shoulder.

"Yes, it is." I take a calming breath. "So, I have to stop him."

As I step into the bunker, Graham hisses, "Get back here."

Jackson looks up at the sound of my entrance. "Liddy," he smiles adoringly at me.

"Jackson." I approach him as I would a dangerous animal. I take a quick glance back to make sure Graham's hidden out of sight. *Good.*

"Did you get my ring?" Jackson asks hopefully.

"I did."

"I'm glad."

I stop a few feet from him, and turn my gaze to the sixteen bodies lying next to us, all desperately clinging to life. "Why did you do this?"

He surveys the girls huddled among the moth-eaten mattresses. "I told you, I'm protecting them. I stopped what happened to you from happening to them."

I stare at him. "What happened to me wasn't so terrible."

"How can you say that?" He takes a step forward. "Your life was perfect."

I step back, maintaining the distance between us.

"You were happy. We were happy. Then you turned thirteen and everything was ruined."

"Removing these girls' souls didn't protect them from being cast out. It destroyed any possible future for them."

"You're wrong." He turns back toward the bodies.

"Do you understand the consequences of what you've done?" I demand.

"How can you not see the value?" he challenges. "I'm letting them stay innocent, keeping their childhoods intact—forever."

"Value? These girls are dying because of you. Count your victims. Do you seem to be one short?"

He counts the bodies. "Where is she?"

"In the ground, six feet under. I just finished burying her lifeless body."

He shakes his head. "No, she's not dead, I saved her." He pulls a satchel I hadn't noticed around his shoulder. He unzips it and displays eighteen glowing vials of silver and gold. "See. They're all right here."

Staring at the souls swirling in their individual glass prisons, I take an involuntary step forward. "Put them back. Put them all back, right now!" I rush at him, attempting to grab the satchel.

"No," Jackson steps back, protectively swiveling the satchel behind him. "No, I'm not going to end their lives. They're safe with me."

"You moron!" I scream. "You're not protecting them. You're *killing* them!"

"No, I'm—"

"I don't care what you think." I step forward, my hands curling into fists. "You're going to show me how to revive them one way or another."

The bunker is silent for several breaths.

"Why are you so angry?"

"Oh, I don't know!" I throw my hands up in exasperation. "Maybe because you've endangered eighteen kids' lives in an attempt to win my affection, or your blindness that you're killing them with your twisted acts of devotion, or your denial that you've actually killed someone. Do any of those answer your question?"

"I didn't think you'd be upset."

"Upset? I'm way past upset!" I swiftly pull my arm back.

"Stop!" Graham rushes in and grabs my arm, preventing my attack. "Reese, think about this," he says, restraining me.

"No!" I break out of his hold and step away from him.

"Think about what you're doing," Graham says calmly. "We don't know what would happen if those vials break."

I stare at him, trying to let my logical side clear my blinding rage. I try to shift all the puzzle pieces into some sort of positive outcome.

"What will it take?" I stride toward Jackson. "What will it take for you to realize what you've done? Do I need to show you the headstone Graham carved? Or the fresh earth we've just dug? What?"

"I just want you to love me," Jackson answers.

"And you'd stop? You'd stop extracting souls if I loved you."

His brow scrunches in confusion. "No."

I break out into a harsh laugh. "Then why? Why would I ever love you, when the very thought of touching you repulses me?" I stare directly at Jackson, then abruptly throw myself at Graham.

"What the—?" Graham catches me. He attempts to finish his question, but I silence him with a kiss.

"What are you doing?" Jackson screeches.

"Go with it. Don't stop me," I murmur against Graham's lips. I pull out the knife sheathed in his belt and continue making out. I can feel his confusion, but he doesn't pull away.

"Stop! Stop kissing him!" Jackson wails. I hear him rush toward us. I turn, the knife pointing at his throat. He stops a millimeter too late and a drop of blood wets the tip of the blade.

"Tell me how to return the souls or I will slice you to ribbons."

"Y-you c-can't kill me," he stutters. "If you do, y-you'll never know."

"You have a point." I step back, still threatening him with the blade. "But there is someone I can kill. Someone you love very deeply."

I twist the blade around and hold it steady an inch above my left breast. "If you don't tell me, right now, I will plunge this knife so deep into my heart that I will be dead before I hit the ground."

"No," Jackson gasps.

"Reese, what are you doing?" Graham's voice is full of warning.

I spare Graham a glance. "Remember what I said." I return my full attention to Jackson. "Well?"

"No, I won't let you do this," Jackson reaches for the blade, but Graham seizes his arms and twists them behind Jackson's back.

"Only one way to stop me," I threaten. "Clock is ticking. Five…" I press the tip to my skin.

"No! Stop!" Jackson cries out.

"… Four…" I dig the tip into my breast, leaning over in pain.

"You're bluffing. It's over. Just stop!" Jackson struggles against Graham's grip.

"…Three…" I twist the dagger, drawing a small trickle of my own blood.

"NO!" His eyes roll at the sight.

"…Two…" I tighten my grip, preparing for the plunge.

"STOP!" He goes limp in Graham's arms. "Stop. I'll show you. I'll show you, just for the love of God, please stop."

"Then show us," I command.

"Can you put the knife down?" Jackson begs. I only raise an eyebrow, not moving an inch. He deflates. "Ok, ok. I need my hands."

With a practiced movement, Graham replaces his grip for his pair of handcuffs. "No need. Walk me through it."

"Get a vial," Jackson sniffs sadly as he begins to instruct Graham. "Unscrew the cap, then cover it back up after a single orb floats out."

Graham does so. A tiny golden light floats out of the glass vial and starts to flutter around the room, looking for a place to land.

"Why just one? You're not trying anything funny, are you?" I demand.

"No. You have to let the first one out alone. If you make each orb search for their body, the soul becomes too weak."

The shining orb hovers over the solar plexus of each cold body one by one, working to find its owner. On the seventh body it doesn't continue on. Instead it nestles for a moment on the girl's navel. The light seeps into her, causing her whole body to momentarily brighten from within.

Jackson nods toward the girl. "You can pour the rest of her soul over her now."

Graham walks to the girl and tilts the vial. Hundreds of silver and gold orbs spill out, blanketing the girl's body. One at a time they are each absorbed.

I remove the blade from my chest and stand before Jackson. "Jackson Raveanie, you are hereby under arrest for the attempted murder of seventeen girls and the murder of one." I drag his satchel from his arm.

"I'll always love you, Liddy." His eyes longingly trace the movement of his satchel.

"Well, now you can love me from your prison cell. Graham, can you lock him in your hover? I can't deal with him anymore."

"Sure." Graham gives Jackson a shake to start walking. "Oh, and before I forget," Graham turns back to me, "don't ever do that again." Then they disappear into the hallway.

The girl whose soul was returned begins to move. "What's going on?" Her voice cracking from disuse.

I rush to her side, "You're waking up from a coma, but you're gonna be ok."

Each vial is labeled with an exact date, time, and location. I match the order the girls were found in with the dates and quickly wake-up all the girls in the bunker. This leaves only two souls still imprisoned. Once all the girls are awake and moving, we make the three-mile climb to the surface.

Graham pushes off the edge of his hover and jogs over. "You all right?"

I look over his shoulder and see Jackson locked in the hover. "Better than yesterday," I answer.

"You saved them."

I stare at the grave. "Not all of them," I remind him. I open one of the remaining vials. An orb floats out and sinks into the ground. I pour the remaining soul over the freshly turned earth. I'm not sure what returning a dead girl's soul will do, but I hope she finds peace.

"Let's go," Graham says softly.

"Yeah, let's go." I turn to him. "Here," I sigh, handing over the remaining vial. "It's Sara's soul, the girl from your Metro."

"Thanks." He curls his fist protectively around the girl's soul. We head toward his hover.

I turn back to take one last look. A golden orb floats up from the grave. "What?"

"Hmm?" Graham turns. "Oh, wow," he breathes.

Hundreds of silver and gold orbs float into the night sky. We stare in awe: sixteen victims, their attacker, and their two rescuers, covered in the glow of a lost girl's soul.

Nine - Reese, One Week Later

I stare out the small window of my office, lost in thought.

"Knock-knock." Logan pokes his head in, breaking my concentration. "Whatcha' thinkin' about?"

"Nothin' much, just everyday stuff," I answer, still watching the view beyond my window.

"Like what?" He steps in.

"Like…" I release a deep exhale. "How do we become who we are? What are the choices, events, and actions that really matter? Which decisions truly define us?"

"That's easy." He closes the door and sits. "All of 'em. They all matter."

I turn toward him. "All of 'em, huh? Can't narrow it down from there?" I swirl the dregs of this morning's coffee in lazy circles around the bottom of my cup.

"Unfortunately, no." A moment of silence passes. "Do you remember the day we met?" he asks out of the blue.

"Vaguely."

"I'll never forget it. Eighteen years ago, you walked in here wearin' a torn, dirty, and very expensive dress. I could've just turned you away, but I thank God every day I didn't. You know why?"

I shake my head. "No idea."

"'Cause you've become a person I didn't know even existed. Someone who actually cares about the wellbein' of others and doesn't give up on 'em. Someone who believes in justice for those who've been wronged, and will fight like hell to get it."

My cheeks grow warm. "Thanks for the flattery, Chief."

"It's not flattery; it's truth. Every day you show up to work, you help someone. You help someone who would have otherwise been left hopeless."

Fidgeting with my coffee mug, I smile and nod. "Thanks."

"Anytime." He stands and opens the door.

"Oh." Graham has one hand in mid-air to knock, the other holding a folder.

"Lieutenant." Logan nods.

"I thought you went back to Metro C?" I say without getting up.

"I did," Graham says. "I returned Sara Norrington's soul. My chief doesn't really believe the story that someone created a drug that prevents its victims from awakening. But, as agreed, the less people who know the truth, the better."

"Right." Logan gives a sharp nod. "And don't worry, we did our part, too. Me and Reese burned Jackson's satchel and everythin' in it. No one is ever gonna use, or recreate, that device again."

"Good," Graham states.

After a minute of silence, Logan asks, "So whatcha' doin' here?"

"I've been re-assigned."

"Here?" Logan and I both ask incredulously.

Graham hands the folder to Logan. "Yup, it's all in there."

Logan looks over the contents of the folder. "Why'd you get re-assigned?"

He shrugs his shoulders. "As I said, my chief thinks I'm lying and maybe a little too full of myself. So, he thought I should 're-learn my manners' down here."

"Well then." Logan claps Graham on the shoulder. "Welcome to Metro W." With that, Logan leaves us alone.

I stare at Graham. "I don't buy it."

"Which part?"

"The part about it being your chief's idea."

"Can't get anything by you." He sighs. "They have more than enough people up in C. Figured I'd be more useful down here. Plus, you've got a lot on your plate. Thought you could use the help."

"You think I need help?"

"No, but I think it might be nice for you not to have to carry the weight of this entire Metro on your own. Maybe I could take a few pounds off your hands."

"You think you can do that?" I challenge.

"Won't know until I try."

"Reese!" Logan calls from the hallway. "Got'a new one for ya!"

"Then let's find out," I say to Graham. Standing, I yell out the door, "Detective Reese and Lieutenant Graham are on it!"

THE AUTHORS

Mike Cervantes

Dinosaur in the Triassic

Mike Cervantes is a graduate of creative writing and communication from The University of Texas at El Paso. He is a humorist, a cartoonist, a steampunk enthusiast, a regular contributor to Denver's many local conventions, and just a swell person. He writes and publishes stories featuring his steampunk hero characters "The Scarlet Derby and Midnight Jay" regularly on his website, TheScarletDerby.com.

Heather Crowley

Clown in an Alternate Future

Heather Cowley was born and raised in Northern Colorado where she currently resides with her loving boyfriend and three, adoring fur babies. She discovered her love of writing in Mrs. Girardi's 2nd grade class at Washington Core Knowledge, and from then until high school graduation signed up for every creative writing class offered. In order to break through the inevitable writer's block that plagues all writers, she spends her time reading, crocheting, and boxing. She is currently holed up at a desk in the library working on her novel.

Jason Henry Evans

Dinosaur in an Alternate Future
Imaginary Friend in an Alternate Future
Robot Assassin in Space

Thomas A. Fowler

Dinosaur in an Evil Laboratory
Dinosaur in the Human Mind
Dinosaur in Space
Imaginary Friend in Space
Kaiju in an Alternate Future
Kaiju in Space
Psycho Killer in an Evil Laboratory
Robot Assassin in an Alternate Future

Thomas A. Fowler (Author & Crash Philosophy Creator) saw Jurassic Park at the age of 11. It was all nerdy as hell from there. Especially when he stuck around for the end credits and saw "Based on the novel by Michael Crichton." He went straight from the movie theater, walked down the mall to a Walden Books. Since then, he's written movies, plays, short-stories and books. While he sticks primarily to science-fiction, he dabbles elsewhere. He holds an MBA in Marketing from Regis University and was a former Content Creator at a full-service ad agency in Denver, Colorado. Now, he devotes that skill set to a freelance career and to helping authors live their dream of getting published. Somewhere, between writing and advertising, he tries to be a loving husband and responsible father.

E. Godhand

Psycho Killer in the Triassic

E. Godhand is a dark fantasy author who lives in Denver, Colorado and runs Black Rat Books. Her office staff include her three rats, Chaos, Order, and Illuminati, and a black cat who bribes her with socks. Read all about ghosts, chaos magick, and surviving death, and ignore the subsequent nightmares. Despite the rumors, Emily does not worship the Elder Gods and is not responsible for the strange bumps in the night. Learn more at EmilyGodhand.com.

H.L. Huner

Alien in Space

Kimberly Keane

Psycho Killer in an Apocalyptic Wasteland

Kimberly Keane lives a secret life playing with data sets, caring for her four-legged, furry dragon, and answering non-existential questions for her adult children like: "How do taxes work," "What's a copay," and "Should I opt out of my 401k plan?" She also writes speculative fiction and spends an inordinate amount of time in coffee and tea shops.

Jason Kent

Alien in an Alternate Future

Jason Kent is an Air Force veteran, Amazon Best Selling author, and military space expert. From launching rockets to great, new sci-fi, he's got you covered! Combating government bureaucracy and military budgeting cycles, he became an expert at systems engineering, designing space systems, and launching billion-dollar rockets. Along the way, Jason nurtured a passion for exploration beyond Earth's atmosphere and yearned to go where no one has gone before! Unfortunately, the U.S. Space Corps has yet to be formed, leading him to the inevitable conclusion the best way to visit the stars was to write about them. Jason is a licensed professional engineer with experience in diverse mission areas such as reconnaissance, engineering, space and launch vehicle operations, space system acquisition, and missile defense. Each of his assignments broadened his experience in real-world space technology and space business ventures. Jason's books include Kindle #1 Best Seller New Sky: Eyes of the Watcher, New Season: Sparrow's Quest, Rifter: Traitors at Teteris, Colony Zero: Quarantine Protocol, and Far Space.

Melissa Koons

Dinosaur in an Apocalyptic Wasteland

Melissa Koons (Proofreader & Formatter) has always had a passion for books and creative writing. It may have started with *Berenstain Bears* by Stan and Jan Berenstain, but it didn't take long for authors like Lucy Culliford Babbit, Tolkien, and Robert Jordan to follow. From a young age, she knew she wanted to share her love for stories with the world. She has written and published one novel, multiple short stories, and poetry. She has a BA in English and Secondary Education from the University of Northern Colorado. A former middle and high school English teacher, she now devotes her career to publishing, editing, writing, and tutoring hoping to inspire and help writers everywhere achieve their goals. When she's not working, she's taking care of her two turtles and catching up on the latest comic book franchise.

Aylâ Larsen

Dinosaur in the Ocean

Aylâ is the creative mind and copywriter behind numerous, award-winning and nationally-recognized advertising campaigns for Colorado-based clients. When she's not being clever with words, she can be found discussing great film and television, singing like an angel, and ranting about mayonnaise. Right now, Aylâ is probably wearing a Disney t-shirt and laughing about a pun she heard two days ago. Learn more at AylaWithaHat.com.

David Munson

Clown in Space

David Munson is an American fantasy author born in October of 1982 in Bountiful Utah. He graduated from Layton High School 2001. Later he went on to attend The University of Utah and Weber State University, both in Northern Utah. David now lives and works in Northern Colorado with his wife Cara, and four children. Ben, Alex, Emily, and Zach. With the encouragement of friends and professors, David began creating the world of Ellspire. It all started with a sheet of paper and some colored pencils, and of course unrelenting imagination. David enjoys all kinds of fantasy writing and fantasy art. He is open to almost any form of fiction and loves a new adventure. When his hours are not spent on writing they are devoted to geeking out over movies, board games, or the latest video games. David is mechanically minded and often can be found working in the garage on just about anything that can be taken apart and put back together. He also enjoys time spent with several different writing groups and encourages creative writing in any form. Imagination is a wonderful gift that needs to be cultivated and shared.

Jennifer Ogden

Psycho Killer in an Alternate Future

In September 2017, Jennifer Ogden finally listened to the call to write that had followed her around since she was a little girl. She took a leap of faith and quit her soul-sucking nine-to-five job. Now, she enjoys spending her days crafting words into stories. She believes it takes courage to live life, laughter to bring joy, and love to see hope. Check out her blog at SoManyBooks.info.

M.M. Ralph

Psycho Killer in the Human Mind

M. M. Ralph is an author and all-around creative intuitive living in Denver, Colorado. She is grateful to be a part of *Crash Philosophy*, major thanks to Thomas A. Fowler and thanks you for your interest. She invites you to connect with her on social media for more information on upcoming projects.

T.J. Valour

Psycho Killer in Space

T.J. Valour's invisible, pet dinosaur landed her in the principal's office in second grade and it has been a rollercoaster of adventure ever since. At work she dances with death and has the honor of recording her client's last chapters of life. When not working, TJ is crafting fantastical urban stories from the safety of her desk. TJ lives in the Rocky Mountains with her wonderful spouse and handsome, but thick-headed, doggo.

Rob Walker

Psycho Killer in the Ocean

Rob Walker is a failed birthday magician and former funeral DJ, probably best known for his animated sketch comedy series Victorian Cut-out Theatre. He writes stories, jokes, sketches and screenplays. He currently lives in Colorado with his wife, son and their two socially inept cats.

Made in the USA
San Bernardino, CA
30 June 2019